IN A
NEW YORK
MINUTE

IN A
NEW YORK
MINUTE

KATE SPENCER

FOREVER

New York Boston

Forever
Hachette Book Group
1290 Avenue of the Americas, New York, NY 10104
read-forever.com
twitter.com/readforeverpub

First Edition: March 2022

Forever is an imprint of Grand Central Publishing. The Forever name and logo are trademarks of Hachette Book Group, Inc.

The publisher is not responsible for websites (or their content) that are not owned by the publisher.

Library of Congress Cataloging-in-Publication Data
Names: Spencer, Kate, 1979- author.
Title: In a New York minute / Kate Spencer.
Description: First edition. | New York : Forever, 2022. | Summary: "When Franny meets Hayes, it's the opposite of a meet-cute-she's just been laid off, and her dress is caught in the subway doors. As if her day could get any worse, the flimsy fabric rips, and she's left in the hipster equivalent of a hospital gown. Hayes is the stuffy suit who offers to give Franny his coat-alongside an unwelcome zing of attraction. He may have saved her from showing her butt to (more of) the city, but that one act is his only redeeming quality. Franny is eager to forget the whole embarrassing encounter. But thanks to a fellow rider liveblogging the whole incident, Franny and Hayes are NYC's new favorite love story with their very own hashtag: #subwaybaes. While Franny is quick to dismiss Hayes as just another rich guy, whose nicest assets are hanging in his closet, she's forced to re-evaluate her opinion when their paths keep crossing. Both are desperate to move past their fifteen minutes of fame-enough so for the one-time "subway baes" to form a grudging alliance. But the more time they (reluctantly) spend together, the more Franny begins to wonder if the line between love and hate is just a subway stop away..."— Provided by publisher.
Identifiers: LCCN 2021041422 | ISBN 9781538737620 (hardcover) | ISBN 9781538737613 (ebook)
Subjects: LCGFT: Romance fiction. | Humorous fiction. | Novels.
Classification: LCC PS3619.P4653 I53 2022 | DDC 813/.6—dc23
LC record available at https://lccn.loc.gov/2021041422

ISBNs: 9781538737620 (hardcover), 9781538737613 (ebook), 9781538723722 (Canadian pbk.)

Printed in the United States of America

LSC-C

Printing 1, 2021

To Anthony, who makes up one half of my New York City love story. And to Teresa and Sarah, who make up the other.

IN A
NEW YORK
MINUTE

CHAPTER ONE

FRANNY

NO ONE PLANS on getting laid off when they wake up in the morning.

No one sips their first drop of coffee and thinks, *Today's the day, fifteen minutes into checking my morning email and drafting a reply to that pain-in-the-ass client Melinda, that I'll get a notification in Slack telling me to head down to the main conference room for an "important chat."*

No one imagines that the super successful interior design start-up they work for—you know, the one that had a massive hiring blitz four years ago, keeps fridges full of organic cold-pressed juices, has beanbag chairs in all the conference rooms, and hosts weekly rooftop happy hours—will lay off half their staff in a matter of forty-five minutes.

No one dares to consider that the venture-capitalist money that had poured in, so much endless cash that it had instilled an overblown sense of possibility and security and allowed the twenty-six-year-old founder to increase staff from twenty-seven to seventy-four people over just the last year (and buy a cherry-red Maserati along the way), would be mismanaged by the team at the top, and totally gone, just like that.

1

At least, I didn't.

In fact, it seemed impossible that the same people who once had excitedly told me about their standard four weeks of vacation for all employees, even entry-level ones, would be one day sitting across from me on multicolored midcentury-modern chairs (not ones I'd ever choose for a client, if I'm being honest), with giant cups of Starbucks in front of them, uttering these words:

"We're so sorry, Franny. We've really valued everything you've contributed to Spayce. But we need to consolidate the digital and design team. Even marketing is taking a big cut. This is just part of working in the start-up space. You know how it is. We grew too quickly, and now we need to scale back."

I should have known that when you're working for a company that promises to "disrupt" things, they might just mean your life.

The promotion that I'd been assured was right around the corner—for over a year—never came. Instead, I'd been unceremoniously sacked, all before ten in the morning. It felt like I'd just been dumped by someone I thought was about to get down on one knee and propose.

I walked back in a daze to the massive bright-white worktable I shared with six other junior designers, tears stinging the corners of my eyes. Tightness spread across my chest, panic settling into my body. My brain was suddenly a running list of numbers and bullet points, ticking across a screen in my head.

Student loans.

Phone bill.

Food.

Those custom checkered Vans I had forked over one hundred dollars for while doing some late-night online retail therapy last week.

Rent.

My apartment was "affordable" by New York City standards, but on my salary it was still a stretch, an expense I justified because

I loved the space so much. Tiny, yes, and occasionally visited by a cockroach or two. But it was all mine.

And, of course, I had big plans to knock down some of my credit card debt and pay off that trip I took to Miami three years ago, where I ordered a $300 bottle of wine by accident at dinner and was too embarrassed to tell the waiter I'd made a mistake.

I'd put all my hopes and dreams for the year on the vision board I'd made alongside my two best friends, Cleo and Lola, and a mound of bagels from Russ & Daughters on a Sunday morning in early January. A promotion at work, financial freedom, a vintage black Chanel purse made of soft buttery leather with a gold-chain strap. Losing my job had definitely not been on there. And I still didn't have that Chanel bag. I guess at least now I could definitely say vision boards were 100 percent BS.

Doug, the head of IT, circled our communal desk with an awkward look on his face, logging us out of our computers with a few quick taps. Melinda was never going to get a reply from me about the bright-red velvet couch I'd sourced for her Austin living room. The fact that she'd be sitting there, irritated and awaiting my reply, was the only bright spot in this otherwise garbage day.

A stack of cardboard boxes was now in the center of the office, strewn atop the bright-pink couches that served as our design team's morning meeting gathering space. Ramona, my quiet, introverted, and brilliant coworker, who created life-size papier-mâché sculptures at her art space in Queens on the weekends, stood across from me, sniffling as she placed a few items from her desk into a box.

"Ramona," I said as I caught her eye. "I'm so sorry."

She wiped her eyes on the back of her sleeve and gave me a weepy smile. "I haven't told anyone here yet, but I'm pregnant."

My mouth fell open. "Oh god."

She nodded. "And Chris—" She got choked up again as she

said her partner's name. "He just quit his job so he could do culinary school full-time. We're so screwed."

My stomach flipped with that about-to-puke feeling at the thought of how they were going to afford everything they needed for a baby.

"It's so messed up," I said. "My student-loan bills are already a nightmare. I don't know how I'm going to pay them down now."

Conversations around us were muted and whispered, but the panic was tangible. Most of the office was under thirty, and almost half of us were now out of work, sent into the wilds of the New York City job market with whatever severance we'd been given. I'd spent four years plugging away at a job that maybe hadn't always stimulated me creatively, but it had paid well, and my coworkers were fun and easy to be around for nine hours a day.

And now, like me, they were reduced to shoving what was left of their time at Spayce into a sixteen-inch cardboard box. A cube-shaped crystal award for Best Digital Design Start-Up. A small green turtle figurine my coworker Raphael had brought me back from Mexico. The framed photo of Keanu Reeves someone had left on my desk as an April Fool's joke. The branded stainless-steel water bottle everyone at the company had gotten last Earth Day.

The last four years of my life, packed up in ten minutes, ready to be lugged home on the subway.

With my vintage bejeweled purse on one shoulder and my canvas Spayce tote bag still packed with my lunch of pasta leftovers on the other, I grabbed my box, mumbled some hushed goodbyes, and headed to the elevator, pressing the neon-blue call button with my knee.

We were in the middle of a heat wave in New York City, one of those bizarro stretches where it goes from sixty to ninety degrees in the middle of May. At seven thirty in the morning, just hours earlier, a billowy blue-green tank-sleeved silk dress (my best friend

Cleo called it my "fancy sack") paired with black high-top Chucks had seemed like a perfectly reasonable outfit choice.

But huffing the three blocks through Times Square while weighted down with all this crap turned me into a sweating tangle of bags and clothes, armpits damp and sweat beads clinging to my curls. And a blister was rubbing itself into existence on my right heel.

After what felt like an hour of digging around, I found my MetroCard and gave it a swipe through the large metal turnstile at the station. By the time I'd made it down a flight of stairs and maneuvered around the late-morning wall of humans still rushing to work, I was a seething, irritated mess. I walked toward the downtown 2/3 train, only to be greeted with a sign by the stairs that declared NO DOWNTOWN TRAINS AT THIS STATION DUE TO CONSTRUCTION.

Everything that could possibly go wrong today was happening. I shifted directions, grumbling curse words under my breath, and headed toward the Q train. This would at least get me to Brooklyn, and then I could loop back on the 2/3 from Atlantic, which would suck. God, I just wanted to get home.

As I tried to catch my breath, I inhaled the pungent stink of the subway that was set free the second warm air descended upon our fair but smelly city. "Oh my god," I muttered, holding in a gag.

And then I heard it: the squeal of brakes, a sure sign that my train was arriving at the platform, which was down yet another flight of stairs in front of me. I dared to breathe through my nose—ugh, everything smelled like urine—and took off jogging, the tchotchkes in my box bouncing with every step. I hit the stairs and caught a glimpse of the silver glint of subway car. It was still in the station.

Ding ding, the subway doors announced. Any New Yorker knew what that sound meant. It was time to run.

"No, no, no!" I shouted, and sprinted onto the platform just as the doors were, mercifully, opening a second time. The train was a blur, but I could see through the scratched-up windows that it was packed—bodies next to bodies next to bodies. An entire barricade of humans stood just inside the doors.

"Excuse me," I huffed, wedging myself next to an older woman with a wire grocery cart, who shuffled forward into the center of the car, and a giant of a man who was long and lean and all suit.

"Sorry. Thank you," I said, angling myself sideways to squeeze on. There was no way to shrink myself with this stupid box in my arms. But still, I was inside, with inches to spare. And I was finally heading home to escape this god-awful shit show of a morning.

As the train lurched forward, I sighed with relief and leaned my back against the doors of the car. Wrapping my right arm around the edge of the box, I reached my left arm for my purse, hoping to grab my phone so I could text Cleo and Lola with my news. Just as my fingers grazed the hard plastic of my phone case, I felt a firm tug behind me.

"What the hell?" I muttered, trying to shift again. But I couldn't move. It was like something had pinned me to the doors of the train, securing me in place. I stepped forward, inadvertently leaning my weight against a pregnant woman who was holding on to a handrail for balance. *Why didn't anyone offer her a seat?* I thought as I apologized for bumping into her. My brain was skipping around between worrying about her to wondering why I couldn't move, and then suddenly my ears connected with something else:

The sound of my dress ripping down the back.

My heart rate picked up, beating its own chant of *Oh my god, oh my god.* My dress—the gorgeous locally-made-in-Brooklyn, cost-a-small-fortune soft silk dress that I'd splurged on at Alter in Williamsburg—had gotten stuck in the subway doors and ripped straight down the seam, from the back of my neck right past my butt. My fancy sack was now a fancy mess.

"Oh my god," I said out loud.

New Yorkers are well practiced in the art of not staring, but dare to step into their personal space and their eyes turn into lasers that can incinerate upon contact. Unfortunately, no one's personal space was safe around me as I frantically tried to grab the back of my dress with my free hand and hold it shut. At first, my elbow smacked into someone's arm, and I was met with a "Jesus Christ" from the skateboarder who'd been on the receiving end.

"Sorry!" I stepped forward to recalibrate and squashed someone's foot underneath mine.

"Excuse me," hissed a woman in fancy athleisure wear as she recoiled.

"Sorry!" I squeaked again. God, my arms ached. I shifted the box onto my left side and shimmied as far as I could against the door, hoping I could buy myself some time before the next stop. But as I grabbed the material by my butt and held it shut, the dress started to slip off my shoulders.

Is it possible to laugh and cry at the exact same time? Because just as tears pricked along the edge of my eyes, hot and huge, I let out a guffaw. This day.

"You okay?" the pregnant woman asked, a look of genuine concern on her face.

"My dress." I gestured toward my back. As I did, the right shoulder strap slipped off my body completely.

"Oh no," she said, horrified.

"I know," I replied, the panic evident in the high octave of my voice. "I'm having a massively shitty day, and in a few minutes I'm going to be mooning the station when the doors open." All it took was one blink before the tears began dripping down my face. Everything awful that had just happened to me was spilling out, in the most public place possible.

Before I could stop her, the pregnant woman shouted into the crowd of commuters, "Does anyone have any safety pins?"

Her voice was loud enough to startle almost every person nearby. "Safety pins? Anyone?"

A few people looked up and then looked back down at their phones. A girl in an NYU hoodie, her hair in a giant topknot on her head, glanced over and offered me a sympathetic smile. The older woman began to dig into her massive purse.

"It's fine. I'm fine," I tried to assure her, even though I was obviously not. I pressed myself against the door as we chugged toward the next station.

"Here, honey!" The older woman waved, and the pregnant woman reached out her hand. "It's not a safety pin, but it might help."

When the pregnant woman stepped back toward me, she opened her palm and revealed a small hair clip.

"Do you want me to try to close it up with this?" she asked me, a skeptical look on her face. But before I could tell her no, a deep, calm voice shot through the din of the subway.

"Here."

It was the giant suit standing next to me, except now he was just crisp white shirt and soft blue tie, his shoulders hitting right at my eyeline. His navy jacket was dangling neatly from his hand. "Here," he said again, clearly perplexed by my inability to understand exactly what he wanted me to do with his coat.

I looked up to meet his eyes.

Even in my *Holy shit, my dress has ripped open straight down the back, and I'm in the one thong I own and never wear, because thongs are miserably uncomfortable, but I bailed on doing laundry last night, so here I am, and to top it all off, I just got let go from my job and I still have at least five more years of student loans to pay* state, I could register that he was handsome. The kind of good-looking stranger that causes you to think *Whoa* when you pass them on the street.

I knew just by the confident, assured way he held himself—

shoulders back, chin just slightly tilted to the sky—and by the cut slopes of his jaw and his thick brown hair, that this was a man who had never known an awkward phase. While the rest of us were running around seventh grade with oozing zits and blinding metal braces (I had to sleep in headgear, for god's sake), he breezed through with ease, all long muscles and creamy, clear skin and enviable cheekbones and dark lashes, from the day he was born.

And then there were his eyes, stern and serious but also big and beautiful. At first glance, they looked brown, but with a second look I realized they were so inky and dark that they came closer to matching the navy of his suit. He had the body of a runner or a cyclist or—it clicked then—a triathlete. I could see him in one of those skimpy running suits now, muscle pulsing against spandex, not caring that everyone in the world could see every angle and curve of his perfectly sculpted body.

"Please." His voice was caught between concerned and annoyed, and the slight wrinkle between his brow underscored his tone. "Take it." He even had good eyebrows, the kind that somehow looked well-groomed even though he was surely too cool to wax them.

"What?" I said, my voice shaky. "You want me to take your jacket?"

He nodded and offered a small smile. "Yes."

And then he blinked, holding his eyes closed an extra beat, showing off those lashes, the kind women revered with both jealousy and awe.

"I have five more of these at home." He said this firmly, like it should be obvious. "It would be of much more help to you."

Five more? If I wasn't half-naked on the subway living through my worst nightmare, I'd make some crack about selling his fancy suits to pay my rent. But instead, I pursed my lips together, which I'd painted in my bright-red all-day lip stain just hours earlier. It was an attempt to push down the tightness in my throat, but it was no use. The misery of this morning was rushing out of me in heavy sobs.

"That's really nice of you. Thank you." I sniffed, my nose stuffy now. Good lord, why does snot need to be a part of crying? I already looked like a newborn sloth when I cried, and the dripping nose only made things worse. "But I can't take it. Your suit jacket. How would I even. Get it back to you?" My breathing was choppy, and the words came out in gasps.

Before he could reply, the train lurched forward and I stumbled a step, my left arm instinctively shooting out to stop myself from falling. I reached for a pole to grab on to, but there was nothing there, and instead I face-planted into him, my left cheek smooshed against his chest, which was warm and solid. My arm that had searched for the pole slid along his side instead, and I wrapped it around his back just to have something to hold on to, my fingers gripping his shirt like a steering wheel. The jolt sent my dress flapping behind me. He took a step forward to balance himself, and his hand landed on my butt where my dress hung open, his fingers firm on my skin.

"Oh my god, I'm so sorry," I heard him say from somewhere. Something about the soft press of his palm—hot and brief on my bare skin—was both electric and comforting, all at once. We stood like this for what felt like minutes: two strangers awkwardly embracing, my cheek still flush against his chest, so close that if I actually stopped to listen I could probably hear his heartbeat.

"It's okay," I babbled into the cool relief of his shirt.

He pulled his hand off me and steadied it on the roof of the subway car. "Excuse me," he said, taking a small step back, holding his hand out like it had just been burned. "That was an accident. My apologies."

Then he glanced down, first at me, and then at his shirt, where

I'd left two wet blotches where my eyes had been. And right below it—oh god—was a trace of snot. Suddenly, getting laid off didn't seem like the worst thing to happen to me today.

I backed away from him, and the pregnant woman gave me a sympathetic look as I accidentally bumped into her. Again.

"I would take it," she said as I muttered another apology. "Unless you want—" She gestured to the clip in her hand.

The conductor's voice crackled over the loudspeaker as the train rolled to a slow stop in the tunnel. "Ladies and gentlemen, we're just holding here as we wait for a train to leave the station ahead of us."

"Okay, yeah." I nodded at the stranger on the subway. "Thank you so much."

He held up the jacket in front of me by the collar, like the men did for their dates in the black-and-white movies that my grandma and I used to watch. Gingerly, he draped it over my shoulders, tugging it ever so slightly so it hung snug over my body, his cheek coming dangerously close to brushing against the top of my head. I breathed a sigh of relief that I was no longer showing my ass to the entire city. As I did, I caught a whiff of his scent lingering on the collar. Apparently, this man's neck smelled like an afternoon spent with old books stacked on wooden shelves as icy rain cracked against the window, with hints of spicy pine and a fireplace that roared with hot flames and flickering coals. It was heady and decadent, steady and dark.

Someone handed me a tissue, and I blew my nose into it until it was too damp to use. "I just got laid off," I blubbered. "And now this." I gestured with my head, as if I could somehow point to my dress with my forehead. "It's really been a bad morning."

He offered me a small smile and a nod but said nothing.

I tucked the tissue into the pocket of his coat and noticed a small grimace ripple across his face.

"I'll get it dry-cleaned and back to you as soon as I can."

He shook his head. "I swear, I'm good. Besides, I think you need it more than me."

I nodded. He wasn't wrong. I did not want to ride the subway all the way to Brooklyn and then make the twelve-minute walk back to my apartment with my dress ripped open down the back.

"I really appreciate it," I said, and I could feel the sobs hovering at the back of my throat, ready at any moment to make another appearance. I gritted my teeth and took a breath, calming myself, reining the tears back in. "This is worse than the time I peed myself from laughing too hard outside Cherry Tavern and had to buy a sweatshirt on Saint Marks to wrap around my waist and wear home."

"I'm sorry, what?" He looked genuinely confused. "You peed yourself?"

It was a bad habit, a tic, the thing I did when other people just bit their nails or twirled their hair. I tried to change direction with humor. "It's nothing. Anyway, I'm really grateful. You quite literally saved my ass."

But he didn't laugh; he barely cracked a smile. Instead, his brow tightened in response, his cheeks pinkish and bright. His mouth was a straight line, and as he glanced away, I noticed the hint of his tongue running across his bottom lip.

God, I wished Cleo and Lola were here to witness this. Laid off. Humiliated in front of an entire subway car. Butt cheeks bared to the world. Topped off with a hot guy coming to my rescue—a hot guy who was clearly not impressed by my ability to rip an entire article of clothing in half without even using my hands.

One day, this would make an amazing story, retold through swells of laughter over pitchers of beer. The kind of tale that earned a declaration of "*This is going in my wedding toast for you,*" which was the highest praise we awarded the mortifying moments we shared together. I'd literally lost both my job and the clothes off my back, and my dignity was not far behind.

Thinking of my friends calmed me, and my breathing steadied a bit. *Inhale, exhale.* The train lurched forward again and roared into the Canal Street station, in the heart of downtown Manhattan. I stayed focused on Cleo and Lola and imagined what we would all nickname this guy when I told them the story. Hot Suit. He was definitely a Hot Suit. Maybe not my best work. Certainly, not very original. But it was to the point and easy to remember. He was hot, and he wore a suit. Done and done.

I glanced back toward him, the man formerly known as Stranger on the Subway, as he bent to pick up a leather briefcase that he'd planted between his feet. It was smooth, polished brown leather but still looked vintage. Well loved, even. I'd never met anyone under the age of sixty who carried a freakin' briefcase, but then again, I didn't mix much with men who wore suits to work either.

When the train rolled to a stop and the doors opened, Hot Suit offered me a polite nod. "Well, good luck," he said. "With everything." I was so dazed by the whole experience that it took me a beat to realize he was getting off.

"Hey!" I shouted out the door as he stepped onto the platform. He angled his head back toward me, and our eyes met again. "Thank you! Seriously. I owe you one!" He shook his head and gave me a slight wave of his hand, a curt goodbye from a stranger who had just swooped in and saved me—my butt included—without even blinking an eye.

"I'm sorry about crying all over your shirt!" I yelled again, but he didn't turn around. And then, Hot Suit was gone, swallowed by the crowd pushing off the train.

~~~

Back in the safety of my tiny apartment in Brooklyn, I dumped the box onto my sliver of kitchen counter and dropped my bags to the ground before shrugging Hot Suit's jacket off my shoulders. I held it in front of me, examining it skeptically. I hadn't found anything in the pockets besides my crumpled tissue (yes, I'd checked on my walk home), and it looked and felt either brand-new or impeccably cared for. My finger brushed against the edge of a tag stitched along the collar. Gucci. Wow. This was now officially the nicest piece of clothing I owned.

Hanging it on a hook inside my closet, I let my ruined dress slide off my body and then collapsed onto my bed in a heap. I was achingly exhausted. **Having the worst day of my life**, I texted my friends. **pls send bagels.**

Lola responded immediately. **BRB meeting will text asap!!!** I knew this meant I might not hear from her for hours. When your job is breaking celebrity news on the internet, reporting about the latest divorce or scandal usually comes before texting your friends back. But Lola was loyal; even if she couldn't always respond right away, she never failed to show up when it counted.

A minute later, my phone rang. I hit the green button, and Cleo's face popped up, slightly obscured by a giant coffee raised to her lips. "You okay?" she asked before taking a swig.

"You are never going to believe what happened to me this morning," I said, skipping a greeting to get right to the point. "Spayce laid me off."

"Oh shit, Fran. That's terrible!" Her eyes widened behind her vintage tortoiseshell cat's-eye glasses that I'd helped her pick out at Fabulous Fanny's in the East Village just a few weeks ago.

"I thought you were about to get promoted."

"Yeah, so did I. But, listen, that's not the worst of it. On my way home, my dress ripped wide-open on the subway. Half of Manhattan saw my butt."

"What?!" Cleo grimaced, nose wrinkled in horror. "Wait. Hold on—I'm almost in my office." I watched the angles on my screen change as she balanced the phone on her coffee cup to shut the door behind her. "There," she said, her face coming back into view. "Now everyone won't hear about your butt."

Cleo tucked a strand of her stick-straight black hair behind her ear, which only made her angled bob look more chic. She was a lawyer at the Legal Aid Society and also worked as an adjunct professor at Fordham. Lola and I liked to tease her that her students were obviously all infatuated with her, but she always brushed us off with a pointed glare. That didn't stop Lola from serenading Cleo with "Hot for Teacher" at our last late-night karaoke session at Winnie's a couple of months ago.

"Don't kill me," she said, pushing her glasses up her nose. "But I have, like, five minutes before I need to get back to teaching this seminar. So give me the quick version, and I'll be over as soon as I can."

I raced through the tale of my train ride, the box of stupid work mementos, the pregnant lady with no seat, my sweaty armpits, and, of course, him.

"Wow," said Cleo. "You know how I feel about the whole stupid idea of chivalry."

I did indeed know how she felt about it.

"And I'm sure you would have been just fine without his help," she continued.

I nodded in agreement.

"But," she added, "something about this is very hot. I mean, who even looks up from their phone on the subway? Much less comes to someone's rescue?"

"And get this," I added. "It's freakin' Gucci."

Cleo whistled through her teeth. "Good lord," she said, drawing out the words for effect.

"I know. Maybe the jacket is a bad talisman and he's using me to get rid of it," I joked, dragging my comforter up and over my body.

"Well, whatever it is, you can sell it on Poshmark for a small fortune."

"I'm going to have to when my severance runs out. I only got eight weeks."

"We'll figure out a plan." I could hear Cleo's brain working through the phone line. "And hey, Fran, maybe it's for the best. I mean, you've been so sick of working there for a long time."

"Yeah," I said. "But what does it say about me that I got laid off? Maybe this whole time I've been terrible at my job and I had no idea."

"Franny, layoffs happen. You decorated my whole apartment, so I have actual proof that you're fantastic at your job."

"You have to say that," I said. "All I did was find you better throw pillows. Anyone can do that." I was joking, sure. But there was a familiar, insecure voice in my head that wondered if maybe that was the truth.

"And besides," I continued, "I liked the paycheck. The stability. The free snacks. The paycheck."

"I know," she said. "And I'm not saying everything happens for a reason—"

"You totally are!" I cut her off. Cleo had the brain of a lawyer but the heart of someone who believed in the magic of the world around us, the stuff we couldn't see. The vision boards had been her idea.

"Look, all I'm saying is that maybe getting laid off is a gift. I feel like I've heard you say a million times how bored you felt not really getting to do anything hands-on at Spayce. Never getting to be in the rooms you designed, putting chairs in the right spot, moving things exactly how you want them."

Cleo was right. I had complained about this. A lot.

"You know what I mean," she continued. "Now you can go crazy and do things your way."

"Now you're just quoting *Laverne and Shirley*," I said. I had long ago tucked away the fantasy of a career defined on my own terms, one that filled both my creative soul and my bank account. I'd made peace with the fact that work would always be just that for me, the path to survival, a means to an end. That's how it had gone for my mom and Jim, my stepdad, and they were happy enough. There was no shame in working just to work and doing what you love on the side. Or at least, that's what I'd told myself to justify my career choice up until this point.

Cleo laughed into the phone. "You're going to make your dreams come true," she sang. And then with a quick goodbye, she was gone, leaving me to remember the dreams that had pushed me to move to New York City in the first place, and wonder if I had anything at all to show for them.

—~~~—

There's an endless list of things a person can do after getting laid off: punch a hole in a wall, meditate, search for jobs, get drunk. I fell asleep. I wasn't even consciously trying to do it, but somewhere in between texts and WhatsApp chats with my fellow spurned former coworkers, I zonked out. Two hours later, it was my phone that woke me, the *ding ding ding*ing of my text alerts jolting me from sleep.

I flicked on my phone. I had thirteen new texts from Lola, her most recent: **Fran r u ok? I'm here! Let me in!** I grabbed my faded bathrobe off its hook and raced toward my door.

"Hey," I said, out of breath as I swung the door open. "I'm so sorry. I totally passed out."

Lola, in all her bleached-blond, smudged-eyeliner glory, shoved a giant brown paper bag into my arms. It was still warm to the touch.

"I brought bagels," she said, her voice serious. That was our Lola. She brought the bagels, every time.

"I'm so sorry you've had such a terrible day," she said as she kicked off her black ankle boots and closed the door behind her.

"I know. Laid off." I placed the bagels on my stove, my counter space still occupied by my box of work mementos.

"I mean, yes. That's awful. But your dress, and the guy on the subway," she said, pulling me in for a hug.

"Did Cleo tell you?" I asked, letting her squeeze me tight. "He was like movie-star hot, and I basically blew my nose on his shirt. I'm not good at first impressions."

"Cleo?" Lola pulled away from me and held me at arm's length. "I haven't talked to her. She's still teaching that stupid environmental law seminar that lasts all freaking day."

"Oh, sorry. I guess I forgot I told you about the subway nightmare."

"Franny." She eyed me with a peculiar examining look. "Did you not read all my texts?"

My brain buzzed as I tried to remember. "I don't know. Why?"

She rolled her eyes, clearly annoyed that I'd missed her messages.

"Okay, so at work today, we've been tracking this Instagram story that's going microviral," she said. Being the deputy editor of the pop-culture-focused website LookingGlass meant that she was always "tracking" things—who unfollowed whom on social media; who favorited which photos; which TikTok stars might be hooking up—and looking into rumors and gossip sent anonymously to her DMs and email. "And I think it's you."

"What do you mean, 'you think it's me'?" I asked, my voice taking on a slightly panicked pitch.

"I mean, I…know it's you. You've got that crazy vintage bag, the one with the rhinestone flowers all over it. Your Spayce bag too. Also, I'd know your beautiful face anywhere. Your butt too." She smiled, trying to lighten the mood. It didn't work.

"Photos?!" I was 100 percent screeching. I was no longer a human; I was now a very loud bird inside a human's body.

"It's you and this insanely hot guy with a blue tie, who looks like he's leaning in to give your ass a squeeze. Smelling your hair," she said. "And you're, like, full-on embracing him. It's PG-rated but very hot. Someone posted the whole thing with photos. And made it into GIFs too, which I have to admit is genius."

My face froze in a horrified, mouth-open look.

She continued. "You guys are flirting. Your hands are all over him, rubbing his chest. And then he leans in for a hug, or maybe a kiss—I couldn't quite tell. Did he kiss you?"

"What?" I shrieked, racing to my bed to grab my phone. "The train stopped short, and I fell into him, and he lost his balance. We definitely did not kiss, Lo. Or rub. Or hug and rub. Why would I do any of that with a stranger I literally just met on the subway?"

My voice was a growl now. I had morphed from bird to cougar in an instant.

Lola raised her brows at me, biting her bottom lip. "I don't know—for fun?"

I turned and waved both my middle fingers in her face.

"Oh, Fran, I'm just teasing. Of course I believe you." Lola sat down next to me on the edge of my bed. "But I also spent like ten minutes staring at photos of someone who looks exactly like you crying in a hot dude's arms as he wrapped his coat around your shoulders."

My stomach didn't flip anymore. It dropped dead. I pounded at my phone, my fingers too slow to keep up with what my brain wanted them to do. I found her texts gently telling me I was possibly about to become an internet sensation, with the screenshots to prove it.

"Holy shit." I tossed the phone next to me. Then I stood up almost immediately. I sat back down. I had no idea what to do with my body, other than run to the bathroom and throw up.

"Some girl posted it all on her Instagram Stories," she said.

"I wanna see it," I demanded.

Lola pursed her lips and, with a reluctant sigh, picked up my phone, unlocked the home screen, and started typing away.

"How do you know my password?" I asked.

"You told it to me once in college when you were drunk and wanted me to order you a pizza," she said, like it was the most obvious reason in the world. "You should probably change it at least once a decade."

When she passed my phone back to me, my hands were shaking. Because there I was, on my own phone screen, in an Instagram Highlight titled **SubwayQTs**.

I said the words slowly, out loud.

"That's what they're calling you," she said matter-of-factly. "SubwayQTs."

"What?!" I was back to being loud and squeaky.

"QTs, like 'cuties,' and because you were on the Q train," she explained in an overly kind voice. "It's a pun."

"Lola, I get the freakin' pun!" I snapped. "I just— That's not what happened. I ripped my dress, and this guy on the train insisted I take his suit jacket, which, I'll have you know, turns out to be Gucci. And he was, like, weirdly nonchalant about the whole thing, and I didn't get his name, and he doesn't want it back, so now I'm just stuck with it."

"Ooooh. Well, that makes much more sense," Lola said with a smirk. She was enjoying herself.

"Your sarcasm is not helping."

I looked back down at my phone and clicked on the story. Someone who'd been near us on the subway had—oh my god— snapped a whole series of back-to-back photos of me on the train, sweaty and blotchy with tears, and clearly freaking out. **OMG this poor woman just got her dress stuck in the door of the Q train**, she had written over a blurry photo of me, mouth agape, with a line of crying-face and shocked-face emojis under it.

I scrolled forward. **Always look for the helpers** was typed on a photo of the pregnant woman leaning toward me, offering the hair clip. A GIF of Mr. Rogers waved in the upper right-hand corner. Jesus, this was embarrassing.

Super hot guy now saving the day!!! is what she captioned a picture of him leaning over me with his jacket in hand. In another, I'm smiling up at him through my tears—I don't remember smiling—and it actually looks like we're having an intimate conversation.

"Holy shit, this is not what happened." I gave Lola a panicked look, and she instinctively put her arm around my back. "Like, at all. I mean, kind of, but I just want to reiterate that I did not mean to touch Hot Suit. I fell into him because the train moved! And he gave me his coat because my dress ripped, which honestly was a lifesaver."

"Hot Suit?" Lola repeated with a laugh.

I crossed my arms in a huff. "He needed a nickname," I explained.

"Okay." She tilted her head in exaggerated thought. "It's kinda literal for my tastes, but I'll give you a B for effort."

I leapt up and paced the length of my bed, which wasn't much bigger than my entire room. In New York terms, my place qualified as a junior one-bedroom, a glorified way of saying it was a studio that came with a corner nook, where you could shove a full-size bed—a queen, if you were lucky. I'd managed to get a queen in there, plus a bedside table next to it. Making furniture work in tiny spaces was my superpower.

"Whose Instagram is it?"

"Some girl who goes to NYU. But it's getting shared everywhere. And I mean, the Stories will disappear, but she added them to her Highlights, and she also put a picture of you two in her grid. Which surprised me, if I'm being honest. I mean, the grid is, like, a sacred space." She shook her head, her digital-media-dork brain coming into focus.

"I truly don't get how this generation uses social media," she said disapprovingly, as if she were an aging grandmother and not someone who had gotten One Direction lyrics tattooed on her back as a dare just last year.

"Can we contact the girl who posted it?" I said, trying to come up with some plan of attack for getting the photos removed immediately. "I need to get this taken down."

"So I already sent her a DM. But if you just search the hash-tag #subwayQTs, all the posts about you come up. They're being shared."

"There's a hashtag?" I said, my voice teetering somewhere between panicked and horrified.

"*You're* a hashtag. I mean, look, it's not a bad thing. Maybe it will help you find a new job?" She was a slick saleswoman now, making her pitch.

"Oh yeah, because that's what everyone looks for in their new hire," I hissed.

"Influencers make a ton of money, Fran." Lola's voice had a schoolteacher edge to it. "You should see what contestants on *The Bachelor* make with their Instagram accounts alone."

I ignored her lecture on Social Media Moneymaking 101.

"You okay?" Lola asked, but I was too stunned to answer. I clicked back through the pictures again. There was a photo of my face pressed against his chest. And even though I'd bumped into him so awkwardly, in the picture it looked like I was de-liberately snuggling him, resting on him, smiling at him, enjoying him. A giant GIF of a cartoon face with heart eyes blinked in the bottom right-hand corner of the screen. **PLS LET THIS BE A SUBWAY LOVE CONNECTION!!!!!** the caption screamed in neon pink.

I clicked again, and there I was with my hand on his chest, but now I was gazing up at him with wide doe eyes. **I am watching 2 ppl fall in love on the subway and I am officially ded**, she wrote. Next pic, me standing next to him with the jacket on, with a crude heart hand-drawn over both our figures. **#SubwayQTs Forever**, she'd written in bold pink lettering.

And finally, a photo of me calling out "Thank you" as he got off the train. **Pretty sure they exchanged numbers and are going to live happily ever after**, she wrote, covering the bottom of the photo in a sea of heart emojis. And then again, the hashtag. Jesus fucking Christ. Exchanged numbers? I snotted all over the guy, and he practically ran off the train to get away from me. But Lola wasn't wrong; in the pictures, it did look like we were very, very into each other.

I clicked again and saw a series of screenshots of messages the NYU girl had received from people following her story. **So many people love #SubwayQTs!** she'd typed triumphantly. I clicked over to the hashtag, and there were more people sharing her story, commenting about #subwayQTs with heart emojis and crying-face emojis, and even one eggplant emoji. I mean, sure he was tall, but come on.

When I was done, I clicked back over to the girl's account, which had been updated while I'd been searching the hashtag. The last image was now a black screen with **OMG THE NY POST JUST CALLED ME ABOUT SubwayQTSSSSS!!!!!!!!!!** written in giant red text. It was time-stamped three minutes ago.

"Ugh, the *Post*," Lola muttered as she peered over my shoulder. "They love stuff like this."

Just as she spoke, my phone rang.

"Let it go to voicemail," she advised, her voice ominous. "And turn your ringer to silent."

Crap.

It didn't take long for people to find me. After all, like everyone my age, I'd been leaving an identity trail of bread crumbs on the internet since I was thirteen. When I was done listening to the voicemail from a reporter at the *New York Post*, I opened up my inbox to find messages from Refinery29, *Cosmopolitan*, BuzzFeed, the *Daily Mail*, and *Bustle*. I'd been easy to identify, my Instagram and Twitter had been set to public, and both listed Spayce in my bios. Someone had discovered my LinkedIn profile and used the photo there to confirm that I was, indeed, most likely one-half of SubwayQTs.

The owner of the suit jacket was still anonymous. Because of course. He was probably one of those *"I don't do social media"* types, too busy helping people around the city, a Clark Kent who couldn't be bothered to change out of his suit. Not to worry, though. Someone had figured out the exact brand and make of the jacket and had linked to it on Instagram, complete with info on where to buy it.

Cleo made it over after class with two bottles of wine in hand, I changed into sweats, and we moved to my blue velvet couch to discuss how to handle my newfound fame. As we talked, BuzzFeed published "SubwayQTs Is the Love Story We Didn't Know We Needed but Now Can't Live Without." I locked my Instagram account, deleted my already dead Twitter page, and deactivated Facebook. We opened the second bottle of wine.

"I swear this will all be over soon," Lola said reassuringly from the floor, where she sat on the giant gold throw pillows that doubled as chairs in my tiny space. "No one will remember this in a week." She was using one of my hardcover books of Italian Renaissance art as a tray for a plate of crackers and cheese. My head was in Cleo's lap, and she stroked my hair gently, raking her fingers along my scalp as if she could massage my infamy away.

"It's just so embarrassing," I moaned, shifting onto my back and pressing the heel of my palm against my forehead.

"Which part?" Cleo asked.

"Um, all of it?" I said rhetorically, as if it should be obvious.

"But I mean, what's really upsetting you?" she pushed, shifting into lawyer mode. "Is it being fired, the fact that your ass was on full display, or slow-dancing with Hot Suit?"

"Losing my job, of course," I replied honestly. I was out of work, and I basically lived paycheck to paycheck. I was screwed. "I know it's just a job, but it felt like such a big part of my identity. Of who I am. And you know I already struggle with that stuff."

Over the years, Cleo and Lola had listened as I worked through the challenges of not knowing much about my birth father. He was a vague entity, a tense subject with my mom, captured in one photograph I kept in the drawer of my bedside table. For my whole life, half of me had always felt like it existed in the shadows.

"And also," I started, and I saw Cleo raise a brow in Lola's direction. "Yes. Hot Suit. It's never fun to be completely humiliated in front of someone, much less a person you'd ogle at in a normal situation. And I told him about that time I peed myself outside Cherry Tavern."

Cleo winced. She'd been there to see that happen in real time.

"I mean, you all have seen every guy I've dated for the past ten years. None of them were 'I carry a briefcase' level of hot."

"Nick the Graffiti Artist was hot," Lola said.

"Nick who gave me a framed picture of himself for Valentine's Day?"

"Oh, right, I forgot about that part." Lola's lips curled in horrified laughter.

"And then there was Rock Climber Aaron," Cleo said. "Remember how his bed was in the kitchen of that apartment he shared with Jasper?"

Cleo had dated Jasper on and off in our midtwenties, and Rock Climber Aaron had been his roommate for a few months before moving back to Colorado for the ski season. His bed had been so close to the stove that his pillow caught on fire once while he was cooking us Kraft Macaroni & Cheese. Cute butt, though.

"He literally told me he didn't want to be exclusive, while his penis was still inside me."

"Definitely not 'I carry a briefcase' hot," Cleo said.

I sat up, pushing myself back against the other side of the couch and tucking my knees in toward my chest. "I just wish I could say thanks, you know?"

"And get his number," said Lola.

I grabbed a pillow and tossed it at her in response.

It wasn't his looks that had unraveled me. Something about him seeing me at my most vulnerable and not turning away, but rather stepping in to help, had felt both mortifying and thrilling all at once. For better or worse, he had seen the real me, and there was something about his expression in that moment that had told me he knew it. And even though the whole world could now view what had happened between us, it had also been something just the two of us shared.

"Lo," chimed in Cleo, sensing my desire to change the subject. "I told Franny we'd help her come up with a plan for work." The only thing Cleo loved more than making a plan was executing it.

Lola's posture straightened, ears perked. She leaned forward in anticipation.

"My plan is to eat a big-ass bag of salt-and-vinegar potato chips and watch every episode of *Law and Order* for a week," I told them. "I'll ride out my severance, apply to as many jobs as possible, and hopefully I'll land something."

"Or you could use this fifteen seconds of fame in your favor," Cleo said matter-of-factly.

"Yessss." Lola clapped her hands together, bouncing in her seat like a toddler. "Come on, you've wanted to do your own design work forever. Remember when you got hired at Spayce? You were convinced you'd stay for a year and then bail and go work on your own."

"Yeah, you stayed for way too long," Cleo blurted. And then, realizing she'd overstepped, she muttered, "Sorry. But you know what I mean."

"It was a good job." I picked at the corner of my sock, where the cotton had rubbed almost bare. "I lucked out. And I've only done, like, five freelance jobs on my own."

"And they were all amazing," Cleo said confidently. "I was at Patrick and James's housewarming party, remember? It was perfection. James literally cried over that French wallpaper you picked out for their bathroom."

"James was drunk," I reminded her.

She ignored me. "I'm sure he'd write you an amazing review. Make some referrals. He knows, like, every rich artsy downtown person in the city."

"Franny, Franny, Franny," Lola cheered, shaking her fists in rhythm with her words. "I love this for you."

"Me too," said Cleo, pleased with herself. "If we help you find some clients, will you at least think about it?"

"Oh my god, you two are too much," I groaned.

"Sorry, we can't help that we're your biggest fans," Cleo said, a faux-defensive tone to her voice.

"Yeah, it's too late because I already made FrannyIsFucking-Awesome.com, and our fan club has, like, a billion members," added Lola, with extra sass.

"Who, you two and my mom?"

"Yeah," Cleo quipped. "And Hot Suit."

"Oh my god, Hot Suit. He's probably somewhere living his best life, in his town house on the Upper East Side, eating caviar with his equally hot model wife."

"And their fifteen perfect golden retrievers," Cleo added, chuckling.

"And his butler, which he spells with two *t*'s." Lola paused for comedic effect, arms outstretched. "Get it?"

"Oh my god, Lola." I buried my face in my hands, half

cringing, half laughing. "You literally have the same sense of humor as Jim."

My stepdad was stoic, but he always laughed at dumb jokes, especially when they were slightly dirty.

Cleo stood then, stretching her arms overhead. "I should get home. I have a conference call at eight tomorrow morning before I go in to teach, and I have to participate in this one. I can't just put myself on mute and fall back asleep."

It was after nine, which, ten years ago, would have been right when we were heading out to a bar. But tonight, work called, responsibilities hovered in the back of our brains. *Except for me,* I thought, excited by the one upside to this whole shitty day: I'd get to sleep in tomorrow.

"I'll go with you," Lola said, yawning as she rose.

"Me too," I chimed in quickly, and they both turned to look at me. I shrugged. "I just need to get some fresh air."

After a round of bathroom breaks, we tumbled out of my apartment, into the small foyer and then out onto the street. Every block in my Brooklyn Heights neighborhood was lined with giant trees sprouting bright-green leaves. Set against the brick town houses and the cobblestone streets, they almost sparkled with color. The subway station was just a few blocks away, and as we walked we chatted about the rest of our week, the possibility of getting together over the weekend, and Lola's coworker who had just adopted a tortoise, of all things.

I headed back home after hugging them goodbye, and forced myself to not look at my phone for the duration of the walk. For the first few steps, it felt impossible, but then I noticed my breathing slowed, my chest unclenched, the muscles down my back relaxed, just a bit. I let my focus fall elsewhere: the places where tree roots had cracked the sidewalks, the ancient gas lamps that still flickered outside some of the austere homes in the neighborhood, the daffodils that suddenly seemed to be everywhere. For the first time today, I felt good. Normal. I was going to be okay.

A few steps from my front door, I reached for my phone out of habit, without thinking. There were alerts everywhere. In my texts, messages from reporters at the *Daily News* and NYN. In my email, messages from a producer from CNN, and from some German newspaper, the name of which I couldn't quite understand. And a message from Lola—**no surprise, the British tabloids love u**—with a link to the *Daily Mail*.

"Holy crap," I said out loud to myself as I stood there gawking at my phone. The world's worst meet-cute had been turned into an adorable romantic comedy that everyone was talking about.

Starring me.

CHAPTER TWO

HAYES

1:07 P.M. MY cousin Perrine was exactly seven minutes late to our standing biweekly lunch date. Not one to waste free time, I waited for her on the sidewalk while scanning through work emails on my phone, tapping out one-word replies and filing every message in its appropriate home until my inbox was back at zero. My shoulders relaxed an inch the second the last email was deleted, only to rise back up when a meeting alert popped on the screen for my call at two thirty.

"Hey," Perrine said with the huff of someone who had just jogged three blocks, tapping at my arm. I gave her The Look—yes, she'd dubbed it this sometime in high school—and leaned in for a hug. The Look was part scowl, part exasperation, part adoration. Perrine and I always fluctuated between laughing at and being annoyed with each other. "Staff meeting ran late," she said with a shrug as we queued up at Greener Things behind every other hungry New Yorker working in Midtown Manhattan. She never apologized for work, and I never expected her to. "I literally save lives, Hayes," she'd said to me the one time I complained about her being late for a breakfast we'd scheduled. I'd kept my mouth shut after that.

"Well, my day has been hellish, so don't worry about it."

I counted the people ahead of us, doing the math in my head as I tried to figure out how long the line might take, plus the minutes spent eating, and then the walk back to the office. Fifty-two minutes at least, which cut it close to the call I had scheduled about possibly expanding to a Seattle office. Plus, I was leaving work early tonight for a dinner honoring what we'd done last year revolutionizing the environmental investing space. And there was a six-mile run penciled into my calendar for five forty-five tomorrow morning that I never missed. I took a deep breath, trying to recalibrate and remember that family time was important too.

"Let me guess—another write-up in the *New York Times*? Too much money being made?" Perrine was so altruistic and kind and painfully polite that most people had no idea how damn sarcastic she really was. Lucky for me, I'd had a front-row seat to her many contradictions my whole life. "And where's your jacket, by the way? Did someone dare you to leave the office without it?"

She also never missed a thing. I gave her the rundown of my weird morning on the subway in a few short sentences. When I finished, her face had gone from unimpressed to utterly baffled.

"Wait, explain this to me again." She had stopped fiddling with her hospital ID badge that hung from her scrubs to stare at me, her head cocked to the side. "Her dress caught in the subway doors and ripped? Dear god, what a nightmare. That's like having your fly down in front of the whole class at school, but a million times worse. Remember when you—"

"Please don't," I interrupted before she could continue with the story of me accepting the Senior Prize in Mathematics in front of our entire high school with toilet paper coming out of the back of my pants. She'd told the whole story in mortifying detail in her toast at my rehearsal dinner. I didn't need to hear it again. "Okay, so if I am following this correctly, you gave her your jacket. A stranger?"

"I told you," I said as the line moved forward an inch. "I was only trying to help. It was no big deal."

I shook my head, exasperated, and paused to order, finally—arugula, beets, cucumber, grilled tempeh, lemon vinaigrette. The man working behind the counter nodded in recognition. It was the same thing I ordered every day.

"You know, you really should try something else," Perrine teased, poking me in the ribs with a laminated menu. "Chickpeas or avocado. Or, oh, I know, maybe add some cheese. Now that would be wild."

I didn't give her more than a quick smirk. The teasing had been the same since we were little kids, because, well, I guess I hadn't changed much. My mom lovingly called me "particular"; Perrine called me a "high-maintenance diva." I was an acquired taste, apparently.

I'd never felt insecure about my personality until I read the documents served to me by my ex-wife's lawyer. *Incompatible.* This had been Angie's reason for our divorce, and the word had secretly haunted me for the past three years, lurking behind me every time I struck up a conversation or considered a first date. *Incompatible.* This was the label I wore every day now, tucked into my jacket like a pocket square. Even, I guess, when my jacket was now on the back of a stranger.

I paid for our salads, tossed a ten-dollar bill in the tip jar, and followed Perrine to a table by the window.

"So, what, you just let her have it?" she asked, shoving a forkful of greens in her mouth.

I nodded, sprinkling just the right amount of salt into my palm before tossing it onto my salad.

"That sounds like jacket-splaining to me." She paused for effect, desperate for me to acknowledge her joke. "Get it? Like mansplaining? Only with your coat."

"Yes, I get it. You're hilarious." I threw a napkin at her head.

It landed on her brow and sat there for a beat before she yanked it off and tucked it in her lap. I held my hand out for a high five, and she begrudgingly reciprocated.

"And let me guess who made it—Armani?"

This was a classic line of teasing between us, and our extended family, even though I constantly reminded them I would always rather have one expensive, well-made thing, as opposed to a ton of cheaper stuff that didn't last. Especially when you considered the impact on the environment. But above all, I just liked things that last. This was why my short-lived marriage was also another punch line among the Montgomery clan. Luckily, Perrine wasn't going there today—yet.

"Gucci," I said before taking another bite. "From their sustainable line that came out a couple years ago."

"You gave a Gucci jacket to a stranger?" Her mouth was caught somewhere between a grimace and a grin.

"It's just a jacket."

"But…" Perrine stared at me. "Why?"

"Because it was the right thing to do." I pressed my lips into a straight line. I wasn't used to this, the strange, self-conscious discomfort that came with having to explain myself.

"And," I added, "it was the polite thing to do."

That would shut Perrine down. My actions were almost always clear-cut, done with precision and reason. These were easy decisions to explain. But it was a lot harder to justify a random act of kindness to a stranger.

The problem was, the woman on the subway hadn't felt like a stranger. Something about her had felt deeply familiar, like slipping into a favorite old sweatshirt. I'd noticed it immediately, right when she stepped on, before her dress fiasco. And then I couldn't stop glancing at her, the way the curls of her hair touched her forehead just so, her delicate lips like a perfectly tied bow. But her eyes were so sad, like a kid whose dog had just died.

What I felt wasn't sexual, not exactly. It was just a feeling, and it scrambled my brain. Like when you see a stranger and you can't stop staring at them, and you want to know what's going on in their head at that very second. And then when her dress ripped, and her expression downshifted into horror, well—I couldn't have stopped the urge to help her if I'd tried. And that uncontrollable, inexplicable feeling annoyed the crap out of me.

"But was she pretty?" Perrine said, interrupting my thinking.

"I mean"—I shrugged—"sure. But it's not like I was trying to ask her out."

The woman on the subway hadn't looked anything like the women I'd dated before or after Angie, or what my mother called my "blond army of exes," a flip remark she'd made last summer while offering her thoughts on the status of my dating life (or lack thereof).

"The Hayes doth protest too much, methinks."

"I wasn't!"

"Fine," Perrine said, narrowing her eyes and letting it go. But I knew thoughts were still churning away in her head. Perrine was calculating, and as inquisitive as a cat. Nothing got past her. Literally, nothing. It's what made her an amazing surgeon. But it's also what made her a pain in the ass.

Now my brain was off and running, remembering the long slope of the woman on the subway's nose, and her bright lips, and the way her short, wavy black hair framed the angles of her face just right. What had Perrine called it when she'd cut her hair short a few years ago? A bob? The first thought that had popped into my mind when I'd turned and seen the woman frantically wrestling with her dress was how my hands would fit perfectly in her curls. I shook my head to get the thought out of my brain, did a few neck rolls to loosen the tension that had settled there. Everything about today was just off.

I was off.

Perrine eyed me curiously as I tried to stretch the thought of that woman out of my brain.

"Look," I said, "I saw a problem, and I tried to help solve it." I pressed my lips into a smile, tilted my head to the side. "It's what I do best."

I dusted pretend dirt off my shoulder, and Perrine rolled her eyes in response. "You are such a dork." She laughed.

"I know. I really am," I said.

"What'd they say at work when you walked in without your jacket?" she asked, poking at a pepper with her fork.

"Nothing," I said, wiping my mouth with the paper napkin that I'd tucked into the collar of my shirt. "We don't have a formal dress code, you know. So even without my jacket, I'm still the most dressed-up person there. Plus, Eleanor's the only one who dares to give me crap about what I wear, and she's out today."

I'd said a silent prayer of thanks about it too, because a story about me swooping in to help a pretty woman on the subway would be like catnip to her. She'd never let it go.

Perrine laughed at this. "Eleanor's right."

"What?" I asked. "I can't help that I got used to wearing suits to work every day. Besides, it's just easier. It's my uniform. Steve Jobs had one. Obama. Hillary Clinton—"

"Okay, okay, I get it." Her voice was rife with sarcasm. "You're in the same category as Barack Obama."

"Thank you," I replied, crossing my arms in smug satisfaction. "Besides, wouldn't you have stepped in and tried to help? Helping people is your thing."

"True." She nodded in hesitant agreement. "But—and please don't take this the wrong way—*you* don't normally notice someone else's emotional state."

"What way *am* I supposed to take that?" I asked, giving her an offended look.

"I'm not saying you're not a nice person!" She raised her voice to make her point, and I gave her a smile to let her know my feelings weren't actually hurt. "I'm just surprised you even looked up from checking your email. Or that you weren't running a cost analysis of the situation first."

This got a chuckle out of me, because she wasn't wrong. I tended to veer into human-calculator territory, overlooking emotions for data, and reason, and logic. And I couldn't fully explain why I'd done it, why this one time my heart and gut instinct had overruled my brain without my permission.

"So what else?" she asked, and I shrugged, trying to act like there was nothing more to say.

"That's the story," I said as I gathered up my trash.

I didn't tell Perrine about the feeling of the woman's skin against my fingertips: hot like a sidewalk in the summertime. Or about the way her mouth shifting into a small O shape as she exhaled had needled my gut. I also didn't mention the story about her peeing herself. I definitely left that out.

I was normally clear on what needed to be done. It wasn't often that I got things wrong. But in that instant on the subway, I just might have, and my miscalculation was nagging at me. Maybe I'd overstepped, assumed she needed help when she was fine on her own. But she'd been so upset. And she'd shouted "Thank you" after me. I'd replayed it all a billion times in my head already, wondering if I'd done the right thing.

Whatever. I needed to let it go. I didn't need the jacket back, and it was long gone now, along with her perfect curls and her torn dress and that cardboard box she'd been balancing in her hands. The beauty of living in a city of eight million people is that I'd never see her again.

—*m*—

Seeing who could get to work the earliest was a friendly, unspoken competition between Eleanor and me. We'd started Arbor Financial Partners three years ago, both of us eager and idealistic after burning out on Wall Street. We'd aim to arrive at six thirty, always with giant coffee cups in hand, bright-eyed and determined. Sure, the competition was fun, but I loved the ritual more. Routine settled me. It gave me the endorphin rush that kick-started my day.

This morning, though, I'd decided to extend my run by a couple of miles, and so I was running late, arriving at 7:34. As I passed Eleanor's office, she glanced at her watch and gave me a self-satisfied smirk through the glass that separated her from the open floor plan. This morning, she was back in full effect: tortoiseshell glasses on, hands waving. She was doing what she did best, juggling fifty things at once, which is why she was simultaneously pounding away at her computer and grilling someone over the phone, her wireless earbuds poised precariously above gold hoops. I offered a casual wave, and she beckoned me inside.

"Uh-huh," she was saying as I walked in, arms crossed. "Yup, yup, I hear you."

I meandered over to where she'd hung framed pictures of all the press we'd gotten, and tweaked the frames that were slightly off-center: the *Wall Street Journal*, the *Financial Times*. *Forbes* had even put us on their 30 Under 30 list two years ago, heralding us for being "a fund that invests with compassion, and donates 1% of its earnings to environmental groups around the world. They're pushing the financial bro aside for something better: the financial do-gooder." Eleanor had the cover and article framed for my birthday; I turned thirty exactly seventeen days after that piece came out.

"Thanks, Luis," she said. "I'll have Tyler send it over by Friday."

She tapped her earbud to end the call. "Opening this Seattle office is going to be a nightmare," she said, and I nodded, already resigned to the stress of what expanding our company would mean. "We're going to need these investors to come through stat if we want any chance of expanding."

I gestured to a stack of photographs leaning against the wall behind her. "You already took those down?" Eleanor called herself an amateur photographer, but her work was stunning. The photos she took on her solo surfing excursion to Costa Rica a couple years ago had added a chill vibe to a space that could often get tense when deals were on the verge of being made— or broken.

"We move offices in, like, three months," she said matter-of-factly. "Might as well get a jump start on the packing."

In addition to trying to open an entirely new branch on the West Coast, Eleanor and I were shifting our whole New York City operation to a bigger, brighter space downtown, to accommodate our ever-expanding team. It was exciting and terrifying all at once, a bold declaration of the growth we were experiencing.

The thought of all the success we'd had the last few years made my stomach churn. It was one thing to be successful on my own, or just alongside Eleanor. But we now had an entire company to answer to, people with mortgages and families and car payments. I rarely doubted myself, but when I did, it was because I was worried about letting our team down.

"I have something for you," she said, her eyes revealing nothing. She reached into her leather tote bag and pulled out a bent copy of the *New York Post*. She pressed at it with her hands, flattening it on her desk and flipping a few pages until she found what she was looking for. "*Saved on the Subway!*" She read the headline out loud. "*Fashion disaster leads to romance with mystery man on the Q.*"

She looked at me again, like she was seeing a wild animal in the flesh for the first time. "You weren't going to mention you went all Hayes in Shining Armor on the train yesterday?"

I grabbed the paper out of her hand, reaching up to scratch the back of my neck.

"You really think that's me? That could be anyone." It was a terrible attempt at a cover-up.

"Don't play dumb with me." Eleanor leaned back in her chair with an exaggerated sigh, kicking her feet up onto her desk and crossing them. She slowly, purposely locked her fingers and cracked her knuckles. She knew I hated that sound. As her hands undulated back and forth, the sunshine pouring in from Fifty-Seventh Street connected with the massive diamond engagement ring on her finger, creating a spiral of light on her desk.

"What I think," she said, enunciating her words as she bent her fingers, "is that you were headed downtown to the new space yesterday morning. But what I *know* is that while you generally present as a curmudgeon—"

"Come on," I protested.

"You are at your core a nice person who wants to help when someone's in trouble."

"Well, thanks for the compliment," I said sharply, crossing my arms.

"Honestly, I'm impressed." She golf-clapped in my direction. "Your Boy Scout side rarely comes out in public."

"Excuse you." I rolled my shoulders, tried to relax. "Did I or did I not rescue a baby bird in college and let it live in my dorm room for two weeks?"

"You did." She laughed. She'd witnessed it firsthand all those years ago. "See, I know the real you that not everyone gets to see," she said with an affectionate smile, and it was true. I'd let Eleanor sleep on the couch in my dorm room for a week after her girlfriend dumped her and she was too depressed to sleep in her own room, and I drove her five hours up to Boston a few years ago, when her sister was hit by a car. And even though she and her fiancé, Henry, could easily afford a cat sitter, she still asked me to feed Luna when they were away, and I always said yes. She knew this side of me, the one that was often hidden behind the more obvious and shiny things that I presented to the world. It felt good, having a friend know me this well. Except right now.

"Also," she said with a wicked grin, "Tyler said you came in yesterday morning with no jacket on." Tyler was our assistant, fresh out of college and whip-smart. They'd mastered the job in one day, and knew every move made in this place. Of course they'd spotted me without my jacket and made a note of it on their mental checklist.

"Look, it wasn't a big deal," I conceded. "It was definitely not romantic."

Eleanor's brow tightened, and she squinted at me. "I didn't ask you if it was romantic."

I waved her off. "All that happened was a woman's dress got stuck in the door and ripped straight down the back—can you believe that? So I let her have my coat to wear." I crossed my arms defensively again. "I didn't know it would make the *New York Post*."

"So you're okay with people knowing it's you in this picture, then?" she asked.

"Yes, of course. It's not a big deal, but for the love of god, please stop badgering me about it. I have work to do."

"Okay, good, because New York News called to book you on their morning show, and I said yes."

She said the words at twice her normal speed.

My mouth dropped open in disbelief. "I'm sorry. What did you just say?"

"Tyler said a producer had emailed the general account. I had them forward it to me."

"You said you got a call."

"Well, first I emailed the producer back. Then she called. They tracked down the woman too."

I shook my head. "Then call them back and say no, Eleanor. This kind of thing is *your* specialty, not *mine*. You're the one who did the Ted Talk." I felt the anxiety creeping across my skin. "You, of all people, should know I have zero ability to speak in front of a crowd. Live television will be a disaster."

"It's a five-minute spot, Hayes. You say hi, she says hi, you laugh, you answer a couple questions. You'll blink, and it will be done." She said this like she was teaching a child how to tie their shoes.

"I don't think I've ever watched New York News in my life," I said, racking my brain for a time when I'd flipped to our local cable news station. ESPN, yes. CNN, sure. But NYN? Maybe for weather, once.

"Well, you're missing out. Pete Killian is a New York icon." She swooned, placing a hand to her heart. "A legend. Statue of Liberty levels of New-Yorky-ness, the Empire State Building of people—"

"Okay, I get it," I said, exasperated. "I get it. But it still sounds excruciating."

"Oh, Hayes, come on. You'll be fine." She shooed a hand in my direction. "But also, Paul thinks it's a good idea. For promoting the business. I looped him in."

Paul, the publicist we'd hired after the *Forbes* list had come out. Of course.

"We're paying him too much money to just ignore him, Hayes," she said in her quiet, firm voice.

"Okay," I said begrudgingly. "For the business. That's it."

I walked out, headed next door to my office, and tried to think about the conference call happening in just a few minutes. But instead, my thoughts shifted back to the woman on the train.

The thought of seeing her again shook my insides like a martini, left me feeling excited, buzzed, nervous. But what was most frustrating is that I couldn't solve the equation, couldn't answer the question of why she was making me feel this way. I needed to clear my head, resettle, reorganize my brain so that I could focus on the day ahead.

For a split second, I thought about heading back outside, pushing through the glass doors and out into the heavy spring air to take a lap around the block. Instead, I sat down, took a deep breath, and did what I did best: I got to work.

CHAPTER THREE

FRANNY

"WHY DID I agree to do this again?" I asked Cleo, who was bent over a plastic folding table set up in the corner of the NYN greenroom, smearing cream cheese on an everything bagel. "I haven't been on TV since I was interviewed by the local news in third grade about why New Haven pizza is the best in America. And I had a crumb under my nose the whole time, and for the rest of elementary school, kids called me 'Booger.' That should have been an omen or something."

"How the hell have I never heard that story before?" Cleo asked with a guffaw. "That's hilarious."

"Because it was traumatizing, and I've tried everything in my power to forget it. And of course my mom texted me about it today."

Wow honey your first time on TV since third grade! Good luck! is what she'd messaged me earlier this morning, followed by **How is the job search going?** It hadn't even been a week, and already I could feel her maternal worry hovering over my shoulder, which always left me feeling stressed, afraid I'd somehow let her down.

My mom and stepdad's opinion had always been that the best kind of job was the one that pays well, not the one that fulfilled your soul. Just the fact that I'd pursued a creative career had always made them nervous, and while they tried to keep that anxiety to themselves, I could still vividly recall them both sitting at the kitchen table, teeth clenched, as I described yet another low-paying internship. Maybe they worried like this because I was an only child. But then again, I had a lot of friends who were the only kid in their family, and none of them seemed to feel like they existed just to make their parents happy.

My job at Spayce had checked all the boxes for them, though, and maybe that's why I'd been comfortable staying put. It paid well. It was steady. Still, if I texted my mom back and told her I was abandoning all my interior design dreams to become an accountant, she'd be thrilled. The practical always won out with her, no matter what, and I hated feeling like I was on my way to disappointing her and also proving her right.

"Well, look, you're doing this because *she* said it was a good idea." Cleo shook her head at Lola, who was wedged into the corner of the couch I was perched on, squinting at her iPhone.

"Lola said you should do it because it's bullshit that someone can take a photo of you on the subway and make up a story about it like it's some sort of movie," said Lola in a chiding tone. She glanced up to glare jokingly in Cleo's direction.

Cleo nodded. "And to give you control over your own narrative. Get your power back. Which is an avenue I appreciate."

"I still wish I could just sue the person who posted this," I said with a resigned sigh.

"Of course you do." Cleo immediately puffed up into scholar mode. "But you actually have no legal recourse here. As we've discussed."

"Just go out there, set the record straight, say thanks, and drop the mic, Fran," Lola said, pausing her endless phone-tapping. "In and out, easy-peasy. You've got this."

I exhaled, feeling a little bit more at ease. In the past forty-eight hours, we'd discussed my "rip-cident" at length. That's what *Teen Vogue* had called it. I called it mortifying, with no chance of going away anytime soon.

"You're right. I can do this." I paced a few steps, as if moving my body could stamp out the nerves.

"You also said you wanted to see Hot Suit in the flesh again," reminded Cleo, in between bites.

"To say thank you!" I protested. "That's it."

"Oh, come on, we all want to see Hot Suit in the flesh," Cleo said with a smirk. "Look, sometimes the universe does provide, in the form of a hot piece of ass."

Lola shrugged at me. "Okay, she's not wrong there."

I twisted my hands together, wringing my fingers. "Seeing him again seems like a terrible idea now. Especially in front of, I don't know, a gajillion freakin' people?"

Cleo's eyes followed me as I fidgeted around the room—sitting down, standing, unsure of what to do with my body. "You should eat something," she said.

"What, and barf all over him after I've already wiped snot on his shirt?" I said, smoothing my dress, an old standby red sheath purchased at Zara a few years ago. "I'm sure he'd love that."

There was a knock at the greenroom door, and Eliza, the producer in charge of my segment, strode in, with Priya, the makeup artist who had done my full face an hour earlier, at her side. "Hey, just giving you a ten-minute heads-up," Eliza said matter-of-factly, as if appearing on TV were the most normal thing in the world. She was one of those people who talked at you but was always busy looking somewhere else. Priya gave me a sweet smile and began dabbing powder across my nose with a giant brush.

"We'll have the jacket out onstage, to the right of your chair, so you can give it to him when he comes out," Eliza said, eyeing something on her clipboard.

"And will someone tell me when to, like, hand it to him?" I

asked, nervously shifting on my heels. I hadn't mentioned it to Eliza—or Lola or Cleo for that matter—but I'd slipped a thank-you note inside the front pocket of the jacket. Nothing elaborate, but in case I was unable to clearly express myself on TV, I wanted to make sure I said thank you. Because if I took away the weirdness of this situation, all that remained underneath was gratitude, and—if I was being honest—the lingering memory of his touch, which still sent electric shocks through my body every time I thought about it.

"Pete will cue you with a question," Eliza replied before briskly exiting the room.

Priya reached into a giant pouch attached at her hip and spritzed my hair deliberately with hair spray. "All set, honey." She winked at me and followed Eliza out the door.

"Promise me," I said, turning to Lola and Cleo, "that we're going out for mimosas after this, no matter how it goes."

"Fran, I called in sick for you," Lola said, offering me a loving smirk. "You're stuck with me today whether you like it or not. Also, worst-case scenario, we can discuss the gorgeous woman I met in the bathroom earlier. I've already slid into her Insta DMs."

"You're unbelievable, you know that?" Cleo shook her head at Lola, but she was smiling too. This was classic Lola: confident, unabashedly brave, ready to flirt even while peeing.

"Maria, my TA, is handling seminar prep," Cleo assured me. "First round is on me."

"I love you guys," I said, my heart racing.

"And we'll start figuring out your new life plan," Lola said, reaching over to grab something out of her bag. "I got you a present that we can all do together later."

She passed a small white box to me, and one to Cleo. "A DNADiscovery kit?" I asked, reading the delicate black font across the front.

She nodded, all-knowing. "Remember when you said the other

night that losing your job felt like losing your identity? Well, now you can get to know more about the rest of you. And *we'll* do it with you. It'll be fun!"

She said this with a shrug of her shoulders, as if spitting into a bottle alongside friends were a typical bonding activity, like a night out playing pool.

"I'm pretty sure I know my results already," Cleo said with a scoff. Both sets of her grandparents had emigrated from Korea.

"And I'm going to be, like ninety-nine percent Ashkenazi," Lola said, laughing. "But you never know! One of my interns found a whole set of cousins they didn't know about."

My stomach churned at the thought of digging into my ancestry. There were some things we just didn't talk about in my family, the main one being my birth father.

"Or we could just focus on the fact that she's a Sagittarius with an Aquarius moon and Leo rising, and get her chart done," said Cleo, who yesterday had very studiously asked me for the exact time and location of my birth.

My thoughts were interrupted by a knock at the door. "We're ready for you," Eliza said with a wave of her hand forward. "Pete will lead the interview, but Jenna, our traffic reporter, is onstage as well. She covers subway delays, so it's a perfect tie-in."

I clasped my hands at my chest, turning back to my friends. "What if he thinks I'm a weirdo?" I lowered my voice in hopes that Eliza wouldn't hear me.

"One, he won't," Cleo said, steady and reassuring. "Two, who cares?"

"Three"—Lola tapped her index finger to her chin, squinting in thought—"do *you* care?"

The swirling sea of nerves in my stomach told me that yes—yes, I did care. I wanted this stranger to like me, to know that there was more to me than the sweaty, snotty mess he met on the subway. But there was no time to have this conversation right now. Instead, I twisted my middle and index fingers into symbols of good luck and gave my friends one last look, stretching my lips wide. "Are my teeth okay?" I asked them.

"Always," Cleo said, beaming, as if she were trying to transport all the love she felt for me into my body.

"Remember, you're a fearless, badass bitch," Lola said confidently.

"Have you met me?" I asked with a chortle, blowing them a kiss as I followed Eliza out the door.

The lights of the NYN studio were blinding, so much so that I almost missed it when the interview started. My stomach was in my knees, which were inexplicably sweating. I kept nervously tucking my hair behind my ear, even though it was firmly held in place with hair spray. In other words, I was a wreck.

"Our guest today has had quite a week," Pete said with a warm smile. He was perched on a stool next to Jenna, who nodded along, auburn ponytail bouncing. "Becoming a viral internet sensation in an instant must have come as quite a shock. Franny, why don't you tell us about it in your own words."

"Okay, well, first, thanks for having me!" I let out a nervous laugh and smiled just a bit too wide for what felt like an eternity. *Calm down, Franny.* I took a breath, attempted to relax.

"So yeah!" My voice was landing at a pitch higher than normal, and I cleared my throat before trying again. "I was laid off from my job that morning. Doing interior design."

I arched my back a little higher, sitting up unnaturally straight. Great. Did I look stiff? Did it look like I was trying too hard?

"There were budget cuts, and I was let go, which was a blow to my ego and my bank account."

Pete chuckled at this sympathetically, and his laugh was

comforting. I took a deep breath and settled into my stool, the nerves starting to slide away. I could do this.

"And then, if that wasn't enough, my dress got stuck in the subway door and ripped open," I continued, and this time I managed a mostly normal laugh. "Even by New York standards, it was kind of a disaster."

"And a stranger stepped in to help," Pete said, encouraging me.

"Yes," I said. "Another passenger on the subway very kindly offered me his jacket to wear."

"His suit jacket!" Jenna said with a big, bright smile.

"Yes, which was so nice of him, because I didn't quite feel like mooning the entire city on my walk home from the subway. Not that I have anything against butts! Butts are beautiful." Dear god, the words just kept tumbling out of my mouth without my brain approving them first. "Just, you know, I want to keep my butt private, for now."

"That's understandable!" Jenna said, and gave me an enthusiastic nod that sent her equally enthusiastic ponytail bobbing again.

"Lots of people were stepping in to help, but the coat saved the day. And that's why I'm here, really. To say thank you. And, of course, to return his jacket."

Pete turned his attention from me to the camera directly across from him. "Well, let's bring out your sartorial savior, Hayes Montgomery the Third, and get his side of things."

Of course a man who dressed like he'd stepped out of a Brooks Brothers catalog had a last name as a first name. But the "*Third*" tacked on to the end was surprising. How fancy.

From out of the corner of my eye, I saw a producer in a headset signal him toward the empty stool next to me. Our interaction on the subway had been such a blur—quite literally, what with my eyes full of tears the whole time—that I hadn't fully taken him in. But now it seemed like he was walking toward me in slow motion. And, wow, was there a lot of him.

He was taller than I remembered, and lean, with an aloof air as cool as the blue of his perfectly tailored suit, which accentuated the angles of his body. I offered a wide smile in his direction but got just a nod in return. He sat down, and I watched his pants pull up at the ankles. His navy socks were peppered with a globe pattern. Huh. Was Mr. Hot Suit the Third a bit of a quirky weirdo? I certainly hoped so.

"Hayes is a nationally recognized pioneer in the field of socially responsible investing." Pete tapped his note cards against his knee. "That's quite a résumé, Hayes!"

"Thank you," he said with a modest chuckle, his smile revealing his dimples. "We're very proud of the work we do."

I felt a swell of nerves bubble in my chest. This guy was not only nice to look at, but he was some sort of superhuman combination of Earth-saving finance wizard and subway do-gooder. I guess that explained the socks.

Jenna leaned in, all confident smiles and soothing tones. "Hayes, most of us ride the subway every day without making eye contact with people." She continued, "What inspired you to lend a helping hand—or jacket—to Franny here?"

I reminded myself that I was on TV and forced a tight smile onto my face. This was almost over. I could hang in for a few more minutes. I just needed to silence the alarm bells ringing out their "*He must think you're a complete mess*" tune on repeat in my brain. I went searching for something to focus on, and my mind traveled back in time to that moment his fingers pressed against my bare hip, and how even in that frantic moment they'd triggered something else in me. Something that had felt a lot like desire.

Hayes cleared his throat. "I just saw someone in need and offered to help."

Jenna gave him a bright, adoring grin in return. "A true knight in a shining *suit* of armor comes to the rescue," she said, cracking herself up as Pete guffawed next to her.

"I really appreciated that Ho—" I thankfully caught myself before the words *Hot Suit* came out of my mouth. "That Hayes stepped in to help."

"And so now you're known on the internet as 'SubwayQTs,'" Pete said with an eager grin.

"Yes, but that couldn't be further from the truth," I interjected quickly. The last thing I needed was Hot Suit thinking I was pining after him like some damsel in distress.

Hayes turned to me, eyes narrowed. For a brief second, I thought he seemed annoyed by my comment, but then he nodded. "Exactly," he said. "We don't even know each other."

"We're definitely not 'QTs,'" I added, shaking my head. "And it's so not okay for someone to make up a whole story about us like that. I appreciate his help. But the person who took those pictures of us, and the reporters who wrote all the news stories, made up this whole ridiculous romance for us. Like he swooped in and rescued me and we fell in love in two seconds."

Hayes crossed and uncrossed his long legs, and when I looked back at his face, his cheeks were flushed pink.

"Hayes, you agree?" Pete asked, leaning forward.

"I do. It's completely unacceptable to post photos of people online without their knowledge."

"And did Franny need rescuing?" Jenna asked.

"I mean, from what I saw, yes." He said this nonchalantly, crossing his arms in front of his chest and shifting in his seat. The double entendre, intended or not, was met with loud chuckles from Pete and Jenna, and Hayes's cheeks flushed a deeper shade of pink. He shot me an awkward look and then quickly averted his eyes.

I gritted my teeth in a tight smile. "Like I said, there were other people trying to help too," I chimed in. I was grateful for what Hot Suit had done, but the message they were hammering home, that I was desperate for this guy's help, was beyond irritating. "A woman offered me her hair clip, which would have probably done the trick."

Hayes raised his brows, and that blush from earlier was gone, replaced with a cocky smirk. He was laughing. Laughing at me, at what I'd said. "I saw...you," he said, his eyes meeting mine. "And I don't think a hair clip could have helped the situation."

And just like that, my gratitude was gone. Just who did this guy think he was, anyway?

"Your story was followed by hundreds of thousands of people online who were sure they saw sparks fly between the two of you," Jenna said.

"That's very flattering," I started.

"I'm sure Ms. Doyle is very nice," Hayes said, his voice low and firm. "But we...I'm...sure she's not my type."

My eyes tried to roll up and out of my head. *Not his type?* What kind of arrogant troll says that in front of millions of people on TV?

"Nor would I be hers, either. That's what I meant to say." He tried, unsuccessfully, to recover from the low blow he had just lobbed at me. "Whatever sparks people saw were all made up by the person who posted those photos of us online."

"Well, we'll let our audience decide if they're seeing sparks today! Franny," Pete said, shifting gears, "what's next for you?"

"Job searching, I assume?" Jenna leaned forward, perked up by the change of topics. She surely didn't mean it to sound belittling, but just the question alone made me feel small, a tiny puddle next to Hayes's waterfall of success. And then there was my mom, already texting me about jobs when I'd barely been unemployed for longer than a minute. I hated the mix of imposter syndrome and fear of letting people down that was churning inside me. So I opened my mouth.

"Actually, I just started my own business!" My voice was chipper, my smile so wide the edges of my lips felt like they could touch my ears. "I've always wanted to strike out on my own. I love getting my hands dirty and being involved in all parts of designing a space. Helping people realize that their decor can really be a bigger reflection of who they are and what they love."

"Girl!" Jenna's hands flew up in the air in delighted surprise. "That's amazing!"

"Thanks," I said, and for a moment I felt wildly bold and self-assured, as if I were really doing this and not telling a lie on TV. "I just finished a job with a bathroom I'm obsessed with. It's amazing what some truly great wallpaper can do to transform a room, especially one that's mostly used for—you know."

Thank god I somehow managed to stop myself before I said "pooping" on live TV.

"So what's your website?" Jenna asked excitedly. "Where can we find you?"

"Um." My brain stalled, frenzied. Because I did not have a website. I did not have clients, or a business. That bathroom with the great wallpaper was from that job I'd done for James over three years ago.

I gulped. What the hell had I just done?

"FrannyDoyle..." I was reaching for something. Anything. "Design...dot-com." *Great job, Franny. Very creative.*

Pete gave me a congratulatory nod. "Well, we wanted to get the opinion of someone who knows you well, and so we've got a special commentator to give us thoughts on your adorable subway meet-cute."

He waved at a video screen that hung overhead. "Joining us live on satellite is Franny's mom, Diane."

"Oh my fucking god," I muttered through clenched teeth.

"Hi, honey!" my mom said with a wave, her salt-and-pepper hair tucked back with a thick blue headband. "You two look so nice together."

She was in her kitchen, which was covered in the same floral wallpaper that had hung there since I was in middle school.

"Mom, hi!" I said with a goofy wave, trying not to let any of the horror I felt seep onto my face. Out of the corner of my eye, I caught a quick look at Hayes, who was gazing at me with a face that was all sympathy.

Jenna turned to my mom's giant pixelated head. "You must be so proud of Franny, starting her own business after all of this, and finding success right off the bat."

"I am. She's my only kid, and I always worry, because that's what moms do. So this is great news. Your own business!" The glee was evident in her voice. The relief too.

"And what do you think, Diane—are they cute together or what?" asked Pete, his white teeth flashing.

"I approve!" Mom said, clasping her hands together. "Franny hasn't brought a boyfriend home since college, so I'd love to welcome a gentleman friend anytime."

It was official. I was going to die here, on live TV, in the middle of the NYN studio. Cause of death: utter humiliation. I was certain Hayes would be chuckling along at this just like Pete and Jenna, but when I glanced over at him, he just gave me a small smile.

"Thanks, Diane." Pete waved her off-screen, and then he and Jenna turned their attention back to us.

"Hayes," said Pete, "we tried to get your folks to join us, but they were unreachable. Apparently, they're on a European river cruise."

I swear his shoulders noticeably relaxed at this news.

"Well, we wanted to give these two a chance to see if an actual love connection might be possible." Jenna shifted to face the camera directly, announcing this to the at-home audience. "So we've built our very own romantic date spot right here in the studio." She gestured to an area slightly offstage that I hadn't noticed earlier. A café table had been set up, complete with coffee cups and a tiny vase of flowers.

Hayes didn't reply right away; he just blinked, and for a moment, I saw what appeared to be a look of pure horror cross his face. And I was right there with him. The last thing I wanted to do was spend more time on TV, hashing out the most awkward experience of my life with Hayes Montgomery *the Third*.

"Why don't you two take a seat at our Café NYC, courtesy of our sponsor Folger's, and get to know each other a little bit."

Hayes was smiling, but it was the kind of smile you wore to dress up a grimace. Eliza hadn't mentioned anything about a fake coffee date when she'd reassured me that the interview would be an in-and-out kind of thing. The way his eyes squinted in response was a dead giveaway: He hadn't been told about this either.

"Look, like he said, I'm not his type." I let my sarcasm soak in for a second but forced a laugh to let the world know I was totally cool with what he'd said. Even though I definitely was not. "I really just came here to return his coat and say thank you," I said, grabbing it off the faceless mannequin positioned next to me. "I even dry-cleaned it. To get the tears off."

I handed the jacket to him, my arms stiff, and he took it, a begrudging look on his face.

"Let this be a lesson to all the gentlemen out there," said Pete knowingly. "Or anyone who wears a suit! Could be ladies too. If you want to meet a nice match, just give them your jacket. I know *I'm* taking notes. A smooth move, Hayes." He leaned over and playfully elbowed him, like they were sharing an inside joke.

"That's not what I was trying to—" Hayes started, only to be interrupted by Jenna, who wisely seemed to sense it was time to change course.

"Well, that's just wonderful," she said. "All right then, Subway-QTs, we'll let you get to it! Hayes, Franny, thank you both so much for coming on. We'll be back after the break with Weather on the Ones, and some summer fashion trends at a price that won't break the bank."

"We're at commercial!" the director yelled, and suddenly a rush of people were on the floor of the studio.

Jenna's grin shrank the second the cameras were off. "God, that was awkward," she muttered to Pete, but it was still loud enough for me to hear. And she was right. All I could remember from the last five minutes was Hot Suit essentially dissing me on live TV, my mom's giant face, and me lying about having my own business. Dear god, why had I said that?

But before I could collapse in a panicked heap, Eliza was there with an arm on my shoulder, guiding me toward the "café." Priya walked alongside us and fussed with a curl that kept falling in my face.

"Hey, you didn't say anything about this 'get-to-know-each-other' thing," I said to Eliza. "Not that I ever say no to free coffee, but I thought this was supposed to be quick."

"Last-minute change," she said with zero feeling, digging into the mic pack attached to the collar of my dress to switch off my microphone. "Your mics will be off, so we'll just be cutting back to you from time to time in the next segment."

"And we're live in three, two…" Cameras locked in on Hayes and me as we sat facing each other, steaming cups of coffee in front of us. I waited for him to say something—anything—but he just stared at me and the table. "So," I deadpanned, "come here often?"

He offered what sounded like a genuine laugh. "Oh yeah, every morning. I'm a regular. They know my order and everything. Non-fat caramel macchiato with two shots of espresso and whipped cream. See?" He picked up the cup and showed it to me. It was black, but I played along.

"Impressive," I said, brows raised.

Then he brought it to his mouth, taking a small sip. "Mmm," he groaned, all pleasure. "Exactly how I like it."

"So," I said as I reached for the small pot of cream and dumped half of it in my cup. "I'm not your type?" It's not like I needed any more confirmation of this fact, but again my mouth was moving faster than my brain.

56

"Hey," he said, and his tone wasn't jokey anymore. "That wasn't at all what I was trying to say. Sometimes the words get tangled in my brain, if that makes sense."

It did make sense. Too much sense, if I was honest. I felt exactly the same. So much so that I had made up a business on live TV. But I was not going to give this guy any more satisfaction today.

I paused for effect, simply to needle him a little more. "No big deal. Happens to me every day. Water under the bridge."

I waved him off and watched his eyes dart from me to the table, then back to me again. They were so dark and yet so beautiful. Not the sparkly bright kind that populated the romance novels I used to sneak from my grandma Elsie's shelves in middle school, books I later packed up and took to the assisted living facility she'd had to move in to. Books I had to toss last year when she'd passed. His eyes were dark and swirling, murky, like the ocean in winter. Every time they moved, his thick black eyelashes swept across them in a hypnotic, rhythmic fashion, like they were trying to get me to forget what had just gone down.

"What I meant to say was that I didn't think I was *your* type. I don't"—he ran his fingers through his hair—"have a way with words, let's say. I work in finance. I do data and numbers. I don't always know how to articulate what I feel. I meant that…" He was searching. "I don't normally date women like you."

I threw my hands up. "Seriously?" I laughed. "You're only making this worse! Did you not see my mom up there, telling the world I haven't brought a man home in almost ten years? I'm not having a good day."

"No." He waved his hands in front of his chest. "I mean, I don't pick women up on the subway."

How was it possible that a man this handsome was also this socially inept?

"Well, where do you pick women up, then?" I took a sip of my coffee, holding the cup to my lips as I swallowed. It was warm, and the smooth edge of the mug was grounding. "The stock exchange?"

He laughed at this, and nodded his head as if to say "*You got me there.*"

"Well, I'd never be caught dead dating a finance bro, so…" I crossed and uncrossed my legs, which were still sweaty, under the table, kicking his shin in the process. "Sorry," I said. "About kicking you just now. Not about the finance-bro comment."

He waved my apology off with his hand, which was lean and muscular. Could hands be muscular? I'd never even considered this before, but his most definitely were. And again, I was remembering the feel of his hands on my back as he'd braced me on the train. Now it was my turn to blush.

"Do I come across like a bro?" He edged forward in his seat, his brow furrowed but not angry. He seemed genuinely curious that this was what I thought of him.

"I mean—you wear suits to work, you're on some *Forbes* list, you have a last name for a first name. I'm just hypothesizing here, but you probably also played lacrosse in high school and graduated from an Ivy League college."

"Soccer," he replied, raising one of those beautifully lush brows. "And I definitely didn't go to an Ivy."

"Oh yeah? Where'd you go?"

"Stanford. And Cal for grad school."

I raised my hands in defeat, flopping them in my lap. Those schools may not be in the Ivy League, but they sure as hell were just as hard to get into. Was he for real?

"Look, let's just pretend this whole thing never happened, okay?" I poured a bit more coffee into my mug, and then another generous slug of cream. "I mean, you're not wrong. This"—I gestured between us—"would never be a thing."

He nodded in agreement, though there was a slight flush to his cheeks, and he looked away as he responded. "I think we can both agree that the girl who thought we were QTs was a total idiot."

"Oh, completely. We are not QT material." I leaned back in my chair and looked over to where a tween girl was modeling some sort of sundress for Pete and Jenna.

"I'm sorry you were let go from your job." His voice was softer, almost kind. "But it's great you've already started your own business."

"Yeah, that's me!" I said, mustering up some faux confidence. "Always on to the next risky thing. I'm excited to…go out on my own for a bit. See how it feels to work for myself."

"So you decorate rooms, then? Buy furniture for people?"

"Not exactly," I said, and for the first time today I could feel genuine excitement hitch in my chest. I loved talking about interior design. "That's what everyone thinks, but it's about more than just decorating. It's about creating experiences. Capturing and expressing and inspiring emotions within an environment."

He nodded. "My mom's been trying to get me to hire someone to decorate my apartment for years now. She says it lacks personality."

"Let me guess." I studied him—looking at his face, his suit, the slight curl in his hair like I would a floor plan.

"Leather couch. Probably expensive. Coffee table. Modernist, sleek, black. No dresser in your bedroom. Neutral-color sheets. You keep meaning to hang art on your walls, but you haven't yet, and—let's be honest—you probably never will."

He shrugged and took a sip from his mug and then raised it toward me, a toast to my skills. "You're good," he said. "I bet you're already in high demand."

I just nodded, pretending like he was right on the nose. "That's why I do what I do, and you do…whatever it is you do."

He cleared his throat. "Have you read any good books lately?"

I cocked my head to the side. "Why? Do you need a recommendation?"

He shrugged. "I was just curious about what you like to read."

I thought for a moment and then perked up. "Ooooh, do you like cults?"

He appeared very confused by this question. "Why would anyone like cults?"

"Not, like, in a join 'em way," I explained. "Reading about them."

He shook his head, giving me another perplexed look.

"Okay, fine." I let out a sigh, giving up on the cult-book recommendation. "What was the last thing you read?"

"A book called *Getting Things Done*," he replied. "It's about productivity. People are obsessed with it. There are all these meet-ups and classes you can go to for it. I had lunch with a client the other week who told me it changed his brain."

"So it's…" I motioned with my hand, trying to get him to finish my sentence, but he didn't bite. Fine. *"A cult."*

Hayes smiled at me and then shook his head, as if he didn't quite know what to make of me. The feeling was mutual.

We sat in silence for a bit. "Is Franny short for Frances?" he asked, and I had to admit his awkwardness was kind of charming.

"No." I scrunched my nose. "Everyone thinks it is, though. It's Francesca."

"Francesca," he repeated back to me. "I like it."

I shook my head. "I'm Franny, unless you're my grandma, who's dead, or my mom when she's pissed off at me. My stepdad calls me Franny-Bananny, which I hated in high school."

"Maybe I could call you Francesca-Bananesca," he joked.

"Oh yeah, that has a great ring to it." I nodded. "It would sound amazing being screamed during sex."

Oh god. Those words had actually exited my mouth, and there was no putting them back in. I avoided his eyes, letting the horror wash over me as I forced myself to fixate on a camera in the corner, as if it were the most interesting thing I'd ever seen. It felt like an hour had passed when I turned back to face him, expecting him to be avoiding my gaze. Instead, he just smiled and stared directly at me, in a way that was so intimate I had to look away again. And of course not being able to hold his gaze only made me feel more self-conscious, and made my brain start buzzing with the urge to move my body.

I went to chug the rest of my coffee, but somehow the cup missed my lip and coffee dripped down my chin and onto my dress. Before I knew what was happening, Hayes had leaned forward with his napkin, but as he tried to hand it to me, his elbow knocked the creamer over, and it rolled into my lap and then shattered onto the floor.

"Oh god, I'm so sorry," he said, grabbing my napkin and wiping off the table frantically as cream dripped onto my leg.

"Please don't take this the wrong way..." I sighed as I blotted up the coffee that had already seeped into my dress. "But this is definitely the worst first date I've ever been on."

When it was finally over, Eliza steered me offstage and back to the greenroom. I flopped onto the couch, eager to hide. As soon as she left, I flipped a middle finger in her direction.

"Dude," Lola said, running her hands through her yellow-white hair, "that was a small shit show."

Cleo turned a stern eye in her direction. "Lo..."

"I'm sorry. But it was. Your mom?" She grimaced, mouth tight.

Cleo begrudgingly nodded in agreement. "Okay, yeah. Lola's right. That was rough."

"You're lucky FrannyDoyleDesign.com was available," Lola added.

"We bought you the URL," Cleo said, sitting down next to me.

"You two are amazing." I paused for a breath, letting the madness of the morning register in my brain. "I am trying not to freak out, but I am freaking out."

"How the hell did that even come out of your mouth?" Lola looked like she was trying not to laugh.

"I don't know!" I pressed my palms to my forehead. "I just wanted to sound like I had my shit together."

"I can't believe they made you sit there for fifteen minutes and fake-date," Cleo said, incredulous.

"Trust me, it was even more awkward than it looked on TV." I smooshed my face into a pillow. "I told Hayes it was the worst first date I'd ever been on. Turns out he's sort of an asshole."

"Ouch," Lola said with a grimace. "But seriously, how can he be so attractive and also so awkward? He was such a dick."

"He's shy? Or he was just as nervous as I was?" I guessed. "Or maybe he was raised in a fancy mansion by wolves."

"Bingo," Cleo declared with a wave of her finger. "They did say his parents were on a cruise. Seems like a cover-up."

"In his defense, I did make a very dumb sex joke and then spilled coffee all over myself," I said as I sat up and straightened out my dress. "It's not like I brought my A game to our fake coffee date."

"Well, luckily you never have to see him again," Cleo said, wrapping an arm around my shoulder.

I felt a strange twinge of disappointment as she said this but brushed it off quickly. "Thank god," I said with a groan. "Because my track record with the guy is terrible."

Lola bent over the table and smeared cream cheese on a sesame bagel. "You did great, Fran," she said, taking a huge bite as she walked back to the chair she'd been sitting in. "He was terrible."

"Finish that, and then let's go," I begged. "And let us never speak of this morning again."

"Oh, we're gonna speak about it again," Cleo said with a laugh. "Like, every day for the rest of your life."

"We are. Sorry." Lola nodded with an exaggerated apologetic bob of her head. "I am literally going to bring it up every chance I get." She stood a bit taller, puffing out her chest, pretending to chat with a stranger. "What was that? You love watching New York News? Have I told you about the time some dumb guy told my amazing friend she wasn't his type on their morning show?"

"You're hilarious," I deadpanned back.

Cleo stood up and leaned over me, planting a kiss on the top of my head. "You're definitely *our* type, though."

"Like, you're my type exactly," Lola chimed in reassuringly. "And, hey, you didn't have a booger on your face this time. That's definitely an improvement."

"I told you, it wasn't a booger!" I said with a laugh. "It was a crumb."

I rose from the couch, grabbing my purse and throwing it over my shoulder. "Okay, let's do this."

Lola snaked her arm through mine. "Time to toast Franny Doyle Design!"

Cleo grabbed another bagel from the table and tossed it in her tote bag. "Smart," I said, unlocking from Lola for a second to do the same.

Cleo tucked in close to my other side, and we walked out arm in arm, taking up as much space as we could as we made our way down the long hallway. As we emerged into the chaos of Midtown in the middle of morning rush hour, Lola stretched her arms to the sky, then landed one over my neck as we walked, pulling me in close. "Hey, Fran, have we ever told you we love you?"

Cleo, already on her cell phone dealing with work, looked up in agreement. "Big-time. Who needs a Subway QT when you have us?"

I felt awash in love for them, my chosen people, my unrelated family.

"I love you too, you jerks."

CHAPTER FOUR

HAYES

"DO YOU WANT the good news or the bad news first?"

Eleanor somehow managed to get the words out through a mouthful of oatmeal. I was snipping at a hot-sauce packet with a pair of scissors. We normally did our weekly check-in meeting around 4 p.m., but it was the Friday before a long weekend, and so we'd pushed it to the morning.

"What kind of question is that?" I asked, dumping the hot sauce onto my egg-white wrap. "You know I'm a bad news first sort of person, always."

You were better off assuming the glass was half-empty, I liked to reason, because then it was a nice surprise if you find out it might just be half-full. This logic had driven Angie nuts. "Where's the joy in that?" she said to me once, exasperated on a car ride out to Montauk for a long weekend with my parents. I had been complaining prematurely, assuming it was already a wash of a vacation. "That way," I'd explained matter-of-factly, "I'll appreciate it more if it doesn't suck."

I'd eventually come to find out that by then, almost everything I did had driven Angie nuts, my obsession with work topping her list. It wasn't lost on me that this memory was sneaking into my brain during an early work meeting.

"The good news, then!" Eleanor said as she sprinkled a packet of brown sugar on her oatmeal. "I had Tyler compile all the inquiries we've gotten since your lovely appearance on New York News." She spun in her chair to face her computer, clicking away at the keyboard.

"According to their tally, we've had"—she scrolled through an Excel spreadsheet—"twenty-six cold inquiries, total. Now, granted, at least ten of them were marriage proposals or some sort of other proposition."

"Well, I guess that's better than people calling me an asshole," I said, with a hint of relief.

"Oh, you sweet dummy." She rolled back toward me in her chair, an overly sympathetic look on her face, playing it up for effect. "We had plenty of those too. I asked Tyler not to include them in the document." Eleanor reached forward to pat me on the head, but I swatted her hand away and ducked before she could get to me.

"I really came across like a jerk, huh?" I slouched forward to lean my elbows on my knees. For the last few days, I'd been replaying my conversation with Franny in my head, which was something I rarely did, even after a terrible business meeting.

"I've definitely seen you have better moments," Eleanor said with a laugh that was full of affection.

"Thank god the audio from our coffee date wasn't recorded," I said with a sigh. I didn't normally get hung up on stuff, and it was starting to annoy me that I couldn't shake the weird feelings our fifteen minutes of fame had stirred up. "It was so uncomfortable. I asked her what books she read."

"And?" Eleanor asked.

"I don't know. She said something about a cult book, and I kinda froze," I said.

Eleanor cringed, her shoulders shooting up to her ears. "I love books about cults," she said, and while Eleanor's reply didn't surprise me, I was still having trouble wrapping my mind around Franny and cults. The fact that I was trying to was worrisome in and of itself.

"Well then, *you* should go on a televised coffee date with her," I replied, the snark evident in my tone.

"I would," she said as she sipped a can of seltzer water. "We could discuss wallpaper. She seems supercool. Definitely *my type*."

Eleanor raised her brows at me, waiting for my reaction. Instead, I just took a giant bite of my food, not giving her the satisfaction of getting a rise out of me.

"Maybe you just need to go on a real date," she suggested. "Like a palate cleanser."

I shook my head. "I can't deal with dating apps right now."

"Let me set you up, then." She perked up at this idea, a smile on her face. "It'll be fun. I still have some cool, hot friends you haven't met yet."

The idea of recalibrating sounded appealing. I needed to get rid of this awkward, restless feeling, and fast.

"Go for it," I said. Eleanor relished a challenge. "Do your best."

We ate quietly for a minute until I realized we hadn't actually discussed her bad news. "Hey," I said through a mouthful of food. "What was the other thing?"

Eleanor sighed, a resigned look on her face. This wasn't a good sign. "Damien Yi just quit."

My stomach dropped. "What do you mean, he 'quit'?"

"He got hired to go do some socialite's new apartment in London," she explained, clearly annoyed.

"But we had a contract." I kept my voice calm, steady. Even when the news was panic-inducing, I never panicked. At least not in front of other people. But my brain was already in overdrive, working at a clip to try to figure out how we could solve this.

"We did, but the new offer was competitive, and in his favor. We had a cancellation clause in the contract, so we're getting our money back, if that's any consolation."

"Fuck." I ran a hand through my hair. Our new office space was set to open the first week of August, and we'd already pushed back the move by five months because the architect needed more time.

With all the disruption of the impending move, we'd let most of our small team work from home, but the office was the heart of our operation, and I was eager to get everyone back and in person in our new space. The build-out had just wrapped, and we were scheduled to have a call this week with Damien, the darling of the sustainable design world, about furniture and load-in dates. It was all supposed to culminate in a party showcasing our new office, which would highlight our commitment to sustainability, right down to the desks we used.

"I didn't put up a stink, because he's someone we're going to want to work with in the future," Eleanor explained pragmatically.

"I get that," I said, "but we've already had the kickoff meeting. He'd said he was planning to source all the deliverables this week. It's a huge pain in the ass."

Eleanor took another bite and nodded in agreement, tapping her fingers against her lips in thought.

"We can figure it out," I said, trying to muster up some blind confidence. After all, this is what Eleanor and I did best: problem-solve, throw water on fires, tackle a crisis and bear-hug it to the ground without anyone noticing. But Damien's leaving was an enormous—and unexpected—challenge, and it threw our perfectly curated timeline and schedule off track.

My mind flashed back to what Franny had said as we sat across from each other, coffee steaming in those stupid NYN-branded mugs: *It's about creating experiences.* I wondered, just briefly, how she might shape this one. She said she was booked solid, though, so that was out of the question. Also, I'd insulted her on TV. Not just in front of half of New York City, but her mom too. There was no way she'd ever want to talk to me again, much less work together. I tried to steer my mind in another direction, but it got stuck imagining what her hair looked like right this second. If it was tucked behind an ear or falling into her eyes.

"Oh, totally," Eleanor said, jolting me out of my thoughts. "We just don't have much time. Especially if we're also trying to figure out the West Coast office logistics. But I've already pinged Paul, since he knows every interior designer in the city."

We needed Paul to come through. The guest list for the party included the most important people in the financial and environmental worlds, people we wanted—no, *needed*—to impress. If we didn't pull this together, we'd look like amateurs, which wouldn't be good for our business or our bottom line. Or my stress levels, for that matter.

Suddenly, a cocktail seemed very necessary. "Hey, do you and Henry want to grab a drink tonight?" I asked Eleanor.

"I'm going out to Montauk, remember?" she replied, a sympathetic look on her face. "I'm meeting Henry at the Jitney after lunch."

Eleanor turned back to her computer, tapping her inbox open. "Are you getting together with Perrine this weekend?" The question was casual, but I knew what was up: Eleanor was searching for info.

"I think so," I said, not looking up from my phone screen. Perrine was on call all weekend. But maybe we'd get together. So not a lie, in theory.

"Hey!" She paused to look up at me as she stood and began piling the trash on her desk. "Why not take the rest of the day off? Give yourself a little break to chill?"

"Didn't we just establish that we have a ton of shit to do?" I leaned back in my chair, arms crossed.

"We did, but the entire city will be shutting down at one o'clock today for the long weekend. You need a full day off, but I know you won't give yourself that, so at least take a couple hours."

"I'll think about it," I said to placate her as she grabbed a bottle of Tums she'd placed on her desk earlier this week and twisted the cap off, popping two pale-pink tablets into her mouth.

"One afternoon to relax, Hayes," she said, and I could tell she was annoyed that I was resisting.

I shrugged. "I've been up since five. I got all my relaxing done already." I'd gone for my run. Showered. Scrolled through every social media app on my phone.

There was nothing left for me to do but work.

"I know, but…" She shook her head in irritation. "One afternoon! The company can survive without you for one afternoon, I swear."

She was right. The problem was, I couldn't survive without work. I had figured this out thanks to the four therapy sessions I'd had after Angie and I first separated. She had blamed my career, and the hours I spent devoted to it, as the reason our relationship had stalled out, dried up.

I'd never pushed back on this; I'd wanted things to work between us more than I'd wanted to be right in the situation. But she had also devoted long hours to a career she loved. Maybe it was easier for her to blame work than to tell me the hard truth, which came out later: She had fallen out of love with me and was questioning if she'd ever been in love with me at all.

And so I'd thrown myself back into work as my relationship crumbled and was left in the hands of lawyers to resolve. I quit therapy, because I was too busy at the office. I focused on building Arbor into something bigger than we'd originally imagined. Without my job, and this company, I felt purposeless and bored. Eleanor knew this about me too. That's why she stopped pushing it.

"But look," I said, holding my hands in front of my chest as if to say "*Ta-da!*" "I didn't wear a tie today. Doesn't that count for something?"

She laughed but didn't otherwise respond, choosing instead to plop back down in front of her computer and take a giant sip of her seltzer.

"Hey." I cleared my throat as I stood to toss my food wrapper in the trash. "Do you think I should contact Franny and apologize for how weird I was on New York News?"

"What is this about, exactly?" Eleanor squinted at me and pursed her mouth to the side, her telltale sign that her brain was chewing on something.

"I've been feeling like an asshole since I made those stupid comments on TV." I rubbed a hand along the back of my neck. "And clearly I was, if people emailed us about it."

I really didn't want to rehash our awkward televised conversation again, but I also hadn't been able to let it go.

"I'm sorry I pressured you do to it," she said, a regretful look on her face. "But I didn't think it was that bad."

"Trust me, I was…" I blew out a sigh, trying to figure out the best words to describe myself. Instead, I went with: "You know…how I can be."

"Yes, I do. Proud and stubborn and occasionally an idiot when it comes to expressing anything that even resembles emotion." She leaned forward and gave my arm a squeeze.

Well. Leave it to Eleanor to find all the words. I opened my mouth to protest, but she waved me off.

"But I also know how truly kind you are, Hayes," she continued. "And I know this whole thing blew up in your face, but try to remember it started from you doing something nice."

"If I recall correctly, you and Perrine agreed that I acted, and I quote, 'borderline chauvinistic.'"

"Well, yes, that too, maybe," she said. "But you're good to the core, Hayes Montgomery. I know that, and don't you forget it."

She smiled at me, one of her serious smiles that she didn't offer up too often.

"Maybe she knows someone," Eleanor said, her brain shifting back into work mode. "For our space. She's a designer. She definitely has contacts."

She turned to her computer but then twisted around toward me almost immediately. "Or!" She waved her index finger to signal that a brilliant idea had just arrived. "We could just hire her," she said. "Money is better than an apology, right? Plus, it could be cool to work with an up-and-coming designer."

"Are you insane?" I tightened my grip around my coffee cup. "I asked if I should send a quick apology, not hire her."

Eleanor shrugged. "Suit yourself."

Later that afternoon, long after Eleanor had grabbed her canvas duffel bag and hustled out of the office, I walked home, the air muggy but slightly cool, the city already emptied out. I plotted my weekend in my head: work, run, work. Central Park would be quiet, which would be nice. Maybe get my ass in gear and hang some art. (Franny had been right about my apartment lacking personality.) Watch the Yankees–Red Sox series. I could order food. I'd check in with Perrine.

There was plenty to do. And I'd always told myself that I didn't mind the quiet, thought I was built for independence, that from isolation grew ideas and innovation. I'd accepted it as the consequence of a failed marriage. It was what I deserved, even, for not noticing things had gone off the rails until it was too late to save our relationship.

But recently, the quiet of my life was starting to feel too quiet. I had people who loved me and whom I loved too, and yet every time I got home to an empty apartment at the end of the day, the loneliness that whispered at my back turned into a roar.

Maybe, I reasoned, as I turned onto Central Park West, that was what had been so thrilling, so maddening about that morning a few weeks ago on the subway. And why, even though I'd said a bunch of dumb stuff to Franny in our interview together, I couldn't push her out of my thoughts. It had been a jolt of something frustrating and exhilarating all at once. For a second, my life had skipped a beat. And I'd liked that feeling. I'd liked it a lot.

—︁ɯɯ︁—

"What's this?" Eleanor stared at the folder I'd left on her desk. It was the day after the long weekend, barely 8 a.m., but we were already operating at warp speed.

"A list of possible designers. Some images of their work. There's a really cool woman in there who did Tesla's new office."

"Look at you, jumping into action." She gave them a glance and nodded at me approvingly. "Not bad."

I passed her compliment off with a shrug.

"I had some free time this weekend." Free time, no plans—same thing.

"And now I need you to do something else for me." Her smile was wicked, glinting. She was enjoying this. "You have to go on a date with Henry's coworker Serena."

When she said she wanted to set me up, I hadn't realized she meant immediately. "And subject another unsuspecting victim to my winning ways?" I scoffed, shaking my head.

"Oh my god," she grumbled with an eye roll. "We've already established you were a dick to Franny."

"On live TV," I added. Yes, it was still bothering me.

"Hayes, it's in the past. It's time to deal with it and move on," she said, as if that were an easy thing to do.

But my brain wasn't letting me move on. Instead it was circling the memory over and over again, still.

"It doesn't need to be about romance," she continued, her voice shifting into life-coach mode, peppy and confident. "Become her friend, for all I care. You need to see other people besides...you know."

She gestured broadly, waving her hand through the air as if she were presenting our office as a prize on a game show.

"You," I said, my voice monotone. I didn't quite feel like playing along.

"And Perrine, yes." Her gaze shifted from mischievous to kind.

"I'm not trying to be a pain in the ass, you know," she said, pushing back in her chair to get a good look at me. "You're my friend. I'm allowed to worry about you sitting alone in your apartment every night."

"I'm not," I protested, but she wasn't wrong.

"You know what I mean," she said, and I did. "And look, you know I love to matchmake, and I've kept my mouth shut since you and Angie broke up. That's been, like, seven hundred years."

"Three," I corrected.

"Whatever," she said, waving me off.

I sighed. "Fine." Maybe it would be nice to meet someone new. I'd been mostly relying on dating apps this past year, and I hadn't made it past the fourth date with anyone I'd met there.

"She's a big runner, like you, and she's training for the New York City Marathon." Her eyes lit up, excited by possibility. "She's very into her job, and she does all this volunteer work. Real type A. She's great. Also she's hot and she's blond. She's like your perfect woman."

Apparently, I'd given everyone in my life the impression that I only dated blond women. But still, she seemed interesting, and appealing in a way that calmed my swirling brain.

"One date," I said.

"Don't get too excited there, buddy."

Her words were playful, but I took them as a dare. *Okay, fine,* I told myself. *I accept.*

CHAPTER FIVE

FRANNY

Thoughts?

A selfie of Lola in a short black dress and studded, heeled ankle boots popped up immediately after her text. Her bleached-blond hair was slicked back, her lips painted an inviting bright red. A rock star, this one.

Cleo responded with a heart-eyes emoji before I could finish typing my reply, which was a short and pointed **YESSSSSS**. And I meant it. Lola looked like a sex bomb. But she always looked like a sex bomb, even when she was on my couch in her NYU sweats and streaky day-old mascara, inhaling a Gatorade and an egg-and-cheese on a bagel after a raging night out.

Whenever we teased her—part in awe, part out of jealousy—that she looked sexy no matter what she was doing or wearing, she'd just offer, "I'm a Scorpio," with a shrug. Cleo had helped her figure out her astrological chart a couple of years ago, and now that was her excuse for everything. Overdramatic? Scorpio. Quick to flip a finger at taxis that run through yellow lights? Scorpio. Fiercest, most loyal friend on the planet, who also holds a grudge like nobody's business? Scorpio, baby.

So yeah, it was no surprise that she would stun on a first date.

Do I also look .4% French? According to my DNA test results I'm tres chic.

We'd all spit into the little DNA containers at brunch after my NYN appearance, and Lola had sent them off in the mail. It was shockingly easy; a few weeks after getting your sample, the company emails you back with DNA results, health predispositions, and any connections to relatives that may be in their database. Cleo's results had come in a few days ago, and as expected, she was all Korean. Lola had just gotten an email and was apparently the tiniest bit French and now milking it for all that it was worth.

I still haven't gotten anything, I wrote back.

Did you tell your mom yet? asked Cleo.

No. I'm operating on a need to know basis with her.

It was only fair, honestly. That was how my mom had always approached the info she gave me, especially when it came to the identity of my birth father. "I met him at a bonfire party, down at the beach," she'd said when I first pressed her about it, around the age of twelve. "He was visiting family, from out of town. We only knew each other a week."

She'd raised me on her own until she met my stepdad, Jim, at work when I was four. By the time I was six, he was a permanent fixture in my life, and they were married when I was eight. Jim was quiet and dependable, like a lighthouse, and he completed our little family unit.

Still, I'd always been the oddball out, plastering my bedroom walls with old black-and-white fashion photos, collecting art books from yard sales, boycotting the affordable path of UConn for the debt-inducing NYU. I was constantly veering off the course of what was expected of me.

So while these looming DNA test results felt like an intrusion into my mom's past, they also seemed a potential doorway to my own. I checked my email again. Nothing.

Have we met this date? I asked, changing the subject, digging around for dirt.

Nope! was all she offered.

Well at least something good came out of that nightmare, I wrote back, cringing as I remembered the look on Hayes's face when I'd made that dumb sex joke.

Cleo chimed in with a GIF of Kevin from *The Office* laughing.

It was also no surprise that Lola was being somewhat coy with the details. She was often tight-lipped about her sex life, and her day-to-day in general. She fed off other people being open books—and she'd made a career of it—but sharing someone else's drama gave her cover to hide her own.

OK so you guys will come bail me out if this date is a bust? she wrote. **I'm meeting her at Firefly at 7.**

Yes. The period at the end of Cleo's reply hinted at her irritation. "*Duh,*" it seemed to say.

We all know the drill! I added.

Here's how our friend code worked: First, we texted each other the locations of our dates, because safety first, obviously. Then, a postdate check-in, mostly just to review the levels of awkwardness that ensued, with the occasional hot make-out story mixed in. And if things were truly going to shit, we always bailed each other with a text or a phone call, or hell—both.

Back in the day when we all lived together, we'd slide into a booth at the dive bar down the street from our fourth-floor walk-up, order a round of tequila shots, and share the gory details about what had gone horribly wrong. Which—let's be real—first dates often did. Throughout the years, we'd even gone so far as to check on each other in person, peeking our heads into bars and clubs, coffee shops and parks, just to make sure everything was cool. This, after all, was what friendship was about.

Teaching until 9, will check my phone on my break, Cleo texted.

I'm about to meet Grant and Nate in Soho re: nursery, I wrote back. I was headed to meet Lola's coworker and his husband at Cafe Gitane, a tiny café off Prince Street. She'd connected me with them over email, because they were looking for someone to design a bedroom for their new baby. It was my first real meeting about a job after getting laid off, and I felt giddy with possibility.

Well if you don't hear from me in an hour or two, send out the guard dogs, Lola replied.

I sent her a GIF of a golden retriever sniffing a cupcake, which she liked with a heart, and then she went radio silent.

—*mm*—

Cafe Gitane was quiet at 5 p.m., before the dinner rush started in earnest. It was a tiny spot, and we were now crammed together at a small circular table right next to the front window. Nate's arm was wrapped tight around Grant as he sipped a cappuccino.

"I'm so pumped about possibly working together." I shifted in the wooden chair, sitting up, trying to look like someone who'd had meetings like this a million times before. "I'm envisioning something bright and colorful, but minimalistic. I think we could have a lot of fun playing up colors and shapes, which can be both childlike but also very chic. And possibly adding a mural of some sort."

Nate and Grant both "oohed" at this idea, and it felt amazing to get positive feedback in real time. At Spayce, we'd get a request from a client through our app, do a consultation over text or chat, and then create a mood board with links to items and suggestions for layout. This would finally be an opportunity to shape a space with my own hands, from start to finish.

"So our gestational carrier is due in two months," Grant said, pushing his gold wire-rimmed glasses back up the bridge of his nose. "Not a ton of time, especially because we know you have your plate full."

Nate slid his free hand across the table to tap my wrist playfully. "We saw you on New York News," he said, a knowing smile on his face.

Grant rolled his eyes. "Nate is obsessed with local news," he explained. "That guy who gave you his jacket was a piece of work, huh?"

"He was." I forced a laugh. "Well, the good news is that my schedule is now wide-open," I said, puffing up my chest. I'd had a few inquiries come in through the website my friends set up for me, and one had resulted in a phone consultation that felt promising. But this was my first real meeting, the actual inception of Franny Doyle Design. I didn't want to appear too desperate for work, but I needed something to get the ball rolling. Something to prove to myself that maybe I could actually do this. And more importantly, something to put in my bank account.

Nate leaned forward with his chin on his hand. "And do you feel like you know the ins and outs of what a nursery needs?" he asked. "I know you don't have kids, but have you ever worked in kids' spaces before?"

"No, but I like to think that I'm still kind of like a kid myself," I said, "so even though I haven't designed a kid's room, exactly, I try to approach everything with a child's heart." I exhaled and smiled, but I felt a slight sinking feeling in my gut. I had bullshitted my way through that answer, and I could tell it hadn't done much to impress them.

"Great," Grant said with a quick nod. "Let's get into it, then. I want to hear more about this mural idea of yours."

An hour later, we were hugging our goodbyes. Aside from my ridiculous "child's heart" speech, the meeting had gone as well as I could have hoped.

"I'll send over my rate and contract, and we can go from there,"

I said to them before we headed off in different directions. I didn't rush, taking my time to savor every little thing I saw along the way to the subway: The parents swinging a small kid between them, arm in arm. The busboy from the restaurant on the corner, lugging in a giant crate of lemons through the front door. The window on the second floor of the apartment above me sliding open. New York felt possible tonight.

My phone buzzed in my bag. An email from my landlord, thanking me for sending my most recent rent payment in on time. I scanned her words until my eyes stopped at the last sentence. "We have to raise your rent a hundred dollars starting next month."

And in an instant, everything felt impossible again.

Pizza. This was the only appropriate solution to the end of this day. Plus, I could afford it, for now at least. I turned around on Mott Street and made my way back down to Spring, swinging a right toward my favorite spot in the city, Famous Ben's.

Twenty minutes later, I was face-to-face with two perfect slices of vodka sauce pizza—covered with a dusting of parmesan and red pepper flakes—and a frothing cup of root beer. Heaven. I placed my phone next to my paper plates, so that I could scroll and eat at the same time, and dug in. A text from Cleo popped up just as I opened Instagram. **Any word from Lola?**

Nope, I wrote back. **Must be a hot date.** I looked at the time on my phone. It had been almost ninety minutes since her date started. Lola hardly went that long without touching her phone, much less texting.

Should we be worried? Cleo asked.

I think she's a few blocks from where I am. I'll walk by on my way to the subway.

Cleo replied with a row of thumbs-up emojis, and I clicked back over to my Instagram feed. I scrolled past pictures of a newly adopted puppy, someone's meticulously drawn bullet journal, and a slideshow of a home renovation with way too many sliding barn doors. Nothing about this mindless parade of images was soothing tonight. How did I know so many people in loving relationships, with enough money to buy gorgeous houses, who also happened to look impossibly good in wide-brimmed hats?

I swiped over to the Search page and typed the name Hayes Montgomery. A private account popped up. It was probably better that I couldn't get a firsthand glimpse into his perfect, gorgeous life. It would only make me feel worse. And besides, why was I still fixating on Hot Suit, anyway? I needed to get this guy out of my brain.

My skin crawled with the temptation of insecurity, the urge to listen to that voice in my head that liked to tell me I couldn't carve out the career I wanted, couldn't make it in New York, could never look good in impossibly wide-brimmed hats. I knew deep down that that voice was lying—though maybe not about the hat—and that it did me no good to believe it. But sometimes self-doubt was an easier path to take than blind confidence.

As I was staring at my phone, a text from my mom popped up: **Thought you might like to know that Jeremy and his wife are expecting their first baby! A girl. Saw his mom at Stop & Shop. Love Mom.**

But I did not, in fact, want to know that my high school boyfriend and his wife were having a kid while I was sitting alone, unemployed, eating the only meal out that I could realistically afford. I didn't respond.

Slices finished, root beer guzzled, Instagram accounts muted, bathroom visited, I mapped out on my phone the bar where Lola was and realized it was even closer than I'd thought. I'd walked by it a million times when I used to work in SoHo at the Anthropologie store on West Broadway, right after college. Five sweaty blocks later, and I was standing out front. No windows for me to peek through. Crap.

From the outside, it seemed like a regular old bar, but opening the door revealed it to be one of those spots tailor-made for first dates. Red velvet lined the booths and barstools. The shelves behind the dark wooden bar sparkled with bottles of liquor. It looked cozy, and romantic, and dark. There was no way you could hang out in this place without making out with someone.

I wandered up to the bar, where a tattooed woman with a short black pixie cut was slowly twisting a cork out of a bottle. Next to me, a couple leaned in close to each other, knees touching, and it took me a second to recall the last time I'd been on a date. It had been over four months ago, with a guy I met at a trivia night at a bar downtown with some work friends. We'd gotten drinks in the East Village, made out on a bench in Tompkins Square Park, and set up plans to meet for dinner the next week. He texted me three days later to cancel, because he was moving back in with his ex-girlfriend.

"Just a club soda with lime," I said, and the bartender nodded, expressionless. I left ten dollars on the bar and scanned the booths but didn't see Lola anywhere. The front lounge area extended back into what looked like an even more intimate space, the walls lined with flickering candles. I grabbed my drink and walked into the darkness, past the bathrooms, as Morrissey's wail drifted from a speaker somewhere. I stood there for a second, letting my eyes adjust.

Soon, the shapes of people turned into actual humans, and I spotted her, tucked into a corner, all sparkling and blond against the bloodred velvet booth. Her hand was gently resting on the thigh of a dark-haired woman with a long ponytail, whose dimples were bright enough to spot even in the murky, low light. She was leaning into Lola, her lips dancing dangerously close to her neck, at that spot where even a breath feels like an invitation for more.

My eyes rested on them for only a few seconds, but it was long enough for an odd pang to split my chest. Their intimacy was erotic, electric, and something I hadn't felt in a long time. Lola was in trouble all right—just not the kind that called for a best-friend intervention. I turned to walk back toward the bar, grabbing my phone out of my bag to text Cleo, but I had no signal. Stupid sexy dungeon of wine and hot people and romance.

I stepped toward the hallway, drink at my lips, the hint of melancholy toying at my stomach. And then—*slam*. I walked straight into the side of someone's body, my soda splashing up onto both of us.

"Oh my god, I'm so—" I looked up to apologize, and the eyes looking back at me were familiar.

I was too surprised to make it to the word *sorry*. There was Hot Suit Hayes Montgomery the Third, standing right in front of me. What kind of cruel joke was the universe playing on me tonight?

He blinked once. I opened my mouth to say something—like "Hi" or "Hey" or "What the hell are you doing here?"—but instead, I just laughed.

"Hello," he said, biting his lower lip as his eyes studied me, puzzled.

"You're here!" I managed to squeak out, still laughing. *This night.* I shook my head.

"Were you waiting for me?" he asked with a smile, looking down at the huge wet spot seeping across his shirt and then back up to meet my eyes.

"Oh my god," I said again, waving a hand at where he was now dabbing his chest with a cocktail napkin. "I'm sorry about...that. I just wasn't expecting—"

"To ever see me again?" His gaze was hard, and the edges of his lips curled into the smallest hint of a smile, which felt more sinister than sweet.

"Well. Yeah." I laughed as I said it, because it was true. I glanced at the spill again and noticed that this time he wasn't buttoned up within an inch of his life in some bespoke suit. Instead, he was in a heather-gray T-shirt that was damp across his chest, in spots where my drink hadn't splattered. "Why aren't you in a suit?"

I could have sworn that in the darkness, he blushed. "I don't only wear suits."

"You have every time I've seen you. That's, like, your thing, right?" He was somehow even more handsome dressed casually; not that I'd ever tell him that.

"I have other things." He ran the back of his hand across his lips. "I was out for a run and decided to stop by to check on my—"

"Excuse me!" We were interrupted by a woman with short blond hair leaning back in her chair, waving us over toward her table. "I know you. Both of you!"

I tried to place her, racking my brain to remember everyone I'd attended class with in college, or maybe met during an internship somewhere. Did I work with her at Spayce?

"Subway QTs!" The woman next to her clasped her hands together as she shouted, figuring it out in real time.

"Oh my god," shrieked the third member of their group. "Oh my god! I followed that whole thing!"

She lifted up her phone and took a photo of us.

"Can I take a picture with you guys?" the blond woman asked, and before either of us could answer she had chucked her phone at her friend and shimmied out from her seat. She wedged her body between us, slung an arm around my waist, and twisted her body to the side to get what I assumed was her preferred angle. I could smell the wine on her breath as she smiled.

I glanced over at Hayes, who was not looking toward the camera. Instead, his gaze was aimed toward where Lola sat in the corner.

"Hayes?" I heard a voice say at the same time as the woman holding the phone directed, "Look here!"

I froze with a tight smile on my face, in posing mode. "Okay," said the woman behind the camera, handing the phone back to her friend for photo inspection and approval. Relaxing, I turned to see what Hayes had been looking at. He was still staring in the direction of the sweet-faced brunette in the corner with Lola. The one with the dimples that glowed. Dimples just like his. Somewhere in my brain, a warning signal sounded: Something was off.

"Hayes," the voice said again, and now I could see it was coming from Lola's date.

I shifted my gaze from Hayes to the brown-haired woman to Lola, who met my gaze with a *"What the hell are you doing here?"* look. I tried to respond with just my eyes, but it was hard to say *"First-date rule! I was just checking on you!"* with facial expressions alone.

I looked back at Hayes, who was staring at me, perplexed.

"Do you know Perrine?" he asked.

"Huh? No, I…"

"My cousin," he said, like it was the most obvious thing in the world. And then suddenly, it was.

"I think your cousin is on a date with my best friend," I continued. They were walking over toward us now, maneuvering their bodies around the candlelit tables to get to us. Crap.

"What?" He swallowed, his voice incredulous.

"I'm not sure why *you're* here," I said, "but *I've* definitely been caught spying on their first date."

"Oh my god, he's not even facing the camera," Drunk Blonde interrupted, squinting down at her phone. "Do you guys mind if we do another photo really quick?"

"Sorry, we've got to go say hi to our friends," I said, and grabbed Hayes by the forearm, which was warm and firm under my hand. I steered him over to where Lola and his cousin were standing, a few feet away.

"Franny," Lola said when I arrived, looking both irritated and amused.

"Hi." I wiggled my fingertips in a wave and then smiled at Hayes's cousin. She reached out her hand to shake mine. Her nails were short and painted a clean white, the same color as the pearl studs dotting her earlobes.

"Perrine," she said, introducing herself, her voice calm and smooth. "I see you found my cousin. Again."

I turned and caught him out of the corner of my eye, large and looming at my side.

"He likes to check on me whenever I go out with strangers. It's very kind, and also totally obnoxious and protective." She gave me a knowing smile, and I liked her immediately. "He's like that."

"I'm sorry, how did the two of you...?" I looked between them like I was trying to solve a two-thousand-piece jigsaw puzzle, trying to figure out their connection. "Wait, Lo, this is the woman you met in the New York News bathroom?"

"I'm sorry, what?" Hayes said, sounding like a clueless dad discovering what TikTok was for the first time.

Both women suddenly looked sheepish. "We bumped into each other before your segment," Perrine said, offering Hayes a smile.

"Before we shared that memorable cup of coffee together," I said to Hayes, who was still processing what was unfolding before us.

"I slid into her DMs," Lola added with a wicked smirk, like it was the most natural thing in the world to do.

"When did you figure this out?" Hayes asked his cousin. He was chewing on the small red straw that must have come in his drink. I watched his long, tan finger tap on the glass, just below a slice of lime teetering on the rim. Water fizzed in his cup. We'd ordered the same thing.

"Right when we got here, it clicked," Lola said, leaning in close to Perrine, their shoulders touching.

"It took us a second to put it together," Perrine added.

"We agreed that if we decided to go out again, we'd tell you both first."

"And we've decided to go out again," Lola said. "So now I guess we're telling you."

Well, this was a turn of events. I opened my mouth to say my goodbyes and let them get back to it when Lola cut me off.

"Wait," she said, her eyes shifting from apologetic to suspicious. "Why are you here?"

"I told Cleo I'd peek in. I had no idea this was happening."

Lola dug her phone out of her purse. "No signal," she said, holding the screen in my direction.

"Okay, well. Have fun, you two," I said, giving Lola one last "*holy crap*" look.

"Yeah, enjoy yourselves," Hayes said next to me, which made me laugh. I'm sure they'd do more than that. "We'll leave you to it."

His hand ever so gently rested on the small of my back, a slight nudge toward the door that lasted just a second—so barely there I almost missed it. But in that instant, it had felt both achingly familiar and shockingly new. His touch sent a ripple of excitement through my body so strong that the aftershocks bounced around my stomach as we walked out of the bar and into the arms of the city, together.

CHAPTER SIX

HAYES

OUTSIDE, THE SUN was long gone but the city was still bright, lit up against the backdrop of the night sky. Franny's mouth was agape as she fished around in her bag for something. "Well," she said, her attention focused on finding whatever it was she was looking for. "This is not how I expected my night to go."

I patted my pocket to make sure my key and credit card were still there. I caught her eyes, and for the first time since we met on the subway that morning in May, I got a clear look at them. Somehow, though they were the coolest of greens, they were lit up, bright and electric. "I didn't either," I said in agreement. I looked at my watch; this little detour had knocked twenty minutes off my run.

"So, your best friend…," I started, not knowing exactly what I was going to ask.

"I mean," she said, and her mouth opened in a confused smile, "what the hell?"

"Well, it sounds like they didn't make the connection until—"

"Until after they started making out?" she said, giggling.

I stood there, hand at my neck, still slightly stunned by the entire situation.

"Of all the women in New York, she picks up your cousin. In a bathroom. *Your* cousin."

She seemed surprised, but also like this was the best news she'd heard all day. "Sometimes this city is magic."

My brows raised as I dug a hand through my hair. Still sweaty. "New York City is just a small town with a lot of people in it."

"Didion?" she asked, a pleased look on her face.

"Didion?" I asked back. "No. I just, made that up."

"Wow, impressive. You should consider switching careers." She gave me a look and then stuck her tongue out at me.

"Cute," I said. My voice was sarcastic, but it was also true. She *was* cute.

"Sorry, I'm just...," she said; then her tone shifted into something more serious. "Today's kinda turned into a bummer. Though seeing your face as you figured out what was going on back there did make it a lot better."

And with that, she perked up again.

"Oh yeah?" I asked. "What did my face look like?" I was genuinely curious.

She opened her mouth in a wide, horrified O and shifted her eyes back and forth. She looked absurd, like that Kit-Cat Klock, with the moving eyes, that Perrine had in her kitchen. I laughed, not just at the ridiculous face she was making, but at the way she did everything so freely. I wasn't used to being around someone like her, a person who sparkled so bright it felt like their energy could rub off on you, just a bit.

Her mouth shifted into a smile. "I should head back to Brooklyn," she said.

"Where do you live?" I asked.

"Brooklyn Heights. I'm going to walk over to the N train."

"Let me," I started, then rephrased what I wanted to say after she caught my eye, her brows raised. "May I walk with you?" I asked. "I'm going uptown."

"Okay," she said, nodding her head along with the syllables, her lips pressed together.

We walked an entire half block together in silence. I tried to avoid her gaze, keeping my eyes on the lush green of the trees, my focus on the infectious sounds coming from outdoor cafés: laughter and clinking of drinks. Normally, I loved New York City when it hinted at summer. But my thoughts quickly switched back to my empty, sterile apartment, and I racked my brain for something else to think about. I was about to ask her how work was going when she stopped abruptly and gasped.

"What?" I asked, looking around, genuinely confused.

"Italian ice," she said, like it was the most obvious thing in the world, pointing to the white food truck parked on the corner. "This is exactly what I need tonight. If I'm gonna go broke, I'm gonna do it with Italian ice."

She started toward the truck. "You don't have to wait," she added. "But I'm getting some."

I wanted to wait, since it would mean more time with her.

"I don't mind," I said, though I couldn't remember the last time I'd gotten ice cream or a Popsicle from an actual ice cream truck, much less Italian ice. Middle school?

"Do you want something?" she asked, shrugging that giant handbag off her shoulder and zipping open a side pocket to pull out a small leather wallet.

I shook my head. "I'm good," I assured her.

"Why not?" she asked, her eyes lifting, hinting at an eye roll. "Oh no. Are you keto? One of those weird sugar-free people?"

"I'm definitely not keto," I said, a defensive edge to my voice. "I just save sugar for special occasions."

"Hayes"—she clasped a hand to her chest, faking a dramatic gesture—"are you suggesting that the discovery of your cousin on a date with my best friend is not a special occasion?"

"I'll let you know when the occasion is special enough," I replied, chuckling at her performance.

"Your loss," she said with a shrug.

"Or gain, since I won't be torturing my body with a carcinogenic substance that's purposefully manufactured to be addictive," I said playfully, knowing instinctively this would needle her.

"Oh my god." She gave an exaggerated grimace. "You are worse than I remembered."

I laughed. She was beautiful, especially when she was joking around. At least, I hoped she was joking.

I stood back as she ordered, watched as she chatted with the mustachioed older man who leaned out of the truck's window. She handed over her money, and moments later he passed her a cup steeped in red and yellow, the scoops already bleeding together in the hazy nighttime heat. She took a small wooden spoon and dug it into the ice with zero hesitation.

"Mmm." Her eyes disappeared for a second, rolling back in ecstasy. She was so...simple. No...Understated. No...Elegant. That was it. Even as she stood there devouring a sweating cup of ice. Snarky too, and chock-full of emotions and colors and thoughts, which seemed to tumble out, unrestricted. But above all, elegant.

For some reason, my mind went to the pewter candlesticks my grandmother Beverly kept in the center of her dining room table. Beverly was known in our family for her extravagance, the one over-the-top member of our usually deliberately reserved family. She liked her eyeglasses huge and her jewelry even bigger, chunks of gems and raw stones, collected from all corners of the world. And her house matched her outfits, all color and glass and flowers and art.

But there, in the center of an antique twelve-person dining room table, surrounded by art painted by her grandkids and a Keith Haring painting that I'm sure was worth more than my entire company, were two small pewter candlesticks. And while she was constantly changing the design of her house, those damn candlesticks never moved. I asked her why once, when I was in high school, helping to clear the plates off the table on Christmas Eve. "Because," she'd said matter-of-factly, "they're the prettiest things in this whole house."

Franny's voice yanked me out of my childhood memories and brought me back to the present.

"My grandma Elsie used to buy me the best Italian ice at this sweet little bakery in New Haven near her house," she said, reminiscing with a smile. "Like homemade. Fresh lemons and everything. It's one of my earliest memories, eating Italian ice in a plastic beach chair in her backyard."

"And how does this one measure up?" I asked.

"It's delicious," she said in between bites. "But it still doesn't even compare."

She spooned up a giant melty scoop and brought it to her mouth, but her timing was off by a second, and some of it dripped onto the front of her dress. "Oh my god," she said. I assumed she'd be annoyed by the mess, but instead she looked down and then up at me, and she let out a laugh, dabbing herself with the tiny single napkin the ice cream guy had given her.

"My grandmother overboiled her broccoli and served it with too much salt," I offered. Grandma Beverly had been a notoriously awful cook. "I would have liked going to your family's house better."

"Well, my grandfather also kept rabbits in the backyard and turned them into rabbit stew. So if you could survive the rabbit murder, you were rewarded handily in Italian ice."

I grimaced. "How did he...?"

She motioned with her hand that held the spoon, twisting it sharply as she made a clicking sound with her tongue. "Broke their necks, without a hint of remorse."

I laughed in disbelief. "You grew up in New Haven?"

"West Haven, but close enough."

"I'm from right near there," I said.

"Let me guess," she said, pausing to stare at me with knowing eyes. "Greenwich."

I let out a small laugh. "Westport," I said.

"Same difference."

I nodded in agreement. She wasn't wrong. WASPy, affluent, filled with country clubs, popped collars. The towns along Connecticut's Gold Coast were one and the same.

"So"—I glanced toward her—"why has it been a not-so-great day?"

"Oh my god, where do I even begin?" she moaned.

"From the beginning?" I replied, and she let out big laugh in response. She had the kind of laughter that made you want to join in, be in on whatever joke she was telling. I smiled back at her and felt myself relax, which was odd, because I hadn't even realized how tense I'd been.

"Okay, so"—she scraped the bottom of her Italian ice cup and dipped the spoon in her mouth one last time—"I had a meeting about a possible design job. A nursery."

"Seems like something you could do in your sleep," I said, attempting a compliment.

She gave me a confused look, brow furrowed, as she stopped by a trash can to toss her spoon and cup. "No, it would actually be a pretty big deal."

"I just assumed you were already swamped with work requests." Great. I'd insulted her again.

"Right..." She trailed off. "But this nursery job would be a major get for me. So I'm nervous. And then, right after this meeting, I got an email from my landlord about my rent going up."

Her voice was higher now, agitated.

"Oof." I brought my hands to my chest in pretend pain.

"Exactly!" she said, her arms open in agreement.

"Well, I believe in you," I said decidedly. "You'll get the job, and you'll figure your rent stuff out."

She looked at me with a perplexed expression.

"Is that weird to say?" I asked.

Of course it was weird. It was too much, too forward. Once again, I was tripping over my tongue around this woman. I never said stuff like this to Perrine, much less to people I didn't know.

I stopped at the crosswalk as the cars whizzed by, and when I turned to look at Franny she was smiling. Phew.

"I mean, yeah, because you barely know me," she said. "But also it's really what I needed to hear right now. So, no, it's not. And thank you."

And then, the bulbous green lights denoting the N and R subway station were in front of us. We walked down the steps side by side.

"You're going uptown?" she asked.

"Yes." It wasn't a lie. Not exactly. I lived uptown, but I had been planning on running home. It felt weird not to be up-front with her, but I really wanted to keep the conversation going.

"Hey, so, I've actually been meaning to contact you about something."

"Okay." She had her MetroCard already in hand. "What's up?" Her gaze narrowed. "Is something wrong with your suit jacket?"

"What? No." I had hung it up in the back of my closet after she handed it to me and hadn't touched it since. "The jacket is fine."

She wiped fake sweat from her brow with a smile and then dropped her hand, eyeing me expectantly.

The words were bottlenecked in my mouth. My brain tried to force them out, as if it were slapping the bottom of a ketchup bottle. "I wanted to apologize if I was weird, when we did the interview. I mean, I *was* weird. Not if. I was. And for what I said about you not being my type. I just felt very out of place, and my words got all mixed up. So. I'm sorry."

She studied me, sucking her cheeks in, shifting her frown into a scowl. Just as my stomach started to twist with nerves, her face blossomed into a smile.

"We're cool," she said finally, giving me a playful push on my shoulder.

"Yeah?" My face flushed with relief.

"Of course. That whole morning was weird." She fiddled with her MetroCard in her hands. "Well, obviously not for some of us." Her eyes widened, and she ran a hand through her hair, tucking it behind her ear. It was shorter than I remembered. Darker too.

I realized I was staring, and blinked to recalibrate. "Oh, you mean my cousin and…"

"Lola," she said.

"Lola, right. Yeah, they've only made it weirder."

She laughed at this, which felt like a win.

"Well, hey, I accept your apology—again." She leaned toward me and gave my shoulder a gentle squeeze. "And I hope you have a nice life."

It was a funny thing to say, yet her voice was completely sincere.

"I hope you have a nice life too, Franny. And a nice night."

And then, with a swipe of her MetroCard, she was off through the turnstile, lost back to the city that had given her to me.

✳

Franny was still on my mind the next morning, our conversation on replay in my brain, ready for me to analyze and obsess over. I couldn't stop thinking about her, and that alone felt off for me. Even work wasn't distracting me like it normally did. And so I texted Serena and asked if she was able to bump up our first date by a few days and meet after work today instead. We'd talked briefly on the phone last week, introducing ourselves and making plans to meet in person. Talking with Serena had been easy and familiar, which was exactly what I needed right now to quell this off-balance feeling Franny had stirred up in me.

We had planned a run around Central Park, which was definitely a departure from my usual meet-for-coffee-or-a-cocktail first-date routine. I felt a slight pang of guilt using a date with Serena as a way to pull my brain out of my thoughts about someone else, but as soon as we hit the pavement I was convinced it had been a good move. She was outgoing and did the bulk of the talking, but she also seemed to genuinely enjoy the run and she laughed at my dumb running jokes.

"I'm in charge of understanding fashion trends, picking jewelry and accessories for shoots and features, scouting the market so I know what should be in the magazine each month," Serena said, her blond ponytail swinging gracefully down her back.

"Wow, I had absolutely no idea what an accessories editor even was," I huffed, trying not to let on that I was out of breath. She was pacing for a race next weekend, which meant she was trying to keep her miles under eight minutes each. I was a nine-minute-mile guy, and I was definitely hustling to keep up with her.

"I style photo shoots too."

"That seems like a lot to do on top of training for the marathon," I marveled.

"Well, that's not even all of it. I'm also on a committee for a charity gala happening at the Museum of Natural History in August. All the proceeds go toward ALS research. My sister-in-law was diagnosed last year."

"God, I'm so sorry to hear that."

"I tend to channel my grief into productivity. I'm probably a little type A," she said with a small laugh, though her face hinted at sadness. "Did Eleanor mention that?"

Eleanor had, in fact, mentioned that. But she'd also said Serena worked closely with her fiancé Henry's group at the magazine and that he thought she was also "generally nice," which was as good of an endorsement as any. And true to Eleanor's promise, she was "hot." Beautiful, really—with long tan limbs and sharp cheekbones and pale-blue eyes.

Serena was easily someone I'd normally be attracted to, and I could see why Eleanor thought she'd be a perfect setup. So why was I feeling absolutely no spark? It was probably work, and the stress of Damien quitting, I reasoned. I had too much going on.

"You have to come," she continued. "We've sent out the formal invites, but I'll email you the info and get one out to you."

Six miles later, we leaned over a bridge by Sixty-Fourth Street, stretching. My calves throbbed, my arms ached, but still—I felt good. Serena was amiable and chatty, making me laugh once or twice. Our conversation was easy and familiar. Enjoyable, even. This had been nice. Perfectly nice.

"Oh!" she said, unstrapping her phone from around her bicep. "I almost forgot. Do you mind if I take a photo of us for my Instagram?"

"Oh god, I dunno," I said. "I don't exactly have the best track record on Instagram."

"I saw." She laughed knowingly. "But social media and influencing is literally my job."

She opened up her phone and began scrolling through her feed. "I have to photograph my outfits every day. I have this hashtag called #SerenaStyle, and basically it's become this whole thing."

"How so?" I asked. It wasn't like I didn't get how Instagram worked, but I'd found that people used the phrase "whole thing" to describe, well, lots of very different things.

"I just have this specific pose, and now people copy it and do their own SerenaStyle shoots. Look."

And, sure enough, there was photo after photo of people jumping in the air, all tagged back to her.

"Come on." She waved me over with a massive grin. "It'll just be in my Stories. Just a shot of our sneakers."

She snapped the photo and pocketed her phone; then she leaned forward for a stretch, crossing her legs and bending at the waist, letting her hands touch the ground. "Would you wanna go grab a drink?" she asked, not turning to look at me. "I know a place with killer burgers and cheap beer."

"Yeah, sure." I crossed an arm in front of my chest to stretch it. I could go for some dinner, and I was genuinely interested in getting to know her better.

She stood up and smiled at me, and I smiled back, because after weeks of not quite feeling like myself, it felt like I was finally on my way back to the old Hayes.

CHAPTER SEVEN

FRANNY

MY ALARM WENT off the next morning, yanking me out of a dream. I'd been in Florida, riding on the back of a motorcycle with Hayes, and I was also working in a circus. It was ridiculous, but it had all made sense while I was sleeping. And the sensation of my arms around his waist, muscular and hard through his T-shirt, had felt incredibly real. I cursed as I yanked my eye mask up, mad that I could no longer feel his body against mine.

As usual, I reached for my phone the minute my eyes cracked open, and I saw a notification that I'd gotten a new email overnight. From the circus perhaps?

No, not the circus.

From: DNADiscovery.com
Subject: Your Results Are In!

"Oh my god," I said out loud, opening the email with frantic, nervous fingers.

Hello, Francesca Doyle! Your results are in. Log in below to discover your ancestry, explore your health history, and trace your roots.

I clicked, and the site popped up, my log-in information saved and ready for this very moment.

Welcome, Francesca! You are:
  10% Scottish
  40% Irish
  50% Southern Italian

Well, duh, I wanted to say. It was instantly underwhelming. I already knew my mom's side of the family was Irish; I could trace them back generations. My grandma even knew the name of the village her family had left when they immigrated to the US. The southern Italian part was interesting, I guess, but there were tons of Italian Americans around New Haven. If my bio dad was there on vacation visiting family, chances were he was some part Italian too, just like most of the kids I'd gone to school with growing up.

My mom had told me my birth father's name, Carmine (another reason I'd always assumed he was Italian American), but because I knew she didn't want to talk about him, I'd always just left the topic alone. And maybe that was for the best, anyway. Because mixed in with the disappointment was relief that I didn't have to actually deal with the fear of hurting my mom by digging into her past. Just this alone always outweighed my desire to know exactly where I'd inherited half of my DNA, even if it could explain why I'd always felt like an outsider in my own family.

Sure, they loved me unconditionally, but that didn't mean they quite understood me. I'd always been a little bit louder, a little bit more emotional, a little bit more creative than everyone else. It had felt confusing and isolating knowing exactly who I was while also never quite feeling like it was good enough. But no matter what my issues were, I didn't want my mother to feel like she wasn't enough for me, or for her and Jim to think that I didn't appreciate them and all they'd done for me.

Still, I'd always existed at arm's length from the more intimate parts of their lives. It was just how it was; we didn't share deep feelings, big emotions, hard things. And my birth father fell squarely into that last category.

When the second email came through about thirty minutes later, with the subject *"Hello from your half sister"* and a link to my DNADiscovery inbox, my first instinct was to assume it was spam. I forwarded a screenshot to Lola and Cleo. *This is fake, right? Someone scamming me for something?* I wrote.

But then Cleo responded immediately with *It looks real to me,* and Lola added, *I told you this happened to my coworker! Anytime there is a DNA match they alert people.*

I read the subject again, and said, "Are you fucking kidding me?" out loud to my empty apartment. I was in the middle of getting ready for a spin class. I stood there, pants bunched around my knees, and clicked on the link to the message, which opened on the DNADiscovery site.

Hello,

I know this is a very strange message to receive on here. I am your half sister, living in Italy. Our father died in 1993, not long after he returned from America. I was two at the time. He was never married to my mother, and there were always rumors of other children. I live and work in Milan now but grew up in Sorrento, not far from where our father is from, and I studied and worked in London after university. My job is in interior design and architecture. I have my own firm and work all over the world. I have also found some cousins I did not know existed through this site. I would love to connect with you when you are ready.

Warmly,
Anna Farina

I read it again.

And again.

And then one more time, as if by doing so the words might disappear. But they did not. I shuffled over to the bed to sit down, pants now around my ankles, and typed her name into Google, misspelling it three times because my fingers were so shaky.

Sure enough, a link to her design firm popped up, a visual orgasm of modern homes and sleek, angular spaces. My heart pounded, knocking around my entire body.

I'd only ever known the barest-bone details of my father's existence, and he was so far removed from my life that he never seemed entirely real to begin with. Most of the time it felt like my mom got knocked up by a ghost who then chose not to haunt me. And it never dawned on me that he could have had other kids. People who might look like me. Act like me. *Get me.* The new realization had left me unable to act, hands frozen, gripping my phone.

And while it felt ridiculous to admit, I had never even considered that this could happen. It had always been easier to not give him much thought, place the idea of him on a shelf and let it collect dust. But of course he had been a real person, with a life, and a family, and people who cared about him. And kids. He had kids. More than just me.

And he was dead. *Dead.* This thought devastated me, in a way that felt totally unexpected. Why was I sad about the death of someone I'd never even met? I was overcome with the weirdest feeling in my chest, tight and hard. Then I blinked and realized why: I was about to cry.

In a panic, I did the only thing that made sense to my brain. I pulled up my pants, shoved on my sneakers, grabbed my bag, and ran out of my apartment.

"Cleo!" I shouted into the phone the second she picked up. I knew she'd be awake; she was always up early to meditate and go through emails before work.

"Holy shit! What's wrong?" I could hear her spring into friend-emergency mode through the phone.

"I think I'm having an anxiety attack. Or is it a panic attack? What is it when your heart feels like it's beating in your head?" I raced down the street toward the subway, power walking.

"What happened?"

"That DNA-test thing we did? I just got mine back. I have a fucking half sister." The words were coming out of my mouth at twice their normal speed.

She let out a drawn-out "Holy crap."

"In Italy. I'm not half–Italian American. I'm half–*Italian Italian*."

The lady standing in the doorway of the Laundromat gave me a strange look as I passed by, still shouting.

"Wow, your mom got knocked up by an Italian dude. Way to go, Diane."

"Cleo! He's dead." There was that tightness in my chest again, crawling back up my throat.

"Oh my god," she gasped. "Okay, look, where are you? I can hear outside sounds."

"I'm going to spin class! I already paid for it, and I don't want to eat the cost."

"Franny, what? Can you just stay where you are and I'll come find you? You don't need to go to a spin class right now."

"I'm going to that place on Atlantic. I need to pedal out this energy."

"What time does class start?" she asked, her breathing suddenly huffy, like she was running.

I whipped the phone away from my ear to check the clock. "Thirty minutes."

"'Kay. I'm on my way."

"What? Seriously?" I shouted as I jaywalked across the street. But all that was left on the other end of the line was silence.

—~~~—

Twenty-seven minutes later, I was clipping my shoes into the pedals on a bike, Jay-Z pumping from a speaker that was turned up entirely too loud for an 8 a.m. class. Here, in this dark room full of bikes and sweaty strangers, I could avoid the unsettling reality that awaited me. I didn't just have new genetic info to wrap my head around.

I had a sister. And a dad I'd never get to meet.

I was already breathing heavily and was only sitting on the bike, barely moving my legs. The panic was still here. My plan to pedal it out of me was beginning to seem absurd, and I leaned my head onto the handlebars and watched as a petite woman in bright striped leggings hopped on the bike next to me.

"Excuse me, would you possibly mind switching bikes?"

Cleo. I would know that determined voice anywhere.

"I was hoping to be next to my friend," she continued, talking to the woman next to me. "She's getting over a terrible case of food poisoning, and I want to make sure she doesn't pass out in class. Or barf."

"Of course," the woman said, eyeing me suspiciously. "What bike were you on?" Cleo pointed to the row behind us.

"Thank you so much," Cleo said, before turning her attention to me. "Hey." Her voice was lowered, her face shifting into one of total concern.

"I cannot believe you're here right now." I shook my head in amazement.

"You know me. I love making the impossible happen." She raised a brow, always so confident. "I enjoyed the challenge, to be honest. I took a cab and ran two blocks."

"Gooood morning, everybody!" The instructor's voice crackled through the loudspeaker. She came in with her fists pumping, tattoos cresting over biceps, her reddish-brown hair as bouncy as her mood. "Before we get started, I want you to introduce yourself to your neighbors on either side of you!"

She cranked up the volume on a Rihanna track as people in the room started chatting. I quickly high-fived a man next to me. "Andy!" he shouted in greeting. I nodded with a tight smile and turned back to my friend.

"Hi, I'm Cleo," she said again loudly as I turned, enunciating every word over the music. "I'm here to keep my best friend from freaking out too much!"

"Okay, everyone, crank your resistance up five turns!" The instructor's voice boomed overhead. "And let's get ready to power through these hills together!"

The class erupted in cheers. Apparently, everyone had showered in Red Bull this morning.

"So!" Cleo leaned in toward me so I could hear. "It's all gonna be fine!"

"You don't know that!" I huffed out my reply, already exhausted from the climb. "This changes everything. I have a whole family I didn't even know about. That my mom doesn't know about. It feels crazy."

"Up to third position!" shrieked the instructor. I rose to my legs, my hands reaching forward on the handlebars. Cleo stayed seated on her bike, sweat already forming along her hairline.

"I have to tell my mom." It took me a minute to get the words out. "I feel like I owe it to her to let her know."

"No, you don't! You get to tell her whatever and whenever you want," Cleo shouted back. "This is your journey."

"Please do not use that word around me ever again," I said with a laugh, and Cleo smiled. Clearly, she had been trying to perk me up, and it had worked.

"I don't even know if I want to respond," I yelled back, trying to be heard over the pulsing bass. "It's just a lot."

Overeager Andy next to me gave me a clear *Please shut up* look and pressed a finger to his lips.

Cleo mouthed the word "*Asshole*" at me, and I let out a guffaw.

"Remember, we're a pack," our instructor wailed from atop her bike at the front of the room. "We ride as one!"

"Look, whatever you decide to do," shouted Cleo, wobbling through push-ups on the handlebars, "I'm here for you. And Lola will be too, obviously."

She paused for a beat.

"God, this fucking sucks," she said with a laugh as the instructor announced it was time to grab weights for the arm workout.

I nodded along in agreement, and on behalf of my quads, which were very pissed off. "I really can't believe you're here. When was the last time you took a spin class?"

"Last time? Um, that one time I did it with you."

"That was almost a year ago, Clee." I started laughing so hard I almost dropped my weights.

Cleo was still cursing as we stood outside the spin studio minutes later, slurping water.

"I should have just stayed in bed and tried to go back to sleep," I grumbled. "I was having this very weird dream where I was on a motorcycle with—" I stopped myself. I didn't want to tell Cleo about my Hayes dream. It had been totally G-rated, yet it had felt so erotic at the same time.

"With who?" she asked, water bottle at her lips.

Busted. "Don't laugh," I said finally, and she nodded. "With Hayes."

"Ooooh." She pursed her lips and did a little sexy dance with her shoulders. "Someone's got Hot Suit on the brain. Was it a sex dream? On the motorcycle?"

"No!" I insisted. "We just rode around on the motorcycle." I purposefully neglected to add how turned on it had left me.

"Okay, well, listen, as much as I want to hear more about your road trip with Hayes, I have to go home and get ready for work. You can call me anytime to talk about this sister stuff, okay? Dad stuff too. You know I know what it's like to lose a dad."

Cleo's dad had died when she was in high school, and it had impacted her in ways I know I couldn't begin to understand. I pressed my lips together. "What if I'm..." My voice trailed off. It felt too embarrassing to say out loud.

"What if you're what?" she asked, digging her hands through her sweaty hair as she gave me an expectant look.

"A disappointment? She finds out this sister she's all excited to meet is some unemployed American weirdo?"

"Okay, Franny." Cleo planted her hands on my shoulders, a stern look on her face. "I want to validate your feelings while also reminding you to speak kindly about yourself, as if you were talking about a friend."

"Fine." I rolled my eyes with a sigh. "But she's an architect and a designer. She does what I do, but, like, for real."

"You're not the Velveteen Rabbit, babe." Cleo dropped her arms and nudged me onward. "I promise you, you're already very real."

CHAPTER EIGHT

HAYES

SATURDAY NIGHT, I showed up at Eleanor and Henry's apartment for dinner with a bottle of wine and, oddly enough, a giant box of saltine crackers. The latter hadn't been my idea; Eleanor had texted me as I was leaving my place, asking me to grab them, and so I'd stopped off at Gristedes.

I rapped on the door, and Henry greeted me in an apron, a tomato-sauce-covered spatula in one hand. "HM Three," he said with a wicked grin, grabbing my forearm and yanking me in for a hug.

He was the only person who called me that. Hell, he was the only person I'd even *let* call me that. It had been one of the first things out of his mouth when we met. Eleanor had started talking to him at a party, a hot, sweaty Halloween thing with way too many people, at a loft downtown. Henry had been dressed as Han Solo, and she had shown up in full Princess Leia cosplay, and their outfit connection had won Eleanor over in an instant. After they'd spent two hours together chatting in a corner, I'd wandered over to say hi. Angie had been dressed up as a Freudian slip that night, in an actual white slip with words like *ego* and *Oedipus complex* written on it. I'd been...well, I'd been dressed as myself.

"Hayes," I'd said that night, extending my hand.

"Montgomery the Third," Eleanor had added, her nervous excitement dancing in her voice. Eleanor's past boyfriends and girlfriends had all been skeptical of me, certain there was something suspicious going on between us when they weren't around. But Henry hadn't seemed fazed by our friendship.

"HM Three," he'd said, clasping my hand firmly in a shake, his eyes bright with excitement and liquor. Henry was confident, cool with everyone, unafraid of anything and everything. And his accent only made him sound more polished. Born in Hong Kong and raised in the UK before moving to the States for college, Henry oozed worldly sophistication without an ounce of douchebaggery. He was a real unicorn.

"Do you have my saltines?" Eleanor called from the living room.

"Yes," I said, furrowing my brow when I discovered her in the fetal position on the couch. "Are you sick?"

I turned to Henry, who was standing next to me, clutching an oven mitt, a stupid grin on his face. "Is she okay?" I asked him, worry creeping into my gut.

"Hayes, you dummy," Eleanor moaned, not lifting her head. "I'm pregnant."

"Oh my god, El." My jaw went slack with shock. "That's... that's..."

"It's a surprise is what it is," she said, tearing into the saltines. "But a good surprise."

Henry let out a little whoop next to me. The grin on his face could have stretched to the ends of Manhattan, it was so big.

"That's amazing. Congratulations." I leaned down to hug her and plant a kiss on her cheek. This felt monumental, exciting in a way I'd never experienced before. "I've always wanted to change careers and go into nannying, so—"

"Good lord, no." She shook her head. "Besides, we need you as our cat sitter. Luna might get jealous."

"Have you told your parents yet?" I asked, plopping into the armchair across from her.

"Not yet. It's still early," she added, "so we're not telling many people. You should be freakin' honored to be in such an exclusive group."

I fist-pumped to show my enthusiasm. But my mind was also racing through everything Eleanor had coming up this year. Our big move, possible new clients, wedding planning with Henry. And now, a kid. Her life was chugging ahead, checking boxes I thought I'd have filled by now. I felt a pang of envy and sadness mixed in with the joy.

"Congrats, man," I said to Henry as he motioned for me to follow him into the kitchen. "You're going to be the coolest dad in all five boroughs."

Henry laughed and then paused in thought. "Yeah, you might actually be right." He took the wine out of my hands, sticking it on the counter next to a giant colander. "Change of menu tonight. Eleanor can't stand the thought of chicken right now, so I'm making spaghetti, with a nice arrabbiata sauce for us. Hers is gonna be plain."

"You know I can hear you, Chef!" Eleanor shouted from the living room, just a few feet away.

"I'll crack this open," Henry said, grabbing a corkscrew out of a drawer. "If you could bring this to my lovely fiancée."

He passed me a glass of purple liquid.

"Gatorade," he muttered, his voice low. "This is the only flavor she can stomach."

"Again, I can hear you," Eleanor called. "Pregnancy has given me endless nausea but also supersonic hearing."

"I love you!" Henry replied, turning back toward the bubbling pot on the stove.

I wandered into the living room, Gatorade in hand.

"Hayes," she groaned, now lying flat on her back with a pile of crackers on her stomach. "I'm sorry I went and got pregnant right before our big office move."

"How dare you," I said dryly with a smile. "How far along are you?"

"Almost eight weeks. The barfing started just a few days ago." She gagged a little as she said it.

"Eleanor," I said, my voice gentle as I sat back down. "This is huge. The work stuff will figure itself out."

I said the words for myself as much as for her. We'd figure it out. We always did. But it still left a small ripple of nerves in my gut.

"I know," she said, tilting her head toward me in a smile. "And I am excited."

"For our move, or for the baby?"

"Oh my god, I hate you." She tossed a saltine at me to prove her point. I popped it in my mouth.

"Does it change your wedding plans at all?" There had been talk of a destination wedding when they'd first gotten engaged. Something about their favorite vacation spot on a remote beach in Sayulita.

"Yeah, we'll either move up the date or postpone. Keep it small, maybe. And definitely do it in New York now."

"Well, you'll get to be the first person at Arbor to try out our parental-leave policy," I said.

"Six months!" she cheered, raising her fists triumphantly. When Eleanor and I had sat down together at a Starbucks in Chelsea four years ago to brainstorm what our own firm would look like, one of the first things we landed on was that we wanted to give employees lots of time off for big life changes, fully paid. I felt a twinge of excitement at the realization that we had actually made it happen, and then a strange, haunted feeling, wondering if I'd ever get to use it myself.

"Oh, and get this." She lowered her voice. "Henry offered to move all his gamer crap out of the office so it can be the nursery."

Henry was known for spending late hours shouting into a headset while playing *Call of Duty*. This was big.

"You know what," I said, before I could stop myself. "Franny could design it. She was just telling me about a meeting she had with potential clients about doing their nursery."

Eleanor slowly repeated my words back to me. "She was *just...telling...you*?"

"We ran into each other the other night." I rolled my eyes, trying to brush it off as not a big deal. "I walked her to the subway."

"Wow." She stuck out her bottom lip, nodded her head. "That's kinda romantic, you know."

"It was totally innocent," I insisted.

"And you didn't say anything to me about it?" she said, eyeing me inquisitively. Almost like she knew I hadn't mentioned it on purpose. "Do you two just follow each other around the city, waiting to bump into each other?"

"I guess so," I muttered. "Her best friend was on a date with Perrine, and we ran into each other."

She sat up, mouth agape. "Hayes Montgomery the Third, you clearly have a lot you need to tell me."

I gave her the briefest recap possible and then tried to change subjects by giving her the details of my date with Serena, right down to the photo of our shoes.

"Okay, an Instagram picture is a big deal," Eleanor said knowingly, looking at it on her phone.

"She said a photo in her Stories wasn't a big deal," I said nonchalantly, playing it cool. An Instagram expert, even. After all, I was the one with a viral story under my belt. "It disappears after twenty-four hours."

"Hayes, you sound like my dad," she scolded, bursting my bubble. "People are going to notice that she tagged you. And she's saved it in her Highlights, so anyone can see it anytime."

"But it's literally just my shoes. Why would anyone care?"

My Instagram account had a total of three photos on it. A grainy shot of the Empire State Building that I took in 2011 and filtered within an inch of its life, a picture of Angie hugging my parents' goldendoodle in front of their Christmas tree right before we got engaged, and a photo I snapped from the top of a hike I took in Vermont a couple years ago. And it was set to private. It was, quite possibly, the least active account on the site.

"People read into the stuff they see online, Hayes. I can't believe I'm still explaining this to you after everything." She gave me an exasperated look and shifted, tossing the saltines next to her on the couch and swinging her legs around to sit cross-legged on the cushions. "But you like her?" she said, giving me a coy smile. "It's going well?"

"Yeah," I said, trying to muster up some enthusiasm. "We're running again tomorrow, and she invited me to some party."

"You sound like you're describing a dental appointment," she teased.

"I'm excited, I swear," I said. And it was true. I liked Serena, and it was easy to be around her. Comfortable, even.

"Well, not to completely switch gears," she said, "but I've got another bad news/good news situation for you."

I leaned forward, elbows on knees. "Didn't you just give me good news?" I pointed at her belly.

She waved her index fingers back and forth, shimmying her shoulders and swaying in her seat. "There's more!"

I clapped my hands together, bound to my fate. "Lay it on me."

"Paul lined up some press for us, and it's killer." She was giddy with excitement.

I raised my brows coolly, not wanting to give her the satisfaction of having one over on me. "Well?" I said finally.

"*Vogue*'s covering the opening party, sending a photographer and reporter. And *Architectural Digest* wants to do a video tour of the new space and a piece in the magazine. Ah!" she shrieked with glee, waving her hands again.

"Whoa," I replied. "That's a big deal."

"Huge," she said.

"Well, this is amazing," I said, no longer trying to play it cool. "That's major press. What could be bad about it?"

"Those eighteen interior designers Tyler called?" She leaned against the couch, resigned, and I knew where this was going. My stomach sank.

"Oh no," I said, bringing my hand up to the back of my neck, fidgeting.

"Oh yes." She had gone from ecstatic to deflated in an instant. "All booked. So we need to figure out something in the next forty-eight hours, or *Vogue* will be photographing us in an empty space."

CHAPTER NINE

FRANNY

A DAY AFTER the big DNA reveal, I was snuggled into the corner of my couch, laptop nestled on my thighs, plugging numbers into a budgeting app in an attempt to plan for the rest of the year. I'd taken a break a few minutes ago and smeared a green mud mask all over my face, as if skin care could somehow solve my problems. All it did was dry so tightly on my face that my lips could barely move, which made it that much harder to eat the Wheat Thins and cheddar slices I'd grabbed from the kitchen earlier.

I reached for a cracker, and the plate, perched precariously on the edge of the couch, began to slide toward the floor. *Shit.* I caught it just in time, and once again admired the way the plate matched not only the vibe but the bright and cheerful colors I'd used to decorate my apartment. It was vintage ceramic, part of a set purchased off a website and sent to me from a small second-hand store in San Francisco. I'd been obsessed for months with finding these plates: hand-painted Italian majolica, covered in bright-orange peacock feathers that spiraled outward. They were pricey, but I excused them as a birthday present to myself, and every time I grabbed one I felt endless pleasure and awe over their beauty.

What would my half sister think of these dishes? I wondered. *Would she like them?* I dropped my head onto the cushion and let out a quiet moan. I still hadn't written her back, even though I'd been googling her nonstop.

On Instagram, Anna's design firm had almost sixty thousand followers. I found photos of her at Fashion Week in Milan all over the internet, balancing in heels as if her feet didn't hurt. It was like looking at photos of myself misshapen in a fun-house mirror. Olive skin, curly dark hair, the same serious set of eyebrows. Just living a much more glamorous, accomplished, better-dressed life.

I forced my brain back onto work stuff, but that only made me feel nauseous with anxiety. Anytime I tried to sit down and think through what it would take to truly work for myself—the budget, the hours, the money I'd need to make to pay my bills, the clients I'd need to have to actually make said money—I was overcome with imposter syndrome, which had only gotten worse since I learned about my cooler, more successful Italian doppelgänger. This was the dark, murky hole of insecurity that I fell into the second self-doubt came knocking at my door.

Not that this was a new feeling, of course. I was good at pushing it aside most of the time, but getting laid off was like a welcome mat, inviting it to show up whenever it wanted. It crept into my brain as my head hit the pillow, sat across from me at my tiny kitchen table as I drank my morning coffee.

This fucking day. Lola's text popped up as I was pacing my apartment, brainstorming, and I sent back a GIF of Daniel Radcliffe screaming "**HELP ME**" and went back to my pacing, plotting my business trajectory in my head.

My phone chimed again. **Teaching until 9**, Cleo wrote. **McManus later?**

One of our favorite dive-bar haunts. My mind skipped over to my three-alarm fire of a budget. **I gotta stick to a tight budget these days**, I wrote, capping it off with a sad face.

Roof then? Lola responded.

Cleo's roof had been a meeting spot for us since our early twenties. Not that it was easy to get to. It involved crawling out onto the fire escape of her fourth-floor walk-up on the Lower East Side and climbing a short but rickety ladder. We'd gotten very good over the years at juggling bottles, bags of takeout, and beach chairs in one hand while guiding ourselves upward with the other.

ROOOOOFFFFFFF, Lola wrote back.

"Well, that settles it," I said to the walls of my apartment. I thumbs-up-emojied back, just as an email alert popped up on my phone. I clicked on the notification to open it, and it was from Lola's coworker Grant. I held in a breath; this was the message I'd been waiting for, the thing that would be both my creative and financial lifeline, a rope to pull me back to the safe comforts of my old life. My eyes scanned the words on the screen.

"We so loved meeting you, Franny," the email read. *"But we've decided to go with a designer who's also a parent, to really capitalize on their expertise. Thank you so much for your time and thoughtful consultation. We hope our paths cross again soon!"*

Goddamn it. My heart sank. Now what the hell was I supposed to do?

Hours later, we were spread out on towels doubling as picnic blankets. The roof was dingy gray and covered in bird poop and leaves. There was nothing nice about it, other than it gave us the opportunity for fresh air and a stellar view of the Williamsburg Bridge. For us, that was enough.

While Cleo and Lola sipped from cans of Pacifico, I slurped out of my metal water bottle. We passed around a bag of Pirate's Booty between us. Technically, it was a free meal. I applauded my frugalness without letting myself get too depressed that I was thirty years old and eating white cheddar puffs for dinner because I was terrified the business I hadn't even officially started yet was doomed to go under. Not that I was going to bring that up tonight. I needed this time with my friends to decompress, forget for a moment that I was screwed. Besides, my friends worried enough about me already.

"Franny?" Cleo said. "You okay?"

And…that's the problem with good friends—they know when something's up, even when you don't tell them.

"I didn't get that nursery job. With Grant." I squeezed out a small, sad smile, in an attempt to act like I was okay.

"No!" Lola gasped as Cleo leaned in to give my arm a squeeze.

"I was kind of counting on that for…well, I guess for everything," I said slowly. "And I really need to figure out how to get some actual clients this year if I want to…you know."

They stared at me. "Want to what?" Lola asked.

"Really and truly start my own business." I sighed. "Not go broke and totally fail at this and humiliate myself in front of everyone I know. Keep my apartment and not have to move back home."

"Franny…" Cleo's voice was calm, her judicious, pragmatic side kicking in. "You just decided to do this. Don't put so much pressure on yourself right off the bat."

"Yeah." Lola nodded in agreement. "You're gonna set yourself up for failure." She reached out to touch her toes, thinking. "And, honestly, what you're doing is seriously brave."

"Thank you," I said. "But bravery doesn't pay my rent, you know? I've got some feelers out to my old clients at Spayce, but maybe I was naive to think I could just pivot and work for myself."

Cleo waved the Pirate's Booty bag at me, and I grabbed it, digging in.

"I'm just saying, keep your ears peeled for rich people with tons of money who want to blow it all on handwoven Turkish rugs, okay?"

"Those are basically the only kind of people I know, so…," Lola joked as she stretched her legs out in front of her, shaking them. "But, hey, seriously, Fran." She turned her eyes toward me. "You've had a bizarre time lately. Go easy on yourself."

Cleo nodded. "Work. Your sister. Your *birth dad*. It's a lot."

"And," Lola chimed in, "you know we can always help you figure out what to say to—"

"Anna," I said as Cleo shoot her a look.

"Right." Lola nodded. "If you decided to respond."

"I haven't yet, but I'm working on it."

I didn't have any more energy left to dig deeper into Franny's Box of Icky Feelings. *Quick, Franny, a subject change,* I said to myself.

"Things have been so nuts I haven't even told you about my walk to the subway with Hayes the other night." I dangled this in front of them like a carrot.

At the mention of his name, they both stopped what they were doing to stare at me. For a quick second, they were frozen in that shocked look you give a friend who has held on to a juicy tidbit for way too long.

"Whad did you thay?" Lola said through a mouthful of Pirate's Booty.

"Hayes walked me to the subway the other night, after we went all *Spy Kids* on your date."

"And?!" Cleo gestured at me to keep going, splashing beer on her shirt as she did. "Damn it," she muttered to herself, dabbing it with the edge of the towel she was sitting on. "I can't believe you haven't told us about this yet!"

"Didn't we just all agree that my life has gone off the rails? I forgot!" I held up my hands defensively.

"Ahh, go on, please," Lola said in a ridiculous fake British accent.

"I don't know. It was fine," I said honestly. "He grew up kinda near me. We talked about our families. Oh, and get this—he apologized for how weird he was during the interview."

"And what did you say?" Lola urged me on.

"I let him off the hook. He seemed very sincere. It was sweet. He doesn't seem as horrible as I originally thought."

"So it was basically a date," Cleo said excitedly.

"It was like a ten-minute walk!" I protested.

"I've been on dates that haven't even lasted that long," Lola snarked.

"Did he remind you that you're not his type?" Cleo asked, scooting forward to sit closer.

"Yeah, how did Mr. Smooth Moneybags charm you this time?" Lola chimed in as she dug around the bottom of the Pirate's Booty bag for crumbs.

"Look, I know this sounds crazy, but he's kind of nice."

I expected some sort of salty joke back from at least one of them, but they both just stared at me.

"What?" I said, staring back at them.

"You have the hots for Hot Suit." Cleo said the words as if she were discovering the answer to a riddle, and she tacked on a little gasp at the end, for effect. "You had that motorcycle dream too, remember?"

"I just said he was nice! Because he's nice! What's wrong with me thinking he's nice?" My voice got the teensiest bit higher.

"You just said 'nice' three times in a row." Lola was also using the riddle-solving voice, slow and studious.

"So?" I waved them off defensively. "I can think he's nice if I want."

"Mm-hmm, sure." Cleo raised a skeptical brow at me. "Nice. That's all. Just nice."

"I totally support you being hot for Hot Suit," said Lola. "Then we can double-date."

"Oh my god, will you stop? We're not going on a double date, because I'm not dating him," I insisted, taking a swig of water.

"But I bet you would, if he asked you out," Cleo went on, giggling. "And you'd have a *nice* kiss at the end of the night."

"Yeah, I wonder." Lola tilted her head in thought. "Do you think he's *nice* at the sex?"

"Ooooh yeah, Hot Suit would give it to you *nicely*, Fran," Cleo said, and now I was laughing along with her and Lola. And even though the attention was still on me, it felt good for the conversation to be light and easy. I kept laughing, hoping that neither of them would detect the truth: that underneath it all, I was scared shitless about just about everything happening in my life.

CHAPTER TEN

HAYES

"HAYES!"

A few days later, Serena greeted me on the sidewalk outside a downtown bar that I'd never heard of until she texted me the name and address. She seemed to tower over me, even though I was taller than her by a few inches. Sure, she was in heels, but it was her electric confidence that seemed to rocket her to the sky. Oh, and the skintight jeans didn't hurt either.

"Hey." I leaned in for a hug and landed my lips on her cheek. "It's nice to see you again."

She laughed at this, even though I hadn't intended it to be funny.

"It's kind of a scene inside. I hope that's okay."

"Of course," I said, unsure of what a "scene" would entail. It was only a Wednesday night. "This is your sorority sister's party?"

Serena nodded. She'd invited me last weekend during our run, and I'd expected a quiet gathering, a few friends.

"Hayley has the whole place rented out for her birthday," she said, reaching for the door. "I've never seen anyone go this hard for their twenty-ninth birthday, but I'm into it."

We walked up the steps and through the giant arched doorway, where overhead floated giant gold balloons that spelled out

121

HAYLEY. Just inside the front door was a wall with Hayley's name printed on it in pink and black, with brand logos all over it. People posed for photos in front of it, hugging and waving peace signs as a bored-looking bearded guy with a camera snapped away.

"Let's go take a photo in front of the step-and-repeat!" She gestured toward the name wall.

Serena pulled me forward and waved the photographer over to us. She angled herself next to me, chin tilted to the right, hips jutting toward the camera, elbow crooked just so. I made the same face I always do. I had decided in middle school that smiling made me look ridiculous in photos, and so I avoided it at all costs the second a camera rolled around. After a few shots together, she slid away from me and twisted her body in the opposite direction. "Derek, I need one for Insta," she said, as if it were the most obvious thing in the world.

Arms in the sky, right leg kicked up behind her, she smiled widely and held herself there for what felt like a minute, a crane posed silently on the edge of water. It was the same pose she'd done last week in the park, her "SerenaStyle" formation. It was supposed to be this happy, joyful pose, but something about it was stiff and planned, the opposite of spontaneous. It made me think back to Franny and her Italian ice, and the way she hadn't cared at all when it spilled on her.

After a round of flashes, Serena came to life again and approached the photographer.

"Can you text those to me?" she asked as I lingered awkwardly a few feet away in front of the photo wall, examining the brands that had sponsored this birthday party. A vodka company I recognized, a dating app. Some CBD brand specifically for women.

Photos acquired minutes later, Serena grabbed my arm again, leading me into the actual party. The music competed with conversations shouted over passed glasses of champagne. In the corner, a pair of tattooed women stitched people's names onto hooded sweatshirts, the party favor of the evening. There seemed to be a cotton-candy machine somewhere, judging by the amount of people eating it, which was competing with hand-rolled sushi as the meal of the night.

The last birthday party I'd been to had been an intimate gathering on the patio of Eleanor's favorite vegan restaurant in the West Village. This felt like a prom.

Yet Serena moved effortlessly through the room, introducing me to people, touching my arm constantly, including me in conversations, talking me up. I got the feeling she was showing me off. It was something that should have stroked my ego, made me feel good. But nothing revved inside me.

"This is Dominique!"

"Hayes runs one of the most important environmental finance firms in the city!"

"We interned together at *Vogue*!"

"The *Wall Street Journal* did a whole profile on him!"

"Can you believe she's only twenty-two and already shooting in Paris?"

"Yeah, we ran the whole Central Park loop together. It was so fun!"

After forty-five minutes of shouted introductions, forced smiles, and endless head nodding, I excused myself and retreated outside for some air. I dug my phone out and texted Perrine. **Do you wanna hang out? I think I'm going to cut out on this party early.**

Perrine's reply popped up just as I jogged back up the steps and into the bar to find Serena. **Aren't you on a date?**

And then: **Having dinner w Lola at 9, can stop by in a few first.**

I sent a thumbs-up emoji in response.

"Hayes!" Serena waved me over to where she was wedged on the edge of a couch next to a gaggle of long-limbed model types.

"Hey!" I leaned down toward her, and she grazed a hand up

my arm, smiling. When her hand reached my wrist, I flipped up my palm, entwining our fingers. A pang of guilt hit my gut— I should want to stay, but my desire to get the hell out of there was overpowering. "I'm gonna take off. I have an early breakfast meeting tomorrow."

"I'm sorry this ended up being such a zoo," she said with a sincerely apologetic look on her face. "Maybe we can do something just the two of us soon? I could even cook you dinner. Your place or mine."

"I'd love that," I said, though it felt more like I was going through the motions of what I was expected to say. I liked this feeling of being wanted, and Serena was charming and warm, and fun to be around. But whenever I was with her, it felt like I was waiting for some feeling to reveal itself, like a guest to a party who was running absurdly late.

She placed a small kiss on my lips, soft and warm, and I pressed back, trying to feel the connection I was so sure was supposed to be there. "Get home safe."

—*mm*—

Perrine leaned against the counter as I microwaved one of my delivery meals. Salmon with an almond-flour crust over green beans. Perfectly adequate. Possibly even good.

"It seems like a strange choice for a date," she said, pondering. "Who invites a guy they just met to a friend's massive birthday party?"

"Well, in her defense, she made it out to be more of a casual gathering. Maybe she didn't know it was going to be so huge?"

"Or maybe that's just what a casual gathering looks like to her."

I shrugged. "I mean, going out seems to be part of her job. So she must like it."

She peered over as I popped the container out of the microwave, steam rising as I mixed the vegetables with a fork. "There should be a law against microwaving fish," she said with a grimace.

Luckily, the buzzer interrupted her food criticism, and she wandered out to the door. "Hey," she called from the hallway. "Is it okay if Lola comes up?" If she was nervous for the two of us to meet again, she didn't sound like it. I tried not to either.

"Of course," I said, playing it cool. I grabbed a paper towel and can of sparkling water and headed to the living room, sitting on the couch with my plate balanced on my knees.

I listened as Perrine and Lola greeted each other in the hall, voices hushed but tender. Footsteps, and then they were in the living room. "Lola," I said, my mouth full. I stood, putting my plate on the coffee table. "It's nice to see you."

I extended my hand toward her, and she took it in her own. "Hi," she said, looking me straight in the eye. "Fancy seeing you again."

I snuck a look at Perrine, who was gazing at Lola with such wide-eyed infatuation it was impossible to miss. I'd lived through Perrine's dating life for almost fifteen years, and I'd never seen her give away her emotions so clearly before.

"Hayes and I were just discussing his awkward date tonight," Perrine said, sitting back in the armchair in the corner. "Seems only fair to include you, since he got to witness our first date in action."

"Oh, I already saw it on Instagram. I've followed Serena and her crew for years." Lola perched on the edge of the chair, her hand casually draped on the back of Perrine's neck. "You looked good," she said, giving me a once-over.

"Um…" This caught me off guard, and I could feel the heat rising in my face. "Thank you."

I wondered, for a moment, if she'd relay this info to her best friend. Then there was that memory again: of Franny, and the Italian ice, and her carefree laugh as if nothing mattered.

"As I was saying," I continued, trying to focus, "it wasn't awkward." I narrowed my eyes at my cousin. "If it was awkward, would she have offered to make me dinner?"

"Ooooh," Lola said supportively, just as Perrine replied, "Here? You don't have a dining room table."

"We can eat in the living room," I said defensively. "Or do it at her place."

"Have you even brought a date back here yet?"

"Perrine," I said, my voice a little sharper now. I didn't feel like discussing my sex life with my cousin, much less with her new girl-friend, whose only impression of me was as a weird date-stalker who said things like *"You're not my type"* to people on live TV.

"Don't worry, Hayes, nothing can shock me," Lola said with a smile. "I read about celebrities doing bizarre shit all day long."

"Then fine. Yes, I've brought women back here," I said with a curt smile. "And dinner is not shocking."

"Hayes, I have literally been inside a morgue, and even it's got more ambiance than this place," Perrine chimed in. "I told you I'd come over and hang stuff up for you."

She was doing the thing where she acted like my mom, or a big sister, even though I was older. Sometimes I tolerated it. Liked it, even. Not today.

"Yeah, well, this apartment is the least of my worries. We need to find someone to do the interior of our new office."

"I thought you had a guy," she said, crossing her arms as she grilled me.

"We did, and then he got a bigger gig. And now we're scrambling. And our publicist just lined up two huge press hits for us, and both are tied into the design and opening of the new space."

"Oh my god," Lola interrupted, which was probably for the best, anyway, since Perrine and I were on the verge of one of our sibling-esque spats.

Both of us turned to look at her. "Wait, sorry," she said, shaking her head. "I had what I thought was an amazing idea and then realized it probably isn't."

"What?" Perrine and I said at the exact same time.

"Okay, well, I think you know Franny is an interior designer." She said this like a salesperson, slowly laying out a pitch before the big sell.

"Franny-from-the-train Franny?" I asked, even though I knew exactly who she was talking about. Hearing her name made the hair on the back of my neck stand at attention.

"Yes, that Franny. As opposed to all the other Frannys we both know." I don't think I'd ever met someone more sarcastic, and being on the receiving end was slightly terrifying and also weirdly enjoyable at the same time.

"Right," I said. "And now she's off and running with her own business and clients, and doing great and booked for months."

Lola shifted slightly. "I think she's had some spots open up."

"Ooooh," Perrine said, quickly shutting up when I shot her The Look.

"She's truly talented. Gifted." Lola paused. "And from what I hear, you two hit it off the other night, so no more hard feelings or anything like that to worry about."

Hard feelings? Great. Just great. I could feel my face getting redder by the minute. "I don't think—"

Lola held up her hand to stop me. "Your call. Of course."

Perrine looked at Lola and then at me. "I think hiring Franny makes perfect sense. You definitely need some help, Hayes-y," Perrine said, using my childhood nickname. "Think about it."

Lola grinned. "It sounds to me like you're kind of fucked, and Franny could definitely unfuck the situation for you. She's done corporate interiors before. It's basically her thing. What she's known for."

"Well," I said, "I do need someone to unfuck things right now."

Perrine snorted, and I glared back.

"Okay," she said, turning to tug on Lola's arm. "We should go. I'm starving."

"Good to see you, Hayes," said Lola, smiling at me like she had my number, even though we'd really just met.

"You too," I said as I followed them to the door. Once they'd left, I flopped onto my couch, stretching my legs long, remote in hand, clicking over to ESPN for something mindless to watch.

I thought for a moment of Serena, her hand on mine, her flirty words. But in a second she was gone, replaced by the idea of seeing Franny again. And then suddenly a text alert popped up on my phone. I swiped over to messages and glanced at the screen. It was Perrine. It simply said, **Take it or leave it**.

And then, before my brain could fully process just what she meant, a contact card followed.

Franny Doyle
917-555-5535

CHAPTER ELEVEN

FRANNY

THE CITY WAS already wide-awake when I got to the front of Cleo's apartment building at 9 a.m. on Saturday. **I'm here**, I texted, and then sat down on her stoop until she popped out through the front door, her hair still wet from the shower.

"Let's do it!" she exclaimed, with way too much energy for this early on a weekend morning. We were headed uptown to hunt for something for me to wear to the black-tie gala her mom cochaired every summer, because the secondhand shops on the Upper East Side were always restocked on Saturday mornings. It was either this or renting a dress. But I liked the idea of something all my own—vintage, timeless, and most importantly, cheap.

The plan was for me to tag along with Cleo, try to meet the design team who produced the event, and schmooze with the fancy uptown ladies, see if they'd hire me to decorate one of their many bathrooms. Cleo had even gotten her mom involved, and Mrs. Kim, like her daughter, loved making the impossible happen.

We'd barely made it on to Houston Street when my phone rang.

"Franny, hi, it's Hayes Montgomery. From the train."

"Hayes who hates sugar?" I said without thinking, and Cleo's mouth dropped when she heard his name.

She tucked her arm in mine and leaned close to try to hear the call through my phone. I gave her a playful push away.

I heard him let out a nervous laugh. "Yes, it's me. Hayes who hates sugar."

We stopped in front of Cleo's favorite coffee shop so she could grab us Americanos to jump-start the day. I paced the sidewalk as she blew me a kiss and walked inside.

"Um, so here's a funny thing that happened to me recently," he continued. "The interior designer we'd hired to do our new office space quit on us, and we need someone to step in ASAP. It's been a big fiasco."

"Ugh, that's terrible," I replied, cringing at what a nightmare he must be dealing with. "I'm sorry to hear that."

"I know you're busy with your own work stuff, but Lola was at my place last night with Perrine, my cousin—"

"Oh, I remember her," I said with a chuckle.

"That's right." I heard him laugh softly through the phone. "Well, she mentioned that your schedule's opened up, and I was wondering if you might be interested in meeting about the position."

"Well, that…" I trailed off for a minute, processing. "That was not what I was expecting you to say." Relief, joy, nervousness: a bunch of feelings burst inside me all at once.

"Is that a bad thing? I know it's an insanely quick turnaround, so if you already have too much—"

"I would absolutely love to put some ideas together for you," I said calmly, trying not to sound too eager. But inside I was screaming, "*Yes! Yes! Yes!*" My severance pay from Spayce was about to run out in a few weeks. God, I needed this. "I can have something to you in forty-eight hours."

"Seriously?" He sounded both surprised and relieved.

I nodded confidently, even though he couldn't see me. "One hundred percent."

"Wow. Okay, thank you. Can you text me your email, and I'll get this over to you, then?"

"Of course." I was bouncing in my Vans, unable to control the excitement. "Oh. And, Hayes..."

"Yes?"

"I'm sorry about that sugar comment from before," I said. "I hope I didn't offend you."

"I promise you, I do eat sweet things," he replied. There was a playfulness to his voice that hadn't been there before, a slight purr that was undeniably sexy. "Occasionally."

"I'll believe it when I see it," I said, smiling.

"Okay, well, we'll have to eat dessert together sometime."

"I'd love that!" Ugh. I sounded way too excited. *Tone it down, Franny. Tone it down.* "That'd be fun."

"'Kay. Well, I'll text that info." Hayes's voice shifted. Mr. All Business was back. "Thanks for considering this."

"No, thank you. I appreciate you thinking of me."

Everything out of my mouth felt weird and flirty, flying out of my lips before I even realized what I was saying.

"For the job," I added.

"Of course. Talk soon."

We hung up just as Cleo was maneuvering her way through the door with two coffee cups in hand.

"Well? How's your crush?" she asked, passing over a cup.

I didn't bother correcting her. "He's good," I said. "He wants to hire me? Maybe? To do the interior of his new office space."

"Whoa!" Her mouth dropped an inch.

"And guess who told him I might have availability," I added, drawing out the mystery.

Cleo tilted her head, confused. "No clue."

"Lola."

"Oh my god, she's always got some scheme going on," Cleo said with what could only be described as a loving eye roll.

131

"So now I have forty-eight hours to put something together." Saying it out loud made it feel real, and my stomach bubbled with nerves.

"Fran!" It was all she needed to say. I could hear every bit of excitement she felt for me in just the way she squealed my name. "This is huge. Just make sure Mercury isn't in retrograde when you sign the contract."

I chuckled. "There's not even a contract yet, Clee. Don't worry."

"And just think of how much one-on-one time you're going to get with your Hot Suit," she teased.

"Oh my god, come on," I said, but, oh, I was thinking about it. That, and the way the sound of his voice had made my knees feel weak, like the time my mom took me to the top of Rockefeller Center when I was a kid. I didn't just think Hayes Montgomery was *nice*. I was heading very close to crush territory, just like Cleo had suggested. Or maybe I was already in it.

"It would be a big deal to get this contract," I said, before I took a sip, smiling as I imagined what a job like this could do for me. Not only would it get the word out about my design work, but it would do the thing I needed most: pay the bills.

"Oh, you'll get it. No doubt in my mind," Cleo said firmly, like there was no other option. "Let's hurry up and find you an outfit so you can get to work."

Besides, just the thought of Hayes and me together was ridiculous. This was one of those completely unattainable crushes that never led anywhere but sucked up all your time and energy. A possible job was way more important than some hot guy. I was going to land this thing, I decided, determined. Hayes and his enchanting eyes be damned.

I made it to the front of Hayes and Eleanor's new building fifteen minutes early. I had planned to give myself some time to reapply my lipstick and check over my pitch document, work through my nerves so that I could be calm when they arrived. Instead, Hayes was already standing there, waiting for me. "Franny, hey," he said with a wave.

I tried to give him a once-over without him noticing. He was dressed almost identical to when we first met, head to toe in navy, with a light-blue shirt underneath his jacket. The crispness of his clothes only made the sharp angles of his face more pronounced, and the combination caused the back of my neck to heat up, a sauna made entirely of nerves . . . and pheromones. When I looked up, his eyes caught mine, but he looked away immediately, as aloof as ever.

"Hi," I replied as he opened the door of the building for me.

"Wow," I said, looking around the lobby. "This is great." It was more than great; it was sleek and sophisticated, a modern mix of wood, metal, and huge floor-to-ceiling windows. Not to mention it was right in the middle of the West Village, blocks from the Hudson River. I tried to keep my drooling to a minimum and attempted to play it cool.

"This way," he said with a tilt of his head as he led me to the elevators. "How are you doing?" he asked politely as we stood across from each other on the way up.

Was he nervous? That seemed unlikely. But why else would he be acting like we were meeting for the first time?

Then I remembered what he had said that night we walked to the subway together: "*I just felt very out of place.*"

Hayes was *awkward*. Something I'd interpreted as haughtiness at first. But now that I could see it for what it was, it was kind of charming.

"Good, thank you," I replied. "I'm—"

Thankfully, the doors dinged open just then, saving me from myself.

"Wow."

Walking into the space was like diving into the ocean with your eyes open for the first time. It was vast, bright, and beautiful. Light carpeted the floor, beaming in through a giant wall of industrial windows facing the Hudson.

"Hayes." I turned to him, my mouth wide, voice filled with glee. "This is *beyond*." I was unable to hide my excitement. There was no point in trying to play it cool. I could have gushed more: the high ceilings, the exposed beams, the raw brick. It was untouched, unmarked, a dream canvas that had my creative brain itching for what felt like the first time in forever. Sitting here empty like this was a disgrace to its beautiful bones. They longed to be caressed and loved, draped in art and color, and filled with life.

"Yeah, it's cool," he said, hands in pockets, watching me.

"Cool?" I repeated back to him, horrified that he'd choose such an ordinary, boring word to describe something as beautiful as this. "That's like saying LeBron James is *just okay* at basketball. This place is a dream."

I bent to touch a hand to the floor—real wood, probably original. I sighed with pleasure. "These floors are amazing. I am sincerely attracted to them."

He let out a "Ha!" at this, and I looked toward him, grinning.

"I'm not kidding," I insisted. "I would date these floors."

I walked to the wall of windows, and he followed a few paces behind. The view stretched deep into New Jersey and then down the river, toward where the Statue of Liberty stood, still and stoic.

"It's weird—I can actually see my old apartment from this view." He pointed south toward Tribeca.

"Why'd you move?" I asked, genuinely curious. You'd have to drag me kicking and screaming from living in an apartment on the water.

"My ex-wife got it in the divorce."

Ex-wife. Well, this was interesting. Hayes Montgomery had a past. He'd been *married.* Imagining him twirling a bride on the dance floor, beaming in a tuxedo, settling into a home, shopping for plates and silverware—it twisted something in me that I couldn't identify. Maybe jealousy, possibly sadness. Probably a little bit of both.

I turned to look at him, assuming he'd be facing away from me, but instead he met my gaze, intently, cheeks flushed. I just nodded. I didn't judge anyone for relationships ending, and I wanted to make sure he knew it.

"And you owned that place?" I asked, turning back to admire the view.

"We did," he said matter-of-factly. Another interesting tidbit. A past and money. I mean, I guess I knew that from the way he'd tossed a six-hundred-dollar jacket at me like it was a tissue, but still. It prickled, remembering that this guy was *someone.* He had a successful business, a cushy bank account; even having an ex-wife felt like an accomplishment. Like he had something to show for all the living he'd done.

It all made me feel uncomfortably small, with not much to show for myself.

He motioned for me to take a seat in one of the plastic folding chairs that had been set up around a larger table placed near the entrance, a makeshift reception area. I sat down gingerly and balanced myself on the edge of the chair just so, painfully aware of his eyes on me. Because they were beautiful eyes, and also because I needed to impress him and land this job. I pulled out my laptop, opening a document to take notes. I tried to discreetly wipe my sweaty palms on my jeans before turning my attention to him.

"Eleanor just texted me. Her doctor's appointment ran late, but she's on her way," he said, glancing up from his phone.

"Do you want to wait for her to start?" I asked, my fingers perched on the keys, back straight. My grandmother had always made a point of correcting my posture, and now I did it to myself whenever I was nervous.

"I think we can just get into it."

I nodded and sat up straighter.

"We loved your proposal," he said, crossing his legs. They were so long I marveled that he could even sit comfortably in these wobbly chairs. "If it's cool with you, we'd like to just get the ball rolling."

I pressed my lips together to suppress the grin that was working its way onto my face.

"With me," I confirmed.

"Yes, as long as you're interested and have the time." He was studying me, his gaze direct and clear, but it revealed nothing. I thought about how low his voice had been on the phone, when he'd told me, "*I do eat sweet things.*" Maybe I'd imagined the playfulness. Had he even been flirting, or was I just projecting, looking for things that weren't really there?

I pushed the thoughts aside. I was better off not letting my brain wander into fantasy territory with him and his deep voice, his fancy suits, and his office full of perfect wood floors. What was important is that he'd just offered me a job, something I desperately needed.

"I can definitely make it work," I said, trying not to freak out. I'd seen their budget on the proposal he'd sent me. This one job could sustain me for months.

"But first, I have a few questions I like to ask everyone I work with, to help me better understand their needs," I continued in my best professional voice.

Hayes nodded.

"So," I said, trying not to focus on how handsome he looked sitting there in the sunlight, or how his demeanor was so serious that it almost didn't fit with how beautiful his face was. And then I reminded myself that he'd announced to the world that I wasn't his type. "How do you want to feel when you walk into your office?"

Hayes was thoughtful for a moment. "You know when you get into a nicely made bed with superclean sheets that are also incredibly worn and soft?"

I nodded. This was one of my favorite things in the world, and it was surprisingly sweet, coming from someone who usually seemed so buttoned-up and closed-off.

"I want that," he continued. "Someplace that's easy. Where I can be myself. Where I can relax and focus on work."

His posture was erect, a freshly sharpened pencil. He rarely looked at ease in his own body, and yet it was clear he was craving comfort from this new space. Something about the revelation started my heart fluttering.

"And how do you want other people to feel when they walk in here?"

His forehead wrinkled as he looked at me. "Other people?"

"Yeah. You know, colleagues, clients, friends, girlfriends."

I said the word so quickly it barely had two syllables. If his cheeks had been pink before, they were now definitely red, a summer tomato ready to burst.

"Would *you* want to go on a date with me to my office? Help me file some documents?" he asked.

Oh god, was he flirting? Or was he annoyed? It was so hard to tell with this one. There was something about his words that always felt so deliberate, pointed, lobbed to land directly inside me.

Then he raised his brows and gave me my answer: Flirting. Definitely flirting. There was that flutter again.

"I'm sorry. I wasn't trying to pry into your personal life," I said, backtracking to avoid encouraging that springy feeling in my chest. *Get it together, Franny. You need this job. Be professional!* "But our spaces tell a story—not just to us, but to anyone who walks into them."

"I was joking," he answered, his smile sheepish. "I, uh, I guess I want other people to walk in here and...get a sense of who I am."

"And who's that exactly?" I leaned forward in my seat, genuinely curious.

Before he could answer, the elevator dinged, the sound slicing through whatever tension this conversation was bubbling up between us. The doors opened, and out walked the kind of woman who made me do a double take when I passed her on the street: warm brown skin, enviable thick curls, giant tortoiseshell glasses, a killer red lip. I made a mental note to ask her who made that lip color. I needed it. Cleo and Lola needed it. Hell, every woman needed a red this good.

She was decked out in a black silk jumpsuit and sky-high black clogs, but the simplicity of it all made her seem incredibly fancy. In one hand, she held a bag of crackers; a tote bag dangled from the other. I wanted to be her best friend, and I didn't even know her.

"Eleanor Lewis," she said, bright and self-possessed. "Hayes's cofounder. I hate the term 'work wife,' but that's essentially what I am."

"It's nice to meet you." Her handshake was firm and warm.

"He told you this was my idea first, right?" she said, leaning in conspiratorially. "I don't want him to get all the credit for hiring you."

I laughed at this; I liked her instantly.

Hayes stood and offered her his seat. "I was going to give you all the credit, El," he said.

She waved him off and tucked the crackers into the giant tote— a creamy, soft leather—and dug around, yanking out an ultrasound picture, shoving it toward Hayes. "Look at this cute little alien face."

Hayes lit up in a way I hadn't seen before. Genuine excitement and joy flashed across his whole body all at once. Brows relaxed, jaw unclenched, shoulders back. "Shit, El," he said, grabbing the strip of images out of her hand. Smiling. "Look at that. Beautiful."

"This kid better be a MacArthur genius, considering how much they've made me throw up. Speaking of, I'm due for a cracker break."

It was clear in just that small moment how much they cared about each other. I smiled and offered my congratulations, and—after a saltine break for Eleanor—we walked around the perimeter of the office.

"Okay, so the goal for the open floor plan and communal work-space is to warm it up but not overpower it," I said as Eleanor and Hayes trailed behind me. "We play up the natural aesthetics of the building—the windows, the light, the wood—but add elements that make it more inviting, so you feel good as soon as you enter. Your employees and clients too."

I glanced back to gauge their response. Eleanor nodded thoughtfully. Hayes's face was unreadable; it was impossible to know if he hated everything I was saying or was just processing it all. But then our eyes connected, and instead of turning away from me, he smiled, brows raised, the kind of face someone gives to say "*I like it. I'm impressed. Well done.*"

It kicked something on inside me, sent my confidence whirring. "Hayes and I had a chance to talk about his own office a bit, and, Eleanor, I'd love to connect with you about your space." I led us into the corner office he'd flagged as hers.

"The only thing I have to have are my pictures hanging some-where," she said.

"You're a photographer?" I asked, wondering how much more impressive this already impressive woman would get.

"Amateur," she said, "but way too into it. And I like to think I'm somewhat decent."

She walked over to the wall, running her hand over the ridges of red brick. "I mostly photograph surfers," she said. "The ocean. Beach towns."

"So water, nature," I mused, brainstorming.

"All that. Every time I'm near the water, I feel like I'm in my element."

"You mean more than when you're running a board meeting?" Hayes teased from behind me.

Eleanor snorted. "That's enough, thank you," she said, giving him the finger before turning back to me. "Hayes acts tough, but he cries watching Pixar movies."

"Hey, just in *Up*," he said defensively. Then to me, with a shrug, "When the wife dies."

He turned, hands in pockets, but not before I could see the faint hint of color on his cheeks. I noticed this about him now; he played it cool, but something warmer was always lurking underneath. If he had been looking back at me, he would have seen me smiling in his direction.

Eleanor and I followed him out into the main area. "I think we can create a sophisticated and inviting space for you that's very organic too," I said.

"I trust you," Eleanor said. "Oh, and I'd like to make that spare office a spot for parents. I need a place to use my breast pump."

"Of course," I said, excited about the idea. "A place for the breast to rest."

Oh god. I clenched my teeth, cringing at my ability to always say too much. "Sorry, that came out all wrong."

Eleanor laughed. "Actually, it was just right." She gave me an approving look. "On that note, I need to get home before I have to lie down on the floor here. Great to meet you, Franny. Thanks for taking this on."

She leaned in toward me, grabbing my elbow affectionately. "For taking *us* on," she said.

"I appreciate the opportunity, truly." I offered her a wide smile that instantly felt too eager, but it was too late to rein it in.

Hayes walked with her to the elevator, discussing some client that was blowing up his inbox today. I busied myself on my computer, typing in notes from our conversations.

Then there he was again, clearing his throat to interrupt me. "There's one other thing I want to show you."

I followed him over to a door that he had pointed out earlier, and when he opened it, everything changed.

When you live in New York City, there's a magical feeling you get whenever you run up the steps out of the subway, spin through a revolving door out of your office building at the end of a long day, push open a window to let in the spring scent of blossoms. There's a split second where the city hits you, greets you, slobbers a kiss on your face like a puppy. It's a jolt, and a shock, and then you move on. But there's a part of you, somewhere, that marvels at it every time.

Stepping onto this roof was like that: an inhalation of breath, a moment of wonder.

"Wow," was all I said, bringing a hand to my eyes to shield them from the orange sunset sitting on top of the Jersey City skyline. "This belongs to you too?"

He nodded, and I could see it in the creases of his eyes, which even outside were still a color too dark to read: He was marveling at it all too.

"Can we use it?"

He nodded. "We should, right?"

"God, yes. This is amazing."

"We have no budget for it, so we'd have to do it on the cheap," he said.

It didn't have a ton of room, nor was it especially beautiful—just the raw concrete of a rooftop and then a wall that ran around the edge, hitting just above my waist. But in the city, outdoor space was more valuable than gold. Their office was gorgeous, but this was a jackpot.

"That shouldn't be too hard. I'll come up with some low-cost ideas for you and Eleanor to consider." There was a flurry in my chest of pure excitement. "And we'll get the ball rolling."

Back inside, Hayes hovered a few feet away as I packed up my bag.

"I liked your suggestions," he said, looking up from his phone, "about my office. My taste is pretty simple, and sometimes I worry that I don't have any. But maybe I do."

There was a question hidden behind his statement, and something about it sounded almost insecure. Could it be possible that underneath his fancy suits Hayes was still working out who he was?

"Of course you do. You're minimalistic. Understated."

I studied him, a piece of art hanging in a museum that I didn't quite understand but couldn't help but want to. "There's nothing simple about a well-made suit, for example."

Standing on that roof in the center of the city had made me feel invincible, fearless. I took a step toward him and tugged on his suit lapel. "I mean, this thing is as plain as possible and yet it's impeccably crafted. So maybe that's your taste."

He blinked, and I could swear he seemed to be studying me. I took a step back, immediately mortified, and tried to course-correct the conversation

"What I mean is…" I searched around my brain for the right words. "Maybe you're more interesting than you're giving yourself credit for."

And just when I was certain that I'd ruined everything with my babbling, Hayes smiled at me.

"Maybe," he said as he shifted his hands to his hips, "you are too."

CHAPTER TWELVE

HAYES

PERRINE AND I had a good clip going tonight. We were running north up the east side of Central Park, maneuvering around cyclists, families with strollers, lingering tourists. I would have preferred to run in silence, but Perrine wanted an update on the Serena situation.

"She invited me to this black-tie gala she's helping put together," I huffed through measured breaths. It was Serena we were discussing, but suddenly I was thinking of Franny, and what she might wear to a black-tie gala. She'd had jeans on the other day as we walked through the office, and this delicate black tank top, and when she laughed she— The thought froze in my mind, rewound three steps. The office. We were working together now. I had to be professional.

"Have you even hooked up?" Perrine asked, winded. Oh, right, Serena. The woman I was actually dating.

"We've kissed. That's it. Is that weird? I honestly feel like I've forgotten how to date people."

It wasn't like I'd been celibate since Angie and I had split up. I'd tried every dating app imaginable. But no relationship had ever really gotten off the ground. They either fizzled after the first couple of dates, or were purely physical for a hot second before one of us called it off. And I'd never really wanted anything serious, anyway, especially not right after my divorce. But now something in me felt open to it.

She shrugged her arms as she hustled along. "I mean, no. What even counts as weird these days, anyway? I met Lola in a bathroom."

We kept moving in the darkness, the park pulsing around us. The sound of a concert thumped from the southern side, and bikes whizzed by with the efficiency and speed of a hummingbird.

"And, look, I get why it's easier to have a casual relationship right now." Her voice was lower, more hesitant. "With work being what it is. But it's okay to want to get to know someone first. To have a connection."

But the word *connection* only made me think about Franny again, and the weird electric energy I felt pass between us. Every time I was near her, it felt like the words got stuck in my mouth and came out all scrambled, and yet I kept wanting to be around her more.

"Serena's great," I said, a reminder to myself more than anything. "Her job's also hectic, so really we get each other. We have a lot in common."

"That's awesome," Perrine said, shooting a smile in my direction as we kept running.

"Things with Lola are going well, though?" I asked, eager to get the spotlight off me.

"So good." She looked at me with giant saucer eyes, lit up by the streetlamps dotting East Drive. "I mean, we've only been dating for a little over a month, but I really like her. I think I'm falling in love with her, honestly."

Before I could respond, she asked, "Sprint to Eighty-Sixth Street?"

And we were off, chasing that final bit of endorphins, the last call of a long day.

Perrine dashed to the Reservoir, stopping at the edge and bending over to catch her breath, her hands on her hips.

"Wow, Perr," I said when I'd caught up with her. "That's a big deal."

"It is." She flopped down on the grass, legs butterflied in front of her. "But it also feels like not a big deal at all. It's weird, you know? You just, like, suddenly realize this could be it, and then everything feels easy."

"Yeah," I said, stretching an arm up, grabbing my elbow with my opposite hand. I turned her words over in my head. *Did* I know this? There had been a time with Angie, a moment early on, where I had thought, *"This is it. This is being in love."* But our relationship had never been easy, for either of us. Maybe Angie had been right: Maybe we'd never even been in love at all. And if that was true, what the hell did that say about me?

"Have you told her?" I asked, not wanting to dwell on yet another possible flaw in my character.

She shook her head. "I will, but right now it just feels nice to know it myself."

I sat down next to her, half-heartedly stretching my legs and picking at blades of grass that poked up by my shins. I didn't want to think about my marriage falling apart, because it all fell squarely on my shoulders. And then I'd have to face the insecurity that remained, that maybe I wasn't meant for a relationship with anyone.

~~~

A few nights later, I was pacing the floors of the new office space, anticipating Franny's arrival. It was a relief to know that we had a designer on board, and that things were finally back on track. In the last forty-eight hours, she'd sent over a barrage of emails to Eleanor and me—lighting fixtures to approve, a few different sources for repurposed wood to check out, some article on the best ergonomic desk chairs. And then, a two-page outline on rooftop gardens, and the benefit of a green space within a work environment.

She'd hand-sketched a simple design plan, with planters, a small seating area, and a long industrial table with benches. Utilizing the outdoor space this way was such an obvious and brilliant idea that when she'd first texted me, I'd been embarrassed I hadn't thought of it first.

Tonight, she burst off the elevator like an exclamation point. "Hayes!" she shouted, giant box in hand. A delivery guy from the hardware store pushed a large pallet of wood and bags of soil behind her. *Do not look at her legs,* I told myself, because they were bare and long and tempting in cutoff jean shorts. I turned my attention to her hands, pressed around the box. This was a safe spot for my gaze to land. Her nails were a bright cherry red. I'd never noticed a color on them before, and my eyes shot to them instantly, and then followed her long slender fingers to her wrist, which was curved and smooth and—

"Hey," she said as she got closer.

"Want me to take that?" I asked, outstretching a hand.

"No," she said, enunciating the word as if I'd offended her. "I know the first time you saw me holding a box I was falling apart, but I got this."

She scanned me as she passed, heading toward the door that led to the roof deck. I took a few quick steps to get ahead of her and grab the door to hold it open. "Is that what you're wearing?" she asked.

"Yes, why?" I'd run home and changed out of my work clothes before coming here and into a white cotton button-down and some jeans that Eleanor and Henry had convinced me to buy but I had hardly worn. They made me look cooler and calmer than I actually was, which Eleanor had insisted was "a good thing."

"A white shirt? We're literally going to be moving bags of dirt."

"I can handle a little dirt," I said as I followed her through the doorway. I inhaled deeply as I passed her, and then caught myself. *Jesus Christ, Hayes. Get it together.*

I tipped the delivery man, who had dropped everything off as close to the roof as he could get. Then I followed Franny outside, undoing the top button on my shirt.

"Solar twinkle lights?" I said, grabbing a container out of the box she'd opened.

"Obviously," she answered, giving me a grin. "We'll attach them to a stake in the garden box and string them to the edge of the roof. You've gotta have mood lighting out here!"

One of her tank top straps fell down her shoulder as she dragged a bag of soil to the opposite side of the roof, and she mindlessly reached up and tucked it under the strap of her bra. I couldn't stop lasering in on every small detail of how she moved, how everything about her felt effortless and relaxed.

"Okay, so you saw the photos of the table I sent? All repurposed wood."

I nodded. "I loved it."

"Great, so that goes here." She walked forward, outlining the shape of a long rectangular table with her steps. "Two benches. You can have meetings or lunch out here, or people can just come out to take a break. Two lounge chairs." She waved over to the small corner nook. "And then the garden area."

She turned back toward me to assess my reaction to her plan, a giant grin on her face. Her excitement was so palpable it crackled off her. I'd never realized that just the idea of placing a table and chairs somewhere could ignite someone like this, but then again I'd never met someone like Franny before. The sight of her mixed up the signals in my brain, like they were shaken together in a tumbler, making the most intoxicating cocktail ever.

"So what do you think?" she asked, her face flushed.

"I'm in," I said. "Just tell me what to do, and I'll do it."

"You're cool with me bossing you around?" she asked, brows raised playfully.

"Why else am I even here?" I rubbed my hands together and then worried I looked ridiculous and put them in my back pockets. "I'm ready to work."

"Woo!" She raised her hands triumphantly, tossing her head back as she laughed, her curls bouncing along for the ride. "Okay, well, the first thing I need you to do is drag those big-ass bags of soil out here and stack them in the corner so they're as close to the garden boxes as possible."

I gave her a quick salute and made a move for the bags as she began unpacking the vertical hydroponic lettuce garden from its box. Dusk settled in around us. When the last bag was stacked in the corner, I wiped my arm across my brow and made my way back to where she was working, assembling a giant white tower that contained a dozen or so pockets for plants.

"Okay, I'm ready for my next assignment," I said, admiring her laser focus on the task in front of her.

"Wow, I never imagined you'd be such an eager student." She pressed her lips together in thought as she looked at me.

"My professor's a hard-ass, but I like her," I said, and when this got a laugh out of her, I felt like I'd won prize.

"Well, you get an A-plus for ass-kissing," she said as she waved for me to follow her. "Let's do the seedlings together."

We walked over near the doorway, where rows of seemingly identical sprouts were lined up next to each other. "Are they all the same?" I asked.

"Excuse you, how dare you insult these beautiful plants that way," she said as she bent down to grab one. "There are five different kinds of salad greens here." She began pointing at each one. "Romaine, arugula, butter lettuce, red leaf, Little Gem. Plus basil, cilantro, mint, and parsley."

"I'm impressed," I quipped, and she turned away, but not before I caught a small pleased smile on her lips.

"You should be," she answered, but her voice was quiet and she still wasn't looking at me. And then something clicked. Could she be feeling the same pull that I was feeling when she was around? It seemed impossible. She was sunshine, and I was...Well, I wasn't sure who or what I was anymore, other than a guy who spent too much time staring into the blue-light abyss of his laptop.

Back at the planter, she stood at my side, the teacher to my student. "Okay, it's easy," she explained, eyeing me to make sure I was following along. I was, sure, but I was also distracted by how her hair seemed to smell like the ocean in winter, crisp and salty and clean.

"Here, hold this." She gently placed the seedling, sticking out of a small mound of soil, into my hands. She pressed her hands around mine so that my palms closed around the plant, and then smiled. Her hands were warm and soft, and I wanted them to stay there for the rest of the night. Instead, she turned her big eyes to me. "Good?" she asked.

All I could do was nod.

"'Kay. You just push the soil aside like this." She reached into the planter and dug a small hole. "And then you're going to want to tuck that little guy in there, and make sure the soil covers enough so that it's secure."

"Where did you learn all this, anyway?" I asked, genuinely impressed.

She shrugged like it was no big deal. "My stepdad is very into gardening. Occasionally, I paid attention." She gave me a pat on the back and then got to work, grabbing more lettuce seedlings to plant.

Minutes later, she piped up. "Oh my god, Hayes!"

"Yes?" I said, confused at what could be so urgent.

"I forgot to tell you the best part." She was peering around the

149

side of the planter, and she looked like a kid at a birthday party about to devour a cupcake. "I got you a compost bin!"

Before I could respond, she added, "Two, actually. A gorgeous, sleek one for the kitchen—you're going to love it—and then a worm-farm composter for out here."

"I don't think I've ever seen anyone this excited about worms before." I put my hands on my hips and watched as she practically rocketed off the roof in delight.

"Well, you've clearly never hung out with anyone who loves worms as much as I do," she said, like it was the most obvious thing in the world. "They're the key to a successful garden."

She smiled, a wide, blindingly white smile. Then her gaze fell, and she clucked disapprovingly. "Oh no," she said, stepping toward me.

"What?" I asked.

Her expression was one of genuine concern. "I told you white was a bad idea."

She leaned forward and studied a blotch of dirt on my shirt, right over my heart. She dabbed at it with her hand, swiping it off until all that was left was the shadow of a stain.

"There," she said, looking back at me. "All better." But she didn't move away.

There it was again. And there was no mistaking it this time. There was an electric, energetic force field crackling between us. It suddenly felt like the thing so many random people on the internet had insisted was between us might actually be there. Was this flirting? Attraction? I couldn't name it, but I could feel it.

The sound of my phone ringing cut through the moment, like someone shattering a glass in a restaurant. "Excuse me," I said. I stepped back and tripped over two of the wooden planks we'd brought out for the garden beds. They went toppling, with loud bangs as they hit the ground. Franny just stood there staring at me as I wrestled my phone from my back pocket, both annoyed at the interruption and relieved that I had an excuse to turn away.

I pressed the button, and Serena's face popped up on the screen. "Serena?" I asked, perplexed.

"Hey! I was in the neighborhood, so I thought I'd stop by. Surprise you with dinner. Eleanor told me you were at your new office and gave me the address."

Serena knew how important the opening was for me, and I wasn't surprised she wanted to see the space for herself. It was nice of her to take the time to come here, but all I could think about was how disappointed I felt that my time alone with Franny was over. "One sec. I'll come down and meet you at the front door."

"Sorry." I turned to Franny. "This woman I'm"—*The woman I'm what? Hanging out with? Dating? Seeing?*—"spending time with just decided to drop by."

"Wow, so you *are* having an office date." She gave me an exaggeratedly shocked smile.

"Oh, I…" I got stuck on my words. "This is…not that. I wouldn't really do that."

"Hayes, I'm teasing." Her words were lighthearted, but her voice was oddly flat. The vibrating electricity that had been flowing between us was now zapped, completely gone. Maybe I'd imagined it altogether. "It's time for me to leave, anyway," she said, and turned toward the doorway that led back into the office.

Our elevator ride to the lobby together was silent.

When we got to the front door of the building, a new kind of force field entered. "Hey!" Serena was dressed for a run but was still impeccably put together, in a crop top and leggings. In her hand was a giant pink box. "Tacos," she said, eyes sparkling. "From my friend who just opened a new spot downtown. Gluten-free, of course."

"Serena, this is Franny. She's in charge of—"

"Oh my god, you're the dress girl! From the subway!" Serena

shoved the box into my hands and leaned forward to clutch Franny in a hug. "You're a legend."

Franny laughed as she peered at me over Serena's shoulder, giving me a bewildered look.

Pulling away, Serena shot me a glance. "I didn't realize you two were real-life friends."

"Oh, we're not," Franny interjected, a bit too quickly.

"It's a long story," I offered. "But the short version is that Franny's an interior designer, and she's come on board at the last minute to do our new office space."

Serena nodded, completely unfazed. "So nice to meet you, Franny," she said, flashing bleached-white teeth.

"You too," Franny said, looking from Serena to me, then back to Serena, trying to connect the dots. "Okay, well"—she offered us a small wave, and now her voice had shifted to an unnaturally cheerful tone—"have fun, you two!"

"Come show me your new office," Serena said, dragging me back toward the elevator. "And we've gotta get a picture of these tacos for Instagram before we eat them."

CHAPTER THIRTEEN

FRANNY

MY PHONE RANG while I was in the middle of multitasking, too many tabs open across my computer screen to count. In one, I was confirming my orders for Hayes and Eleanor's office. Load-in was in a month, and everything was on rush order. Then there was the response to Anna that I'd started but never sent, which I kept in my Google Docs and mostly just stared at. And then tab after tab of financial stuff: bank account, credit card balance, student loans. I'd been staring at those too, but not shockingly, the balances still remained unpaid.

"Mom, hi," I said, tucking the phone between my ear and my shoulder so I could keep working.

"Hi, honey." Her voice crackled on the other end; they had terrible service at their house. "Just calling to check in on things."

"Everything's good here," I said, fudging. Technically, things were fine. I had clean underwear on and had managed to drink at least one glass of water so far today. That counted for something, right?

"I was just telling Marianne how in demand you are," she said.

Ah, Marianne, her best friend since high school. They seemed to spend most of their time discussing what their kids were up to.

153

Marianne's daughter, Ruby, a year younger than me, worked as an RN at the local hospital's pediatric ward and was pregnant with her second kid. Plus, she and her husband lived ten minutes away from Marianne.

By Mom Measurements, Ruby was always beating me handily. Even as kids, it always felt like we were held up against each other, her very active school sports schedule compared to the time I spent doodling in notebooks. Needless to say, we spent our childhood in very different friend groups and never had much to say to each other when our moms got the families together.

"I'm working on a big office opening right now," I said, giving her information that would hopefully make her stop worrying. "I'll send you and Jim pics when it's all installed."

"I'd love that," she said. "Honey, I wanted to see if you had time to help plan Ruby's baby sprinkle. I'm hosting it, but you know I don't know the first thing about decorating. I thought maybe you could send me some ideas, make one of those Pinterest things of what I should buy. And then come help me set up at the house. It's on a Sunday."

"A sprinkle?" I asked. It sounded like some sort of sex-fetish party.

"Yes, you know, it's like a baby shower, but for the second kid. A sprinkle."

I rolled my eyes. The last thing I had time for was putting together a mood board for a baby shower, much less taking the train out to their house for a day spent dragging plastic tables around. But she was my mom, and I couldn't shake the feeling that letting her down would be worse than saying yes.

"Okay, yeah. Sure," I said. Saying yes felt like a good way to reset the cosmic balance of me not yet telling her about Anna's existence.

A text interrupted us, and I glanced at my phone to see what it was. **I'm officially in a committed relationship!** wrote Lola, followed by a row of shocked-face emojis.

"Mom, that's a work thing I gotta go answer," I lied. So much for cosmic balance, I guess.

"Okay, sweetie. Bye."

Phew. That was easy. Back to Lola. I sent off a row of bright-red exclamation-point emojis. For anyone else, a committed relationship might not have been a big deal. But this was Lola, who had always leaned into her reputation as someone who never settled down, who preferred ending things before they got serious, who couldn't stand the feeling of being tied down. For her, proudly declaring herself off the market meant something.

Big deal! Cleo responded seconds later. **Who knew Fran bumping into a hot weirdo on the subway would get YOU a girlfriend LOL**

Without even thinking, I typed out **He's not a weirdo** and then let my finger hover over the little blue arrow that would deliver the message to my friends. I tended to avoid conflict; I'd always rather steady the boat than rock it. But something about the phrase "*hot weirdo*" got under my skin. I mean, sure, he was a little awkward. And, yeah, he wore a tie like 95 percent of the time and refused to eat sugar. But the Hayes I'd gotten to know was also kind and witty, quiet and thoughtful. I liked those things, and I liked them enough to finally hit SEND, conflict be damned.

I took the train back into the city on Thursday afternoon to finalize measurements for the window shades we were installing. Hayes and Eleanor had given me an extra set of keys to the office, as well as the alarm code, so I could come and go as needed. Yesterday, I'd been there bright and early with my coffee, to oversee the electrician handling the fixtures and wiring. Finally, I was doing the hands-on work I'd dreamed about, getting to dork out about every step.

"Hello?" I called, even though I knew no one was there, feeling both relieved and disappointed that I wasn't going to see Hayes today. Inside, the office was lit up by the sun, and the tall palms that had been brought in for the reception area cast lightning-bolt shadows across the floor. Already, the space had the soothing energy of a spa, and my breath immediately settled in my chest. But the quiet was interrupted by the sound of someone walking across the wood floor, and Hayes emerged from his office, in light-gray suit pants with a white collared shirt tucked into them. No tie or jacket to be seen.

"Franny, hi." He ran a hand through his enviably thick hair.

"Hey," I said, smoothing the front of my wrinkled overalls. Suddenly, I could feel the sweat on my forehead, smell the body odor coating my armpits. I tucked my hair behind my ear and desperately wished I'd remembered to put on some lip gloss before walking into the building. "I didn't expect you to be here."

"Sorry, I had a long day of meetings. I needed to get out of the office," he said, sliding his hands into his pockets and smiling. "My brain was hurting. On top of this new office and the party, we're figuring out the strategy for opening a West Coast office, in Seattle. Plus all our other work on top of that."

"So you got out of the office and came to . . . your office?" I said, teasing him.

He shrugged with a bashful laugh, which was low and husky and hit me in a way that felt like longing, igniting parts of my body that ached to be touched. I stuck my thumb between my teeth and bit it, taking a deep breath. It didn't help.

"Hey, I get it," I said, not wanting him to feel self-conscious by my joking around. "When I need to think, I go to the Laundromat down the street from my apartment."

He gave me a skeptical look.

"Seriously," I insisted. "It's a habit left over from college. I even have a washer and dryer in my place now, but there's something about being out in public, watching clothes tumble around. I dunno." I shrugged. "It helps my brain calm down. Especially if I'm stressed or angry about something."

"Well, the next time I piss you off, I'll be sure to leave my dirty clothes with you," he said as he pushed his sleeves up his forearms.

"I mean, didn't you kind of do that once already?" I teased.

My eyes caught his as he let out a surprised laugh. I loved that we could go back and forth like this; he could dish it, but he could also take it. And it dawned on me: Talking to Hayes was fun. So fun, in fact, that I'd forgotten why I was there in the first place.

"Well…" I trailed off. "Um…I'm just going to measure your windows so we can finalize the shades so…"

You're here to work, Franny, I reminded myself. *And he's dating a blond skyscraper of human perfection. You need to let it go.*

"Of course. Don't let me hold you up," he said with a curt nod. We were back to being cardboard cutouts, two paper dolls dancing around each other. It was probably better this way, I reasoned. This was work, nothing more. But I couldn't help but hate the quiet left in the wake of our laughter.

I gave him a small wave and walked toward the endless windows beckoning me, ushering in the late-afternoon light. I snuck a look back to see him sitting on the floor of his office, leaning against the wall, legs long and crossed in front of him, laptop on his thighs. His focus was intense, singular, direct, and watching him stare at his computer reminded me how much I liked it when that focus was squarely on me.

I stuck my wireless headphones in and got to work measuring, photographing, and flipping over to my iPad occasionally, refer-ring back to the mood boards I'd made. The light shifted on the wood floors below me, the shadows disappearing as the sun set lower in the sky. I got into a groove, plopping down on the floor to work, so involved in what I was doing that when I felt a hand on my shoulder, I shrieked in shock and yanked an earbud out of my ear, tossing it across the floor.

"Whoa," was all I heard behind me. I twisted around, and there, overhead, like the sun, was Hayes.

"Sorry, you surprised me." I shook out my shoulders, that sudden adrenaline rush still coursing through me. "I can kind of get lost in my work."

"I get it," he said, and then he laughed. "I thought you were about to kick my ass."

"Maybe later," I said, giving him a grin.

"Are you doing anything else with the roof today?" he asked. "I wanted to see if you needed help."

I had actually planned on coming back in the morning to do more work on the garden area. But the extra hands now wouldn't hurt, I reasoned. It only made sense. Or maybe the lusty, salivating part of my brain had stepped in and overpowered my frontal lobe. Either way, without hesitating, I said, "You think you can handle another work session with me in charge?"

He gave me a confident look. "I think I can manage one more."

"Okay, great. I'll meet you out there in thirty," I said, that smile still stuck on my face.

He nodded, but before he could reply, his phone rang in his hand. "Excuse me," he said as he walked toward his office, shutting the door behind him. Through the glass, I watched as he paced and talked, all business. Now that I knew how funny he could be, I liked it when he turned serious, focused, intense.

He looked up and caught me staring, waved a hand hi at me. I gave him a forced smile, waved back. Oh god, was he on to me? Somewhere along the path from meeting on the subway to today, things had become easy between us. He'd been so cool and aloof that day on the train, even more so during our TV interview. He'd quite literally announced that we were not each other's types. *And he's dating someone,* my brain hissed, back to being all logic and facts.

We were two strangers from different corners of the city, who were not meant to meet, much less enjoy each other's company. But that had all changed, and somehow I'd missed the moment things shifted. And now it was too late: I was stuck liking him, and I couldn't shake it. As I walked out through the door to the roof deck, I felt a shock of sadness. I felt silly for even feeling it, but I was going to miss seeing him when this was over.

I let out a sigh and shook out my shoulders again, as if that somehow could get rid of these feelings buzzing around inside me. *Time to focus on work, Fran.* I took another deep breath and got to it.

Jim and I had put planter boxes together two summers ago for his garden, and the muscle memory reignited the second I held the drill in my hand. Instead of letting my mind rehash all the reasons I should not be attracted to Hot Suit, and all the reasons he almost certainly was not into me, I concentrated on putting the small planks of wood together.

Almost exactly thirty minutes later, Hayes appeared. "Hey." I turned to find him behind me, eyes expectant.

"Hello," I said as my stomach gave a weird rumble. "Ready to start pouring in the soil?" I gestured over to the corner where two boxes were now fully built. "We just need to line them, and then they're good to go."

He nodded. "I was going to get some food delivered. Can I interest you in anything?"

His gaze was unreadable, set in that steady, motionless poker face, but then it shifted into a full-on smile, doing that lusty thing again to my body. His mouth was so lovely, and every time he smiled at me I imagined what his lips would feel like against my own.

"I'm so hungry I would literally eat some of this dirt right now," I said, clutching my stomach.

"Well, you definitely don't need to do that. I can pull the menu up on my phone."

I shook my head at him. "I'll just have whatever you're getting."

"You don't want to look?" he said, but again, I shook my head.

"Surprise me," I said. "I want to get back to work. I'm serious—I'll eat anything." I offered him a smile, and shockingly, he didn't argue.

We'd just finished pressing the radish and carrot seeds into the soil when his phone dinged on the newly installed table. "Thank god," he moaned, and then bolted for the door. Minutes later, he returned with a white plastic bag stacked with containers.

"Surprise," he said, his voice playful.

I wiped my hands on my overalls and walked over to where he was placing everything out neatly in a row on the new table. Two giant paper containers, ketchup packets, napkins. Sliding onto the bench next to him, I cracked open the corner of a container. "No way," I said as the scent of steaming hot, greasy French fries wafted up into my face. They were piled next to the biggest, crispiest-looking grilled cheese I'd ever seen. Perfection. "I thought you didn't eat, like, anything bad for you."

He shrugged. "I was having a craving."

"I'm always craving a grilled cheese, so thank you," I said, digging in. We ate in silence for a bit, and as it hit seven, the solar lights I'd hung sparked on, and suddenly our little rooftop was bathed in an otherworldly glow. I lifted my face to look up, and as I did, Hayes did the same, smiling.

"This really is the perfect meal for this view," I said, squeezing two packets of ketchup all over my fries.

His brow furrowed. "Would you have preferred something else?" he asked, clearly concerned.

"No," I assured him. "I'm being serious. A diner grilled-cheese sandwich and fries doesn't get nearly as much NYC cred as a bagel or pizza, but it's New York to the core."

"Pizza is the best, though, right? We both agree?"

When I nodded, he said, "Good, 'cause I was gonna make you leave if you said no. Especially since I'm assuming you're Italian."

I squinted at him. "How did you know that?"

"Your name's Francesca," he said, like that alone made it obvious. "And your obsession with Italian ice."

"Ah, well, yeah. My dad's side is Italian." I nibbled on a fry and tried not to show how pleased I was that he had been trying to figure me out.

"*Interessante,*" he mused.

"Show-off." I grinned at him. I liked how his voice sounded speaking Italian, melodic and low.

"I studied abroad in Bologna and Milan," he said. "I've lost most of my Italian, except when I need to order food."

Milan. The word struck me in the chest. That was where my sister lived. Worked. Hayes had been there too. I considered telling him, unloading this new part of myself. But anytime I thought about telling anyone about what I'd discovered, it felt too real.

"Well, that's the most important time," I replied. "You probably speak more of it than I do."

"Your dad never taught you any?"

"I didn't know my dad. So." *And now my dad is dead,* I thought, *and I'll never get the chance.* I swallowed, trying to release the lump that had just taken up residence in my throat.

Hayes nodded, and I could tell he expected me to continue.

"I actually never met him, or his side of the family. I went to college for art and design, so I didn't take any language classes. And my high school only offered Spanish and French." I took another bite of my sandwich, chewing for a moment. "I can understand it some, though, now. I play around with it on language apps."

I grabbed a napkin off the table and began shredding it slowly. "Anyway..."

"Well, Italian's way overrated." He gave me a warm smile. "So overrated I don't even know how to say that in Italian."

I laughed and went back to eating. And then it occurred to me—he was following my lead, giving me space to open up if I wanted. This was new. I was used to meeting people's expectations, going along with things out of obligation. But I didn't have to do that with him. He wasn't pushing to go anywhere with the conversation, other than where I wanted. And this alone made me want to keep talking.

"So get this," I said, the words almost falling out of my mouth. "My mom and my birth dad basically had a one-night stand, and she never saw him again but she got pregnant. So cliché, I know. But I've never really known much about him."

There was no gasp, or shock, or awkward joke. Instead, he just leaned closer to me. "That must have been hard," he said. "For you."

"Yeah, I guess it has been. I mean, that's where I've landed after a couple years in therapy."

As usual, I'd tried to lighten the mood with a joke, but he just nodded thoughtfully. As I shifted on the bench, the napkin I'd been fiddling with went flying onto the ground, and I reached down to grab it just as Hayes made a move for it. Our heads collided like two soccer players going for the same ball, connecting in a thud.

"Ow," we said simultaneously.

I sat up, clutching my forehead, just as Hayes leaned toward me, my torn napkin in his hand. "Are you okay?" he asked, softly pressing his index and middle fingers to my brow.

I startled at his touch, and he pulled his hand back quickly but kept his eyes on me. They were concerned and caring and gentle, just as his touch had been. I gulped, and then played it off with a smile. "Yes, yes. I'm fine. Are you?"

"Just a mild concussion," he said, smiling as he rubbed his forehead.

He handed me my napkin, and I tucked it in my lap. "Anyway," I continued, "I took one of those DNA tests recently. Just on a lark, with my friends. And I learned I'm Italian and Irish, with some Scottish mixed in. Kinda cool to find out, but no big deal. But then someone tracked me down through the app and sent me a message."

"Who?" His brow furrowed as he bit into his sandwich, listening intently.

"Apparently, I have a half sister in Italy. In Milan, actually."

"Wow. That's wild."

"I know!" I said, my voice rising. "It's bonkers. And honestly, there's a part of it that feels amazing, if that even makes sense. But it also kind of freaked me out, and I haven't responded yet."

He nodded, giving me the space to talk.

"She also told me that my…our dad died a long time ago. And just knowing that has felt really…"

I swallowed, still trying to figure out my feelings in real time. "It's heavy," I said eventually. "And sad. It's really sad."

"I am really, really sorry for your loss," he said in a quiet voice. I'd never thought about it like that: a loss. The word hit me deeply.

"My whole life, one side of who I am has been a literal blank space," I continued. "And that can kinda mess with you growing up, when you don't entirely know who you come from. Especially…"

I had never said this part out loud before.

"Especially when I've always kind of been the odd one in my family. You know…" I waved my hands at myself, as if this explained everything, and Hayes just laughed.

"I don't know. You seem very normal to me."

"Thank you." I tipped an imaginary hat to him. "But I'm the

talkative, artsy weirdo who left my hometown and moved to New York City. My mom and stepdad met at the bank they worked at, and that's the same place they retired from a few years ago. Their idea of a fun night is sitting in matching recliners watching *CSI*."

"Wait, that actually does sound like a fun night to me," Hayes objected, and then bit into a fry.

"True," I said. "But you get what I mean."

"Yeah," he said thoughtfully. "I do."

"And the crazy part is," I added, "I think this sister might also be an artsy weirdo. Just a very successful one. So I'm intimidated by that, but also I'm dying to know what she's like, and what my dad was like, and if…"

Hayes let me go silent, and then finished my thought for me. "And if you're at all like them."

I nodded and felt annoyed at how easily he got me. I was trying desperately not to be into this guy, and then he had to go and understand exactly what I was trying to say. "But there's a part of me that worries—what if I'm not like them at all? And then what? It'll be like I don't fit in anywhere."

I turned my attention back to my food, dragging a French fry through the pile of ketchup I'd made in front of me. I didn't want him to see that my eyes had filled with tears.

Hayes was quiet for a moment, thinking. "Do you wanna hear what I think?" he asked gingerly, like he was trying to pull out a splinter without hurting me. I nodded.

"You're under no obligation to respond, just because you're related. Family is what we make, not what we're born into. At least it is for me."

I took a swig of my water, listening.

"And maybe, instead of this revealing something new about yourself, it will help you connect to what you've always known about yourself all along."

Well, that was…deep. Not what I was expecting. It almost

sounded like he knew what he was talking about. But that was ridiculous. Hayes was the kind of person who clearly had it all figured out. Maybe I was way off. Maybe he was still learning too.

"Thanks, Hayes. I should pay you for this therapy session," I joked.

"Whatever choice you make will be the right one," he said knowingly, like he'd told himself this same thing before. "And if you do end up going over to Italy to meet her, I can definitely tell you how to say 'Subway QTs' in Italian."

I let out a guffaw then that was such a relief the smile lingered on my face long after I'd stopped laughing. When we were both finished eating, neither of us made an effort to move, despite the darkness beginning to settle in. Instead, we sat in comfortable silence as the sun disappeared and the city woke back up for the night. For the first time since receiving Anna's message, I felt calm about it, no matter how I decided to move forward. But my heart was still racing. Because another thing had become frighteningly clear to me tonight: I had it bad for Hayes Montgomery the Third.

CHAPTER FOURTEEN

HAYES

"YOU DID ALL this?" I probably should have opened with something smoother, but the spread in front of me was too amazing for my brain to catch up to my mouth. Luckily, Serena laughed, glass of white wine in her hand as she waved me in, an entire restaurant-worthy vegan meal laid out on the long white dining table just off her kitchen.

"I did, yes!" she said, completely unfazed by my clunky entrance.

"I brought red," I said, lifting the bottle in my hands. "Sorry."

"Perfect for after dinner," she replied with a flirty wink.

"Thank you for having me over," I said as she took the wine out of my hands and walked into the kitchen. I stood there for a moment, assessing the scene. Candles lit. Serena in a lacy white off-the-shoulder top and ripped jeans, feet bare. Casual, yes. But also wildly sexy, in the most intentional way possible.

Everything with Serena, down to the smallest detail, was deliberate. And tonight, I knew it was all done for me, but it only made me feel tense, stressed. It was the opposite of how I'd felt with Franny during dinner a few nights ago, and I couldn't stop circling back to that. I was here on a date, romantic and intimate. But the place I really wanted to be was back on the roof deck of my office, surrounded by potting soil and composting supplies, with Franny and her beautiful curls and bright eyes and big laugh.

"I was just looking at the final seating arrangements for the gala," she said, tracing her hand along my collar, interrupting my thoughts. "I put us with a fun group."

"I like fun," I said, forcing a smile onto my face.

"Well, thank god," she said, stepping back to grab another wineglass off the counter, handing it to me. "My ex-boyfriend was a buzzkill, and I'm still learning that it's okay to live exactly how I want."

She said this decisively, without hesitation, and motioned for me to take a seat at the table, in front of a delicious-looking beet salad.

"Would it be okay to ask why you and your ex split?" I asked, sliding into my seat and pouring her more wine.

She waved me off. "Please, Hayes, I'm an open book. I literally shared my last microneedling appointment on a Facebook Live."

"That's a face thing?" I asked as she reached forward to clink her glass against mine.

She nodded. "Anyway, I broke up with him when I realized that I liked the *idea* of us way more than the *actual* us. You know what I mean?"

"Yeah, I think so," I said, taking a sip of wine. Her words hit me unexpectedly, almost like she was looking inside my brain and could see what I was thinking—that this was exactly how I felt about the two of us.

"We looked great together. We did all the right things. But, god, when we were alone, we had nothing to talk about. It never felt easy. And I was bored. I hate being bored."

She looked directly at me, and in a panic, I blurted out, "We're going to be growing lettuce at our new office." Which was the completely wrong thing to say in the moment. But I needed to get out from under the feeling that was brewing in me.

I'd been so hung up on this idea of being "incompatible" in relationships that I never took a second to think about what it really meant to connect with someone. I wanted it to be easy, like Serena has said. But more than anything, I didn't want to be bored. I craved the excitement, the passion, and all the highs, of course. Yet I wanted to be with someone for the deep, dark lows and the hard stuff too. I was looking for a roller coaster, a relationship that left me wanting more, always ready to go again. But could I handle that? And could I even be that for someone else? I wasn't sure, and I took a giant sip of wine, focusing on Serena's story about her latest training run, and pushing aside questions I'd rather not think about.

An hour later, satiated and slightly buzzed, Serena and I stood next to each other at the sink. I rinsed; she loaded the dishwasher. I clicked the faucet off as we finished, and Serena put a dishwashing pod in and shut the door, actually hitting it closed with her hip—like some sort of starlet in a movie—before pressing a couple of buttons and setting the machine whirring. She casually draped a hand on my neck, nails scratching gently where hair met skin. "So," she said, her voice lower than I'd ever heard it, her face tantalizingly close to mine, "what should we do now?"

"Wait, you had a nice dinner, which she made. And you started making out in the kitchen. And then because it was going well, you panicked and left?"

Perrine said the words through a mouthful of lettuce.

I let out a long sigh. I'd been replaying the entire date with Serena in my head since I'd left her apartment last night. "Okay, first of all, I did not call it 'panicking,'" I said, giving her The Look. "It was really nice. I just realized last night that she's not who I wanted to be with. And once that hit me, I knew I couldn't stay. So when she invited me into her bedroom, I told her I had to go home."

I didn't mention to Perrine that Franny had also been in my thoughts the entire time, and that I'd been comparing every move Serena made to her. I couldn't stop thinking about the way Franny had made me laugh the other night at my office—at myself, and the world. And how then, later, our conversation had shifted to things that were deeply personal. I was never bored when I was with her. In fact, I couldn't think of anything else when she was around. And also, apparently, when she wasn't.

"Because you said you had a doctor's appointment."

I nodded.

"On a Sunday morning."

"It's not impossible!" I protested.

"Hayes, I'm a freakin' doctor. Most of us stay home on Sundays, unless we're on call."

I tilted my head back. Maybe staring at the ceiling would save me. I wasn't sure how to explain this to Perrine, who rarely pushed me on dating but still had a hard time hiding her eagerness for me to "find someone." The date had been good. Great, even. It's just that the feeling I'd expected—some uptick in pulse, a quiver of excitement, a deluge of nerves—never happened.

Even just the sight of Franny working on the floor with her ear-buds on clawed at something animalistic and raw inside me: the urge to confess all my feelings, to feel the weight of her on top of me, right there on those wood floors. And when that feeling never materialized with Serena, it didn't feel right to stay.

"So you would have rather I'd slept with someone I'm not entirely into?"

"No! No, I'm definitely not saying that. And I'm not trying to criticize you. Just getting to the bottom of what was going on."

Freakin' doctors. Always trying to solve things.

"I guess I just kept thinking about how much I enjoyed having dinner with Franny the other night. And how dinner with Serena wasn't that."

Perrine's eyes morphed into laser beams, narrowed at my head. "You didn't tell me you had dinner with Franny."

Wait, hadn't I?

"Yeah, I did." I crossed my arms in front of my chest.

Perrine shook her head, clearly pleased that she'd gotten this information out of me.

"We had dinner at the new Arbor office." I tried to make this sound as if it were no big deal.

"Like a date?" The high pitch to her voice told me that Perrine did indeed think this was a big deal.

"She was working!" Why did I suddenly feel defensive? "You're the one who set this whole thing up, remember?" I continued. "She's been dealing with stuff at our office. And I happened to be there and ordering takeout, so I asked her if she wanted some too."

"Mm-hmm," Perrine said, raising her eyebrows at me, forever a skeptic. I ignored her and dug back into my salad.

"I'm going with Serena to her gala event on Saturday." My voice was resigned. "So maybe after that, I should end things."

"Um, you like someone else. You definitely need to end things." She said this as if she wanted to also add "*you dumbass*" but had refrained.

"Even if I did like Franny"—Perrine rolled her eyes at me as I said this—"I'm not even sure she'd be interested in me. I don't know anything about the type of people she's dated. They're probably all, like, graffiti artists or famous musicians."

She studied me, an amused look on her face. "Just what do you think her type is?"

"I dunno, cool people?" I imagined Franny with skateboarders and artists, punk drummers and moody poets. Free spirits who could keep up with all the magic that flew out of her brain.

"You're cool," Perrine said, and then laughed to herself. "I can ask Lola what Franny's type is. Drop some hints."

"Oh my god, Perrine, please do not say anything to Lola." My heart picked up speed, panicked.

"Hayes, you're a grown man. What are you so afraid of?" she asked.

Everything, I wanted to say.

But instead, I snapped back, "Nothing," and left it at that.

CHAPTER FIFTEEN

FRANNY

I WAS SUPPOSED to be finalizing the last bit of load-in needs for Arbor's new office, but instead I was hunched over my laptop, troubleshooting a challenging new client. My mom. Since asking for my help figuring out decorations for the baby shower—excuse me, *sprinkle*—that she was hosting, she'd invaded my inbox with nonstop one-line emails from her AOL account.

19 people have RSVPed, read one.

I'm renting three round tables—is that enough? read another.

Wait, honey, scratch that—it's 18 people. Donna just canceled because she needs to go wedding dress shopping with Morgan. xxxooo Mom had arrived in my inbox just minutes ago. I had no idea who Donna even was, much less Morgan, but they'd just screwed up the order I was trying to place for folding chairs, so obviously I hated them now.

Helping her plan a casual afternoon gathering at her home now included sourcing enough tables, chairs, and place settings to rent for twenty people, a tent to cover her backyard, decorations, a cooler, and party favors. What I'd thought would be one quickly pulled-together Pinterest board had morphed into an Excel spreadsheet that took up the whole screen of my laptop, and an entire day on my calendar now reserved for helping my mom throw a party for a woman I didn't even like. I could think of eight million other things I'd rather be doing on a Sunday.

My email alert let off a ring. *Do you think you could run to Costco before the shower to get the cake and drinks? You can take my car.*

I had finally had enough of the emails, and picked up the phone. "Mom," I said when she answered after one ring.

"Hi, honey, is this about Costco? You should pick up some snacks to bring back into the city too, of course," she said, and the kind offer melted away most of the annoyance I'd felt building up in my chest, even though I could barely carry anything back to the city from Costco, much less fit it in my apartment.

"Yes, I can go to Costco," I said, my voice peppy in an attempt to mask my reluctance. The only thing bothering me more than the amount of work this had turned out to be was the fact that I hadn't been honest and just said no to her in the first place. I'd said yes to make her happy, but the result was that I was miserable. "I'll try to get out there at ten, as long as you can pick me up at the train station."

"I'm really excited to see you, sweetie," she said. "You know you can stay for dinner—even spend the night too if you want."

"I appreciate that, Mom, but I think I should just come back into the city." I leaned against the couch, my hair sticking to the back of my neck. Even though the air-conditioning was blasting inside, it was still sticky and warm. You'd think the summer heat would make me tired, lethargic, but instead I felt jumpy, ready to crawl out of my skin.

Ever since Hayes and I had talked on his new office roof, I'd wanted to call him, text him, anything to force us to have to connect, to see each other. Instead, we'd exchanged a few polite emails with Eleanor and their assistant Tyler about building logistics and the delivery of a fridge for their office kitchen.

I'd spent a lot of time analyzing the most recent email, which he'd signed with *Best, Hayes*. It had sent me into a small spiral. Nothing was worse than getting an email from the person you can't stop thinking about and having them end it with a *Best*. There was no way he signed his emails to Serena with *Best*. She probably got something like *Desperate for your touch,* or a GIF of an erupting volcano. As she should, I reasoned. They're dating— she deserved all the sexual-innuendo GIFs in the world. But I was still silently pining for Hayes, and there was nothing even remotely flirty about a *Best,* and it made me wonder if everything I'd felt between us was just in my head.

"Okay, kiddo," my mom said. "Have a good rest of your day."

"'Kay. You too," I said, feeling guilty for the relief I felt as I hung up the phone. Stretching out long on my couch, I let out a loud moan. I hadn't seen Hayes in a few days, and now every magical, flirty interaction we'd had was starting to feel like that motorcycle dream—pure fiction, created by my brain.

My phone pinged again, but this time it was a text from Lola, a photo of the spread she'd prepped for our picnic later today. Gooey Brie, crackers, salami, grapes, cans of wine. I looked at my watch. It was almost time to head into the city to meet my friends. This would be exactly what I needed.

One sweaty subway ride later, I was let out into the sauna that was Midtown Manhattan in the middle of July. Cleo and Lola were already waiting for me on the corner of Fifty-Ninth and Fifth, sitting on the edge of the fountain. Cleo had a giant ratty blanket tucked under her arm, and she was using her other hand to fan her face. I waved at them and held up the bag I'd brought, containing my contributions to our feast: hummus, pita chips, and olives from

Sahadi's in Brooklyn. Lola cupped her hands to her mouth when she saw me, shouting "Woo-hoo!"

"There she finally is!" Lola said as I wandered up to them. "Our queen of Brooklyn."

"I will never live in Manhattan. Leave me alone," I quipped back, long accustomed to this teasing about my borough of choice. "I don't care how annoying the trains are on the weekend."

"Shall we?" said Cleo, rising with a stretch. We followed the winding pathway into the park, which was lush and green. Just the shade of the trees made it feel a few degrees cooler than the rest of the city. We walked along the road, up toward Sheep Meadow, where we planned on spreading out on the grass, snacking our faces off, and hanging out together until dusk.

We were standing at the crosswalk on Sixty-Fifth Street, about to head into the meadow, when a bolt of blond dashed by us. She stopped a few feet away and whipped her head around. She jogged back toward us, waving both hands excitedly.

"Oh boy," I heard Lola say quietly. We were standing face-to-face with Serena, the woman I'd met at Hayes's office. The woman he was "*spending time with.*"

"Franny!" she exclaimed. She was now directly in front of us, in black running shorts and a cropped tank top, the only thing someone could wear on this disgustingly hot day while exercising. "Serena," she said, pointing at her chest, her smile so big it could block the sun. "I'm dating Hayes?"

Cleo let out a small "Whoa" under her breath as my heart raced, rattling around so loudly I was sure the entire city could hear it over the din of traffic and sirens that surrounded us.

"Hi," I said with a polite nod. "It's nice to see you again."

"I knew it was you! How's the office coming along?" She said this with a smile on her face while jogging in place.

"Okay," I said, still trying to process what was happening. "It's almost done."

"Well, I can't wait to see it," she said, raising a hand to her brow, which seemed to have less sweat on it than mine, despite the fact that she was the one out for a run. "Maybe we can chat sometime? I've been thinking of redesigning my place."

"Sure," I said. "Hayes has my info." I smiled, putting on my professional-Franny face.

"Wonderful!" She was still bouncing on her toes. "Okay, off I go."

"Okay!" I said, matching the pep in her voice, giving her a wave as she took off again.

"She's even hotter in person," Lola said admiringly.

I gave her a look, and she shrugged back. "What? She is. And she's the worst kind of hot person too."

"Oh yeah?" I said. "What kind is that?"

"A nice one," Lola said, like she was revealing some sort of universal truth. "She's apparently genuinely great."

Once we'd found a free patch of grass and settled onto Cleo's blanket, Lola whipped out her phone and pulled up Serena's Instagram page. Over a hundred thousand people were following her every move, which included a video of her running that must have been taken sometime today.

Cleo peeked at it and then handed it to me. "I've never even heard of her," she said, before grabbing some salami and taking a bite.

Lola gave her a look. "Clee, I love you, but your pop-culture knowledge is not the most impressive."

"Hey!" Cleo protested.

"Name five microinfluencers," Lola countered, and Cleo gave a resigned laugh.

"Okay, fine," she said. "You're right."

We ate in silence for a bit, people-watching. Finally, after popping open a can of wine and taking a few sips, I said the thing that was gnawing at me in the back of my brain.

"Let's say I did have a thing for Hayes," I said, and they both turned to face me as I chewed on a fingernail, nervous to put this out into the world.

"Mm-hmm?" Cleo said, eyebrows raised expectantly.

"Why would he even consider going out with me when he's already dating her?" I said, awkwardly scrunching up my face in embarrassment. "I know, I know, I sound like I'm twelve. But she's so..." What was the world I wanted to use? *Beautiful? Accomplished? Flawless?*

"Much?" Cleo volunteered.

"Yes!" I said. "It's so hard to be around someone like that, who's so *much*, when I'm always feeling like I'm not enough. And before you say anything"—I held up my hand—"I know that I am enough. I know that I am beautiful, and smart, and talented, and a reasonably good cook, and all the other nice things you're going to tell me. But you know what I mean. Sometimes you can't help but compare yourself to someone like that."

"What's that quote? 'Comparison is the thief of joy'?" Lola squinted in thought.

"Something like that," I said. "And it's true! It's so dumb. But I can't help it."

Cleo patted my thigh affectionately. "It's totally normal to think this way, but try to remember she's probably comparing herself to you too."

I rolled my eyes at this, which only made Cleo annoyed. "I'm serious, Fran!"

I pointed at my hair, which was frizzing wildly in the humidity. "Oh, really? You think she's jealous of this mess on my head?"

Cleo laughed and then built herself a little cracker sandwich with cheese and salami. "You're all the things you said you are, and a lot more."

"One hundred percent agree," Lola said, as if there were no other answer. "And if you're feeling like you have a thing for

Hayes, I bet you he's also feeling a thing for you. It's not like he's exclusive with her."

She tossed a grape in her mouth. "I dig around for dirt from Perrine sometimes," she said with a coy smile before I could question her about how she knew such a thing.

"If he was at all was interested in me, why did he sign an email to me with *'Best'*?" I posed to them.

"Everyone knows that *'Best'* is the sign-off you use when you don't want the person you're into to know that you're into them," Lola replied, like it was obvious. "Especially someone you're working with."

Cleo laughed at this. "Oh my god, you're so right. Whenever I want to make out with someone, I always make sure my emails are superformal, so it seems like I don't."

"How often does this happen to you?" I asked her, truly curious.

"I don't know, I've met a lot of hot lawyers!" she said defensively.

"If he signed his email *'Best,'*" Lola said confidently, "what he means is 'I can't stop thinking about putting my mouth all over you.'"

"Especially between your legs," Cleo added, and Lola snorted.

I covered my face with my hands and laughed. "Okay," I said as I balled my fingers into fists and pressed them to my chin. "Then what does it say that I sent an email today and signed it *'Can't wait to talk soon!'*"

"Oh, girl," Lola said with a shake of her head. "It means you've got it bad."

CHAPTER SIXTEEN

HAYES

THE NEXT DAY, at the office, I tossed my giant binder outlining our launch party on Eleanor's desk.

"Well, look at you," she said, lowering her glasses to gaze at me approvingly. Taking a sip from a glass of ginger ale, she opened the cover, her eyes skimming the first page.

"Tyler did most of it—let's be honest." I slid into my chair, flipping open my laptop. "That famous DJ they're friends with agreed to spin for a couple hours for half their normal rate. Tyler knows everyone."

"The guy who has the residency in Stockholm?" Eleanor asked, legitimately wowed.

"That's the one," I said with a nod.

"Maybe Tyler should be COO," Eleanor joked.

"Not so fast," I said. "I signed off on everything. Double-checked the budget. And I hired these caterers Serena recommended."

Eleanor applauded.

"Oh, and Citi Bike is giving everyone a discount code to use so they can ride to and from the party."

"Ooooh," Eleanor said, sounding excited.

"I knew you'd like that." I felt slightly smug.

"So if Serena gave you her preferred caterer, things must be getting serious," Eleanor joked, poking around for info.

"I have to go prep for this call with Luis about the space he found for us in Seattle," I said, grateful for the excuse not to discuss my romantic life. Especially because I'd decided after my conversation with Perrine that I needed to break things off with Serena. I didn't want to do it right before her big event. She'd been working on the gala for months, and I knew that it was more than just a party for her; it was personal. I couldn't decide which was a crappier move—calling things off before we went, or right after.

I sat down at my desk to send a quick email, but instead I picked up my phone, and found my finger hovering over Franny's name.

Hi Franny, Just wanted to see if you'll need to stop by the office anytime this week.

I hit SEND on the text before I could stop myself.

Her reply was immediate. **No, I'm good! I'm waiting on the final greenery order for your main offices and lobby.** She followed up with a completely benign thumbs-up emoji.

I popped my head back into Eleanor's office. "Hey," I said.

"Yeah?" She looked up from her computer.

"Do you want to grab lunch?" I asked. "It's so nice out today. We could eat in the park."

She tilted her head to study me. "You okay?"

"Of course. Why?" I crossed my arms, waiting impatiently for her answer.

"You"—she pointed a manicured finger at me—"never take lunch breaks."

"What do you mean? I have lunch with Perrine, like, twice a month."

Oh. That's what she meant. She raised her palms at me. "See?"

"Okay, well, I'm going to eat my lunch outside today," I said. "I might even take a full hour."

"I'm impressed! And I'm in." Eleanor smirked, clearly amused. "You can tell me all about your dinner with Serena. It sounds like from what she's told Henry, she's into you."

My stomach dropped at the thought of dipping back into my feelings and figuring out how to navigate them. It had felt way easier to just focus on the launch party and the Seattle office plans than deciding what to do about ending things with Serena. Not because I was worried about breaking it off, but because once I did, I'd have to deal with my feelings for Franny.

The steps of the natural history museum were lit up like a beacon, photographers hollering at the top of their lungs at people I didn't know to turn this way and move that way. I checked in with the press person managing the guest list, who shouted something into a headset. Minutes later, Serena was gliding toward me, in an eye-poppingly low-cut red dress, her hair sleek and long in a ponytail down her back.

"I didn't think it was possible for you to be more handsome, but here you are in a tux," she said, linking her hands with mine and leaning in for a kiss on the cheek.

"You look stunning," I said into her ear. It was the absolute truth. It wasn't just the dress; Serena was magnetic.

The red carpet was louder than I'd expected. Brighter too. The click of the cameras and the furiously shouted demands of the photographers created an overwhelming cacophony of noise. "This way, please, Serena!"

And then it was done, and Serena led me into the museum. But instead of following the flow of people to the Hall of Ocean Life, she pulled me aside, into the shadows of a giant marble pillar.

"Listen," she said, giving my hand a squeeze, "I really appreciate you coming tonight, and I don't want to make things awkward."

I squinted, my mind working quickly, trying to track where this was going.

"But I think you and I are probably better as friends." She looked at me, waiting for a reply. "And I think you might feel the same way too?"

I did feel the same way. Exactly the same. But this announcement, here, was still not what I was expecting.

"I do think that, actually. Yeah," I said, processing my surprise. "I think you're great, but I'm just not…" *I'm not here,* I wanted to say. *Even when I'm with you, in my brain I'm always with someone else.*

"Feeling it?" she finished, smiling.

I smiled back, appreciating her bluntness. "I guess that's one way of putting it."

"Look." She placed a hand on my forearm. "I don't want to waste your time, or my time, if this isn't working. And I was thinking about how I was going to introduce you to my friends tonight, and I realized it didn't feel right to say 'boyfriend.' And that got me thinking."

I nodded. "How about 'guy your coworker set you up with that didn't totally work out'?"

"That has a nice ring to it." She released her hand and sighed. Even though the conversation was drama-free, it was still awkward. I shifted in my shoes, which suddenly felt a half size too small.

She pressed her lips together, her face serious. "I'm sorry if I've made this night uncomfortable for you. I'd totally get it if you want to leave."

"It's not, and I don't. I really appreciate your honesty." I ran a hand through my hair and exhaled.

"You're a good guy, you know that?" She tilted her head, gave me a kind smile.

I shrugged her off with a smile. "It's the tux."

"Well, we're still sitting together, so"—she looped her arm through mine—"shall we?"

As we moved through the hallway, we passed small exhibits set up along the way: a giant chunk of jade in a glass case, some fossils immortalized in stone. But nothing could ever fully prepare you for the moment you stepped into the Hall of Ocean Life, which was a stunning, mind-blowing place at any time of day. The walls were full of exhibits, but the real showstopper was the life-size blue whale that hung from the ceiling of the massive room, looming over everyone and everything below.

The dinner banter with Serena's friends was easy, and she booked it to the dance floor with a group of girlfriends once the band started. I decided to check out the silent auction in the back of the room, and I wandered slowly, past tempting descriptions of cabins in Vermont, weeklong wine-tasting trips in the South of France, a brand-new Jeep Cherokee. Finally, I paused in front of a listing for a Tuscan villa and a tour through southern Italy. *Franny should get to see Italy someday,* I said to myself. *She should get to experience that side of who she is, firsthand.*

I was so distracted by the thought of her twirling pasta on a fork and smiling at me over a glass of Chianti that I almost missed the sound of someone sighing wistfully next to me. Something about the sound sent my gut reeling, and I twisted my head to the left. I had to blink to be sure she wasn't an illusion, that my eyes weren't taking this already strange night and making it stranger still. But the darkness opened back into light, and she was still there.

Franny. Always appearing when I least expected her.

She caught my eye, her head tilting back a bit in surprise. "Hayes."

"Hi."

"If you're coming to save me from yet another disastrous wardrobe malfunction, you're going to be sorely disappointed. This dress is basically glued on." Her red lips curved up just the tiniest bit. I gulped and tried to play it cooler than I felt in my gut.

"Well, we're both in luck, then," I said, grinning back. "I only have one tux, and I'd like to keep it."

I fiddled with my bow tie and attempted to subtly take Franny in, head to toe. She was wearing a sleek strapless black dress with a satin ivory bodice. It was elegant and timeless, a delicate necklace her only adornment. Her hair was still in a halo around her head, but it was secured with two small pearl barrettes, and her eyes seemed even brighter than usual.

"Cleo—one of my best friends—her mom is one of the cochairs of the gala. Has been since Cleo's dad died of ALS thirteen years ago," she blurted out, even though I hadn't yet asked why she was there.

I nodded, and she continued, talking quickly. "This is how her mom has some control over the situation, I think. Trying to help people."

"That makes a lot of sense," I said, trying to sound calm. The last thing I wanted was for her to know how nervous I felt. Admitting how I felt about Franny to Perrine meant those thoughts were now out there in the world, alive. And that felt terrifying.

"I'm tagging along to 'network.'" She said this with air quotes. "Cleo's mom is hopefully going to introduce me to some fancy people." She wiggled her eyebrows as she said this. "And maybe even the team who decorates for the event."

"Well, I hope you can have a little bit of fun too," I said, before glancing back down at the Tuscan villa. "What are we bidding on tonight?"

"*We* are not bidding on anything, because we just started our own business and we need to make money, not spend it, and also we are not nearly as loaded as the rest of these rich uptown types," Franny scoffed, complete with a full-on smile that sent my heart bouncing.

"But if we *were* bidding…" I leaned in, not letting it go. "Italy?"

She rested her lips on the edge of her glass of champagne. "Definitely Italy." She thought for a moment. "I've always wanted to go, but now more than ever, you know?"

I nodded, and we stared at each other.

"I hope you get to go someday," I said finally. "Well, um…I'll let you get back to it."

"Wait," she said, her hand suddenly on my wrist. "What are you doing here?"

"Oh." I wasn't even sure where to begin. "Well, you know that woman I was seeing?"

"The pretty one who brought the tacos?" I wasn't sure if it was my brain playing tricks on me, but I swore that there was a sharp edge to her voice when she said this.

I let out a laugh. "Yes, that one. She's on one of the committees for the event."

"Cool. I actually ran into her in Central Park the other day." She nodded, a polite smile on her face. "Small world."

"She also broke up with me the second I got here," I said, leaning toward her with a smile, hands in my pockets.

"Shut up!" Franny's arm flew to my chest this time, giving me a small shove. "Oh my god, who does that?"

"It's not nearly as scandalous as it sounds," I said with a small laugh. "It was completely mutual. But, yes, she ended things."

And then I noticed: Her hand was still there on my chest. Almost instinctively, I reached up and covered it with my own, holding it there before my brain jolted awake. I realized what I was doing, and I dropped my arm back down to my side.

"Well, I'm sorry, even if it wasn't that big of a deal." She crossed her arms in front of her chest, then dropped them, then clasped her hands. "I dated this guy once who told me he didn't want to be exclusive while we were—" Her eyes shifted to mine and then she blinked, recalibrating. "You know what, never mind."

"What?" I asked. I liked how she did this, spilled too much info and then tried to backtrack. Her brain and her heart were always so wide-open, for everyone to see. I was dying to know what she was about to say.

She shook her head. "It's TMI. And I've told you too much about myself already."

"You mean the Saint Marks story?" I said, chuckling as I remembered everything she'd said that morning on the subway.

She gently smacked her forehead with her palm. "I had sincerely hoped you'd erased that from your memory."

"Never," I said. "Anyway, I'll let you get back to your not bidding on things."

But she didn't move. Instead, we just stood there staring at each other.

I kept talking, unsure of what to do next. "And I'll see you next week, right?"

Did I sound too hopeful? Too eager? I didn't know how to juggle the feelings sizzling inside me, mixed with the need to hide them from her, lest she think me desperate, or boring. Or maybe she already thought those things. It was possible she didn't enjoy my company at all. My brain was on fire.

But then she smiled.

"Definitely."

CHAPTER SEVENTEEN

FRANNY

I HUSTLED AS fast as I could in heels toward Cleo, to give her the details of my latest interaction with Hayes. I found her next to her brothers, Sam and Wes, identical twins, standing in a circle of partygoers on the edge of the dance floor. Sam kept his hair longer and slicked back, and Wes never went anywhere without his thick black glasses, so it was easy to tell them apart.

Cleo looked elegant and classic as always: Her hair was sleek and straight, and her dress, short-sleeved, tight, and navy, draped every curve of her body just so. She'd picked it because it was impossible to stain and she could wear her regular bra with it—in which she'd tucked a crystal to bring her calm throughout the night. Even in her stunning black-tie best, Cleo was both pragmatic and otherworldly, as always.

"There you are!" she said, wrapping an arm around my waist. Her brothers greeted me with sheepish college-boy waves.

"I need to talk to you," I whispered in her ear, but before I could elaborate, her mom pulled me in for a hug.

"Franny!" Miriam said as she kissed me on the cheek. "Let me introduce you to everyone. The twins you know, of course." I gave a nod in the direction of Sam and Wes, who were seniors at

Brown and the University of Virginia, respectively, and starting to look like actual grown-ups in their tuxedos.

"Franny, Sam has an internship in the city coming up, and he's looking for a sublet, if you hear of anything," Miriam continued. "He doesn't want to live at home with his mama. Imagine that."

"Mom, you know I love you even if I don't want to be your roommate," Sam replied with a bashful grin. Wes grabbed him by the shoulder and they headed in the direction of the bar. Miriam turned back toward me and Cleo.

"Franny is an interior designer who just launched her own business," she announced to the group. "And she's incredibly talented."

Miriam offered me a proud smile, and my posture straightened under her gaze. She'd always treated Lola and me like daughters, welcoming us into the Kim family and home as awkward new-to-New-York college kids. The Kims lived just north of the city, in Rye, and we'd escaped to her house numerous times over the years.

Cleo had filled her in on my new business, and my need for clients, and she now began pointing around the group, ticking off names and job titles, which I tried to retain.

A woman named Ellen, with crystal-studded glasses and a martini in one hand, leaned in for a handshake with the other. "I saw you on New York News," she said knowingly. "I met my husband when I was getting on the A train on Forty-Second Street. He accidentally stepped on the heel of my shoe—some atrocious loafer; it was the seventies, after all—and he kicked it onto the subway tracks. He tied his sweater around my foot so I could get home, and the rest is history."

"Oh my goodness!" The silver-haired woman next to her who had introduced herself as "Catherine Ratcliffe but everyone calls me Duffy" laughed. "I had no idea Bobby was that romantic."

Duffy then leaned in toward the group, her face ready to gossip.

"My first husband and I met in high school." This was said with an eye roll, and the group tittered in response. "But Ray—number four—and I met on a double date. We were both set up with other people and went home with each other."

The story swapping continued—tales of first glances, drunken kisses, and lackluster anniversaries—until suddenly Ellen pushed her glasses up her nose and reached to grab my arm across the group. "Your man is here," she said, her mouth rounded in gleeful shock. "From the subway."

Cleo turned her head and then whipped back toward me. "Oh my god, Franny," she murmured in my ear. "Hayes is here. Like, right behind you."

I swiveled out of her reach to look, and, sure enough, Hayes was walking toward us.

"Hello again," he said, offering me a small smile as he fiddled with the sleeve of his jacket.

"Hi," I said, feeling the same nervous giddiness bubble up in my stomach that had appeared when I laid eyes on him earlier.

He turned to Cleo. "I don't believe we've met yet. Hayes Montgomery."

She shook his outstretched hand. "Cleo Kim. Nice to meet you. I've heard a lot about you. Obviously. Oh, and this is my mom, Miriam Kim."

Hayes greeted Miriam politely, but before she could respond, Ellen had cut in. "I'm a fan," she said, all toothy smile and charm. "It's so nice to see the two of you are actually an item."

Hayes glanced at me, ran a hand through his hair, and smiled back at Ellen.

"Ah, well, I hate to disappoint you, but Franny and I are just working together, actually. She's designing my new office space."

There was much oohing and aahing over this. He chuckled and looked back at me, a hint of red popping up on his lovely, smooth skin.

"Franny, I, uh, wanted to see if you might want to dance when the band picks up again."

His eyes, dark and serious, stared directly at me. Into me.

"Oh! Oh." My brain spun like a Ferris wheel.

"This is how my second husband and I met," I heard Duffy say to Miriam. "A gala just like this one. Danced all night. Then he left me for one of the partners at his law firm."

"Sure," I said, straining to remain calm and cool. "That would be fun."

"I'll come back over in a few minutes, then," he said as he tugged on the edge of his collar.

"Okay." I nodded, exhaling as I smiled. My heart was racing.

As soon as he was a few feet away, I turned toward Cleo. "That's what I wanted to tell you earlier. I saw Hayes at the auction table, and he told me Serena dumped him tonight."

Cleo squeezed my bare arm, her lips pressed together, holding back a smile. "Now *this* is exciting," she said.

"Is it?" I asked, my brain racing to pick apart tonight's inter-actions with Hayes so far. "Maybe he's just being polite."

"Oh, Franny." Cleo patted me on the tip of my nose with her index finger. "You're so clueless sometimes."

"Excuse me, I once came very close to qualifying to be on *College Jeopardy!*"

"Which is why it's extra-adorable when you're this dense." Cleo tilted her head and gave me a loving stare. "Franny, didn't we discuss this in the park the other day? All the evidence is right there in front of you. Connect the dots, please."

She paused for a beat, staring at me expectantly. "He's into you. Am I right?"

She opened the conversation up to the group, all of whom were watching us, with an open-palmed wave of her hand.

My insides twisted. "Um, no, he's not."

"Trust me. I can tell," Miriam said, nodding at her daughter.

"Mrs. Kim, I literally work for him now. He's just being polite."

"So you're spending a lot of time together," Ellen said. "Getting to know each other."

"Talking about desks and light fixtures," I clarified.

"And he must find that very interesting, because he just asked you to dance," Duffy chimed in now, manicured, diamond-covered hands studiously clasped under her chin. "Get ready, dear. He's on his way over."

The dance floor glowed, lit up in a dim-blue hue and the soft flickering light of candles. I knew that later in the evening—according to Cleo anyway—things would get raucous, with this crowd of hedge fund CEOs and bankers dancing past midnight. But it was only nine, maybe a little bit past that, and the band was playing a soft, jazzy tune, like something you'd hear in a café at brunch. All around me, couples were dancing closer than I'd realized from the sidelines. I'm not sure what I'd thought we were going to do when I agreed to this—a choreographed eighties-style number?—but dancing cheek to cheek was not it.

Hayes's hand pressed gently on my lower back, guiding me through chatting couples, close talkers, and laughing circles of friends around the room, until we reached the edge of the dance floor. He leaned in closer to talk, but his voice was still quiet over the din of the music. "Do you want to lead?"

I turned to give him a look and was met by a grin more wicked than I'd ever seen on his face. I poked him in the shoulder as retaliation. "Normally, I would, but I literally have no idea how to do this."

A slight panic was setting in. I couldn't recall the last time I had slow-danced with someone. Middle school? Ninth grade, maybe? Sure, I danced at weddings, and at bars or parties when I'd had the occasional tequila shot or two. But *danced* danced, with my hand in someone else's, their arm around my waist? There was no memory of this in my brain.

"I'm guessing your mom didn't make you take ballroom dancing in the basement of a church in fifth grade?" Hayes said with a soft laugh.

"God, no." I chuckled. "In fifth grade, I was only expected to mow the lawn."

"Well, I could either teach you the box step," he said, reaching for my hand, "or"—he rested his other hand firmly at the curve of my back—"we could just move, Ms. Doyle," he said, and his words fizzed inside me, verbal champagne.

I'd never heard him say my last name before, and the sound of it on his lips heated me from the inside out, his voice rich and low. He bit his bottom lip as he looked at me—not smiling, just staring. My eyes moved from his mouth to his jaw, then back to his eyes, which were still on me. My body felt like a Slinky, coiled tight, on the edge of being let go.

"Hayes?"

"Yes?" There was that soft smile again, and he inched a step closer to me.

"Do you think there will be a time where people will stop recognizing us from our dumb moment on the train?"

He pulled back a bit and gave me a perplexed look. "I didn't think it was dumb."

I shook my head. "That's because your clothes didn't betray you in front of the entire world."

"That's fair," he said with a chuckle. "And there's definitely a solid over-sixty demo here, so clearly we've got some New York News fans lurking about. They probably don't know what Instagram is, though."

We were so close I could feel his words landing on the sensitive part of my neck, right below my ear. I was listening to him, but I was also imagining how it would feel if his lips moved just a hair closer, until they were pressed against my skin.

"If it's any consolation," he continued, "I'm glad it happened. I mean, for purely selfish reasons, of course. You've done such a kick-ass job on the office. You're literally a lifesaver."

"Thank you," I said, beaming. I was genuinely proud of how it was turning out. "It's been fun."

"And Perrine wouldn't have met Lola. I've never seen her happier."

I nodded. "Lola too," I said.

"Not that I take any pleasure in what you went through on the train," he said. "But, hey, it also means I get to dance with you tonight, so."

I had to look down at the floor. Because his words had swooped into me and stirred everything up, and I was afraid he could see it on my face. "Well, the truth is," I joked, "I look better in this dress than in your suit jacket."

He laughed and relaxed against my body, and I was so consumed by that feeling that I didn't even notice that the song had changed. And then again, minutes later, the next one played. Slowly, with each change in music, our bodies got closer and closer together, until his breath was a light wind on the nape of neck, my cheek pressed softly against the warm curve of his shoulder.

I was acutely aware of how every cell along the front of my body lit up against his, and the feel of our bodies so close pulled me back in time, to just a few months ago, when I'd slammed my hands against his chest as the train jolted. How firm and solid he'd felt, a comforting wall to land against as the world around me flipped on its axis. And now I felt it again, things suddenly shifting and changing, and yet here he was—something steady to hold on to. And it scared me just how much I didn't want to let go.

I woke up Sunday morning with my body on fire, the fuse lit the night before by the feeling of Hayes's breath on my neck. I couldn't get over the sensation of how muscular he was through his tux, and the idea of just how that firm, smooth skin would feel against my body with no clothes between us was making me squirm. I tucked myself under the covers of my bed, a cup of coffee close by, and reenacted every moment, trying to recall the glint in Hayes's eyes, the occasional hint of his dimples, the warmth of his body. And then on top of all this, Cleo's words played like a song on repeat: "*He's into you.*"

His hand. That's what I kept circling back to. His hand on my back, the first place I'd ever felt him touch me, in that instant on the subway. He had held it there, still and firm, for most of the time we were dancing. Even through the satin of my dress, I could feel him there, as if we were skin to skin. But there was one instance where he'd started tracing small circles on my back, and it had felt so wildly erotic, like his hand was between my legs and not palming the spot where I'd had a small butterfly tattooed in bright blue ten summers ago.

I clenched my eyes closed and opened them wide, willing myself out of my fantasy. There was a chain of texts from Lola and Cleo sitting unanswered on my phone. Cleo recapped last night—and filled us in on the handsome Columbia PhD student she'd met at an after-party. I sent through a string of thumbs-up and heart emojis, and then tossed my phone aside. There was something else I needed to do.

Leaning over the edge of the bed, I grabbed my computer from the floor and powered it on. It had been weeks now since that note from my half sister had landed in my inbox. I wasn't sure what it was about last night that had infused me with courage, but I clicked on the Reply box below her message and finally, *finally* began typing.

My response was short, but it took me almost an hour to write what I wanted to say and hit SEND. I'd expected the feeling of the message going through to offer up some sense of relief, or calm, but instead I felt utterly terrified. What if I was too forward? Too needy? Not friendly enough? What if she decided not to respond? I had finally taken the step to connecting with this person, who would in turn connect me with parts of myself that had always been a mystery. And now I was plagued with worry about rejection, with the thought that I might not actually get to know this side of myself at all.

Anyone wanna grab pizza? Ramen? Something easy and cheap? I have a sister update, I texted Lola and Cleo. I could kill two birds with one stone tonight: fill up my stomach and fill them in about responding to Anna.

Hanging with Perrine! Lola responded. **Rain check? Update us here?**

Paper-grading hell, is all Cleo wrote. **Rain check pls, and I want to hear everything.**

Before I could respond, my email alert rang, and I frantically switched over to my inbox, assuming Anna had gotten my message and written back quickly. Instead, my heart jumped. There was a message from Hayes.

F –

Just signing off on the fridge delivery time. I can be there to meet them, no problem.

There was nothing erotic, or flirty, or sexy to it. No mention of last night, our dance, the way our bodies seemed to naturally gravitate toward each other every time we were near.

I fumed. A robot could have written this message. I was so annoyed I didn't even notice his sign-off at first. But once I did, it was all I could see.

Can't wait to talk soon.
—H

CHAPTER EIGHTEEN

HAYES

I WAS STANDING shirtless in the bathroom, postshower, trying to shave while also eyeing my phone, waiting for another message to come through from Franny. We'd been texting, which, oddly, felt even more intimate than seeing her in person, and I'd basically glued the phone to my hand so that I'd always be ready when another message popped up. Normally, I tried to give myself some space from my devices. I always slept without my phone in my bedroom—I didn't have much work-life balance beyond that, even though I tried—but the past few nights I'd been heading to bed with my phone in hand, eager to see what she'd written.

I was sliding the razor down my face when my phone buzzed, and I moved my hand so quickly I nicked my chin. "Ow!" I flinched. It didn't stop me from grabbing my phone in the other hand.

So let me guess, her message said. **You're deciding between a suit and . . . a suit to wear tonight.**

I sent back a series of emojis, a face with a tongue sticking out, and then the **100**, for good measure. She was exactly right. I dabbed at the cut on my face with a tissue, and then typed.

Heads up there will be a couple reporters at the party, I texted her. **Maybe we can get your business some press.**

You've seen me in an interview, she wrote back. **You sure? LOL**

I sent one of those laugh-crying emojis, but once it went through it felt childish and embarrassing. Would she think that was dumb? Ugh, I was agonizing over the stupidest things these days. **Any word from your sister?**

Not yet, but that's fair. It took me weeks to respond.

We'd been swapping stories about the things that were currently keeping us up at night—for her, it was her sister. Never any mention of work stuff, though I always assumed she was busy with her next project. For me, anxiety about this launch party had been brewing all week, topped with nerves about the interviews we'd scheduled and worry that it would be some sort of unmitigated social disaster. And then there was my looming Seattle trip, and the stress of trying to expand our business to the opposite coast.

The only thing I wasn't nervous about was our office itself. Franny had pulled together a space that was warm and inviting. Most importantly, it felt like us. I'd never thought about how much I hated the gray walls of our old space, but now they felt cold and oppressive, and I couldn't wait to be in this new world of wood, brick, and light all the time. And the best part of all, at least in my opinion, was the garden and the roof deck outside. It didn't just feel like part of the office; it felt like a space I shared only with Franny. I was going to miss seeing her out there, laughing, hands in the soil, telling me what to do. I was getting ready to say goodbye to her, and then it dawned on me—maybe I didn't have to.

"Please don't give me that look," I said to Eleanor as our Lyft sputtered to a stop in traffic on Eighth Avenue.

"Sorry, sorry," she said, taking a sip of her sparkling water. "You're just uncharacteristically jumpy today. Are you nervous about the party, or because Franny's going to be there?"

"How do you know I'm even nervous?" I snarked back, though she was, of course, right. I was nervous about all of it, really. But especially about seeing Franny.

"Well, I invited Serena, in case you want to take your turn dumping her at a party you're hosting," she said, a devilish gleam in her eye.

"Honestly, I wouldn't put it past you," I said, knowing full well she was teasing. "Also, we left things on good terms. I actually did invite her, but she's out of town."

"Brave of you," Eleanor said with an admiring look.

We stepped out in front of our new building, gliding through the lobby and up to the fourth floor, where Tyler was directing people lugging in the trays of charcuterie and cheese we'd ordered from a small catering business deep in Brooklyn.

"Wow," Eleanor said as she circled the space. "It looks amazing in here."

"I'm inclined to agree," Tyler said, in full party-planner mode, clipboard in hand as they hovered over a platter full of fruits and vegetables organized like the colors of a rainbow.

Members of our team started trickling in, fresh from the pregaming that had taken place at a bar down the street. The reporters from *Vogue* and *Architectural Digest* checked in, along with photographers from *New York* magazine and *Vanity Fair*.

Out of the corner of my eye, I saw Perrine and Lola saunter in, hands linked. And behind them, Franny, red-lipped, hair everywhere, arms crossed, face beaming. She was in some sort of olive-green jumpsuit that I knew instinctively Eleanor would love. I made my way over to them, beer in hand, trying not to appear as nervous as I felt inside. I was excited to see her, but I still couldn't figure out how to show it, or if I should at all.

"Hayes-y!" Perrine yelled as I approached, which was the absolute last thing I wanted her to call me in front of the woman I couldn't stop thinking about.

"Perrine," I replied as she grabbed me with both hands for a hug. "Please don't call me that in public," I muttered as I leaned in.

She just laughed in response.

"Hello, Lola," I said as she also came in for a hug. I guess I hugged now.

"Hayes," she said, planting the slightest kiss on my cheek.

"Hey!" Franny said from behind Lola with a wave.

"Franny, hi!" I leaned forward and then stepped back, unsure of how exactly to greet her. Should I also hug her? Was that too much? Or was it weird if I hugged everyone else and not her? I couldn't figure out the right move. So we just stood there, staring at each other.

"I'm so glad you—" I started, just as she said, "It looks amazing in—"

"You first." I gestured her on with a slight wave of my hand.

"I told Lola how hard you've been working on this night," she said with a small smile. "And it looks awesome."

I shook my head. "We would literally not even be here if it wasn't for you, so…"

"Well, it looks great," Lola chimed in, with a side-eyed glance at Franny.

"Thank you," I said. "I'm glad you all could make it." I snuck a look back in Franny's direction. She was beaming as she surveyed the scene, her hands on her hips. This night belonged to her as much as it did Eleanor and me.

"Well, we'll let you get back to schmoozing," Perrine said. And with a knowing eye roll to Lola and Franny, she muttered sarcastically, "His favorite thing to do."

Franny shot me an amused look and then turned and followed them toward the bar.

Eleanor came over and dragged me into a corner for a thirty-minute chat with some investors well-known in the environmental space. I tried to stay focused on our conversation while also watching Franny out of the corner of my eye: Franny sipping a drink, and then another. Franny grabbing two portobello sliders and handing one to Lola with a smile. Franny chatting with Tyler and nodding along thoughtfully as Tyler pointed to different pieces in the giant floral arrangement on the new reception desk. Franny.

—*mn*—

An hour later, she was next to me, chatting with the reporter from *Vogue*. "You two have an amazing origin story," the reporter, a woman named Alicia, with short pink hair, said into her iPhone. "Could you tell us how you met?"

"Hayes helped me out of a sticky situation on the subway," Franny said, looking up at me with a smile. "So it was only natural that I return the favor."

"Let's just say we bumped into each other," I said, beaming. Every move I made felt too big, too obvious, too clear about the fact that Franny occupied a permanent home in my brain. I'd tried to rein it in for so long, out of not wanting to look foolish, or silly, or too in my feelings for her. But now that's exactly where I wanted to be. I wanted to be obvious, to make it clear, not just to Franny, or myself, but to the world: I liked her.

"Sure." Franny nodded. "I like that way better."

"And when we lost our original interior designer at the last minute, Franny seemed like a natural fit. She came in and whipped this place into shape in no time."

"Honestly, this was a dream space to work on. I mean, look at it." Franny waved a hand around, and the reporter's eyes followed.

"And Hayes and Eleanor made it easy." She said this with a playful pat on my back, and when she released her hand I wanted to grab it and put it back. Unlike our last interview together, this felt easy. Fun. We'd gone from being totally out of sync to feeling completely in tune. I'd never felt like this with another person before, and I wasn't ready to let it go.

Later, Eleanor and I stood by the windows, surveying the scene. "We should try to get a photo with Franny in it too." Eleanor's voice was in my ear as she waved at the *Vanity Fair* photographer, gesturing them toward us.

"Yeah, I was just thinking we should grab her."

"Mmm, yeah." She nodded. "That must be why you keep looking over there at her."

Eleanor narrowed her glance at me, and it was knowing and sharp. Before I could come back with something smart, the photographer was upon us, shuffling us over into better light.

"Okay, look," I said through my teeth as we smiled for the camera. "If I tell you everything, will you promise to be cool just this once?"

"Of course," she said, staring straight ahead as the photographer finished shooting, then meandered back into the crowd.

I turned toward Eleanor again. "I like her," I said as I dug at the collar of my shirt, which seemed to have shrunk two sizes over the course of this conversation.

"That's it? You *like* her?"

"I like her, and I'm thinking about asking her out to dinner now that she's done working for us, yes."

"Well, you might want to go show off your charm and wit, because I think she's about to head out the door."

I followed Eleanor's gaze across the room, to where Franny was hugging Lola.

"Crap," I muttered under my breath.

"Tell her we want a photo with her!" Eleanor shouted after me.

I wove my way through the crowd as I watched Franny disappear toward the elevators. I took off for the entrance, trying to walk at a fast enough pace to reach her without looking like a weirdo running through his own party. But once I got there, she was nowhere to be found. I pushed the button, but the elevator was stuck at the first floor and didn't seem to be moving. Luckily, I had walked the building weeks prior, and knew that the stairwell was always unlocked in case of a fire. I made a dash for it.

Four flights later, I flung the door open directly onto the street. I could see her curls, bouncing just twenty feet ahead of me. So close.

"Franny!" I shouted, cupping my hands to my face to amplify my voice. She turned back, glancing around as she tried to determine where the voice was coming from. I gave her a wave and then slow-jogged to where she stood.

"Hey," she said, a confused look on her face.

"I was going to grab you for a photo for *Architectural Digest*," I said. "But you're leaving."

"Oh, don't worry. I made sure to connect with them," she said. "They took a few photos already."

"Oh." I tried to keep the disappointment from my voice. "Good."

She tucked her hair behind both ears. "It's just that I can only play fake extrovert for so long," she said. "You might not believe it, but underneath this"—she waved a hand up and down her body—"lurks a secret introvert."

"Well, I'm just a straight-up introvert, so I get it." I squeezed the back of my neck with my hand.

"The space looks amazing, Hayes," she said. "I'm really happy I got to be a part of it."

"Can I get you a Lyft?" I asked, unsure of what else to say. "Or a bike?"

"I'm just going to walk to the subway," she said, her face bright. "Though if you wanna lend me your jacket just in case, you can."

I laughed. I liked that we could joke about it all now, that whatever awkward weirdness that had hovered over our initial meeting had transitioned into something relaxed, playful. Intimate, even.

And yet at this moment, I still didn't know what to say next. All I knew was that I didn't want her to go. I wanted to do anything to make this night last, to keep her here, drenched in the light of passing cars and buildings. She was all color, a painting so lovely you couldn't help but stop and marvel at it.

"Well," she said, adjusting the bag hanging off her shoulder. "Good night"—she gave me a sweet smile and raised her brows—"Hayes-y."

"Good night, *Francesca*," I offered back, crossing my arms smugly across my chest.

She looked at me, brows still high, and let out a laugh.

"What?" I asked.

"I wasn't expecting a Francesca," she said. "You surprised me."

"Well, hopefully, it won't be the last time," I said, stammering slightly. "That I surprise you. Or you surprise me. Or we surprise each other? I don't know where I'm going with this." I couldn't figure out the right words to say to her.

"Good night, Hayes," she said with one final smile. I stood there as she headed down West Thirteenth Street, losing her to New York City once again.

Feeling the weight of her absence deep in my chest, I turned toward the building and headed back to the party inside. I still had at least an hour of schmoozing left. I let my hand graze the edge of the building, feeling the cool cement against my fingertips. Anything to bring me back to reality.

Just as I reached to pull open the doors to the lobby, I felt someone tap my shoulder. I turned to find Franny, slightly out of breath. She exhaled as she took a final step, meeting me almost toe to toe.

"Surprise," she said, still breathless.

I furrowed my brow in confusion and opened my mouth to reply. But before I could get a word out, her lips were there, soft against mine, lingering for what felt like years or a split second— it was hard to tell. Time didn't so much stop, but rather sped forward, blasted me off to space and back down to Earth again. The tips of her fingers brushed my cheek, and the sensation of her skin against mine set off an electrical fire inside my skull. I reached for her face, her delicate curls brushing against my fingers.

Before my brain could catch up with my body and process what was happening, she leaned back with an enormous smile, her eyes alight with something feral. And without a word, she dashed down the street and into the night, leaving me standing dumbstruck.

CHAPTER NINETEEN

FRANNY

"WAIT, I'M SORRY. I'm going to need you to repeat this story again," Cleo said from the couch, where she lay splayed out, chopsticks in one hand, takeout container of dumplings in the other. "You said, 'Surprise,' and then you kissed him?"

I buried my face in my hands. It had been twenty-four hours since I'd made the decision to run back and kiss Hayes. It had been quick, a flash of skin, a skip of the heart. So fast it almost felt like a figment of my imagination. But it had happened. I'd done it, and I hadn't stopped thinking about it since, with a strange mix of horror and thrill. Horror because—what if he was horrified? And thrill because, well…it had been thrilling. And in between all the panicked thoughts, I'd been imagining what it might feel like to do it again.

Lola squealed and kicked me with her socked feet in a pitter-patter motion, like a cat getting its stomach rubbed.

"I had had two glasses of prosecco," I moaned. "You know sparkling wine is one of my biggest enemies."

"Oh, don't blame it on the booze," Lola said. "We've both seen you truly hammered, and this was not one of those nights. Remember the Halloween when we all dressed up like the Spice

Girls and you made out with Wall Street Greg at that Gowanus loft party?"

Cleo raised her head. "Oh my god, Lo, and *you* clogged the toilet at that after-party?"

"Okay, forget I said anything." Lola grimaced. "Besides, this is about Franny. Franny kissing Hayes."

"Ooooh, and liking it!" Cleo piped up. "Remember when she thought he was a jerk?"

"I believe she said 'asshole,'" Lola said, dunking a dumpling in soy sauce and vinegar. "I never bought it. You were smitten the second he forced his coat on you on the train."

Cleo mm-hmmed in agreement from the couch.

"Wow, you are very insightful," I replied sarcastically. "Seriously, though. I need to call him, right? And make sure he knows it was just an accidental in-the-moment kind of thing?"

Neither of my friends said anything. Instead, they each snuck a glance at the other. "I can see you both looking at each other. You know that, right?" I waved my hands at them. "I am literally two feet away from you."

I looked at my phone for what felt like the five hundredth time today. So far, the only person I'd heard from was my mom, sending me pictures of possible floral arrangements for Ruby's baby shower next weekend. I ignored her.

"I'm seeing Perrine tomorrow for yoga and dinner," Lola said. "I could ask her to try to get some info out of him."

"No!" Cleo and I said at the same time. Lola laughed.

"Great minds," I said, leaning over to pat Cleo's leg gingerly.

"This great mind is ready for that Advil you promised me earlier," she moaned. "I hate my period."

"It's honestly a wonder our cycles are not synced," Lola said.

"Well, I'm on birth control, so y'all will need to sync up with me," I replied, a finger pointed to my chest.

"Hey," said Lola, sitting up. "We're all supposed to go out to dinner on Friday, remember? So you two can get to know Perrine better? Hayes is going to be there."

Oh crap, right. She'd mentioned this over text at some point, and I'd said yes. Now her face was so eager it was clear this meant a lot to her.

"You'll still come, right? Even if things with Hayes are weird?"

"Of course," I assured her. I pushed back up off the floor and shuffled my slippered feet into the bathroom, digging around in the drawer I kept telling myself I needed to organize. Finally, I found the giant bottle of store-brand ibuprofen shoved in there next to my hair dryer and a box of organic tampons.

I walked back to the living room, bottle in hand, when I noticed both my friends sitting upright, erect, and slightly tense. "What?" I asked.

"Check your phone," Cleo said quickly. "You got a text."

I glanced at my phone on the floor, stomach leaping up to my throat. I looked back at my friends, who were staring at me expectantly. "You read it, didn't you?"

"The whole message was just right there, on your screen." Lola scrunched her face apologetically.

"Legally, we're fine, because the text revealed itself to us," Cleo said matter-of-factly.

"Don't use your law degree against me!" I bent down and grabbed my phone off the floor, pressing the home button to reveal the screen.

Francesca, hi. Could we talk?

I stared at the screen, crafting my reply in my head. So far, all I had was "Yes." Suddenly, another message popped up.

In case it's unclear, I was using "Francesca" because you commented on me using your full name last night. I think

> this is me trying to be funny or perhaps even charming,
> but I am not particularly good at it, so.

My cheeks turned red, like a stovetop set to high. Seconds later, this:

> I'm going to stop now.

I smiled, a small laugh escaping my lips. "Oh my god, what?" said Lola, her voice laced with the kind of urgency only a best friend coaching you through a postkiss text-message exchange can possess.

"He's just somehow even more awkward over text, and it's oddly charming."

Cleo flopped back down on the pillows behind her. "It's like he's so handsome he never had to learn social skills."

I took a sip of water. "I'm just worried that I've now put both of us in a strange position. And, like, way to go, me—kissing the first client I've ever had." I shook my head, frustrated at myself. I couldn't figure out what I wanted.

"You've really set me up here." Lola's eyes twinkled. "Should I say what I want to say?"

Cleo kicked at her playfully. "No!" she scolded.

Lola snorted in reply. "Fine. But you make it too easy sometimes, Fran!"

"No, but seriously." I frowned, thinking things through. "I've started my own business. I don't need to be making out with my clients, especially my first one. I should be using him for referrals, not his body."

"That's fair," Cleo mused. "But in your defense, you did meet him outside of work. In a totally random and also cliché-to-the-point-of-being-absurdly-romantic way. So it's only fair that this happened."

"I'm just second-guessing everything now," I said, nervously chewing on a fingernail.

"And technically, you're done working for him. The party was last night." Cleo leaned forward, and I could tell she was excited by this work-around. Solving things wasn't just her specialty; it made her giddy.

I nodded. "I'm just waiting on my final payment from them."

"So there's your out. As long as you both consent to moving forward with some sort of physical relationship, you're fine. You can, in fact, use him for his body."

"Agreed," Lola said with a slow clap. Cleo bowed in the most exaggerated way possible.

"So can I make my strange-position joke now?" Lola asked.

"No!" Cleo shouted, throwing a pillow at Lola, who ducked so it landed behind her.

My phone sounded again, and we all jumped. I peered down, expecting more from Hayes. Instead, it was a number I didn't recognize.

Hi Franny, this is Serena!!! Hayes gave me your number. I'd love to hop on a call to discuss possibly working together. I moved a couple of months ago and my apartment needs major tlc. I'm in a 2br right on Gramercy Park. Xoxoxo

"Oh boy," I said with a big sigh, and read it out loud to my friends. She lived in one of the most exclusive parts of the city, where residents got a key to a private park.

"Wow, it's like she has a sixth sense," Cleo mused.

"This is crazy," I said, unease settling in my bones. "What now—I'm going to make out with the guy she was dating and then also decorate her apartment?"

"I mean, yeah." Lola gave me a confused look. "That's exactly what's going to happen."

KATE SPENCER

"Nope. No." I shook my head. "This is who I'm supposed to follow in the Hayes Montgomery dating pool? A hot woman who can afford to live on Gramercy Park? I should have never kissed him."

"I'm sure it's family money. No one our age could afford that on their own," Lola grumbled with a knowing eye roll as Cleo gave me a serious look.

"Franny, please don't get in your head comparing yourself to her again," Cleo said as she leaned closer. "He asked *you* to dance at the gala, remember?"

"Yeah, after she dumped him! I was probably some in-the-moment rebound." I closed my eyes to think for a minute. My face was hot. I felt so foolish.

"Did I like kissing him? Yes," I said finally. "But it feels like a mistake. And I have to be my own boss here, and boss Franny is saying a client/designer relationship is a no."

"But a Hayes/Franny relationship is such a yes," Lola said, hands in the air, as if it were obvious.

"I know we can't tell you what to do...," Cleo said.

"You can't," I interjected.

"But I think it's a mistake not to pursue this with him," she finished.

Lola nodded in agreement. "Also, we never even got to double-date," she said with a pout.

"Obviously, you should do what you think is best," said Cleo, sounding resigned. "And we'll support you no matter what."

"Great," I said, crossing my arms in front of my chest. "I'm gonna nip it in the bud now."

"Can we at least help you craft this text back to him?" Lola asked.

"Obviously," I said, and we huddled around my phone.

Forty-eight minutes later, I hit SEND.

210

Hey! Happy to hop on the phone, or we could meet up tomorrow somewhere if you feel like coffee. Brooklyn Bridge Park?

I'd spent fifteen minutes debating a reply to his comment about being charming, but decided against it. Better to set up this boundary now. Even if it was cute. And charming. Which it was.

Damn it.

A couple minutes later, my phone rang: Hayes. "Oh my god, it's him," I whispered to my friends.

"Ooooh boy," Lola muttered as she reached for the container of scallion pancakes at the same time as Cleo said, "Why are you whispering?"

I waved them off with my hand.

"Hi," I said, trying to sound nonchalant and like I hadn't spent almost an hour composing a two-sentence text with my best friends.

"Franny, hi," Hayes said, and his gentle voice instantly hit a soft spot inside me.

"Hi," I said again.

"I thought hopping on the phone might be easier?"

"Sure," I said, my voice chipper. But I felt a twinge of disappointment that I wasn't going to get to see him in person, which was not at all what I wanted to be feeling. I pushed it aside. Not now.

"Hayes, look. I'm sorry for being so wildly unprofessional last night."

Oh god, I sounded absurd. And he sounded... quiet.

"It's just that," I said quickly, desperate to fill the awful, humiliating silence, "I think I should stick to being professional with you for now, if that makes sense."

"Oh," he said, like he was trying to figure out a puzzle. And

211

then, "Of course. I totally understand that." His tone had shifted quickly. Now he was all business.

Was he relieved? I couldn't tell. "Just 'cause, you know, I'm trying to focus on my work and business," I added.

"Yes, I completely get that. And I am, as well. Working…and all that."

"Oh, well, cool. Thanks for understanding."

We were both quiet, and when he didn't say anything, I added, "Good talk."

I heard him chuckle at this, and I winced. Why did I always say the weirdest things?

"Good talk indeed."

"'Kay. Well, bye, Hayes."

I hung up before I could hear how he decided to say my name.

"Ugh, that was so awkward," I groaned, letting my head collapse in my lap. "Did I really just say 'Good talk'?"

Lola leaned up off the floor and squeezed my knee. "It happens to the best of us. Remember Gaby? When I broke up with her, I told her to 'Keep fighting the good fight.'"

"Well, whatever," I said, my voice shaky. "At least that's over with."

Out of the corner of my eye, I saw Lola shoot Cleo a look, but neither of them said a word.

Later, long after they'd left, I played last night's kiss over in my head, just one more time. The feeling of his suit against my hands, the calm I felt just leaning against him, the moment when I turned around to run back to kiss him, soft and quick but with an undeniable urgency. The thought of it left me thinking throughout the night, analyzing and doubting my decision. The last thing I remembered thinking as I drifted off to sleep was that I'd made a huge mistake.

CHAPTER TWENTY

HAYES

IT WAS 5:30 P.M., and the sun was still high in the sky. My mind should have been focused elsewhere. I was supposed to head out to Seattle in a few days, for a big pitch meeting with possible investors. We needed them on board to grow the company, and Eleanor, salesperson extraordinaire, was staying behind in New York on her doctor's orders. It was on me to nail the pitch and get them excited about working with us. Plus, we'd gone ahead and planned a bunch of walk-throughs of possible office spaces, along with meetings with analysts, the first people we'd hire to add to our new team.

But despite all the craziness at work, my thoughts were only filled with Franny. It had been five days since she'd ended things before I'd even had a chance to ask her out, six since she kissed me in the middle of the sidewalk, and approximately 98 percent of those waking hours I'd spent replaying our interactions in my head, reimagining the soft curve of her back under my palm, the brush of her hair against my chin, the warmth of her hand wrapped in mine.

I'd been so nervous on the phone with her that day that I hadn't been able to get out the words I wanted to say: *I like you. I'm glad you kissed me. I want to do it again and again and again.* Maybe my silence had pushed her away. Or maybe she didn't want anything to do with me romantically.

Either way, it was all-consuming, this urge to just lay eyes on her again, rewind things to the beginning, start all over, before the gala, and the kiss. I would go right back to that moment she walked into my subway car. I would steer her away from the door so her dress didn't rip. I would give her my number, invite her to a proper meal out.

But I also wanted to respect Franny's wishes. She was just starting her business; she had important things to focus on. I got it. And maybe her kiss was just an in-the-moment thing, the mix of alcohol, and the party, and the energy of the night.

Yet I still hadn't been able to stop thinking about her, and the excitement I felt that I'd get to see her tonight was causing my heart to race. I still wanted to bask in her light, in whatever way I could get it. Perhaps that made me greedy, but I'd rather have a little bit of Franny as opposed to none at all.

Knowing I'd see her soon made me move quickly, and I zigzagged my way across the West Village and SoHo at a clip until I arrived in front of the small Mexican restaurant Perrine had invited me to for this "getting-to-know-each-other" dinner.

"Hayes." I spun around quickly, worried that if I took my time the voice—and the person it belonged to—would disappear. I blinked just to be sure, but she was standing in front of me, her hands propped on her hips, one of which was jutting out ever so slightly. She was in a flowy light-blue floral dress that billowed around her. She looked like an annoyed toddler, and I loved it.

"Hey." I tried to force myself to sound casual and friend-like, and not like someone who'd been nervously anticipating this moment all week. "You're early too, huh?"

"Did you not get a text?" she said, her brow furrowed like she was trying to piece together a puzzle. "Lola said she and

Perrine needed to cancel. Something about them both having food poisoning."

I nodded. "I see."

"And then Cleo also conveniently got dragged into some emergency at work."

"Huh." I nodded again and pulled my phone out of my pocket. Indeed, there was a text from Perrine. **Sorry for last minute text but sick and need to cancel dinner**, was all it said. I held the phone up for Franny to see.

"Wow. Is your cousin as cunning as my best friends?" she asked, a look of disbelief on her face.

"Apparently," I said, still putting the pieces together. "We've been set up."

"Oh, big-time." At first, I thought she was pissed off, but then Franny's head tipped backward, and the most beautiful, uproarious laugh poured past her lips, which were lined with that rich red color of hers. Just that sound of pure joy from her set off a spark inside me, and I couldn't help but smile.

"I'm honestly kind of impressed," I said, running my hands through my hair. "This is not Perrine's style at all. She's much less obvious with her forcing of people to—"

To be together, is what I wanted to say. But I cut myself off. We'd both agreed that this thing between us wasn't going anywhere, and the last thing I wanted to do was seem like I hadn't gotten the message.

"Oh, well, this is classic Lola, so you might want to get used to it." She said this with an affectionate smile, and it hit me how much she adored her friends. It was another thing I liked about her.

There was a lull, and in that brief quiet moment, it dawned on me. I'd made a mistake trying to convince myself I didn't want this to go further. I was desperate for Franny. And, god, I liked how I felt whenever I was around her. Like my brain was on vacation and my whole body was warmed up by the sun.

"All right, well…" She gave me a small nod, like she was about to leave. This was my last chance.

"Wait," I said, my throat suddenly sand-dry. "When you called me last weekend"—the words rumbled out, raw and honest—"I should have told you how I felt. I like you. I haven't been able to stop thinking about kissing you."

Franny just stared at me.

"Let me try this again," I said, clearing my throat. "First and foremost, I respect both your professional boundaries and your personal space, and will honor them completely. But I wish I had been more clear with you about how I felt after we kissed. I wanted it to happen, and I'm so glad it did."

"I'm glad it did too," Franny said slowly, eyes firm on my face. "I just thought maybe I'd misread you, or the situation. I wasn't sure."

I shook my head. "You didn't misread anything. And I'm sorry—I should have told you how I've been feeling. I only came here tonight because I wanted to see you. I hope we can still be friends."

She nodded, her eyes searching mine. "But you'd also be okay with, like, more than friends?"

I laughed at this. It felt like my feelings were so obvious they were tattooed on my forehead. Clearly, I needed to do a better job expressing them out loud. "Yes," I said firmly. "Yes."

I took a step closer to her and watched as her chest heaved with a breath, then released, as she dragged her teeth, so slowly, over her bottom lip. I had known her long enough now to know that her brain was moving at a mile a minute, processing fifty different things she could say to me, all of which could slice me open in a second. Everything she said to me, no matter the nicest words or a cutting dig, burned through my veins like venom. She was my poison, for better or for worse.

And then I saw it. That thing that happened on her face

whenever she shifted into a smile. I felt silly even thinking it, but there was no other way to describe it. She sparkled.

"Should we get a drink?" she said finally.

"I'd love that," I said. There was a relief in letting these words go, in putting it all out there in front of us.

"You don't want to go home and run ten miles?" She was teasing me now, and it felt amazing.

"I can do that tomorrow morning. I can even do it with a hangover." I let out a breath, let my tongue run over my bottom lip.

"I don't think you even *get* hangovers," she said, and she reached up and ran her hand gently across my cheek, down my jaw. From her words, it was clear she'd intended it to be a joke, but her voice was lower than normal, serious. "Sometimes, you seem superhuman."

"I promise you, I'm not superhuman. Just anal-retentive and addicted to routine." I tried to say this jokingly, but I felt weirdly self-conscious. "I'm assuming there's still a dinner reservation for our group. Clearly, our friends were hoping we'd use it."

She blinked up at me then, her pupils wide and bright and open. Something about her face hit a place so deep in my gut that I hadn't known it existed until very recently. I raised my hands, unsure of what I was doing until they found hers, and she brought them close to her chest, her fingers intertwined with mine.

"Okay, then," she said as she tugged me closer. "Let's go get that table."

CHAPTER TWENTY-ONE

FRANNY

RELIEF. ALL I felt was relief. What a strange, intoxicating sensation. Why had I resisted this in the first place? It was warm, and easy, like the summer air outside. The first margarita slipped down my throat like an oyster, smooth and fast and without thought. By the second drink, brought out with our dinner, Hayes's cheeks were bright and red, the edge of his calf resting between my legs under the table. It felt electric and daring, a breaking of the rules. They were just our legs, and having them touch was totally G-rated. But something about the heavy weight of him against me below the gray marble top of the café table, while our hands rested chastely above, felt more erotic and dirty than anything I'd ever done before.

"I've never seen *Grease*." Hayes wrinkled his nose in embarrassment. We were swapping stories, small facts about ourselves, our families. A few minutes ago, he'd asked, "What is something that everyone else has done but you?"

So far I had seen his "I've never played golf, even though I look like I have" and raised him with "I've never been to Disney World and don't want to."

And now, this horrifying reveal. "*Grease*," I gasped, in exaggerated horror, "is a classic."

He shrugged and took a pull of his beer. "I'm a monster, what can I say."

"Do you know any of the songs at least?" I asked, truly horrified.

"Something something summer romance, something something at the high school dance?" he guessed, shimmying slightly in his seat, dancing along to a totally botched attempt at "Summer Nights." The sight of him like that, the top of his collared shirt unbuttoned, his hair slightly ruffled, the small hint of sweat on his brow, being so unabashedly and unselfconsciously silly, tripped my heart up. I burst out laughing.

"Oh my god," I said in between gasping hysterics. "You're a disaster."

Hayes was doubled over too, his grin wider than I'd ever seen it. It revealed an entirely new face, one that was bright and boyish. It made me do a double take, like when you see someone you think you know on the street, only to realize it wasn't them at all. Except in this case, it was still him.

"That's probably why my marriage ended," he said, swinging his drink back again.

I stared at him, surprised. "Sorry," he said. "Too much gallows humor? TMI?"

"No, not at all." I reached my hand across the table, gave his forearm a squeeze. "And I know that you're joking, but I don't really think you're a disaster."

He smiled at this. "Ever since my marriage ended, Perrine's constantly trying to psychoanalyze why my relationships never last long. Doctor brain."

I ran a finger along the bottom of my glass, where the base met the warm, stained wood of the table. "And what has the doctor concluded?"

Hayes shifted uncomfortably in his chair and laid an arm across his chest, stretching it with the other. "Oh, you know, some di-agnosis that involves me needing to open up, work less, consider being more vulnerable."

"Well," I said dismissively. "She's just a surgeon. What does she know?"

And with this, Hayes straight-up *snorted* and let out a laugh so hard the couple behind us turned their heads to give a disapprov-ing stare. We made wide, obvious eyes at each other, mocking our neighbors, and sat in an easy silence for a moment, drinking.

"And what do you think?" I asked quietly, taking him in.

He was silent for a minute, looking over my shoulder and then back at me. "I spent a long time after my divorce thinking I was a person who just wasn't good in relationships. But lately, I've been realizing it was because I was with the wrong people. Not that I'm not partially responsible for things not working out, of course. But I'm learning to ease up on myself a bit about it."

"Is that what happened with Serena?" I kept a cool face as I asked this, but inside I still felt that swell of not-quite-good-enough nerves.

"Oh yeah." He nodded. "We were not at all a fit. But what I realized is that sometimes it can feel safer to be with the wrong person than to find someone who really feels right."

He looked at me and then looked away, taking another swig of his beer. Thank god he couldn't see how my heart was thundering around my chest. He pointed his glass at me. "That was too serious. Your turn."

"Okay, don't judge," I said. "I've never had gelato."

"You're half-Italian." Hayes gave me a puzzled look, his brows pinched. "How is that even possible?"

"When I was a kid, I just preferred Popsicles over ice cream. Italian ice, remember?"

"But gelato." He was still aghast. "Not even once?"

"Nope." I shook my head. "I mean, my mom's family is Irish!"

Hayes tipped back his cup and gulped down the dregs of his beer. "Come on," he said, pushing his chair back and grabbing his credit card from where the server had left it.

I stared up at him from the table. "You're going to make me go get gelato, aren't you?" I felt a smile sneaking out from behind my pursed lips.

"This is urgent, Franny," Hayes said, folding his arms and squinting at me. "These are your roots! You can't be Italian and never try gelato. That's basically the same as never having pizza."

"You're not even Italian." I gave him a sassy, disparaging look. "Who made you an authority on what I'm supposed to eat?"

He tilted his head at me, like he was trying to figure out just how serious I was. When I finally stuck my tongue out at him, he snorted again, that relaxed laugh still so unfamiliar to me that it made me grin every time.

"Wait a second," I said, leaning back in my chair to give him my best analytical look. "You never eat sugar. What's the twist?"

"I told you." He extended his hand, and I took it, letting him pull me up out of my chair. "I just like to save dessert for special occasions."

He gave my hand a squeeze and then dropped it, and as he stuck his wallet in his back pocket, I let his words soak in. He'd been saving it for a special occasion. For *me*.

Fifteen minutes later, we were standing in line inside an Italian bakery crammed with tiny wood tables and rows of perfectly sprinkled cookies behind the glass counter, their sweet smell wafting through the air. Old men in white paper hats and aprons worked quickly behind the counter, with serious expressions on their faces. Hayes looked at me expectantly. "Well?" he asked, his brows raised, hands open to the space around us.

"I love it," I sighed, taking a minute to inhale the mix of sweet desserts with the lingering smell of espresso.

He smiled, revealing those dimples that made his whole face shine.

"And," I said, "I'd been sure you were going to drag me to that trendy gelato place on Ludlow, so I am pleasantly surprised."

He held out his hand for a high five, and instead of slapping his palm, I reached up and interlaced my fingers with his. Maybe it was just liquid courage again. But the alcohol was burning off, and this desire I'd felt to yank him closer and closer seemed to only get stronger. His cheeks burned, I could tell, their pink tint spreading to his dimples. But if he was flustered, he didn't let on.

His eyes followed our hands as I lowered them between us and leaned in to bump my shoulder to his. "Thank you," I whispered. Our heads were so close I could smell his scent drifting off his shirt, that woodsy mix of shampoo, deodorant, laundry, aftershave: daily life. It was a smell no bottle could contain. It was purely him, a scent that had wafted by me so many times before but only now seemed to permeate the air around me.

Minutes later, we were outside, cups of gelato in hand and a small box of warm pignoli cookies in my bag. "Shall we walk?" he asked, and I nodded in between bites of two scoops of pistachio and chocolate, stacked high. "Aren't you going to ask me what I think of my first gelato?" I asked, toying with the spoon in my mouth.

"Nah, I'm pretty confident that you love it already," he said. I pushed my shoulder into his side but said nothing else. He was right, of course. He seemed to always be right. Jerk.

―⁓⁓―

Deep into downtown New York we went, past parks lit up with late-night soccer games and cafés overflowing with couples and groups enjoying the magic of a warm city night. This was my favorite time of day in New York, the hours before midnight, when everyone in the city reemerges after work, and a week's worth of stress, to celebrate Friday in the darkness. Somehow, the city seemed even brighter and more bustling at night, electric with energy, one giant caffeinated surge of life. Before we knew it, we were standing in front of City Hall.

"This is my favorite building in the entire city." Hayes's voice was full of reverence.

"I would have expected something more modern, or minimalistic, from you," I mused. "Energy-efficient. Solar panels. Should I keep going?"

"No, thank you. You've made your point."

He took a couple steps forward.

"In all seriousness, though," he said, "in another lifetime, I almost became an architect, and when I was deciding whether or not to ditch my finance career and apply to grad school, I used to come down here and sit in the park and just stare."

He pointed to the spires of the building; they looked like fingers dipping into the inky blackness of the night sky.

"I love that this building is a relic that seems to last as everything around it changes," he added. "That dichotomy is New York to me, in a nutshell. Everything changes, and somehow *it* still stays the same."

I tried to see what he saw; it was beautiful, sure, but it was magic only to him. I didn't mind. I didn't say it out loud, but that was *my* New York in a nutshell: those special things that we share only with ourselves, the treasures whose shine only we can see. The unremarkable street corners or nameless coffee shops that held worlds of their own.

"What would you do after you sat and stared at a building?" I asked.

"I'd run the length of the Brooklyn Bridge and back, and then sprint to my old apartment in the East Village." He laughed. "I had a lot of stress to burn that year."

I nodded. "Cool."

"Franny." He laughed and gave me a look of disbelief. "Don't say it."

"I've driven across it plenty of times!" I said, knowing exactly where he was going with this.

"But you've"—he shook his head, exasperated—"never walked across it."

I shrugged and made a face. "It seemed too touristy."

"Oh my god." He ran his fingers through his hair. "And you've lived here what, nine, ten years?"

"Twelve," I confessed with a grimace. "If you count college."

"Twelve?!" He threw up his hands at me and gaped.

"You're going to really be horrified by this, but my apartment's only a few blocks away from the bridge too."

"Franny, no!" I'd never seem him this animated, and it made me smile.

"Look, I biked across the Williamsburg Bridge once," I said, holding my hands up defensively. "I've been to the Cloisters. I know where to get the best whitefish salad in the city. I'm not a total monster."

"Okay, well, do you have thirty more minutes?"

"I've got all night," I said, my eyes bright, my words obviously flirty. I took a second to try to remember back months ago, when he seemed so cocky and loathsome on that bright NYN morning show set. How had this side of him not been evident all along? My brain struggled to remember exactly what about him I'd found so horrible in the first place.

"Perfect," he said, tugging at my wrist. "Let's go."

We crossed Fulton Street to the sidewalk that led us to the mouth of the bridge. Even though it was nearing eleven, there were people in packs ahead of us, enjoying the unending warmth of the day. The wooden planks of the walkway stretched on for what felt like forever, with the occasional cyclist speeding through the crowds in that no-bullshit way only a New Yorker on a bike can possess.

Up, up, up we went, the buildings around the edge of Manhattan rising to meet us. The farther we walked, the closer the Statue of Liberty seemed to get, almost like she was peeking around the corner, coming out to greet us. To the left of us, a Q train slogged its way over the Manhattan Bridge. Even though the city felt like hot soup, a cool breeze swept by us, and the sounds of the people milling around created a soothing cacophony of white noise. It was oddly meditative, and I wondered if Hayes felt it too. After about fifteen minutes of walking and weaving through crowds in silence, he rested a hand on my shoulder.

"Wanna sit for a sec?" he asked.

I nodded and followed him toward a bench that was, miraculously, empty. Even though I was in Converse, my feet were tired, and it felt good to sit. In front of us, a teenage girl in platform sneakers posed with her arms stretched out overhead, leaping in the air, as her mom snapped a photo. "Lemme see?" she asked, grabbing the phone out of her mom's hand. It took a second to register, but then I realized exactly what she'd been doing: Serena's pose, the one with the hashtag, which her followers did along with her.

At the thought of Serena, my brain immediately reached for all the usual insecure feelings I often clung to, but my heart piped in and pushed them aside. Cleo had said something to me that day we'd run into Serena in Central Park, something like "You're all those things, and more." It was true, and it was time I let myself believe it.

Gazing out at the harbor in front of us, I felt the oddest sense of calm wash over me. So much of the past few months had been filled with tension, and yet in this moment, I was at peace. I was reaching into my bag to snap a photo of the bridge when I noticed I had a new email. I peeked at it, just to be sure it wasn't something work-related. When I saw who the sender was, I gasped.

"What?" Hayes shifted to look at me.

I sat there silently reading for a second. "My half sister in Italy wrote back," I said finally, still not looking up from my phone, where I was rereading every single word.

"Oh my god." I grabbed for his arm excitedly on instinct, like I would reach for Lola or Cleo. "She sent some photos too."

The look on Hayes's face was utterly patient. "Do you feel like sharing what she said?"

I passed the phone over to him so he could read it.

Dearest Franny,

How wonderful that we both work in design. We are connected beyond just our DNA, it seems. My apologies for my delay. I have been traveling for work. Would you like to arrange a time to talk via video chat? My English is much better in conversation than writing. I've attached a recent photograph and a picture from when I was a baby, of me with our dad and our grandmother, Giuseppa. She's 88 and still lives in their village.

—Anna

"Wow," he said, passing the phone back to me. "How do you feel?"

"Okay," I replied, and I could almost feel my shoulders release, relaxing for the first time in forever. "Good, actually. Should I open the photos?"

"Of course," he said eagerly. "I mean, if you want to, then you should. Of course."

I pressed the first attachment, and a face popped up, smiling dark eyes, and curls like mine, only longer. Hayes leaned in over my shoulder.

"It's uncanny," he muttered. "Obviously, you're related. But still." I'd always assumed my hair came from my birth father, because everyone else in my family was walking around with fine brown hair. But to really see it, and know it, felt entirely different. The sureness steadied something inside me.

The next picture was grainy and harder to see, but there was a short older woman, with a handkerchief in her hair, gazing sternly at the camera. Standing next to her was a taller man, with a broad smile and thick jet-black hair that grew long on the sides, a slight mullet. In his arms was a tiny baby, with the same inky hair.

"My grandma's got a real resting bitch face going on," I joked, despite the racing of my heart.

"She looks like she doesn't take crap from anyone," he replied. "Reminds me of someone I know."

He said this with a playful nudge of his elbow to my ribs, and I felt a surge of self-confidence.

"I wish I could meet her." The words got caught in my throat. I knew all along that learning more about my newfound family would be intense, but I still wasn't prepared for the emotion it churned up inside me.

"You have to get to Italy," he said as if it were a thing I could do tomorrow.

"Someday," I agreed. Though I'd never offered up any further information, as far as I knew Hayes was still under the impression that my business was booming, an immediate success story. I knew I'd eventually have to come clean about it. But for now, this night was too good to spoil with my money woes.

"At least I can tell my sister I finally had gelato, so she won't be totally ashamed of me," I said.

"I'm sure she'll be very impressed," he said, a lightness in his voice that matched the smile on his face. "Have you told your mom?"

I shook my head. "I just don't know how she'd handle it. Any of it," I said, thinking of the other things I'd kept from her lately. "I'm seeing her this weekend, but I don't think it's the right time to tell her."

I tucked myself into him, so warm and inviting. I could feel the weight of what was unraveling between us, the unspoken acknowledgment that this—*this*—was something. We were people who shared things, intimate things, deeper than just kissing. All my worries, insecurities, and thoughts of not being good enough, suddenly seemed so pointless now. Because I knew that there was nothing that could compare to this.

"I know it's crazy that I've never been here before," I said. "But honestly, that's what I love so much about this city. That you can live here for years and still not have experienced everything. That there are still surprises left. That it's still..."

I stopped, searching for the right word.

"Magical?" he suggested.

"Yes!" I smacked his leg, and he laughed, my new favorite response to get out of him.

Hayes let out a breath, stretching his arms until they reached out behind us, resting on the edge of the bench and also gently against my shoulders. Warm skin on warm skin in warm air. Heaven.

"God, I love this stupid city." I leaned my head back, connecting to him with the smallest touch, though it felt like plugging into a socket.

"Same," he said with a nod.

"Are we doing that thing?" I asked him, pulling my knees into my chest. "Are we being tourists in our own city?"

"I mean, sure," he mused. "But I think it's good to look up and not take all of this for granted once in a while." He gestured with his free hand, waving it like a magician at the city and the river and the skyline stretching out in front of us. I knew exactly what he meant—New York could be overwhelming and all-encompassing, but sometimes—often—you moved through it without really seeing it.

And then his fingers pressed ever so gently against my neck, as if to say "*This too.*" It sent a jolt through the parts of my body I often forgot existed; I could feel the tendons in my calves come to life. I dared to glance to my right and caught a glimpse of his eyes crinkling into a smile as he stared straight ahead. He kept finding new ways to drive me crazy, and I didn't mind it. Not one bit.

CHAPTER TWENTY-TWO

HAYES

I WAS WALKING a tightrope between not wanting this night to end and not wanting Franny to catch on that I didn't want this night to end. I cared about what she thought of me, more than I wanted to admit, and the idea of appearing too forward or desperate, or annoying—or *something*—terrified me into subduing my excitement. But it was almost midnight, and we were standing on Front Street, pulling piping-hot slices of pizza out of a box and shoving them into our mouths. It had been Franny's turn to gasp in horror when I'd told her I'd never been to Grimaldi's before.

"You lectured me about never walking the Brooklyn Bridge, and yet you have the audacity not to eat the best pizza in the city, located directly *under* the bridge? Shame on you."

Her horror was earned—I'd give her that—but I made up for it by eating three slices without hesitation. The line in front of Grimaldi's had dwindled, and one of the cooks shuffled up to the window behind us and flipped the sign to CLOSED.

Rationally, I knew I should feel exhausted. The past few hours had been filled with food, alcohol, and walking. But I was on fire, fully charged. It felt like with every look in Franny's direction, my body would spontaneously combust or rocket into the air.

She took the now-empty box out of my hand without saying a word and walked it over to the blue recycling bin on the corner, the familiarity of this gesture sending a buzz from my heart to my stomach.

"So," she said, "I should head home."

I stuffed my disappointment down and nodded, opening my mouth to agree with her—perhaps too eagerly—that of course it was time for this night to end.

"Would you want to walk with me?" she said, cutting me off before I could start talking. My eyes darted to hers, and they were wider than normal. "It's not that far from here. Five minutes, tops."

"Yeah!" I sounded too eager. *Rein it in, Hayes.* "Yeah, of course."

I crossed and uncrossed my arms and then stuffed my hands in my pockets. When did my hands become so cumbersome?

"Although please remember that I am definitely going to give you a hard time again for never walking across the Brooklyn Bridge until tonight," I said.

"That's fair," she said, looping her arm through mine. "Although aren't you glad I waited to do it with you for the first time?"

I was.

Franny steered us down Everit, until we made a left on Cranberry Street. "Seriously?" I said as we passed the street sign. "Cranberry Street? That is so quaint it feels like it should be in a movie."

"It *is* in a movie." She turned and gave me the eye.

I shook my head. "I have no idea which one."

"Hayes," she said, annoyed but smiling. "Come on. I'll give you *Grease*, but this is a New York City classic."

"Um…" I actually tried to come up with something. "*Home Alone Two?*"

"Dear god, Hayes!" She let go of my arm and dashed into the middle of the street. "Who am I?"

She started pacing back and forth, kicking the air with her right foot.

"A Rockette?" I asked, genuinely perplexed. "That's literally my best guess."

She dashed back toward me, getting up in my face. "Hayes," she said, her grin wicked. "Snap out of it!"

I shrugged. "I'm seriously trying, but now I am just very confused."

"Oh my god, Hayes, I need you to come with me."

She grabbed my hand and dragged me toward a light-blue wooden town house with a white gate lining the street, and steps dotted with flowerpots that ended at a bright-red door.

"Is this your place?" I asked, marveling at how downright sweet it looked.

"Yup."

"You might live in the only house in New York City with a white picket fence."

She looked up from her purse, where she was digging for what I assumed were her keys. "I know. It's absurdly perfect, and I can never move, even though I should not be paying this much in rent right now," she said, clicking the keys into the lock of the basement apartment, the door swinging open.

"Come on," she said, ushering me in.

I'd be lying if I said I hadn't imagined Franny's apartment many times over in my head. For weeks now, I'd watched her delicately caress plants, sigh over lighting fixtures, and stare for what seemed like hours at empty walls, her brain churning in ways mine could never comprehend. I saw everything in lists and columns, numbers and equations. But Franny saw the world in shapes and colors.

Still, I wasn't expecting how light a space could feel, especially one so tiny and filled with color. Her apartment was about the same size as my new personal office. I followed behind her as she walked in and dropped her purse on a plush couch that seemed to take up the entire wall. In the bay window, a table stacked with books was surrounded by plants that surely clamored for all the light that must pour in every morning. I moved a few steps closer and could see the titles: *Rothko*, *Kahlo*, one simply titled *Uffizi Gallery*. Of course she'd devour art books.

A faded leather chair sat regal but unassuming in the corner, next to a mantel covered in soft twinkle lights and small pots of succulents. I bent to examine her fireplace, only to discover a small flat-screen TV inside, hidden behind a gold screen.

"You put your TV in your fireplace?" I said, marveling at her ingenuity.

She shrugged. "It was the easiest place to tuck it away. When it's behind the screen, you don't even notice it, and when I want a fire, I just find one on YouTube."

Her kitchen was small but spotless—wooden countertops, a small white farm sink. Even her fridge seemed half-size. A bistro table was nestled in the corner with just two chairs, a small pitcher holding crisp white tulips on top.

"Bathroom?" I asked.

"Here," she said, waving at me to follow. A few steps past the kitchen was a small bathroom, with barely room for one person. "This is technically a studio, but I put up this curtain rod so my bed feels like its own space." Her living room was one thing, but seeing her bedroom felt intimate, personal, like knocking on someone's door and having them answer in their pajamas. She tugged the curtain open, revealing a nook as bright and cozy as the rest of her place—a bed draped in a blue patterned duvet, yellow throw pillows, a small side table with a lamp and potted succulent. A book rested on the edge, and I leaned closer as I walked by to get a peek. Nora Ephron. I smiled. We had been trying to out–New York each other all night, but the Ephron book pushed Franny just ahead of me to first place.

Her bathroom: black-and-white tile. I gazed into the mirror as I washed my hands in the tiny sink. What the hell was I doing here, close to 1 a.m.? What I wanted to do—drag Franny to her bed and never leave—was butting heads with what I felt I should do— say good night, head outside, and get a car back to Manhattan. Run. Maybe go into the office tomorrow, prep for my Seattle trip, rehearse my pitch.

Return to normal.

But walking back out into Franny's apartment, I was immediately hit with the smell of popcorn. *Popcorn?* She was standing over the stove, barefoot, shaking freshly popped kernels into a large glass bowl. "Beer? Water?" she asked over her shoulder.

"Um, water's good."

She grabbed two glasses and passed them to me. "Water's in a pitcher in the fridge," she said.

There went my great exit.

"Sure, yeah. And then I'll probably head back into the city," I said, admiring how, for a New Yorker, and a single one at that, Franny had so much food in her fridge. And not takeout containers either—neatly stacked Swiss yogurts and glass containers of sliced vegetables.

"Nice try, The Third," she said, turning to shove the bowl toward me. "I have one more thing to teach you before you can go."

She nodded toward the couch, moving first to slide over the fireplace screen, and then settled into a corner, curling her legs under her and grabbing the remote off the table by the bay window. I followed, planting myself on the other side of the sofa, putting our drinks and popcorn on top of a pile of Italian cookbooks that sat stacked on the floor in front of the couch. Her smart TV clicked on, and she tapped the remote with purpose until she found what she was looking for. "Okay, I'm gonna give you one last chance," she said, fixing her gaze on me. "Tell me you've seen *Moonstruck*."

"Francesca Doyle," I said, "forgive me. But I have not."

"And here you had the audacity to lecture me on my heritage while never having seen what is possibly the greatest New York love story of all time? I am sincerely offended."

"I thought SubwayQTs was the greatest New York love story of all time." I said it as a joke, but as the words left my mouth they felt anything but funny. They were honest and true.

"We're a close second," she said with a smile, running a hand through her curls. "Do you have to be up early tomorrow morning?" she asked, pointing the remote at me.

I shook my head. I was supposed to meet Perrine for a run at seven, but I had nixed that via text when Franny had taken a moment to lean over on the bridge and gaze toward the East River. It wasn't that I'd known the night would end up here, with me on her couch, trying not to show how nervous I was. But something inside me had felt hopeful that the night would just go on forever. And so I canceled plans I would never normally cancel simply because of that feeling. Because of *maybe*. Because of *what if*. Because there was something so *possible* about this night.

"Good," she said. "We're watching *Moonstruck*."

"*Moonstruck*," I said, my mind scrambling to place exactly which movie this was. "With Cher?"

"Yes, *with Cher*. What other *Moonstruck* is there?" She reached for a handful of popcorn and tossed a piece in my direction.

"Hey!" I swatted her away defensively. "I'm game. But what am I missing here?"

Franny's eyes narrowed. "Hayes..."

"What!" I said with a laugh.

"This is not only the most important representation of Italian Americans on film, but it takes place on this very street."

"Cranberry Street."

"Oh my god, *yes*, Cranberry Street. Why are you so clueless sometimes?"

There was something in me that twitched when she called me

clueless, that feeling of fear that maybe I was misreading things. But then she scrunched up her nose and smiled at me as she stretched out in my direction and leaned back into the couch cushions, the popcorn bowl between us. I tried to turn my attention to the TV as she hit PLAY, but my eyes kept betraying me and focusing on her instead. Every lean toward the popcorn brought us closer and closer together, until she finally moved the bowl to the ground, tucked a pillow under her head, and lay down so her hair grazed my thigh, just so.

Could she feel how tense I was? How every cell in my body was sending signals to that one spot on my leg to play it cool? I was barely holding myself together, contemplating whether I should simply ask, "*Is what I think is happening between us actually happening?*" or just bend down and press my mouth against hers, no words said. Instead, Franny twisted in place, looking up at me with a smile, and then grabbed my hand from where it rested on the back of her couch, tense and electric, and brought it down to wrap around her, her fingers laced in mine.

I expected this to undo me, but instead my shoulders relaxed. The sensation of my hand against hers soothed me, like the feeling of a cold washcloth pressed against my feverish forehead as a kid. I could breathe again. I traced slow circles on her skin with my thumb. Everything in my body slowed, as if to say *This is where you should be. Stay.*

And then, to my own shock, I got sucked into the movie unfolding before us. I got why Cher and Nicolas Cage yelling at each other about love was intoxicating. It was loud and passionate and angry, but it was honest and pure too, and watching their back-and-forth made me think of Franny and me. It was messy, but it made complete sense. *We* made sense. About halfway through the movie, I leaned down to tell Franny, but she was folded into herself and fast asleep.

It was nearly 3 a.m. when the movie finished. Franny was still asleep on the couch, our empty glasses and decimated popcorn on the floor, our hands still entwined. One of her legs had stretched out, and I'd stared longer than I cared to admit at the curve of her calf, her smooth skin. I felt delirious, exhausted but still wide-awake. I gingerly untangled our fingers and slid up and off the couch slowly so as not to wake her. There was a gray knit blanket slung over the back of the couch, and I draped it over Franny. I grabbed our glasses and the popcorn bowl, and crept to the kitchen, sliding my socked feet along the old floors so as not to wake her with the sound of creaking wood.

Watching her sleep felt oddly personal and also quietly comforting, but then again—perhaps a little weird. Should I still be here? I looked at her front door; there was no way to lock it from the outside, so if I left now I'd be leaving her door open to the world. I pondered my plan as I rinsed out the cups and bowl, placing them on her dish rack. I felt strange staying, but leaving her here with her door unlocked just wasn't an option.

That was it. I was staying. I took off my jacket and folded it over a chair. Then I grabbed a pillow off the couch to tuck under my head, and I lay down on my back, my body on the floor next to where Franny slept, dead to the world. I closed my eyes and thought about *Moonstruck*, and what it means to remember that falling in love is possible.

— *mm* —

"Hayes?" There was a voice, and a warm hand, and something hard against my back. I kept my eyes shut, determined to stay asleep.

"Hayes." The voice was firm now, the hand, too, pressing into my chest with a shake.

"Mmm."

"Are you asleep on my living room floor?"

The voice jolted me awake. I had drifted off, forgotten that I'd decided to lie down until Franny woke up and I could leave with her safely locking the door behind me.

"Hey, yes." I squinted my eyes open, and there was Franny's face peering over the edge of the couch, lit up by sunlight.

"What are you doing down there?" She leaned over and tousled my hair gently, pushing it off my forehead.

I stretched my arms overhead. Shit, my back was killing me.

"You fell asleep during the movie, and I didn't want to leave, because your door only locks with a key. I figured I'd stay until you woke up."

I pushed myself up to sit. The long, meandering night had finally hit me. It hurt to move. Franny leaned forward on her elbows and then turned to look at her legs before looking back at me. "Did you put a blanket on me?"

I nodded.

"And you stayed here on the floor instead of waking me up and having me lock the door behind you. Or sleeping in my bed."

"Yeah." I ran a hand through my hair, which was sticking up at all angles. Those ideas hadn't even crossed my mind. Just the mention of her bed kicked me awake, imagining the thought of us in it. Not sleeping. God, I felt ridiculous.

"It's"—she squinted at the watch on her arm—"ten twenty-four."

"I haven't slept this late since college," I said, twisting to give my back a crack. "I've normally run six miles and done a bunch of work by now."

"You're a terrifying machine," she said with a laugh.

"I'm sorry I ended up crashing here. I'll head home."

"Okay, or"—Franny's hand was suddenly on me, my shoulder, fingering the edge of my button-down—"you could stay."

CHAPTER TWENTY-THREE

FRANNY

"STAY." HAYES'S VOICE was unsure, and his tone made me realize the gravity of what I'd just suggested. It's why I'd kept extending our night, over and over again. I didn't want our time together to end. I wasn't ready for him to leave; I wanted his hand back in mine for a little bit longer.

"Yeah," I said. "We could get some coffee, go to the farmer's market. Make a day of it?"

And then it dawned on me: I was stalling. I was holding out because I knew where this was headed. And, god, I liked teetering in this spot, that moment when you're strapped in and standing on the edge, about to jump out of the plane. This feeling sometimes felt better than the actual fall.

"Coffee," he said. "And bagels?"

"Oh, definitely bagels."

I grabbed some jeans and a tank top out of my drawers and shuffled into the bathroom, where I blotted my face with a makeup-removing wipe and brushed my teeth. I stared at myself in the mirror and remembered how, just days ago, I had told Hayes I didn't want anything to happen between us. I realized now I'd been afraid, and it had been easier to shut things down than to actually say yes to the thing I wanted. I don't know if it was the gelato, or the moonlight, or the magic of the Brooklyn Bridge, but somewhere over the East River I decided: Maybe it was okay to go for exactly what I wanted for once. And what I wanted was Hayes.

"I promise you it's worth the walk to Court Street for these bagels," I said as we trudged down Henry Street, past the less worthy bagel shops that were closer to my apartment.

"Are you trying to out–New York me for a second day in a row?" he joked, casually linking his fingers through mine, sending my head spinning.

"Aren't I always, Hayes? Haven't you figured this out by now?"

Later, bagels sufficiently devoured (egg and cheese for me, cream cheese and lox for him), we wandered toward the farmer's market with giant coffees in hand. The air was still slightly cool and humid, with an overcast sky hanging low and heavy with gray clouds.

"Do you mind if I grab some stuff for this week?"

"Of course not," Hayes said between sips.

"If you have to go...," I began. I wasn't sure how this time together had started, and I definitely didn't know when it was supposed to end.

"Franny, my day is wide-open."

"What about work? And six-mile runs?" I asked, feeling self-conscious that maybe he had better things to do.

"Those things can wait. Nothing could possibly be better than spending time with you."

He bit his lip, smiling at me. Was he always this romantic? This soft and kind, this intimate with his feelings? Something about him had shifted. Overnight? Or over months? Had romantic Hayes secretly been there all along?

"When did you get so smooth?" I asked with a whack on his arm. He grabbed at my hand and tugged me toward a table full of fiddleheads.

I went overboard, per usual, but still managed to stay on budget, grabbing raspberries and three pounds of peaches, and a container of fresh cavatelli from the pasta guy I loved so much. As badly as I was trying to save my money, this is where I liked to let it all go out the window. Hayes offered to help me lug the bags to my place, and we headed back down Montague Street, window-shopping along the way.

I felt the first drop as we turned onto Hicks Street.

"Uh-oh," Hayes muttered just as I looked to him to ask him if he'd felt it too.

"Rain?"

"I think we're about to get dumped on."

"Should we make a run for it?" I asked, and thunder rumbled overhead in reply. We still had about six more blocks to go.

"Can you run with bags of groceries in your hands?" he asked.

"I mean, I can try!" But the second I said that, they felt ten pounds heavier.

"Let's just commit to it, then," Hayes said, returning to that unnaturally calm and collected person I knew him to be, unfazed by everything. "We're going to get wet whether we run or walk. It's inevitable. It's already happening. I think we just have to embrace it."

His words hung there between us as we crossed Pierrepont, until our silence was split by another rumble of thunder. The skies opened upon us and covered us whole.

I shrieked with laughter, and Hayes lifted his arms, bags in hand. Embracing it. It was moments like this that I wish actually went viral, when joy is so pure and unadulterated that it just comes out of us without thinking.

There was no point in racing home, and so we marveled in it: the utter drenching of the world around us, the crackling of the sky, the way everyone else seemed to race by in an attempt to get cover. But he was right. There was no point in trying to avoid the inevitable. You could seek shelter, but you could never really avoid the downpour. Eventually, you have to surrender to the rain.

Back in front of my apartment, I grabbed my keys out of my canvas purse—sopping like a used rag—and unlocked the door, kicking off my shoes. "Holy shit!" I said, dumping the bags on the floor.

"I mean, at least I don't need to shower today," he said as he gingerly set down the three bags he was holding and shut the door behind him.

"No, that was like a week's worth of bathing," I said, smiling.

He stared back at me, also smiling, his eyes examining my face. "You're soaked," he said, his voice gravelly and low. I nodded, grabbed a dry dish towel from the counter, and stepped toward him. It felt like the space between us was going to explode: another downpour, endless thunder, the fiery crackling of light.

I reached for his face with my hands, grabbing his chin in one and wiping his wet brow with the other. He leaned forward, grasping my waist, his hands firm over my hip bones. I sighed, and all the sensation in my body rushed to where his hands held me, so secure, like if I went limp he could still prop me up. It was everything I'd grown to like about Hayes in one simple gesture—his constant desire to fix things, help, hold things together. No matter what.

There were a million words I could say in this moment. I could make a funny quip about the weather, or thank him for carrying all those groceries, or comment on his clothes—but before I could open my mouth, he was there, his lips on mine. Hayes Montgomery was kissing me, hard.

I threw the dish towel over my shoulder, not caring where it landed. My brain went to the groceries for a hot second—*Should I put them away? Are they perishable?*—before I scolded myself for even thinking of doing anything but this, right now. This felt urgent, important, and, god, his wet hair felt good against my hands. Last night had felt timid and exploratory, a tentative introduction to what might come. But this was frantic, needy, desperate. I pushed him forward with my body.

"We should take off these wet clothes," I murmured in between kisses.

"I don't have anything to change into."

His lips pressed against my jaw, his teeth grazing my neck, my shoulder blade.

"I don't *want* you to change into anything." I felt his teeth nip harder into my neck in response, followed by the softest of kisses. He led me toward the kitchen, guiding me until my body was up against the counter. His hands moved from my hips to the back of my thighs, and he lifted me in one fell swoop onto the edge. I wrapped my legs around his hips, and he ground into me, responding to the pressure of my body against his.

"Is this okay, Francesca?" he asked, and I almost imploded right there at the way my full name rolled out of his mouth.

"It is very okay. It would be even more okay if we went to my bed."

That was all he needed to hear. He lifted me off the counter, my arms around his neck, my mouth on it too, his body stumbling forward. "Watch your head," he said protectively as he moved us down the short hallway.

He lowered me to the floor, and his hands grazed the edge of my tank top. Then he lifted it up and threw it off. I tried to do the same with his shirt, but it was wet and heavy, and it got stuck on his head. He reached up to help me, and we both started laughing. I grabbed at my jeans, but the rain had glued them to my body, and it was taking every muscle in my arms to pull them down. I collapsed onto my bed, pants crumpled at my knees. "Hayes," I said, "I am going to say something incredibly unsexy to you right now, and I hope it doesn't kill the mood."

"Anything," he said. His face was open and patient, and I knew in that moment that there was nothing I could say to this man that he would find uncomfortable or embarrassing. He'd seen the most raw parts of me from the first time we met, and he was still here.

Also, his chest. Holy shit, his chest. I had wondered what was underneath all those perfectly laundered, crisp button-downs. And here was my answer: tight muscle and soft dark hair, smooth skin that stretched on for days. If Hayes's chest was already the death of me, I might not live long enough to see him fully naked.

"My pants are stuck," I said, gesturing at my ankles. "Can you just, you know, yank them off?"

"Is this your version of dirty talk, Franny?" He smirked at me. Fuck, he was hot when he flirted.

I leaned back on the bed and lifted my legs, and Hayes pulled my jeans off in one swift motion. His pants dropped more easily to the floor, and he kicked them to the side and then climbed over me, sliding a knee next to my hip.

"Hi," I said, gazing up at him, his damp hair falling forward and touching my forehead.

"Hey," he said back, holding my gaze.

"Our underwear is wet too. We should probably take that off."

He nodded gravely. "I would hate to get your bed all wet," he said. Together, we slid back, our heads on the pillows, his hand tracing a line down my arm, across my ribs. He unhooked my bra with a flick of his fingers.

"Wow," I said, shifting the straps off my shoulders. "One hand."

"I'm good with my hands," he said, a lopsided grin creeping across his face.

"Oh my god, who are you?" I laughed a kiss onto his mouth.

"You set me up with that one," he said. "But it's also true."

I pushed his boxer briefs down, then let him slide them off his legs as I lifted my hips and dragged my own underwear off slowly, knowing his eyes were on every move I made.

He ran a hand down to my calf and up my thigh, planting soft kisses on my stomach.

"I have condoms in my drawer," I said, cutting to the chase.

He looked up at me, sliding back so our faces were flush. "Is all this okay?"

"This is the most okay thing to happen to me in a long time." I laid a hand on his cheek. "But if you want, we can slow down. Take a break. Go get some coffee from Café New York."

"Oh god," he groaned, remembering our awkward NYN coffee date. "For you, I would." He laughed as he kissed me gently, letting his mouth move from my lips to my brow, to my neck, and then my shoulder. "What do you think," he said, his voice breathy, "that girl who took those pictures of us on the subway would say if she could see us now?"

"I think she'd be pleased at how right she was." I rolled my hips against him, the pressure of his body a pull I was unable to resist. "That we might just be Subway QTs after all."

"Can I call you 'my QT,' Franny?" Hayes asked as he licked my nipple ever so gently, pulling his teeth across my breast in a way that caused every hair on my body to startle.

"As long as if, after that, you promise to never, ever say that word again," I said, before letting out a moan.

"I promise," he said, moving his mouth to my other breast, his tongue hot on my skin, leaving my body cold and wanting the second it left. "Do you promise?"

"Yes." I would promise him just about anything if it meant he would never, ever stop.

―――

Franny: What would you guys do if I told you I just had three orgasms.

Cleo: With an actual person or w your vibrator?

Franny: Not just with an actual person. With HAYES.

Cleo: STFU

Franny: ☀

Lola: omgomg I KNEW THIS WAS GOING TO HAPPEN

Franny: Yes how convenient you all couldn't make it to dinner last night. Nice plan.

Lola: BUT IT WORKED

Franny: Don't tell Perrine!

Cleo: Can I tell the guy from Bumble who I'm about to meet for coffee?

Franny: I hate u both.

Lola: Go ice your vagina, Fran!

Lola: Cleo, report back.

Cleo: I'll let you know if he looks like someone who can go 4 three orgasms

Franny: 🙏

Franny: ♡

CHAPTER TWENTY-FOUR

HAYES

WHEN I OPENED my eyes again, I was alone in Franny's bed. Her room was dark, the rain still pounding outside. I sat up, rubbing the sleep from my eyes. The clock on her bedside table read 6:03 p.m.

I peered over the edge of the bed, but my clothes were nowhere to be found. There was, however, a folded shirt and pair of pants perched precariously on the bedside table next to me with a Post-it on top. *"Drying your clothes. Put me on,"* it read.

I was just yanking the T-shirt over my head when I heard the wood floors creak. "Hey." It was Franny. Still wet, but this time from the shower. She was wrapped in a cream-colored towel, her hair in ringlets around her face.

"Hey," I said. "Thank you for the clothes."

"I thought you'd look good in my high school boyfriend's Dave Matthews Band shirt and my biggest pair of flannel pants." She winked, shuffling by me to her dresser. "I hope it's okay that I put your stuff in the dryer. I read the tags—it's all machine-washable."

"Of course," I said, watching from the bed as she slipped on a pair of gray sweats and a striped long-sleeved shirt.

The whistle of a teakettle piped up from the kitchen. "Be right back."

I swung my legs over the bed, sliding into the pants. They were a little short but did the trick. I stretched, my body aching in the best way possible. I was still too out of it to really process what had gone down this afternoon. I mean, yes, sex. And more sex. But also words uttered. Body parts touched. Moans and sighs and promises of things.

I followed her trail out into the kitchen, where she stood over two steaming mugs. The groceries we'd picked up earlier were spread out on the counter: bok choy and cucumbers, and tomatoes so juicy they looked like water balloons about to explode, a container of fresh pasta, and some hand-rolled pretzels.

"Thanks." I grabbed a mug and leaned against the counter, watching her organize and sort.

"So...," I started.

She glanced at me, a small smile on her face.

"Would you want to hang out tonight?" I asked it at the exact same time as she said, "Do you want to stay for dinner?"

She laughed. "Yes, let's hang out. As long as it involves eating some of this food."

"I'm game." I blew on the tea, inhaling its sharp peppermint scent. "What were you thinking of making?"

"Well, I have fresh pasta, tomatoes, basil, goat cheese, and some arugula, and that baguette I made you lug home."

"It's not soaked through?" I asked.

"I think we can make it work," she said, pressing tentatively on its crust.

"That sounds incredible. You tell me where to start, and I'll sous-chef for you."

Franny set me up with a cutting board and a sharp knife, and I set to work chopping tomatoes into small cubes and tossing them in a large bowl. Next to me, Franny washed the arugula and basil, the latter of which she handed off to me to be minced into small pieces and added to the tomato.

With the two of us working together, it wasn't long before we were setting dishes out on the table, a heaping bowl of fresh pasta with a no-cook tomato sauce between us. Franny had whipped up an arugula salad with lemon and olive oil, and she'd torn the bread into bite-size pieces and toasted it to get a bit of crunch. She poured some wine into a carafe and grabbed two tiny old jam jars from a cabinet. Outside, it was still pouring. Franny shut off the AC and pushed open the windows, letting in crisp air and the sweet smell of rain on concrete. "It's actually kind of cool out there," she said. "The air feels good."

The sounds of the city wafted in as we sat down to eat. Our dinner was simple and bright, full of big, filling flavors. But it was also quiet, with easy banter about our usual weekend activities. Franny liked to catch up on reading and walk around Prospect Park; I tended to run and clean, and watch too much baseball. It was stuff that we did on our own, stuff that suddenly seemed a lot more appealing when imagining doing it with someone else. She told me about the baby shower she'd been dragged into planning with her mom, the endless messages she'd been getting from her for weeks. I gave her the rundown on my Seattle trip and the early talks of maybe opening a San Diego office too.

Later, as I did the dishes, Franny tucked herself back into that corner of the couch, her laptop open and teetering precariously on the edge of the sofa arm as she crafted a reply to Anna's latest email. I liked seeing her like this, her guard down, relaxed. It felt natural, like we did this every weekend. *What if we did this every weekend?* I asked myself. What if sometimes I came out to Brooklyn, or she brought her stuff into the city and we walked along the High Line or sat by the fountain at Lincoln Center and watched the people heading into the opera. I hadn't let myself wonder what it might look like to share the slow moments of my life with someone else again. But they felt immediately brighter imagining Franny there with me.

When I finished, it was inky black outside; the night had somehow snuck up on us, surprised us with darkness. Not that I had been paying attention to anything other than Franny today. I shuffled over to the couch, sitting much closer to her than I had last night. She snapped her laptop shut and placed it on the floor, running a hand down my thigh. "Before you even suggest that it's time for you to go, I want you to know that I'd love for you to stay. Here. And not just because I want to force you to watch more eighties movies with me."

"You mean we're not watching *Sixteen Candles*?" I placed a chaste kiss on the edge of her neck, where it sloped up to meet her chin.

"I mean, that movie is wildly problematic by today's standards, so hell, no. And I don't feel like watching *Grease*, as shameful as it is that you haven't seen it."

"What should we do, then?"

Franny turned to face me, placing her hands flat on my chest. "I have a long list of ideas, if you're open to hearing them."

She tucked her fingers into my waistband, scraping her nails gently along my skin. With one swift movement, she had gone from sitting next to me to straddling my lap, her hands now wrapped around my hips. She placed a delicate kiss on my cheekbone and then traced her lips to my ear, then down my neck. Instinctively, I pressed her into me, wrapping my arms around her back, and let out a long sigh into her neck, resisting the urge to lift her up and carry her to her bed—or, better yet, the kitchen counter.

"I'm listening," I said. The words came out rough, like wheels on gravel.

"Well, the most important thing to know," she said, "is that every one of them involves you completely naked."

The next morning, I woke up again in Franny's bed. But this time, I wasn't clutching a pillow. I was holding her. She was splayed across my chest, face-planted and out, one arm draped over my stomach. My arms were wrapped around her like she was a safety blanket. "Franny?" My voice was a hoarse whisper. I got no reply. She was out, and so I lay there, doing absolutely nothing but enjoying the sensation of her body pressed against mine, the way her bare skin felt against my fingers, her rhythmic breathing lulling me back into a quiet, meditative place.

I wasn't used to lying still, to indulging my senses in what was happening in the present. Normally, I woke up before my alarm, grabbing my phone before my eyes were even open. Scrolling emails. Devouring news. Paying bills. But here, in Franny's bed, I wasn't even sure where my phone was. And I didn't want to leap out of bed, torch my adrenaline, start my day. I felt perfectly content for the first time in maybe forever.

Franny stretched awake and leaned back to face me. "Hey," she said, rubbing her eyes.

"Morning," I said softly, running a finger down her nose.

She rolled over to look at her phone and groaned when she saw the time. "I really do not want to take the train out to Connecticut today."

"Baby shower time?" I asked, trying not to let her hear the disappointment in my voice.

She nodded and slid next to me, her head tucked against my shoulder. "Can we hang out tomorrow night? I could come to you?"

"My flight to Seattle is at six fifteen tomorrow morning. I'm back Thursday night."

"Noooo," she moaned.

"You could come stay at my place tonight?" I suggested, determined to figure out a solution.

"I don't think I get back into the city until, like, ten o'clock." She ran a hand down my chest, then from hip bone to hip bone, and I sucked in a breath.

Franny giggled. She knew exactly what she was doing to me. Suddenly, she sat upright. "Screw it," she said. "I'm not going."

"Aren't you supposed to be helping your mom?" I asked.

"Shh." She pressed a finger against my lips. "Please don't talk me out of this."

She grabbed her phone, and as she typed out a message to her mom, I took my time kissing my way across her shoulder blades.

"Done," she said, twisting around to wrap her arms around my neck, shifting to straddle me. "I told my mom I had a migraine. I didn't tell her that my migraine was gorgeous, and naked in my bed."

She pulled me toward her, kissing me deeply, and every thought in my mind evaporated into dust.

Later, we made pancakes from scratch together as NPR blared from Franny's phone, and topped them with some of the raspberries we'd lugged home in the rain yesterday. We spread out over her tiny table, passing pages from the Sunday *New York Times* across to each other as we ate in silence. It was achingly intimate, and resonated with me just as deeply as sliding next to her naked in bed did. Sex was one thing, but comfort, finding contentment in the quiet, that was something else altogether. Our actions were as unhurried as our day: We read, we sipped, we took leisurely bites. The silence was interrupted when Franny kicked me with her foot and asked, "Am I going to have to fight you for the crossword?"

I sighed dramatically, handing the *Magazine* over begrudgingly.

"Okay, fine, I'll share." She planted a kiss on my forehead as she stood and grabbed two pencils from a cup on the little shelf by the window.

She tried to hand me one, and I waved her off. "Do you really think I do the crossword in pencil, Franny? It's pen or nothing."

"Wow, that's the hottest thing anyone's ever said to me." She leaned forward and kissed me before heading back to grab a pen. Then we splayed out on the couch and spent the next thirty minutes scribbling and debating.

"Well, that was way faster than when I do it on my own," Franny said, looking at our completed work.

"I'm proud of us." I leaned forward for a high five. "Who knew we'd make such a good team. I'll be honest, sometimes I skip Sundays, because it's too hard for me."

"Wow, Hayes has a weakness! And here I thought you were chiseled, nerdy perfection."

I rolled my eyes, but her opinion thrilled me. Even if it was tongue-in-cheek, there was something in her voice that told me she also thought it was true. Just a little.

"I'm glad I stayed here with you," she said, draping her legs over mine. "It's been a while since I did something I wanted to do, just for me."

"I am too." I cupped her face in my hand, kissing her softly. I pulled back slowly. "Was your mom mad?"

She shrugged. "I haven't heard from her, but she's been entertaining twenty very loud women all day. She probably went to bed immediately after."

"Hey, what time is it?" I asked her, leaning forward to tap on her watch.

"Almost six. Wow." She raised her eyebrows at me. We were now going on almost forty-eight hours together, and we had been dancing around some things the entire time: How was this weekend going to end? And when? And, most importantly, what did all of this mean?

I stood and stretched, bending at the waist until my hands touched my feet, decked in a thick pair of Knicks-themed socks Franny had tossed at me this morning.

"So I should probably head back to my apartment," I started, even though I didn't want our time together to end. "I have an entire inbox and a client report I've been putting off since dinner on Friday, and I have to read up on the candidates I'm interviewing this week. And I have to pack."

"Well, that won't be hard for you," she said, pulling on my earlobe with a smile. "Just pack all your suits."

"Rude," I teased, poking her in the ribs as she squealed.

"What if…" I hesitated and then made myself ask. "What if you came back to my place tonight? Bring your laptop, some clothes. We can order in and do some work together."

As soon as the words were out of my mouth, I began to doubt myself, but she smiled. "Okay," she said with a nod, gathering the paper on the floor. "I just need a few minutes to get organized."

"Of course," I said.

"Just so I'm clear," she said as she stood up, "you're enjoying this weekend as much as I am?"

Her words extinguished all the nerves I'd just battled. I rose to meet her, and my hands grazed her jaw, toying with the hair that fell at her ears. "More," I promised, leaning in for another kiss. "Seriously."

We locked eyes, and I could tell she was searching to confirm that I was being honest. Satisfied, she smiled and ducked out of my hands. "Let me just get my stuff together."

I busied myself by tidying up our breakfast spread, walking dishes to the sink, recycling the newspaper, rinsing out coffee cups. I smiled as I worked, marveling at how strange the events of the past few months had been. I'd always thought the idea of fate, of the universe, of the magic of life, to be utter bullshit. But here I was, washing the lip gloss off a mug that belonged to the stranger who barreled onto my subway car one day. Life might not be magic, but it sure was something.

"Wait, say that again?" Franny's voice pierced through my

thoughts, the pitch a bit higher than normal. Urgent. "Slow down. I can't understand you."

Was she talking to me? I peered my head around the corner, dish towel in hand. Franny was pacing in front of her bed, phone pressed against her ear.

"When did this happen?" A pause. "Oh god, okay. I'll get there as soon as I can."

She was pale white, and she crumpled to the ground, leaning her back against her bed and clutching her knees. "That was my stepdad," she said, her voice tense and quiet. "My mom had a heart attack this morning, and she's at the hospital."

"Oh, no, Franny." I dropped to my knees to face her.

"He said she threw up while she was setting up tables in the backyard, and her entire left side was in pain, so he drove her to the emergency room. They caught it early, which is lucky. The nurse told him they call this kind of heart attack the 'widow maker.'"

I clasped her hands in mine, stroked her knuckles with my thumbs. Her face was calm, stoic, and it registered to me then that she might be in shock.

"I was supposed to be there." Her voice was pained. "She could have died."

I helped her up to sit on her bed, my hand on her back.

"Can you take me to the train?" Her voice was practically a whisper. "I need to get out there."

"Of course," I said, nodding reassuringly. "You stay here. Let me figure it out."

I rose to my feet, hustled to the kitchen, grabbed a cup from her dish rack, and filled it with water. She was still on her bed when I handed it to her. "Thank you." She gave me a small smile, and my heart squeezed.

Just as I was about to search for train info out to New Haven, an idea clicked in my brain. I opened Google. Sure enough, there was one of those short-term car-rental places around the corner.

"Hey." I reached a hand to her, and she accepted, letting me pull her onto her feet. "I will absolutely get you to the train if that's what you'd prefer. But it would be just as easy for me to rent a car and drive you there. I'd be really happy to do that. If you want."

Forty-five minutes later, I was behind the wheel of a Zipcar, Franny silent in the passenger seat beside me. I was used to things feeling abuzz whenever I was around her. There was always something coming from her: tears, laughter, excitement, information, energy, sass, new ideas. But she was uncharacteristically subdued: no crying, or texting, or commenting on my driving. Just her arms wrapped around her knees, her face toward the window.

"Do you want to listen to music?" I asked. She just shook her head, and so I kept driving in silence.

We didn't speak again until about halfway into our trip, when she turned to look at me, her voice low. "I just feel so bad."

"Franny"—I glanced at her quickly, trying to keep my eyes on the road—"what do you mean?"

"I lied to my mom," she said, her voice cracking. "Just because I didn't want to help her with some stupid baby shower. What a shitty thing to do to her."

I didn't say anything. I just listened.

She sighed. "I haven't even told my mom about Anna," she said with a sniffle, and I knew she was crying now. "And now I might not even get the chance."

I reached out to rest my hand on her knee.

"This whole time, I've been obsessing over a dead dad and a sister I'll probably never meet. And then I went and blew off the family I actually have."

"I'm so sorry, Franny," I said, giving her leg a gentle squeeze. "It sounds so hard. But I think both can hold space in your heart."

I cringed a little at how cheesy I sounded, but I also believed it wholeheartedly.

"Do you want to text your friends?" I asked. "Let them know what's going on?"

"No." She shook her head. "I don't have the energy right now. I'll do it when I get to the hospital."

She was quiet again. Outside, the sky was black. It was almost ten now.

"I'm glad you're here," she said with a slight press of her hand against mine. I shifted my hand, turning it so that it faced upright against her palm, and slid my fingers through hers.

"I am too," I said. "And I'm here as long you need me to be."

We stayed like that for the rest of the drive, hands connected. And I marveled that even in the middle of this very hard thing, being with Franny was the only place I wanted to be.

CHAPTER TWENTY-FIVE

FRANNY

MY MOM USED to say she knew I was really upset about something when I stopped talking. I wondered, as Connecticut rolled by in the darkness, if Hayes had figured this out tonight. I'd barely been able to find the words to match the grief, panic, and shame that were overpowering my thoughts.

I couldn't even bring myself to let Lola and Cleo know what was going on. Every time I looked at my phone to text them that my mom was in the hospital, that my mom had been admitted for the night, and probably longer, I couldn't. It wasn't that I didn't think they could handle it; they would walk through fire if I asked them to, just to be there for me. But typing the words made it all too real.

Hayes's voice cut through the darkness. "Hey, we're here," he announced. "Let me drop you off, and I'll park and meet you inside."

I nodded and opened the door, not looking back as I closed it.

When I got to the information desk, a woman with kind eyes directed me to the recovery unit. I texted Jim that I was on my way, and he met me in the lobby, greeting me with a quick hug as I got off the elevator.

"You didn't have to come all the way here," he said gruffly. His eyes were red and swollen, and he looked like he hadn't slept in a week.

"I know," I said. "But it's important for me to be here. Plus you need someone to get you coffee."

Jim ruffled my hair after I said this, a gesture that I knew meant *Thank you, I love you, I'm glad you're here.* He and my mom weren't particularly big on expressing their feelings, and Jim especially spoke more through gestures and acts of kindness than he did through words. It had taken me years to learn this, to come to terms that I was the only one of the three of us who needed to verbalize...well, everything.

"How's Mom?" I asked, trying to keep the tears at bay.

"Resting," he said. "But she's awake if you want to say a quick hello."

I followed him down a long hallway, lit up in a dull-yellow light. The sound of hospital machines beeping and ringing around us blended together to form a depressing melody.

We shuffled into a nondescript room, where my mom sat propped up in a hospital bed, her shoulder-length gray-brown hair spread out against crisp white pillows. Her skin was sallow, and an IV stuck out of her arm.

"Francesca Marie," she said. Her voice was hoarse but still, I could hear the disappointment. "What are you doing here? You're sick."

"Mom, you had a heart attack," I said, guilt filling me head to toe. I dragged a gray plastic chair over to the side of her bed as Jim plopped into the armchair in the corner of the room. "Did you really think I wouldn't come the second I heard?"

She smiled at this, and her eyes shimmered with the gloss of tears, though not a single one left her eye to travel down her face. She was a master at holding in a cry.

"I told Jim not to bug you so you could sleep off your migraine."

"I'm okay, Mom," I croaked.

I would need to come clean with her about everything soon, but now was not the time. She reached a pale hand out, and I took it in both of mine and gave her a squeeze.

Her gaze went from affectionate to inquisitive in an instant, her brows sharpening on her tired face. "How'd you get here?"

"A friend drove me," I said.

"Cleo?" she asked, her hand still in mine.

"No, Hayes."

"Your subway boyfriend?" She shifted against her pillows, sitting up a bit. "Franny, this is exciting."

She was smiling, but all I could see was how pale she was.

"Mom, he's just a friend. Please calm down. I don't want you to do anything that's going to make you feel worse."

"Oh, please, Franny, I'm going to be fine," she scolded.

An older woman with short black hair in nurse's scrubs came into the room, pushing a large machine on a cart.

"Hi, Diane," she said. "I've got to borrow you for a bit for vitals, and then you should take it easy."

"I'll wait outside, okay?" I said.

My mom nodded at this.

"I love you, Mom." Every muscle in my throat caught on the words.

"I love you too, honey."

I held in my tears until I got into the hallway. This entire day had been too much. Too much good feeling, too much doubt, too much fear. I found the family waiting room and collapsed onto a worn pink couch. Phone in hand, I opened my text messages.

One from Hayes. **Downstairs if you need me**, was all it said.

I opened up my text chain with Cleo and Lola. **Sorry for this very late message, but I'm out in CT with my mom—she had a heart attack. She's going to be ok I think. At hospital.**

Their replies came back almost immediately, but I closed my

phone and hit the DO NOT DISTURB button. I didn't have the energy for it right now.

I took the elevator back downstairs to the lobby, but Hayes was nowhere to be found.

I looked around for a moment, and then I heard him. He was outside, on his phone.

"I'm going to need to reschedule it, Eleanor," he was saying as I walked out the automatic doors, his voice firm. "I'm still at the hospital, and I don't want to leave her like this."

A pause. He paced, and I stood just outside the door, listening.

"Oh my god, no. You do not need to go." He was agitated and loud, a sight I'd never seen before. "I'll push everything to next week. There's no way I'm going to make my flight now, anyway."

He caught my eye, gave me a quick wave, and then put his head back down, listening.

"The investor meeting is just going to have to be canceled. Yeah. Yeah. I know it looks bad. I don't give a fuck."

He let out a sigh. He looked exhausted. He went silent again, and I started to feel sick, for real, my head throbbing. He was rearranging all his work stuff for me. This was horrible.

I stepped toward him, grabbing his arm. He moved his phone away. "Is everything okay?" he asked, a concerned look spreading over his face. "Your mom?"

"Do not cancel your work trip for me." My voice was firmer than I'd expected. I sounded mad. I *was* mad.

He put the phone back up. "Hey, I'll call you right back," he said, and then turned all his attention to me. "Franny, what's going on?"

"I cannot be the reason you don't go to Seattle." I crossed my arms over my chest.

"You don't get to decide that," he said, mirroring me. "There's no way I'm going to make my flight now. And I'd rather be here with you."

"I can't let you do that," I said, shaking my head at him. Why was he being so stubborn? "You can't cancel an investor meeting that affects your whole company, just because of me."

"Franny," he said, giving me a hard stare. "First of all, I can do whatever I damn well please."

I opened my mouth, ready to snap at him, but he spoke before I could get a word in.

"Look..." He paused, his eyes darting across my face. "I screwed up my last relationship because of work. And"—he sighed, lifted a hand, and dug it into the back of his neck—"I really don't want to do that again."

"Well, then I'll do it. Whatever this is between us, it ends now." My voice had gotten higher, louder. I was almost yelling. "I need to be here for my mom," I continued. "I blew her off, and I lied to her, just so I could stay in bed and sleep with you, and look what happened. I almost lost her today."

"Us being together didn't cause your mom to have a heart attack." His voice was calm but cold. "You said you wanted to be with me."

"Well, I wish I hadn't," I said. "I was stupid for even thinking we could be a thing. We're nothing alike."

He winced. My words had done something—something I didn't quite understand, but I knew that I'd hurt him.

I threw up my hands. I was unraveling. "And I still need to figure out what the hell I'm doing with my career and my business, when I have no jobs lined up and no money coming in."

His eyes scanned my face, trying to find a crack of clarity somewhere. "I thought your business was going well. You've been turning people away. You said so. In that interview—"

"I made that up." My entire body sagged, both from exhaustion and from the relief of finally being completely honest. "They were talking about how successful you were, and I just...I don't know, I just blurted out that I was successful too. I was too embarrassed to tell you I'd fudged all of it."

"So your work—"

"I'm not overflowing with clients, no. You and Eleanor have literally been my only client so far. I'm still trying to build my business, make connections, get whatever jobs I can. It's why I told Serena I'd be available to work with her." My voice broke on her name, and he looked confused. He wasn't the only one. "This is why I should have never kissed you!"

Hayes said nothing. Instead, he walked over to a bench where there were two coffee cups, picked one up and popped the plastic lid flap open, chugging back a huge sip. Putting it back down, he turned to look at me. "I didn't know if you'd want decaf or regular, so I got both," he said, gesturing to the cups. I hated him for being kind right now.

"I don't know what I did to make you think you couldn't tell me the truth," he said finally. "But if that's what you want, fine. The most important thing is for you to be with your mom."

I pressed my lips together, feeling hot and defiant.

"And you're right." He gave me a long, hard stare. "We're nothing alike. I should have known that all along."

"Thank you for everything today," I said, wobbling a bit. My entire body felt numb. "I owe you one."

A flicker of recognition registered on his face. I thought he might share, but instead he leaned over me and planted a kiss on the top of my head.

"Someday, Franny," he said, his mouth lingering, "I'm going to take you up on that."

He stood there for a moment, a pause that felt endless, and I almost expected him to take off his jacket and drape it over my shoulders, just as he did when we first met. But instead he turned without looking at me, digging his hands into his pockets as he left, lit up by the parking lot lights.

mm

I had just woken up when a giant delivery of bagels from Zabar's arrived at my parents' house. I tore into the package like an animal. I had barely eaten anything since yesterday afternoon, and suddenly it felt like everything that had gone wrong in my life could be fixed by a bagel, cream cheese, and lox. I ripped open the card. "*Food = love*," it read. "*xx, Lola and Perrine*."

Whoa. I knew Lola and Perrine were exclusive, serious even, but they were now at the send-a-sympathy-food-basket level of dating? I texted Cleo immediately.

Just got a Zabar's gift basket from Lola and PERRINE, I wrote.

!!!!!! Cleo wrote back. **Wait more importantly Franny how is your mom?**

Jim is going to come pick me up and take me back to the hospital. I think it's going to be a long recovery, but she'll be okay.

A series of heart emojis. **Thank god.**

I paused before I typed out the next thing I wanted to say. I had been up throughout the night thinking about it, agonizing over how I could actually help my mom. I texted Cleo my solution.

I'm going to stay out here for a bit to help out.

You're a good daughter, she wrote back.

Your brother could totally stay at my place for the month while I'm here, I replied.

Ew, Fran, no. He barely knows how to do his own laundry.

I laughed at this, though she was probably right.

I'm serious, I wrote. **I could definitely use the money, and then I can stay here and help my mom. Also I broke up with Hayes**

last night even though we were only together for like 24 hours. It was bad.

I didn't have the energy to type anything else.

Franny WHAT?!

I'll call you tonight I promise, I replied, **but I gotta go do mom stuff xoxo.**

Later, as I lay on my old twin bed, I thought about what it meant to be home. Growing up, I'd always felt out of place: With my mom and Jim. In my house. In my skin. But moving to New York, finding Lola and Cleo, discovering the world of art and design, creating my very own home in my little apartment—those things had shown me what it truly meant to belong. And then Hayes showed up in my life, and he felt both entirely new and utterly familiar, all at once. And all these things together made up the place I wanted to be more than anything in the world.

But I wasn't there, where I belonged. I was here, staring at the cracked ceiling of my childhood home. I flopped around, trying to get comfortable. I turned over, and on the bookshelf next to me was a framed photo of me as a little kid, hair long and tangled, sitting in my grandmother's lap, my mom seated next to both of us, her hand on my belly. We're all grinning, and our smiles look almost identical, a thread connecting the three of us. I let out a sigh, felt the tears creep back into my eyes. Even if this wasn't home—this place, this house, this family—they were still a part of me. And maybe in my own way, I did belong here too.

But there was one piece still missing, floating out there, ready for me to grab it. If I was ever going to truly know myself, I needed to know all of me. And so I grabbed my phone off the floor, opened up my email, and began to type.

Anna,

It's been a crazy week here. My mom is in the hospital after having a heart attack, which has been awful and scary, though she's doing okay. I'm still trying to figure out how to make the career I want in interior design happen.

On top of all of this, I met someone. A guy. Un uomo. (I'm trying to learn Italian!) He's not like anyone I've ever dated, and I ended things in the worst possible way. I hope you don't mind me dumping all of this on you, but it feels good to tell someone. Plus, you're Italian. You all know something about love, right?

I've never had a sister, or any siblings before. But knowing you're out there is really bringing me some comfort tonight. I hope we get the chance to talk more soon and, who knows, maybe even meet one day.

Love,
Franny (your sister!)

CHAPTER TWENTY-SIX

HAYES

ELEANOR STOOD WITH her hand on her rounded belly, eyes following me like laser beams as I walked into her new office and shut the door. She had texted me, **Get in here**, as soon as I'd walked in.

"I know what you're going to ask, and I don't want to talk about it." My voice was hoarse, the result of not sleeping. It was impossible to avoid eye contact with her, but I could at least avoid the conversation.

"Oh, we're going to talk about it." She had that no-nonsense tone, which meant one thing: She wouldn't give up on this easily.

I waved my hands in defeat. I sat down in the chair across from her desk. I had expected the way things ended with Franny to dull me, numb me, make me a shell. Instead, everything felt heightened, too bright, my senses exploding. I could feel every hair on my head, every fiber of cotton pressing against my skin. Losing Franny had only made me more aware of everything going on around me, everything without her in it.

"So on Saturday, you texted me and basically told me you had a girlfriend." She leaned forward, elbow resting on her desk, chin in her hand.

I sighed. "I never used that word."

"I bet you wanted to, though," she replied, her voice all-knowing.

"And?" I replied, impatient.

"And then last night you call from a hospital in the middle of Connecticut and tell me you can't go to Seattle because of her."

"Yeah," I said, like it hadn't been a crisis I'd forced her to get out of bed and deal with in the middle of the night.

"And now you're here hours later, in the office, and you're flying to Seattle tonight."

Eleanor crossed her arms on her desk and looked directly at me. "So are you going to tell me what happened, or am I just going to have to guess?"

"There's nothing to guess about. We were maybe going to be a thing, and now we aren't, and that's it."

"Maybe going to be *a thing*." She repeated my words back to me.

"Not even a thing, really." I couldn't tell if it was a hundred degrees in here or ten. I was sweating and freezing, and kept fidgeting in my seat.

"So you were going to cancel an entire week of important meetings for 'not even a thing'?" She was being tough, but her tone was kind. Eleanor was handling me with kid gloves, which meant she was able to tell what a mess I was no matter how much I was trying to hide it.

I ignored her. "Did you want to listen to me run through the pitch one more time? I'm not leaving for a few more hours."

"Oh, don't do that, Hayes." Eleanor gave me a sad look. "You can't just change the subject. I've known you long enough to know when things are more than 'maybe a thing.'"

I sighed and shrugged. "I'm not ready to talk about it, El."

"Well, finally, you say something you actually mean." She eyed me again, for a beat, and then her face went soft. "I'm sorry, Hayes."

"Me too," I admitted, which felt too raw, too honest. "But it was a bad idea to begin with. We made no sense together. It's for the best."

"And what's the best—you being alone and miserable? A total jerk to all of us because of it?"

I just sighed and crossed and uncrossed my legs. I was exhausted.

"I'm sorry. I didn't mean…" She spun in her chair as she thought. "What I meant is, I like you and her. Together."

"Mmm?" I feigned disinterest, but I was genuinely curious as to where she was going with this. She'd barely seen us together. And Eleanor had never expressed any sort of allegiance to anyone I'd dated, even when it was one of her own friends. She'd obviously taken my "side" through my divorce, but even as I worked through the end of things with Angie she never uttered a negative word about her. For her to come out in favor of Franny felt like a departure from her usual neutral stance.

"Most of the time you rely so heavily on certain…qualities of your personality. You know the things I'm talking about. The…stern side. Protective, analytical. But every time I saw you with Franny, or heard you talk about her, all the hidden sides of you I like even more kept showing up."

"And what sides are those?" I asked, leaning forward.

"You're unfailingly kind and generous. Spontaneous, when the mood strikes. And, dare I even say, funny."

"You didn't think I was funny when you were yelling at me about screwing up this pitch meeting last night," I said, managing to give her a snarky smile.

"God, and moody as all hell too."

At first, I didn't respond. I wanted to do what I always did before Franny entered the picture. Focus. Block everything out. Get sucked into the blue light of my computer.

Instead, I leaned back in the chair and pressed my palms into my forehead.

"I really liked her." My voice was quiet. "But it's done."

"Nothing's ever really done, Hayes." She looked at me with sympathy. "You just have to figure out how to bring it back to life."

—⁓⁓—

As the week went on, and turned into two, three, and then four, I only felt more certain things were over. The seasons were shifting, September was blooming as only it could, the leaves still clinging to trees in all their bright-green glory, wringing out the last vestiges of brightness before the darkness of winter set in soon. Perrine called. Eleanor and Henry had me over for dinner. I bought something called a DockATot off their baby registry in preparation for their baby shower next month. We settled into our new office, began planning for our next round of fundraising. Investors on board, I hired three people for our new Seattle space, and we'd asked Tyler to go out and open the new office there early next year. I ran five miles almost every day, then six. Seven. Nine.

Time moved forward. But Franny did not respond to my texts, or my voicemails. Maybe it was for the best; I wasn't even sure I'd know what words to say if she ever did pick up or write back. And yet I still kept thinking about her: what she was doing, whether she was happy, whether I'd ever get to see her smile again. But it was at home, in my apartment, that I missed her the most. And one day, her voice popped into my head. I could hear her, clear and sharp, accurately guessing all the things I had in my apartment and how sparsely decorated it was. So I went for it.

I hung a photograph Eleanor had taken for me of surfers cresting a wave in Montauk and a painting my grandmother did when I was little, a watercolor of her flower garden in August. I ordered a dining room table after digging through the file Franny had put together of all the vendors she'd used for our office. It was coming in two months from the same sustainable wood source upstate that she'd used for all our desks. I googled "indoor plants that are hard to kill" and made a list. Slowly, my space started to feel more like me, more like a place I wanted to share with people, even if the person I wanted to be there most of all was gone.

One night over Labor Day weekend, after an almost ten-mile run around Central Park, I wandered into my closet postshower, digging around for some sweats to throw on over my boxers and T-shirt. And there it was: my suit jacket. *The* suit jacket. It had been hanging there, untouched since Franny unceremoniously handed it to me at that morning show taping all those months ago. Dry-cleaned and pressed, pocket square tucked neatly in the front. It had felt like bad luck to wear it again, so I'd left it here, pressed between the wall and another navy-blue jacket, a relic of the moment that had set my life off course—or maybe, set it on course. I wasn't sure anymore.

I reached for it, sliding it off the hanger and holding it in front of me, thinking of Franny for what felt like the millionth time. I brought it to my nose, hoping for some hint of her there, but all that was left was the faint smell of chemicals. Suddenly self-conscious, I stuck the coat back on the hanger, grabbing the pocket square so I could stick it in my drawer with the others. As I did, a small folded piece of paper fell out and landed on the floor.

Dear Stranger,

Just in case I don't get a chance to properly say it today: thank you. I don't know why you did it, but you were there to help me when I most needed it, and I truly appreciate it. (Please forget that story I told you about peeing my pants, though.)

Yours,
Franny Doyle

She had been here this whole time, had known what I needed to hear. And, god, how I wished I could figure out how to tell her: I did it because the second I saw her, I knew she was someone I wanted to be near. I couldn't stop myself.

And then, just like that moment on the subway, I knew what I had to do. I dashed back into the living room, flipped open my laptop, and hammered out an email in seconds flat.

I know things are weird, but I'd love to talk. Could we meet for coffee?

I hit SEND before I could reconsider my words. I peeked over at some MLB scores, scanned Twitter, and went to shut my computer down, when I noticed that a reply had come through, only minutes after I sent my message.

Okay.

And then a minute after that, a second one.

Name a place, I'll be there.

―――

"I have to say, this was unexpected."

Lola leaned back in her chair, fingers wrapped around her to-go cup of coffee. Her mouth was set in a smile, her white-blond hair tousled on her head. Next to her, Cleo sat with her chin in her hand, observing me through her glasses. She too was smiling, but it did nothing to quell my nerves.

"I really appreciate you both meeting me." I fiddled with the silicone lid on my travel mug. "And I promise not to take up too much of your time." I bit my upper lip. Let out a breath. "Okay, well. The first thing I wanted to tell you both is that I care a lot about her."

"Are you asking us for Franny's hand?" Lola said with a laugh.

"No. I know Franny doesn't want anything to happen between us, and I get that." I sat up a little straighter, put on my best business-meeting face. "I just wanted to find out how she's doing. Make sure she's okay."

"She's okay," said Lola. "Hanging in there."

"It's nice of you to check in on her," Cleo said with a kind smile, followed by a sip of her tea. "I think it's been a tough month, but her mom seems to be doing much better."

"That's good. I'm really glad to hear that."

Cleo put her cup down and looked directly at me. "How are you doing, though?"

I shrugged. "Busy with work. We're expanding to Seattle, and maybe San Diego, or somewhere in California. So that's exciting."

"I mean, with how you feel about Franny." Cleo looked at me like she could read my thoughts. Lola nodded in agreement and then also turned her attention toward me.

My insides roiled. "Franny wants nothing to do with me, and I respect that. I can't change how she feels. That's not my place."

"God, for someone so smart, you sure are dumb sometimes." Lola's eyes rolled, but she was looking at me with affection. "Trust me, she definitely wants 'something to do with you.'"

She said the last words while waving her fingers in air quotes. A feeling deep inside me pinged with possibility, but I shoved it down.

"What I mean is, I know we're done," I said. "But I still care about her. That's why I reached out to you both."

"And because you want us to like you," said Cleo. Her voice was so gentle that it almost masked that direct hit of her statement.

"Well, yeah." I blinked, unnerved. She'd thrown me off my game. "Yeah, I do."

I cleared my throat and kept going. "You can't help wanting the friends of the person you're in—the person you're interested in to like you. Even if it isn't going to go anywhere." I took a sip of my coffee, trying not to let on how self-conscious I felt about admitting all this to them. "And also because I think you're both cool."

"Aw," said Cleo, taking a sip of her drink.

"And you're dating Perrine." I gestured to Lola. "And it's important for me to know you, and be your friend."

Lola's face softened instantly when I mentioned Perrine.

"Does she know about this?" I asked.

She waved a hand between us. "No. I'll tell her. But first I wanted to talk to you."

Lola shifted in her seat and leaned toward me. "As long as we're here," she said, "there's something I wanted to ask you. I need your help with something."

"Okay," I said, grateful for the attention to be off me. "Tell me what you need."

Lola leaned forward in her seat, sliding her hands onto the table. "I want to propose to Perrine, and I want you to help me to do it."

"Holy shit," I said. This was definitely not what I was expecting her to say. Cleo let out a squeal and clapped with excitement.

"Y-yeah," I stammered. "Wow. Of course I'm game."

"Good." Lola's smile was wide and wicked, and she brushed her bleached-blond hair off her face before reaching her hand across the table to shake mine. "Just so you know, I really wanted us all to go on a double date."

I laughed wistfully at this. "That would have been fun," I agreed.

"Who knows," chimed in Cleo. "Maybe you'll get the chance."

CHAPTER TWENTY-SEVEN

FRANNY

I'D NEVER BEEN more nervous in my life to see someone, and we weren't even meeting face-to-face. But for days, I'd been in a panic, nerves raging. Then finally the day arrived, and I spent hours prepping myself, getting ready. I washed my hair and shaved my legs, and spent a good fifteen minutes trying to do a cat eye with eyeliner before giving up and wiping it off, hoping the smudges on my lid weren't too noticeable. Then I changed my shirt three times, only to end up back in the first one I put on. And now there was nothing left to do but pick up my phone.

"Franny?"

That face, the voice: It was foreign and yet so familiar, all at once. It sent my heart racing, out of my chest, up into the sky, setting off fireworks.

"Hi," I said, my voice cracking. Was I going to cry? The answer came in an instant, tears sliding down my face. I grabbed a tissue from the box on Jim's desk, dabbed it in the corners of my eyes. "I can't believe it's really you."

There, on the screen, was my half sister.

She let out something that sounded like a laugh and a squeal.

"I cannot believe you're real!" she said, her Italian accent adding a melody to every word.

We stared at each other on our screens, smiling. Her hair was long, but curly like mine. Our eyes were different; hers were dark brown and wider set. But our noses both sloped up ever so slightly, and there was something about seeing her that just felt comfortable, like coming home at night to a light left on.

"How's your mama?" she asked, and I could see the concern on her face.

"So much better. Thanks for asking." I exhaled, releasing my nerves a bit. "I'm so excited to see you," I said. "I've been so nervous."

"Me too," she said. And, god, she was beautiful when she smiled. "I've been worried about what you would think of me."

"What?" I leaned back in surprise. "I'm so in awe of you, and all you've done. I've been following along on your Instagram, and you've done so much amazing work."

"Ah, well," she said, pulling a curl down and letting it bounce back up, then repeating the gesture. "A client just fired me from a huge job, but I won't put that on the internet."

"Shut up," I shrieked, a little too loudly. "That's ridiculous. You're so talented!"

She shrugged. "I'm glad that you think so, because I need convincing a lot of the time."

I eased into the chair, my back relaxing. "I know what you mean," I said. "I'm the same exact way." *Maybe it's genetic,* I thought.

"Well, tell me what's going on with work," she said. "Maybe all my mistakes can help you."

Thirty minutes later, after scheduling a date to talk again in a couple of days, I made my way into the living room where my mom was tucked under a blanket, watching HGTV. She'd been home from the hospital for almost a month now, but she still wasn't back at 100 percent.

Jim was at the grocery store, and I sat down at the opposite end of the couch, wrapping an arm around her socked feet.

"I could hear you in there, laughing," she said, turning her gaze toward me. "Were you talking to the girls?"

She meant Lola and Cleo, and I just nodded. "Yeah," I said, and then realized it was now or never.

"Actually, no." My stomach bubbled with nerves. This was it. "I was talking to a woman in Italy who I met through one of those DNA testing sites."

Our eyes locked, and I could see in her face she knew what I was about to say before I said it. "I took one of those tests in the spring, just for fun. But I found a half sister, from my birth father's side."

"Oh, Franny." Her face was unreadable, and all I could think was that I'd disappointed her yet again. "I'm so happy for you."

I leveled my eyes at her. "You are?" This was not what I'd expected her to say.

"I always wanted you to have siblings," she said, a hesitant smile breaking out on her face. "And to know more about that side of your family. I've always felt guilty that I've never been able to tell you much about your birth father. I barely had any info to go on. We didn't do a ton of talking."

She said this with a laugh, and in that moment I could imagine her, young and passionate, swept away by a handsome man with thick black hair.

"You never told me anything about him," I said. "I've always been too nervous to ask."

"It's hard to talk about," she said as she leaned forward and reached for my hand, giving it a squeeze. "You know, it was a different time. There's a lot of shame there for me, I think. And worry. I worry a lot about how I haven't done everything right for you."

This was the most we'd ever talked about my birth father, their relationship, and her feelings about all of it. It was new territory for us, and it felt raw and scary. But it also felt exactly right.

"He's not alive anymore," I said quietly. Delivering this news to her was unexpectedly crushing. Saying it out loud didn't just makes his death real; it made him real too.

"Oh, Franny," she said, her voice breaking. She slid her legs off the couch and scooted over to sit next to me, wrapping her arm around my shoulder. "I'm so sorry."

"I am too," I said, choked up. I'd never get the chance to know him, this person who was a part of me. It was a loss I was still processing.

"Thank you for not being mad," I said, leaning on her, feeling her warmth.

"Franny, how could I be mad at you?" She smiled at me, a look of pure love. My body loosened up the tiniest bit.

"Am I scared of you finding out something that might hurt you, or leave you feeling disappointed? Of course. I'm your mom." She said this with a shrug, like it was the obvious answer to everything. "I've always worried about that. But, no, I'm not mad."

"I'll be okay," I said, swallowing down the lump in my throat.

"I know you will." She leaned forward and patted my hand. "Look how well you've done since losing your job. You know you don't need to stay here for my sake, right? I'm on the mend, and you should get back to things."

And with that, I started to cry. Not dainty, delicate tears, like the ones that had arrived when I saw Anna just minutes earlier. And not the wet, blubbery, messy kind of cry, like what Hayes saw that day on the subway.

This was a full-body, chest-heaving tsunami of a cry, which exploded out of me without warning.

"Franny?" she asked, shifting her body to look at me, her voice alarmed. "What's going on?"

"I've screwed everything up." My voice came out like a wail, and I pressed my face into my hands. "I tried to launch my own business, and I did that one job, which was amazing. But I haven't had enough jobs lined up to keep up with bills and rent."

"But I thought you said on TV—"

"It wasn't the truth. It just came out. I was embarrassed and nervous, and I just wanted everyone to think I was doing okay. I wanted *you* to think that." The words spilled out of me. "I don't want you to think I'm a failure. I know you already worry about me not having a steadier career."

She took her free hand and brought it to my chin, lifting my face until our eyes met.

"Francesca Marie Doyle"—her voice was firm—"I've spent the last thirty years being in awe of you."

I sniffled and wiped my nose on my sleeve, and gave her a confused look.

"Occasionally, intimidated too," she said as she moved her hand to tuck a strand of hair behind my ear.

Surely, I thought, she was joking. But her face was completely serious.

"Nothing about me is intimidating," I said, chest heaving.

"*Nothing about you is intimidating*," she said back to me, chuckling. "Fran, you've known exactly who you were since the day you popped out of me. You worked jobs in high school so you could pay for your own art classes, and then when you got into NYU you were determined to go, even though everyone, including me, told you it'd be easier just to go to UConn and live at home. You moved to New York City at eighteen, and you've never looked back. You chose a career you were passionate about, and you've made it work. You've built a life for yourself—one you love—and you know exactly who you are. That's something most of us can't say. So, yeah, sometimes you are intimidating, in the best way possible. And, god, do I love it. I am so proud of you."

I took in a deep breath, and let it out through my mouth, steadying myself. "But you're always so worried about me."

"I worry about if you're happy. I worry that you're being too hard on yourself. I worry that you're not getting enough sleep."

I let out a small laugh at this.

"But I never worry about *you*, Franny, not really. If anything, I worry about anyone who tries to stand in your way. I know I'm just your mom, but you've always seemed unstoppable to me. The day you stop doing exactly what you want with your life, that's when I'll worry. Because that would be a failure. Not yours, but mine, as your mom."

"It's hard for me to shake this feeling that I just want to make you proud," I said. "And if I don't, I've messed up." I'd never been this honest with her before, and it felt amazing and terrifying, all at once. I yanked down the sleeves of my sweatshirt, and wiped my eyes with them.

"Franny, the only person who you need to make proud is yourself. Don't worry about me. I'll always be proud of you, no matter what."

Her words kicked the tears back into high gear. It was impossible to feel proud of myself when I'd hurt Hayes and screwed everything up between us.

"I lied about having a migraine, that morning. With the baby shower. I'm so sorry."

"Oh, honey, it's okay. I never said thank you for all you did to help me with that." She wove her fingers through mine, placed her other hand on top of my own.

"And I lied because of a guy," I said, finally getting the words out, my voice hoarse from crying. "The one from the subway."

"Hayes Montgomery the Third?" she asked, and I was so taken aback at her using his full name that I laughed.

"You know his *full name*?" I said, still shocked at having heard it come out of her mouth.

280

"I set up a Google Alert for him." She said it like it was obvious. "I have one for you too."

I shook my head at this. What a mom move.

"I screwed it all up." I let out a weary sigh, and she ran her hand through my hair, so gently, like she did when I was small. "I panicked about, well, everything—your heart attack, feeling like I was failing at getting work, how much I liked him. I said stuff to him that wasn't especially nice. I know you said I should be proud of myself, but I'm not proud of how I treated him."

"Well, what would make you proud, then?" she asked, still softly rubbing my head.

I thought for a moment. "Apologizing," I said. "I owe him one."

"Well, I think that's a great plan." She planted a kiss on my forehead, still holding me close.

"I really, really like him, Mom," I said. I could feel the heavy weight of longing for him in my bones. It hadn't left me. Even though our relationship had ended, my feelings hadn't.

"I know, honey," she whispered gently in my ear. "I know. I know."

Later that night, as I washed dishes, I heard a muffled conversation coming from the living room. Then Jim called, "Franny-Bananny!" I shuffled in, with the rubber dish gloves still on, plopping down in his raggedy old armchair.

"Hey," I said. "What's up?"

"Can you go grab the recycling bin off the porch and put it out front?" he asked.

"Sure thing," I said, hopping back up. I walked through the kitchen, tossing my gloves in the sink, and opened the door, stepping out into the sunporch they'd added on after I left for college. There, on my mom's wicker couch, sat Lola and Cleo.

"Oh my god!" I screamed as they rushed toward me, looping me into their arms for a hug. "Am I hallucinating?"

"You wish," Lola said, laughing into my hair. "But we are very real."

"How did you get here?" I asked, pulling back to marvel at them.

"It's bizarre," said Cleo, sliding out of her leather jacket with a smile, "but there are these things called trains."

I snorted. "Oh my god, how is it possible that you've gotten snarkier."

"We have some important things to tell you," said Lola. "And, honestly, we're both sick of texting you. We missed your face."

"Okay." I sat down on the love seat that was positioned across from the couch. I was so excited to see them that I couldn't stop my body from bouncing up and down ever so slightly. "What is it?"

"You first," Cleo said to Lola, whose face broke out into a wide grin. Cleo clutched her hands in front of her face, giddy.

"Cleo already knows," she said.

"What's going on?" I asked, nervous. Was she somehow pregnant? I glanced at the Van Halen T-shirt she was wearing and tried to see if there was any sort of outline of a bump.

She held out her left hand, which had been tucked in her lap, and waved it at me. Just below a dark-blue manicure sat a gold ring with a giant black diamond at the center, flanked by smaller, white diamonds.

"Holy shit," I said, trying to process what I was seeing.

"I'm engaged!" she squealed, in an excited octave her voice rarely hit.

"To"—I was still trying to wrap my head around it—"Perrine?"

She nodded, beaming. "I proposed."

"Oh my god, Lola!" I stood up and moved toward her, and she rose to meet me for a hug. "I am so happy for you."

I let her go and grabbed her hand. "Also, holy shit, that rock is big."

"It was her grandmother's," she said. "She said she'd been waiting for the right time to ask me, but I beat her to it."

"Holy crap. It's so beautiful." My eyes immediately overflowed with tears, for what felt like the fiftieth time today. "Oh my god, of course I'm crying again." I reached over to the side table for a tissue. "It's been a long day," I explained.

"Okay, well, hopefully this won't make you cry," said Cleo as she leaned forward, grabbing something out of her purse. "It just came out."

She passed a copy of *Architectural Digest* across the table. On the cover was a photo of Eleanor, in a long black tank dress and bright-red flats, perched on her desk. Hayes stood, arms crossed, next to her. Even this tiny version of him, so stoic and serious, shot a pang of longing through my heart.

"I've been dying to see this," I said reverently. The magazine piece, yes. But also, Hayes's face. I'd missed it.

"You need to read the article inside," Cleo said, grabbing the magazine and flipping through the pages before sliding it back to me. "Specifically…" She tapped to a paragraph on the page, toward the end.

I scanned the beginning, which was mostly a recap of Hayes and Eleanor's business, and the history of the office space, which was originally an old tannery. And then I followed Cleo's finger to this:

Franny Doyle's use of organic elements to highlight the former industrial space relied on repurposed materials, natural light, and colors that calm anyone who enters, providing a respite not just from the city but from the often dull or overdone design of today's modern financial centers. "Her vision and execution were integral to creating a workspace that represents the essence and soul of Arbor," Montgomery told AD. *"She represents the future of sustainable design."*

"Wow." I looked back up at my friends, attempting a calm and collected face. "That's really nice."

But inside, my thoughts were bouncing around at warp speed. God, I missed Hayes, and that formal side of him that said stuffy things like "vision and execution." But I missed the other side of him more: the patient listener, the thoughtful date, the painfully funny dork.

I missed all of him. So much.

Also, damn, this write-up was a big deal. This was the kind of press that actually translated into jobs. I could put this quote on the front page of my website, follow up with some of my old design contacts from Spayce and share the article. My brain was plotting and scheming about work for what felt like the first time in forever. Excitement was creeping back into my body. God, I'd loved designing the Arbor office. I wasn't ready to give up on that feeling. I wanted it back.

"My mom's friends are asking me for your contact info," Cleo said excitedly.

"Seriously?" I asked. All of this good news felt surreal.

"Yes, they've all been obsessed with you since the gala, and now that they've seen your work they're chomping at the bit. I just wanted to make sure it was okay before I passed on your phone number. I know you've got stuff going on with your mom."

"Yes, oh my god, it's more than okay." I looked at my friends with a stupid smile on my face. "That would be amazing."

"Man, I've missed you," Lola said, smiling back.

"I've missed you too. Both of you." I wanted to wrap my arms around them and never let them go. "When are you supposed to go back to the city?"

"Our train's in a couple hours," Lola said, glancing at her phone for the time. "We thought we could hang out here and bug you for a little bit."

That sounded nice. But what I really wanted, more than anything, was to go back home to Brooklyn. I wanted to put everything I had into getting my business off the ground, and to find the right words to express to Hayes how sorry I was about how things had ended between us. I was ready to make myself proud.

"Or...," I said to my friends, a plan forming clearly in my mind. "Could you help me pack?"

—*mm*—

"Wow, Franny, you got yourself *real* diamonds?" Lola cooed, an inch from my face, reaching up to touch the tiny stud dotting my earlobe. We were standing in my apartment, toasting my return to the city. I was still on a tight budget, but to commemorate this shift I'd started feeling in myself, this next step forward, I'd allowed myself one tiny splurge.

"I just wanted to do something to celebrate," I said, swatting at her. "They weren't that much. It was either this or get bangs."

"Oh, you definitely made the right choice," she said, leaning in for a hug. "I'm so proud of you."

"I'm proud of me too," I said. Last week, I'd been written about on *Town & Country*'s website, with a slideshow about my work designing an art-focused playroom for a summer home in Sag Harbor. The house belonged to the niece of Duffy, one of the women I'd met at the gala thanks to Cleo's mom. And next week, I had my first meeting with Serena about redecorating her entire apartment, which she seemed very excited to go over budget on. When I saw the small diamond earrings at Catbird, a jewelry boutique I loved in Williamsburg, after brunch last weekend, it had felt like a sign. A splurge I not only wanted but could afford. Something just for me.

285

"Wait, hold still—you have, like, the smallest bit of mascara under your eye." Lola was studying my face with the seriousness of a forensic investigator. "Oh, no, it's just an eyelash."

She pressed a finger against the soft skin under my eye and pulled away with the eyelash stuck to the top of her index finger.

"Make a wish," she said, holding her hand directly in front of my mouth. I paused for a moment, considering my options. Franny Doyle Design was starting to truly take shape. Lola was engaged. And Anna and I had been video-chatting weekly, learning more about each other and our parallel lives. We'd even been swapping career advice, sharing work tips and client horror stories. Everything was in its correct place

Well, almost everything. I inhaled and huffed out a breath. For the last few weeks, I'd written emails to Hayes that I never sent, started and deleted text messages, and role-played with my girl-friends about how to best apologize to him. But nothing had ever felt exactly right. And every time I felt brave enough to hit SEND, I panicked or second-guessed myself—and my words. But tonight we were going to be in the same room together, and I couldn't push it off any longer. I promised myself that when I got the chance, I would tell Hayes exactly what I felt: I'd screwed up. I was sorry. And I'd give anything to try it all again.

It didn't mean I wasn't still scared. I knew now that I'd always experience doubt and fear, that I'd second-guess myself again. But I was also Franny Doyle. I was, as Hayes once told me, a woman who didn't take shit from anyone, and that included myself.

Cleo emerged from the bathroom, makeup perfected. I clapped in approval. She responded with a short bow. "Should we pop open the champagne before we leave?"

Lola scurried to the fridge and grabbed the bottle of Dom Pérignon, an engagement gift from her boss.

She passed the bottle over to Cleo, the champagne-opening expert in the group. We shrieked as the cork popped, laughing at ourselves as Cleo filled our wineglasses with bubbly. Eventually we'd all own champagne flutes. But not today.

Cleo kicked things off. "A toast, to the last person any of us thought would get married first."

"Hey!" Lola protested as Cleo gave her a knowing look. "I mean, no one is more surprised than me," she conceded with a grin.

"We are so happy for you, Lo," Cleo continued, her voice now serious.

"We are, and we love you more than anything in the whole world," I said. "To Lola, and love."

"And to friendship," Lola added, lifting her glass. "To us."

CHAPTER TWENTY-EIGHT

HAYES

LOLA AND PERRINE had rented out the entire floor of Adelphi and Willoughby, a buzzed-about new restaurant in Brooklyn. Walking in, I made my way to the bar—all white marble lit up with votives—and asked for a double scotch on the rocks, something to calm my nerves.

When Perrine and Lola had asked me to give a toast at their engagement party, I had said yes immediately. It had taken three different drafts and some coaching from Eleanor, but I'd finally landed on something that felt personal. I just hoped I'd be able to get the words out of my mouth in front of all these people.

In front of Franny.

I tried to push the thought of her out of my mind as I walked toward the crowded room, even though I was checking out every face I passed to see if it was her. Not that I didn't like thinking about her. I visited her in my mind almost every night, remembered how just the touch of her body had made me ache with need, her soft skin against my hands as they tried to touch every inch of her. I imagined what it would be like to go to sleep next to her on a regular old work night, to wake up with her the next day, going about our mundane morning routines, together.

But tonight was about Perrine and Lola, and their love. It was time to put on my game face. So I grabbed some sparkling water from a passed tray of drinks and brought it over to where Eleanor and Henry were chatting with some of Perrine's doctor friends.

"Hey," I said as they opened up their circle to include me. "I got this for you in case you were thirsty."

"Will you look at this guy?" Eleanor said, taking the glass of water out of my hand with an adoring smile. "The best work husband in the world."

She turned toward me as Henry entertained the group with a story about the time he broke his leg while skiing with Perrine, Eleanor, and me.

"You look nice," she said, eyeing my outfit.

"Thanks," I said, running my hands around the collar and adjusting it just so. "I actually bought it for tonight. You would be horrified to know how many suits I tried on trying to pick out the right one."

"Oh, I can imagine," she teased. "Trying to impress someone?"

"Yeah, I am," I said with a nod. My suit was the darkest shade of forest green, and it had reminded me immediately of Franny's eyes. I'd paired it with a white shirt and no tie. I'd thought way too much about it.

"I assumed so, but it's nice hearing you admit it," she said, and then raised her glass. "A toast to you, Hayes Montgomery. I hope you get the girl."

Just as our glasses connected, I saw Eleanor's eyes perk up at something over my shoulder.

"And now's your chance," she said, with a discreet tip of her chin. "Back and to your right."

I turned around slowly, and there she was, only twenty feet away. She was standing next to Cleo, laughing at something someone was saying. I could only see her profile, but even from the side she was beautiful, a black silk dress hugging her in all the right places.

I turned back to Eleanor, who just tilted her head toward Franny with a firm "Go!" It was an order. But before I could even take a step toward her, a clinking of glasses sounded around the room.

Everyone turned to face the front of the bar, where Lola and Perrine stood, arms wrapped around each other in the most assured way, so confident of their love and their life together to come. I knew this meant it was time for my toast, and so I hustled toward them as the crowd erupted in cheers—the brides-to-be were kissing—and made it next to them right as the bartender leaned over to hand me a microphone.

The crowd quieted, and I took a deep breath and then exhaled it slowly, just like the meditation app on my phone instructed me to do. Then I raised my glass.

"I'm so honored to be a part of tonight's celebration, and to offer a toast to the future brides," I said into the microphone. I took another slow, deep breath, then a sip of scotch. I felt a little better.

"I'm Perrine's cousin Hayes, though she's always felt more like a sister to me. Growing up together meant that I got used to having her around, and honestly, I took Perrine and all her amazing qualities for granted. You know, like her sarcastic sense of humor, how she always offers to drive you to the airport, and how she somehow manages to burn every single bag of popcorn she puts in the microwave."

This got a laugh from the crowd, and I smiled, shifting a bit. I was finding a groove, and it was starting to feel good. As I talked, I scanned the crowd for Franny's face, but I came up empty.

"But the one thing I've never taken for granted is her ability to love. She is kind, and generous, and she gives all of herself to the people she loves. And nowhere is that more evident than when she's with Lola."

There was a collective "ahh" from the crowd, and then the room was tinkling again with the sound of people tapping their glasses with silverware. The brides-to-be kissed again, and everyone responded with applause. I raised my glass toward them, and the crowd followed along. If we stopped to do this every few seconds, we'd all be drunk by the end of my toast. I pushed on.

"And, Lola, it's been so fun getting to know you not just as Perrine's fiancée, but as a friend as well."

Lola stuck out her bottom lip and pressed a hand to her heart, mouthing "*Thank you*" at me.

"There's a line in the movie *Moonstruck*"—I paused, nervous about this part of my speech—"which a very smart person once told me is 'the greatest New York love story of all time.'"

I searched again for Franny in the crowd as I talked, but I couldn't find her anywhere.

"Nicolas Cage's character says, 'Love doesn't make things nice—it ruins everything. It breaks your heart. It makes things a mess. We aren't here to make things perfect. The snowflakes are perfect. The stars are perfect. Not us.' Well, you, Perrine and Lola, are as close to perfect as one couple could get. So let's all raise a glass to love, as messy and imperfect as it can be."

And in that moment, as everyone around us was raising glasses and cheering, I spotted Franny, off in the back. Her eyes found mine, and I held her gaze, tried to transport everything I felt for her across the room with that one look. God, she was so beautiful.

I blinked and looked away, stepping back and bumping into Lola.

"Nice job, future cousin-in-law." She leaned in for a hug. "You almost made me cry. Almost."

"I'm going to assume that's a compliment," I teased.

She nodded and gave me an affectionate poke in the shoulder before turning back toward Perrine, which meant I could keep trying to make eye contact with Franny. I looked toward where she'd been standing, but she was gone. I panic-scanned the room and saw her hugging Cleo before walking toward the door. Crap.

I wove my way through the cluster of guests, smiling and nodding at people as I tried not to spill on anyone while also moving as fast as I could in a dimly lit restaurant. By the time I made it past the host's desk up front, Franny was long gone, and I braced myself for the disappointment to come. I pushed the glass door open and stepped out onto the sidewalk.

And there, under the streetlight, she stood, facing away from me, bouncing on her toes. I took a few steps closer, and I could hear her talking. For a second, I thought she might be on her phone, but then I realized she seemed to be talking to herself.

"Franny?" I said tentatively, still unsure of what she was doing.

She whipped around, her mouth wide-open. "Oh my god," she said when she saw me, and her face looked slightly horrified. "Did you just hear what I was saying?"

"No," I said, and seeing her again this close made it hard for my brain to form actual words. "Hi."

"Hi." She exhaled, and then said in a wobbly voice, "I'm just going to go for it."

Her hands were clenched at her sides in fists, and she looked me directly in the eye.

"I'm sorry," she said, with a tilt of her chin. "I'm so sorry. What you did for me when my mom had her heart attack—taking me to the hospital to be with her when you had so much going on—it was so nice of you, and instead of saying thank you, I lashed out at you and said a lot of things I didn't mean."

I cleared my throat, ran a hand across the back of my neck. I searched my head for words but found nothing.

"Look," she said, moving her hands to hold them together in front of her chest. "I was really scared, about…honestly, about everything. My mom, and finding my sister, and losing my birth dad, and starting my own business, and my feelings for you. I really let all that crap get in the way of so much stuff, and I'm trying very hard not to do that again. Also, it was so shitty of me not to respond to your messages. I have no excuse, other than I was just scared and a shithead."

"You're not a shithead," I said, trying to follow along with the words firing out of her mouth at rapid speed.

"Occasionally, I can be a shithead," she said, and I let out a small chuckle at this, because it was so purely Franny, and, god, how I missed her.

"So," she said, blowing out a sigh, "I'm just going to say it. I love you. I'm in love with you."

The words sprang out into the air, wrapped themselves around me, made it so I couldn't move.

"You drive me crazy in all the best ways possible, and spending the last couple of months without you has been the most miserable stretch of my life. I miss talking to you, and how sometimes you say the funniest things."

Her voice was loud, and emphatic, and out of the corner of my eye I saw a woman walking her dog who had stopped to listen to our conversation. Who had stopped to watch Franny as she told me she loved me.

"I miss talking to you too," was all I could get out. There was so much I wanted to say that it was all tangled in a knot inside my brain. I searched for a thread to pull, to yank out the words that could truly articulate how I felt. But there was panic mixed in, too; Franny always knew exactly what to say. What if my response fell flat?

"You're funny, do you know that?" she asked, waving her hands at me, her hair bouncing slightly as she talked. "And you're a great listener, and you're kind. I love how your cheeks do that." She gestured toward my face, and I reached up to touch my cheeks, as if there were something on them. "When you're nervous or thinking. Or both. Also, you're stupidly hot. I know it's shallow, but I can't help it. You're just hot—it's a fact. And you're a good kisser."

She stopped talking and caught her breath. "So yeah," she said, her voice quieting a little. "I think that's all of it."

Every muscle in my body felt tight, pulled like elastic about to break. I had to tell her. Had to find the courage to put my feelings out into the world, just like she had. But instead, I felt stuck, like I'd been planted there, in the cement.

"You don't have to say anything," she said. "And you don't have to accept my apology. I just want you to know that I'm sorry, and that I love you, and that I wish I had never cut you out of my life like I did. But I'm so glad I got to know you, Hayes. Even if it did require my clothes literally falling off my body in public. I would do it all over again just to meet you."

I took a step closer to where she stood, thinking I could hug her. But instead, I shoved my hands in my pockets. "I don't know what to say," I stammered, finally finding some words, though they were all the wrong ones.

"That's okay." Her voice cracked, but she was smiling. Her face was shining like I'd never seen it do before, like a brand-new penny. "I should go."

"Wait, what?" I blinked, trying to process all that was happening in real time.

But before I could say anything else, she bolted, jogging down the block and turning the corner into the darkness of the city. And with her went the opportunity to tell her the one thing I wanted say more than anything: *I love you too.*

CHAPTER TWENTY-NINE

FRANNY

IT'S FUNNY HOW just when you think you know what your brain's going to do, it goes and does the opposite. I thought I was going to spend the night tossing and turning, replaying my interaction with Hayes over and over again. Instead, the second I got home, I crashed. I kicked off my dress and climbed into bed without brushing my teeth. I'd left the party immediately after we spoke, so high and wired from the adrenaline rush of telling him the truth and apologizing that my body just took off for the subway. But then the second it was done and I was back home, something in me hit the mental OFF switch and I passed out before it was even ten o'clock.

And when I woke up at 5 a.m. with a jolt, I didn't feel a drop of regret for what I had said. There was nothing to take back, or do over and change. Who knew it would be this liberating to be honest and up-front, not just with Hayes but with myself?

His silence, though, had stung. I'd wanted him to get down on his knees, declare his adoration, say all of the things that I needed to hear. Instead he'd just stood there. Maybe he didn't feel the way I wanted him to, and I guess it was time to accept that. But even though his reaction hurt, I'd done exactly what I wanted to do, and I felt absolutely at peace with all of it. It didn't mean I wasn't still desperately sad without him, and his shockingly funny jokes and his adorable dorkiness and the way he kissed my neck in the dark like it was something to be cherished, and not just a weird blob of skin that connected my body to my head. I missed everything about him. But I also knew that I was going to be okay. And knowing that felt good.

At six, I knew there was no way I'd be able to fall back asleep. So I threw on some leggings, a sports bra, and a giant NYU sweat-shirt that very clearly had a coffee stain on the front and should have gone into the laundry instead of on my body. I grabbed a ten-dollar bill, my sunglasses, and my key, slapped some sunscreen on my face and a hat on my head, and went out to walk. It was brisk and cool, and the sun was still rising. I didn't have my phone to guide me; I'd left it at home so I could fully clear my head: no music, no texts to friends, no GPS. Just me.

But after an hour and a half taking step after step after step, something became obvious: All this clearheadedness and honesty and expressing myself had made me very, very hungry.

I'd ended up in Carroll Gardens, and I found my way to a bagel shop I'd never been to before. I grabbed an everything bagel and a coffee and sat down in the small seating area. In the corner was a dad making faces at his giggling toddler, and across from me sat an old couple munching on bialys. Overhead, a TV was playing commercials, the volume low. I chewed slowly and watched; it felt strange not to have my phone to stare at for once. Suddenly, NYN's morning show was on the screen, and my old friends Pete and Jenna. My TV appearance felt so long ago now I almost couldn't believe that it had happened. But I still remembered it all in detail, from the sound of my dress ripping to the first time my eyes had connected with his, to the way his leg had felt when I'd nervously kicked it under the table on our on-air coffee date. And now our lives were intrinsically connected, because of one small moment that had set off a chain of events like fireworks.

I was so focused on my memories that it took me a second to realize that Hayes was now on the screen above me. *Hayes.*

"Excuse me!" I shouted to the teenager working behind the counter. "Can you turn up the TV, please?"

She slid a remote across the counter, and I reached for it, pressing the volume button until Pete's voice was clear.

"—former guest who you maybe remember from a viral moment last spring, when he stepped in to help a woman whose dress had ripped on the subway."

Hayes smiled at this, and a full-screen shot of us sitting next to each other during that interview appeared.

"That's me!" I said out loud, without thinking. Everyone turned to look.

"Really?" said the older man, adjusting his cap as if that would help him see better.

"Yes," I said, a little defensively. "I just had a lot of makeup on there. And no hat."

"Hayes," continued Jenna. "You reached out to our producer last night, asking for some help, and lucky for you, we'd had a cancellation and could squeeze you on this morning. So tell us what you need from our audience."

He cleared his throat, and I noticed that his hands were clenched in his lap. He looked nervous, like a little kid in a spelling bee, and my heart ached for him.

"Well, that woman you mentioned, Franny, who I met on the train...," he started. "We actually hit it off. And last night, she told me she loved me."

"How exciting!" Jenna clenched her hands into fists and cheered. *Cheered.*

"Well, honestly, as she knows, I often get a little tongue-tied. And so I didn't get the chance to tell her how I felt."

"Which is?" Pete said, egging him on with a wave of his hand.

"Well, I'm in love with her," he said.

I clasped my hands to my face. Behind me, the teenager at the counter said, "Wait, is he talking about you?"

Hayes kept going. "And I should have told her the second I figured it out, but you know how it is when your brain takes a while to catch up with your heart."

Jenna swooned over this. Even Pete's face went soft with a goofy smile.

"So, anyway, when she told me last night, I froze," he continued. "And so that's why I reached out to your producer, Eliza. We were brought together on your show once before, so I'm hoping maybe you can make that happen again. I guess I just figured, what better way to tell Franny that I love her than to tell the whole world."

Jenna clutched a note card to her chest. "People do wild things for love," she said.

Hayes nodded. "I guess they do."

The camera cut back to Pete and Jenna, and like that, he was gone.

"Oh my goodness!" the old woman near me said, dabbing her lips with a napkin. "You have to go find this young man."

The dad in the corner was pointing at me and then to the TV, explaining to his son what had just happened. Behind the counter, two more workers had joined the first and were staring at me.

I felt surprisingly calm. Too calm. I was in shock. Love-shock. I needed to get to Hayes.

"I don't...I don't know where he is," I stammered. "Also, I spent all my money on breakfast. I don't have enough for a MetroCard."

"Well, if he's on New York News, he's at Rockefeller Center," the dad said, still bouncing his kid on his lap. "Go there."

The old man leaned forward in his chair, pulling a wallet out of his back pocket. "Here," he said, passing a yellow MetroCard to me. "I always keep one on me that has at least ten rides, just in case."

"I want to say that I can't accept this, but I'm going to accept this," I said, clutching it to my chest. "Thank you so much."

"He's cute!" his wife shouted at me as I hustled for the door. "Go get him."

And off I went, to do exactly that.

—*m*—

I had no watch and no phone to keep track of time, but it felt like the train inched from Brooklyn into the city. It was the weekend, so it was making local stops, and the feeling of calm that had settled into me in the bagel shop was long gone. I was now a full-on wreck: a foot-jiggling, nail-biting, sleeve-twisting mess. Hayes was in love with me too, and now every second we were not together was a complete waste of time.

The train chugged into the Rockefeller Center station, and I bolted as soon as the doors slid open. I ran up the stairs, past the shops that lined the hallways of the station, and then I was outside, on Sixth Avenue and Fifty-First Street.

"Crap!" I dodged my way through the throngs of people already hogging the sidewalk. Two breathless blocks later, I was near the NYN studio. I took a minute to catch my breath, hands on my knees, panting next to a lamppost. I looked around as the world moved quickly by me. I laughed, out loud, at the ridiculousness of it all. It would be impossible to find him in the middle of this chaos. I looked down. In my frantic departure from the bagel shop, I'd smeared cream cheese on the front of my sweatshirt.

Of course.

My grand plan of meeting Hayes as he left NYN was quickly being ruined by reality. I turned the corner to walk in the street, past the crowds and the shops hawking tourist wares, and toward the center of the Plaza.

I suddenly felt incredible stupid. What was I thinking, running here smelling like an everything bagel with a stranger's MetroCard in my hand? I had to get back to Brooklyn, where at least I could shower and put on some mascara and shave my legs, and then call him and go to his apartment and strip naked immediately and climb on top of him. That was a much better plan.

I got the hell out of the tourist madness and made my way down Fifth Avenue, to Grand Central Station. The Main Concourse was slow for a Saturday morning. The space always reminded me of a library, with its giant glass windows and arched celestial ceiling.

I was walking across the marble floor, headed toward the long hallway that led down to the subway tracks, when someone a few steps ahead of me dropped a wad of cash. I ran to pick it up and then lifted my head to figure out which way he'd gone.

"Excuse me," I shouted, but this being New York, no one turned around. "Hey!" I said, jogging a few steps to tap the stranger on the shoulder. I'd moved so quickly I hadn't had a chance to even process the man's shape, the long body, the thick hair. But the second I laid a hand on him, I knew, even before he turned around.

It was Hayes.

He stopped so abruptly that I was still in motion, and I lurched into his chest, my head smacking against his shoulder and my right foot stomping hard on his shoe.

"Ow," he grumbled, taking a step back, his hand on my elbow. "Ma'am, are you o— Oh my god."

He tilted his head so he could see my face under my hat. "Franny?"

"You dropped some money," were the first words out of my mouth as I opened my palm.

"What are you doing here?" he asked incredulously.

"I saw you on TV," I explained, as if it were the most obvious thing in the world. "I went to Rockefeller Center to find you."

"But we're in Grand Central," he said, his brows still quizzical, face perplexed.

"I know. I couldn't find you, so I'm on my way home. But here you are." We stood there for a second, still. "Wait," I said, something dawning on me. "'*Ma'am*'? Do I look that old?"

He laughed, as if he couldn't believe what I was saying. "I was trying to be polite—you startled me."

"How do you think I feel? I was minding my business eating when you came on a TV in the bagel shop!"

It was then that I realized his hand was still on my arm, and so I stepped closer to him, desperate to breathe him in.

"Franny," he said, cupping my face with his free hand. "Do you want to go back and finish your bagel?"

His mouth shifted into a playful smirk, and I smacked him in the shoulder and then let my hand move slowly down his chest. "No, you jerk. I just want to be here, with you."

He smiled at this, and then his long arms were around me, pressing me into him, warm and steady, his chin resting atop my head. I reached my arms around him and held on.

"I like your jacket," I muttered into his chest. "Gucci?" I joked.

"No, something new. Birch and Fole."

It didn't ring a bell. "What's that?" I asked, pulling away to look at him.

"A sustainable and gender-inclusive clothing company focusing on ethical practices," he said, planting a kiss on the top of my head. "I thought it sounded cool."

"Wow, I never thought I'd see the day you weren't in some bespoke designer suit.

"Well, I met this woman"—Hayes's voice was soft and low—"and I'm trying to impress her."

"I bet she likes you no matter what you wear," I said, tilting my head up to smile at him.

"Well, that's good, because she's going to be seeing a lot of him, and he mostly likes to wear old sweats from college."

"What if she likes him best when he's naked?" I asked, enjoying this game we were playing.

"I think they can work something out," he said with a nod of his head.

"Good," I said.

I reached a hand to his face and rubbed my thumb against the soft stubble of his cheek. He leaned forward and kissed me softly, letting his teeth graze the edge of my lips.

"Hayes," I murmured as I shifted to kiss his face, then his neck.

"Yeah?" He slid his arms back around my waist.

I pulled back and looked at him. "I love you."

"I love you too, Franny."

"What do we do now?" I asked.

"I don't have any plans," he said, reaching for and finding my hand, giving it a squeeze. "Are you headed back to Brooklyn?" Hayes asked, his eyes studying me.

I nodded. "Will you come with me?" I said. "Is that weird to ask?"

He shook his head, his face so serious it melted my heart. "It's not weird at all."

We walked down the steps to the subway, swiping our Metro-Cards through the turnstile. "A very sweet old man gave me his MetroCard this morning so I could come find you," I said as I put it back in my pocket. "Maybe it's my good-luck charm."

The platform was quiet, the weekend rush yet to pick up. Nearby, a few people milled about, peeking down the tracks waiting for the train. In the distance, a saxophone wailed. It was New York in its purest form, unassuming and peaceful and wide-awake.

"I've replayed the moment we met so many times," he said, his thumb making small circles on the top of my hand. "I would have acted differently if I could go back and do it again."

"Like how?" I asked, genuinely curious.

"I would have introduced myself, for starters," he said. "I thought you were so pretty."

"I thought you were"—I shrugged, made a bored face—"just okay. But I did give you the nickname Hot Suit behind your back."

He laughed and pulled me close to him, nipping me playfully on the neck. "I've missed you so much," he said, lips pressed against my skin.

"I know I told you last night," I replied, "but I'll say it again: I'm sorry I pulled away, and I'm sorry I stopped talking to you."

He leaned back and lifted a hand to my chin, tilting my head so our eyes met. "But you didn't. I found your note in my pocket, after things ended between us. It was exactly what I needed to hear from you, at the exact right time."

The downtown train interrupted us, roaring past until it screeched to a stop. We got on together, stepping through the doors and sitting. The car was almost entirely empty.

"I think about you every time I get on the subway. About the day we met. And everything after." He wrapped his arm around my shoulder, and I leaned into him, so solid and warm.

"Let's try it again," I said, smiling at the idea blooming in my head.

"What do you mean?" He gave me a skeptical look, one I'd grown to know and love. It was the look he made when his brain was working, analyzing, searching for logic. It was so Hayes it made my heart ache with love for him, and all the ways he was exactly, perfectly, himself.

"Meeting each other." I ran my hand down his thigh, giving it a squeeze. "Let's get it right this time."

Hayes laughed as he ran a hand through his hair. "Okay."

"Franny Doyle," I said. I stretched out my hand, and Hayes shook it. "I just got laid off, and I'm freaking out, and I think you are very handsome, even though I won't be able to admit it for a long time."

"Hayes Montgomery the Third. Though I leave out 'the Third,' because it's pretentious and embarrassing. I find you charming and gorgeous, which I also find infuriating, because I like being in control of my emotions, and everything else for that matter."

"Pleased to meet you." We kept our hands locked together even though we'd stopped shaking. "We should hang out sometime. What are you doing next week?"

Hayes paused, the smile on his face shrinking slightly. "Actually"—he held my gaze with his—"I was thinking about going to Italy."

"Wait, what?"

"Remember the silent auction, at the natural history museum? The Italian vacation you kept eyeing?"

"You bid on it?" I asked.

He nodded.

"And I won," he said, and then turned to look at me. "I mean, technically, *we* won."

I gave him a quizzical look. "What do you mean?"

"I had planned on giving it to you," he explained, rubbing his thumb along my palm, his hand still in mine. "But when we...when we stopped speaking to each other, it felt absurd to dump something like that on you. But..." He looked at me, his gaze hesitant. "But we could go anytime you wanted."

I just stared at him, mouth ajar in a bewildered smile.

"You have to know by now," he said, running his other hand over my thigh, "that at my core I'm pathetically romantic and mushy, right?"

"I really, really like that about you," I said, and placed a small kiss on his jaw.

"Anyway, the tickets are yours, and you can do whatever you want with them, of course. But you did tell me when we met that you owed me one. Maybe I can finally collect on that."

"I think we can work something out," I teased. "But I need to warn you, I will definitely sleep on your shoulder on the plane. And I drool."

"Don't worry," he said, giving me that boyish grin of his that made my whole body swell. "I already know that about you, and I don't care. I still like you."

He reached up and turned my hat backward. "You look cute in this," he said, tapping the bill before leaning in to kiss me, his lips soft and urgent. "I also wanted to do this the first time we met."

The subway doors opened at the next stop, and we both looked up. We weren't heading toward Brooklyn at all. In our stupor, we must have gone to the wrong platform. We were on a train heading uptown.

"Franny," he said, pointing to the station sign as the doors closed, "this isn't the right train. We're going the wrong way."

I laughed and looked at him, grabbing his hand and bringing it to my lips with a kiss.

"Well, let's just ride it, then," I said. "And see where it takes us."

ACKNOWLEDGMENTS

I want to first acknowledge all the people who flip right to the Acknowledgments before reading a book. I see you. I am you. Welcome, and thanks for being here.

None of this would be possible without Holly Root, who is truly one of the most fantastic humans on earth, and an amazing agent to boot. I'm so lucky to have you in my corner. Many thanks to the entire Root Literary team for all that you do, and a special shout-out to Alyssa Moore, for being so on top of everything.

My editor, Amy Pierpont, is a brilliant word wizard who gave this book its wings. I am so grateful for your thoughtful direction and support throughout this process, and am better for it. And so is this book!

Estelle Hallick, thank you for being on board since Day 1, and for all you've done to share this book with the world.

I am so fortunate and grateful to get to work with the talented Forever team, including Sam Brody, Daniela Medina, Carolyn Kurek, and copy editor Elizabeth Johnson.

Kate Sweeney, Annie Sklaver-Orenstein, Bridget Maloney-Sinclair, Joy Engel, Gwen Mesco, Eirene Donahue, Emily Barth Isler, and Tanya Doyle-Gradet all read various drafts of this book. Thank you for your notes, feedback, catches (I'm looking at you, Gwen!), and cheerleading. It means the world to me.

Heather Lazare's editorial prowess helped shape this book significantly.

Kristin Dwyer has been a guiding light throughout this process. Laine Hammer shared invaluable insight that allowed me to craft Franny's life experiences in a more authentic way.

Doree Shafrir, thank you for reading a draft of this book and lovingly assuring panicked ol' me that it did, actually, make sense. You are a wonderful business partner and friend and I will happily answer the "What do you like best about Doree?" question until the end of time.

Samee Junio, Sam Reed, Sara Robillard—thank you for all you do to keep our podcast operation up and running, especially during all the book deadlines.

To the entire *Forever35* community of listeners: You all are the literal best. You feel like family to me, and I'm so grateful for all the love you've shown me during this process.

Thank you to The Pile for being there, always, and to Write! Write! Write! for your support and generosity every time I came to you with a question or worry. I couldn't have finished this book without you.

This book would not have been written without the music of Phoebe Bridgers and Katie Crutchfield getting me through endless revisions. The gift that musicians give to stressed-out writers on deadlines is incomparable, and I am grateful.

Thanks to Phish, just because.

To my wonderful extended family of Spencers, Brightons, and Kings—I really lucked out in the family department. Thanks for always cheering me on.

The bond between Franny, Lola, and Cleo is modeled after the many endlessly loving and relentlessly supportive friends I am so lucky to have. Roommate, Biggie, Little One, Goober, Rocky, and Ater—you have especially kept me afloat through the hardest times. All my best laughs are with you.

Teresa Christiansen and Sarah Plimpton, this book would not

exist without you and all the memories we made together. Sister Liberty forever.

Eleanor and Lydia King, you make my world go round. I love you more than everything bagels with scallion cream cheese and sliced cucumbers and tomatoes.

Anthony King, you've been there for me unconditionally since the day you asked me to go out to dinner at a ridiculous German restaurant on the East Side. I'm so glad I said yes.

And to the entire living, breathing, pulsating city of New York: I would be nothing without you. You are impossible to live in and impossible to live without. I will love you forever.

ABOUT THE AUTHOR

Kate Spencer is an author, journalist, and cohost of the podcast *Forever35*. Her memoir, *The Dead Moms Club*, was published by Seal Press in 2017. She lives with her husband and two kids in Los Angeles.